THE
COURTESAN'S
DAUGHTER

THE
COURTESAN'S
DAUGHTER

A NOVEL

SUSANNE
DUNLAP

atmosphere press

To Chloé, my movie lover.

CHAPTER ONE

Sylvie

It seems silly now, as I look back on what my life was like before I ran away, but for a whole year, I used to imagine I was living in a moving picture. It all started the day I found a nickel in the gutter on my way home to Mulberry Street from the Girls High School on Twelfth Street, and instead of rushing back to help my mother finish up the shirtwaists she sewed day in and day out, I skipped north to Fourteenth Street and the nearest nickelodeon. The flicker that afternoon was *Romance of a War Nurse*. One moving picture. That was all I needed. I fell in love—with cinema, with make-believe, and especially with the Vitagraph girl. No, that's wrong. I didn't fall in love with the Vitagraph girl. I wanted to *be* the Vitagraph girl.

Months before I saw her on the screen, I had overheard my classmates talking and gossiping about a mysterious lady whose name they did not know, sharing *cartes de visite* and pages torn out of *Harper's Bazaar* or the nickel weeklies. I peered over their shoulders to get a glimpse of this person. She was very pretty, but I couldn't see why they were so crazy for her. Still, they talked about her as if she was a goddess, arguing over which of her pictures was the best and which was her most moving scene. I laughed at them. I was too smart to be so taken with a pretty face. I could hear my mother's voice: *To be pretty—what is that? To be smart, to be educated. That is most important,* non?

I never really understood how that little French word, *non*, could so clearly mean its opposite.

Anyway, that's what I thought, too, until the time I finally saw the Vitagraph girl for myself. I've relived every moment of that day more times than I can count. I see it now: I give my nickel to the man at the entrance and enter a small, dark room with about a dozen other women and men, mostly in pairs. It's close and smells of bodies, and the floor is sticky. I know people are staring at me—because I was alone? Maybe. I take an empty place on a bench at the very back. I jump a little when a sharp click and then a whir commences behind my right shoulder, but when the screen flickers to life and a pianist starts to play, I lose all awareness of anything but what is before my eyes. It takes no more than a moment for me to recognize the Vitagraph girl, a nurse tending to sick and dying soldiers. And I lose myself, completely, utterly.

It was a miracle. She was a miracle. How could someone say so much without a single word? The captions told the story, but the Vitagraph girl made everyone understand what it meant. I hid in the dark and stayed to watch her a second time, knowing *Maman* was probably worried sick right then, partly because I was late, partly because I wouldn't have time to help her finish the sewing before Mr. Silverstein arrived to take away the finished shirtwaists.

When the ticket man finally came in and shooed me out so I couldn't stay and watch a third time, I floated away on the near-dark streets, ignoring the squeal of trolley wheels, the clopping of hooves, and the occasional backfire of an automobile engine. For that brief time, I forgot that my life was all laid out before me like a drab gray blanket. I pretended I wasn't going to follow my mother's rigid plan and graduate from high school then go to Teachers College. That was the most daring thought I'd ever had. As long as I could remember, we'd talk about that, about how I wouldn't need to marry because I could support myself. *Men,* Maman would say. *What they want is not worth giving them.* But I wasn't so sure of that. I dreamed of being held in a strong embrace, like the Vitagraph girl was at the end of the flicker. Voices overlapped in my mind. My mother saying, *There is only one way not to end up like me,* the other saying, *There are so many ways to be happy.* Then I would think about the families in our apartment building, with so many children they could hardly feed and clothe, and all living in two cramped rooms. Maybe my mother was right. I didn't want to believe it, though.

I never told my mother about going to the nickelodeon. It was the first secret I ever kept from her, but not the last.

On that day, though, my pleasant fantasy of being in the moving pictures crashed down with a thud when I arrived at the bottom of the stoop to our building at twilight and gazed up at the ugly, real world I inhabited. Paint peeling off the front door, which wouldn't close properly ever since one of the Murphy boys had broken it down when he was being chased by the police. The gas lamps in the stairwell managing to be both searingly bright and leave corners unilluminated at the same time. The rats dashing in front of me even in the middle of the day, scurrying away through the many gaps between floorboards.

"*Mon Dieu,* where have you been!" My mother cried as soon as I walked through the door.

"Oh, I...had to stay late and help Miss Foster." It was all I could think of on the spot.

"How could you agree to such a thing? Surely some other girl could have done it," she said. "Mr. Silverstein will be here *tout de suite*, and these three waists—" She held them up, pointing to the dangling threads.

"I'll start right away, and we'll finish," I said, but I knew that only she could do the delicate handwork, that she'd had to waste her valuable time on the sewing machine—normally my job—doing the rough assembly.

Mr. Silverstein considered my mother to be the best seamstress in New York. He said so all the time. When he asked her how she came by her skills, she would say, *from the nuns at Notre Dame de Sion*. She never explained more, but I knew that she'd been an orphan and was unhappy and ran away, and something else happened, and I was born. She never said anything about my father or the circumstances that led us to New York. Mr. Silverstein was polite enough not to ask for more, satisfied with getting the high-quality waists my mother and I sewed, much higher quality than the ones turned out in factories near Washington Square.

My mother was desperate enough that day to let me help her finish some buttonholes and tucks, so I sat down and got to work, my mind whirring like the moving picture projector, flashing images that took me far away.

#

Life had gone back to normal on the outside ever since my trip to the nickelodeon. Yet inside, in my mind and heart, everything was bubbling and confusing. My impractical dream grew stronger every day. If my mother noticed anything, saw me gazing out the window in a daydream or sighing as I sat at the sewing machine, she never said. Maman and I rarely spoke of anything that didn't have to do with schoolwork, sewing, or God. She avoided asking questions, and I'd never gotten into the habit of it.

We worked hard from seven in the morning until six or seven at night—Maman sewing until her eyes burned and her fingers cramped, me going to school and helping her when I got home. Our only day of rest was Sunday. We would wake at our usual time and go to early Mass at the Church of the Most Precious Blood—the Italian church a few blocks away. My mother spoke French to me there and pretended she couldn't understand English. She kept herself aloof from everyone as much as she could, including our neighbors, and discouraged me from mixing with them. "They will never escape this life, not like you," she explained, as if their condition could rub off on me and erase my chances of improving myself.

I don't know how she managed to keep us so isolated. We lived practically on top of one another. The building was never entirely quiet. Cries of, "Where is my necktie?" "Go polish your shoes!" "God will see those dirty fingernails," echoed through the building, even on a Sunday morning, and were almost always followed by the sound of a strap hitting a bottom and wails and shouts.

From the very start, though, that Sunday was special. Maman woke me later than usual, and rather than make a pot of tea with only one spoonful of leaves in it, she put in two. I smiled when I smelled the aroma and tasted the delicate flavor instead of something with barely more flavor than hot water. She smiled back at me over the cracked cup she always took, holding a handkerchief underneath it to catch any drips. Thinking back, maybe I should have recognized that as love. Those little gestures, not meant to be noticed, were as much as she could allow herself.

"You've been out of sorts lately, *ma petite*," my mother said after we finished our tea, and I started to comb the nighttime tangles out of my hair. "Perhaps we'll attend high Mass today, as a treat."

I'll never know exactly why she chose that day. Maybe she sensed my altered mood, noticed, without saying anything, that something in me had changed lately. But at the time, I was so surprised that I stopped with the comb suspended above my head and turned to stare at her. High Mass, with its chanting and readings and long homily, took too much time out of the one day of the week we had to do all our chores— wash clothes, iron, bake bread for the coming week. That's why we rarely went.

Maman had turned away, though, so she didn't notice me staring, and all I saw was her perfect chignon, that marvel of hairdressing only French women seem able to achieve. I went back to combing my own pale blond hair, wishing I could look in a mirror while I did it. A moment later, Mama bustled over, twisted my shoulders so that my back was to her, and started braiding my hair as she did every morning, yanking and weaving it so tight I could feel it pulling at my temples.

"Couldn't I wear it down, just this once?" I asked. I wanted to look more like the Vitagraph girl, whose hair hung to her waist, just pulled up enough at her temples not to obscure her face.

"I've explained all that to you many times, *ma chère*." Mama started weaving the strands of hair again. "It's—provocative." Even after fifteen years in New York, she still sometimes had to pause before a word in English she rarely used, drag it up from somewhere she must have stored it years past.

If I had been younger, I would have let the matter drop and done as she said. But I was seventeen years old then, and I figured I was all grown up. I turned and took hold of her hands. "This is Mass, not out on the streets. Everyone will be praying. No one will pay attention to me." I secretly hoped that was not true.

She shrugged her very French sort of shrug and tugged the

corners of her mouth down in disapproval. "Very well. But I'll tie it back."

I knew not to push her further and let her bind my long hair into a queue that hung down my back and swished against the starched fabric of my shirtwaist.

"We'll have to do the mending before we go, or we won't finish today. And breakfast, you will have to remain hungry until this afternoon."

I said nothing and brought the work basket over to the window where light was just beginning to filter in. It was a small price to pay on such a morning.

All at once, our building burst into life as dozens of feet thundered down five flights of stairs. I covered my ears. My mother smiled for the second time in less than an hour. I wondered why, what had changed.

We finished the mending and put on our warmest coats to shield us from the cold November wind. Our street, Mulberry Street, was like all the others on the Lower East Side, with four or five floors of tenements atop the shops on the ground floor, so close across the street that sunlight only penetrated in the middle of the day. One or two men lounged at streetcorners smoking, their hands stuffed deep in their pockets. We crossed the road to avoid having to go right past them, making our walk longer than it needed to be. Once we reached the corner of Broome and Baxter streets, we joined the parade of smartly dressed families moving toward the church doors, nodding to each other while sizing each other up. Women wore hats decked with feathers and flowers. Men traded their workday caps for fedoras and looked strained and uncomfortable in their neckties and dress shirts.

We avoided the grand front entrance and entered by a side door. I followed my mother to a pew at the back.

Within minutes, the sanctuary filled to overflowing with Italian families: grandmothers and matrons all in black, younger women and girls in their dark coats with severely nipped-in waistlines, bits of ribbon or lace poking out from their collars. I stood and knelt and stood again and made the sign of the cross at the same time as everyone around me. The gestures were so automatic I hardly had to think about them, and I found myself imagining an emotional scene in a moving picture where the Vitagraph girl went to church to mourn her dead sweetheart—who turned out not to be dead after all and surprised her with a bouquet of flowers just before they kissed and the screen went black.

My mother nudged me. It was our turn to approach the altar rail for communion. We joined a line that moved like a train with a schedule to keep, stopping as briefly as possible for the priest to lay the host on each tongue. As we progressed, I glanced to my right, tired of staring at my mother's back.

That's when I saw him.

He sat in the middle of a row about a third of the way to the front, his eyes boring into me like a ray of sunlight on a cold day, right through the fabric of my coat. The girl behind me had to poke me in the back to start me going again. I almost forgot to cross myself after accepting the host and to genuflect before sliding back into my pew.

While my mother leaned her forehead on her folded hands and moved her lips in silent prayer, my mind whirled. Who was that boy? Why was he looking at me? I didn't think I'd ever seen him before. I would have remembered a face like that, with those eyes.

Mass ended soon after, and people started filing out of their pews to the door. I hung back a little, just to see if I could get another glimpse of the boy. My mother remained on her knees as she often did at the end of the service, praying.

But the boy had disappeared. The flutter of anticipation in my stomach faded, and I persuaded myself that the entire scene was just me being too imaginative. Mama stood and started toward the same side door where we'd entered.

"Such a sad face."

The voice, so quiet only I could hear it, came from behind me. I was afraid to look around.

"Beautiful, but sad."

I felt the slightest movement of my hair, as if a breeze had come out of nowhere in the tomb-still church, but I knew it wasn't a breeze. My blood tingled into my cheeks, and I glanced ahead to make sure my mother wouldn't see. I turned, and there he was. Up close, he was even more handsome. And tall. I had to tilt my head up to look into his eyes, dark pools that caught the light as they gazed back at me.

He took my hand and raised it to his lips. I was too shocked to react. He smiled and said, "*Mi scusa.* Paolo Bonnano, at your service. Why have I not seen you here before?"

He'd asked a question. I would have to answer. "We usually attend early Mass," I said, the words sounding strangled and weak. "It's...I'm Sylvie Button. That's my name. Pleased to meet you."

"Not Sylvia?"

"No. We're French."

"Ah. I'm Italian."

"I guessed."

An awkward silence followed until we both started talking at once.

"Do you go to school?" "Where do you live?"

We laughed. Once over the nervous beginning, our conversation flowed easily, and we answered each other's questions as we made our way toward the door. I was relieved to see that my mother had already gone outside, no doubt assuming I was right behind her.

"I'm in business. With my father."

"We live on Mulberry Street. I'm in school."

I asked him what his business was, and he gave a vague answer I didn't understand, something about insurance, or security. As he walked next to me, the shadow of his long, curling lashes against his cheekbones distracted me, and I didn't press him further. We'd reached the door, too quickly, I thought. "I'd better go find my mother. She'll wonder where I've gone."

"Of course. How may I see you again?" He held the door open for me.

Before I had a chance to think it through, I said, "I walk to the girls' high school on Twelfth Street every day. If your business happened to take you across my path, we could meet."

His eyes shifted over my shoulder, and he nodded and took a step back. "Be seeing you," he said and settled his cap on his head before turning and walking away.

It was my mother, coming toward me with a frown on her face. "Who is that?" she said, taking my hand.

"He's just an Italian boy who works for his father," I said, trying to sound calm, to still my pounding heart. I don't think I succeeded.

"So, not in school then?"

"Not everyone my age is still in school." My comment sound testier than I meant it to.

"Not everyone is as smart as you are, *ma petite*," Maman said.

We walked home in silence after that and hardly spoke to each other while we continued our Sunday chores. The rooms of our apartment felt tight and airless with the windows closed against the cold. I wondered if Paolo lived in such a place. Somehow, thinking of him suggested space, a different world, possibilities. I let my mind wander again, imagining us together in a moving picture. His expressive eyes would make other girls swoon, I was certain.

But I was unlikely to see him again, I thought, so I attacked the floor with the scrub brush so hard I thought I might make a hole right through it to the Murphys' apartment on the floor below.

CHAPTER
TWO

Justine

When I saw Sylvie with that boy, my heart stopped beating for a breath or two. I had worked so hard to keep her from being distracted from her studies, keeping her busy all the time. The very last thing I wanted was for her to fall under the influence of some young man of whom we knew nothing, and who could offer her only heartache for the future. Later, I realized I should have spoken to her about it, explained more. It would have been better if I had told her things to make her understand why she must put off *amours* until after college. But I remained silent, my tongue leaden in my mouth. If I started talking, who knew what secret would fly out and tear the delicate fabric of our lives. Sylvie did not mention the boy again.

I let her keep her secrets. I had a mountain of my own.

One of them was Alfonse. My dream. My nightmare. He found me in New York one beautiful spring day, ten years after

I had fled Paris with Sylvie. I had gone out to Sixth Avenue to buy some thread and allowed myself a few extra minutes to enjoy the balmy weather, straying a little farther uptown than I customarily did. I wandered over to the Ladies' Mile, where many of the waists Sylvie and I made were sold in the department stores. Nearly every woman in New York, probably all around America, needed waists. With so many women working now, they had no time to sew their own clothes. That was my good fortune, at least for a time.

Shirtwaists were not what the stores put in their windows to attract customers, however, and I gazed with a mixture of pleasure and longing at the elegant gowns and hats, remembering a time long gone when I would have been able to purchase any of them I wanted. It was a time that, in all other details, I tried not to think of. Along with the elegant clothes came the opera, music halls, exhibits—Alfonse never missed a photography exhibit, and I could still hear his voice saying *You just wait. These moving pictures—they are the future.*

I was completely lost in my memories, seeing them through the softening veil of time and recalling all that had been good. Yet after a while, I had an uneasy sensation that someone was right behind me, about to tap me on the shoulder. I turned to look, but I saw only shoppers minding their own business, walking along in twos and threes and chatting, laughter floating into the air. Still, the feeling persisted. I continued walking, now distracted from the pleasant pastime of admiring dresses I would never wear. I reached a corner and was about to cross when a large, handsome motorcar moving slowly near the curb drew in front of me, blocking my way. An ungloved hand rested on the top of the rear passenger door, a ruby ring on the third finger. I knew that hand.

My legs weakened beneath me. I thought of going quickly into a shop and trying to flee through another door, but that would be foolish, and running was out of the question on the crowded sidewalk. Before I could think of another way to escape, his voice called out, "Justine!"

I stood as still as a boulder in a river as pedestrians flowed around me. A moment later—or was it an eternity—a hand gripped my upper arm and pulled me into the backseat, and I found myself sitting beside him. Alfonse d'Antigny, a man I had prayed to the Virgin I would never see again.

"*Quelle plaisir.*" He lifted my hand to his lips. I shuddered, not entirely in disgust, the ghost of a memory when I welcomed such a gesture from him flitting into my mind. "How is it that our paths have not crossed these several years?"

"Why are you here?" I asked. Fine lines radiated from the corners of his familiar eyes. I, too, must look older, I thought. I pushed a wisp of hair that had come loose from my chignon under my hat.

"After ten years, that is all you say? Not '*bonjour,*' or '*how are you?*'"

I wanted to say a great deal more, and none of it polite, but I held my tongue. "I lead an honorable life here." Despite my best efforts, my voice quavered.

"I am here on business and expect to make frequent voyages to New York in these next years. I invest in moving pictures, and Mr. Edison has invited me to examine his latest invention." He pulled me toward him. "I would much sooner examine you...I hope you are not squandering your consider-able talents by giving them away."

I tried to resist, but he was strong. Through clenched teeth, I said, "I have left that life behind. I earn my living another way."

He let go of me and chuckled. "I see by your clothing that it is a meager living at best. I could once again give you a life of luxury and ease. You could go into that store as a customer instead of merely looking with desire in your eyes from outside. It would please me to have an arrangement much like the one we previously enjoyed."

"No."

"...And if we come to some arrangement, I will never tell the authorities what I suspect concerning the whereabouts of a certain three-year-old girl, whose disappearance has never been solved."

My heart stopped. "I don't know what you mean."

"Don't you?"

"I bore a child, and she died."

"That, *ma chère,* is a lie. We both know it." He gripped my wrist so hard my fingers began to tingle.

"You had no right." But of course, by law he did, and in his own way, though long since abolished, the *droigt de seigneur.* "And I tell you, she is dead." *Dead to you, forever.*

We stared at each other, neither of us willing to be the first to look away.

He shrugged. "If that is true, you killed her. She was in good health the last time I saw her in the care of her nurse-maid. She would have led a charmed life with Madame d'An-tigny and myself."

He had touched on my one source of disquiet about what I had done, that I had taken Sylvie away from a life of luxury and condemned her to poverty and want. "We have no business with each other. Please let me leave now. *Nous sommes finis.*"

The automobile started making its way through the congested streets. "No, I think not," Alfonse said. "I have unfinished business with you." He took a silver pencil and a piece of paper out of his pocket and scribbled something on it. "Meet me here, Thursday."

"And if I don't?"

"Then I will reopen the inquiry into what happened to that little girl all those years ago."

I shrank under the force of his gaze.

16

"That's better," he said.

I knew then that if I wanted to protect Sylvie, to shield her from Alfonse, I would have to agree to what he proposed. With those few words, he proved that he held immeasurable power over me.

And, *grace à Dieu,* I would not let him hold that power over Sylvie.

#

For five years, I kept my side of the agreement with Alfonse, meeting either him or someone he sent in his place once a month at an apartment near Twentieth Street, during the day when Sylvie was at school. He made a point of paying me each time, so that I could make no mistake about the nature of our association. Sometimes he brought wine, but more often he just took me quickly, hardly looking at me. I could not always tell whether he was angry or sad, but he rarely smiled. I was glad. His smile was more dangerous than anything else about him. The most important thing was to make sure he could never follow me home and find Sylvie. I always insisted he be the first to leave, and I never took the same route back to Mulberry Street. I believed he remained in ignorance of where I lived.

#

About three weeks before Christmas in 1910, early in the afternoon before Sylvie came home from school and helped me with the piecework, I heard the familiar sound of Aaron Silverstein's footsteps climbing the stairs, followed by his customary knock. For nearly ten years, this gentle, Jewish man had come, morning and night, six days a week, to bring me work and pick it up when Sylvie and I were finished. We didn't own a clock, but I could tell by the daylight it was too early for him to arrive expecting our completed work. And besides, Sylvie was not yet home from school.

I took off my apron, smoothed down my hair, and walked without hurrying to open the door.

"Forgive me. May I come in? I will only take a moment of your time. I know you are busy."

I couldn't refuse him. He was the bearer of all honest prosperity in my home. "Please, sit," I said, preparing to clear a chair of sewing apparatus.

"No, as I said, I won't stay."

He swung down a satchel he'd been carrying across his back and placed it on the floor. As he rummaged inside it, he said, "I am a connoisseur, of sorts, of fine fabrics. Who knows, perhaps I will one day open a tailor's shop of my own. But I couldn't help noticing..." He stood, holding in each hand a folded length of material, one a soft gray wool, the other a pale pink linen. "...that Miss Button should really be wearing a proper lady's skirt, and that in any case, she has outgrown the one she now wears each day."

The implication was clear. I was not able to see to the needs of my own daughter. "I'm sorry, I cannot afford such fine material, I"—Indignation bubbled up inside me, that he'd noticed and that he presumed to force me to do something about it.

"Oh no, no, no!" he said. "I would like to make a gift of the material to you and your daughter. You have been so diligent and reliable over the years. It has meant a great deal to me." His forehead creased in worry. "If I have offended you, I apologize."

"I couldn't accept such costly gifts," I said. Gifts, in my experience, pledged one to some kind of repayment.

"You would be under no obligation to me, let me assure you! Only I know that in your skilled hands, these materials would be put to good use, and Miss Button should wear clothes that do not make her look like a pauper." He blushed a deep crimson. "I did not mean...I'm sorry..."

I was ashamed of my assumption that he had some hidden purpose. Perhaps Mr. Silverstein was not like other men. He could have imposed himself upon me years ago, and he didn't. "Well, for Sylvie...Thank you," I said, reaching my hands out to take the material.

His brow smoothed, and he broke into a wide, joyful smile. "Please don't tell her the cloth came from me. This can be our secret." Mr. Silverstein picked up the now empty satchel, and said, "I'll be back later for the waists."

As I ran my hands over the material, I couldn't help thinking back to another time when I had handled such luxurious stuff. It was at the convent of the Sisters of Sion, in Paris, a long time ago. I learned my craft sewing wedding gowns for wealthy young ladies, who settled for nothing less than the finest peau de soie, lace, velvet, and such embellishment as was appropriate and fashionable. When it was time for me to leave the convent—for I showed no inclination for cloistered life—the sisters thought they had done me a kindness in purchasing an apprenticeship for me to a dressmaker. I believe that if they had known what was to come, they would have done otherwise. That woman tormented me so much that, after only a few months, I ran away from her.

Then Victor found me. He saw me steal a piece of bread off someone's plate at an outdoor cafe, a desperate measure born of extreme hunger, and took me in. Recognizing someone vulnerable and naive, he taught me a different way to earn a living. I still curse him for it, except that in the end, his introduction to Alfonse resulted in Sylvie—my blessing, the one bright spark of light in my life.

In giving me something that would make Sylvie happy, Mr. Silverstein showed a degree of understanding about me that I didn't expect. The man I only exchanged polite greetings with and considered more a means to an end than a person had observed us quite astutely over the past years. I first met him when I applied at Leiserson's Shirtwaist Factory for a job. He saw me and explained that the factory work would not do for someone with a child and no family to leave her with. But instead of walking away, he gave us the means to survive by bringing us piecework. Most remarkable of all to me, he never appeared to think I owed him anything for it.

Perhaps that was why I hardly considered him to be a man. Men wanted things from women. I knew that too well.

CHAPTER
THREE

Sylvie

"I don't understand why you won't tell me the simplest thing! Where was I born? Who is my father?" I was ready to leave for school, my hand on the doorknob.

My mother whirled around from where she stood rinsing off plates at the kitchen sink. Her eyes flashed with fury. I stepped back. She took a deep breath and closed her eyes for a moment. When she opened them, she said, "You must trust me. I will tell you someday. But now is not the time."

Trust? How could I trust someone who told me nothing! I opened the door fast to rush out and nearly ran into Joey Cooper.

"Good thing you're pretty, or I'd give you a black eye for that," he said with a wink before hurtling down the rest of the stairs two at a time, shoving his arms into the sleeves of his patched coat as he went.

Pretty? Joey was the oldest son in his family. My age, but

already working in a factory and bringing home wages to help feed his five brothers and sisters. I couldn't imagine how they all fit in a space the same size as ours, except that in the summertime, like other children in the building, I'd find them sleeping in the hallways or on the fire escape when I crept out of our apartment to use the commode.

I hurried down the stairs after him, picked my way down the stoop to avoid the patches of ice that still hadn't melted off in the morning sun, and set off at a snappy pace, shaking my head to clear it of my angry thoughts and turn them toward a pleasant, moving-picture fantasy. My walk to school was long enough to accommodate an entire drama. Lately, my stories all involved a tall, dark Italian boy, who usually ended by declaring his undying love for me.

I attended the Girls High School mostly because of Mr. Silverstein, who had told my mother about it and its modern building and progressive methods of teaching. I would get a better education there, he said. That was enough encouragement for her. I was just happy to have a reason to leave our neighborhood and its dirt and squalor. And to be honest, I had to admit that I loved school. I worked hard, my teachers liked me, and I had been asked to submit an essay for a prize. The prize came with a hundred-dollar scholarship to Teachers College.

I was the only girl from Mulberry Street who took the trouble to go all that way. It was a shorter walk to Henry Street School, and those other girls could get home sooner to help watch the little ones or do chores. Since most of them left off school at fifteen to work in the factories, they didn't care so much about learning. The girls in my class at the High School were mostly from the German neighborhood, which was richer than ours.

That morning, although it had snowed the night before, a thaw sent a warm breeze to tease me with a promise of spring when it wasn't yet officially winter. The warmth also melted the light snow, and I had to dodge slushy puddles every time I crossed a street. I was so preoccupied with placing my feet where I wouldn't ruin my only pair of shoes that the tap on my shoulder just as I was about to cross Houston Street startled me. I jumped and dropped my satchel, spilling school books and papers into the wet, dirty gutter. "Oh no!" I cried, madly scrambling to pick everything up before it was ruined.

"Let me help!"

Although I'd only heard it once, I had replayed that voice in my mind so many times that I recognized it instantly. I had met him two full weeks ago and I'd given up hope he'd actually seek me out. I forced myself not to immediately turn around and look at him, just continued scooping up my dropped books and papers alongside him. Every now and again our hands touched, sending electric shocks up through my gloves and into my belly.

"May I walk along with you?" he said.

"I'm only going to school," I said, my cheeks now burning. I could blame it on the brisk breeze if he noticed.

"Do you always walk by yourself?"

"Yes. Why?"

He shrugged. "Only that a pretty girl like you shouldn't be wandering the streets of Manhattan without a man to protect her."

He called me pretty. That was twice in one day a boy used that word to describe me, although I expected Joey had just been kidding me. I was so shocked it took me a moment to realize that I failed to answer his first question, that he must have assumed a yes, and so began to walk with me along the sidewalk toward school. Up ahead was a corner I always tried to avoid, where a crew worked every day putting up a new building. The times I forgot to turn and passed right by it, the ruckus the men created calling out "Darling!" and "Sweetie!"

and things whose meaning I didn't know but could guess, drew unwanted attention to me from everyone who happened to be out at that time. "Let's turn here," I said, already starting east toward the next block to take the long route around.

"Isn't your school just up there?" He pointed along First Avenue.

"Yes, I..." How could I explain my silly detour?

"Come with me," he said, and tucked my free hand into the crook of his elbow.

I braced myself for the jeers and catcalls and embarrassment, fixing my eyes on the pavement in front of me.

But nothing happened. I looked up. Several of the men stared at me, suppressing smirks. One tugged the front of his cap at Paolo and nodded. A satisfied smile tickled the corners of Paolo's mouth. Of course. I didn't know whether to be annoyed or proud. I wondered if being with any young man would have silenced the workers, or whether it was something about Paolo in particular.

"Looks like I better walk with you every day," he said as we shook hands goodbye about a block away from the entrance to the school.

"Oh, I'm sure that's not—"

"And I'm sure it is." He lifted his cap up off his head and winked at me, turned on his heel, and strode away.

And after that Paolo did walk with me every day. I suspended my usual parade of imaginary moving pictures to occupy my mind on the long walk to school, because suddenly real life was much more interesting. When Paolo and I weren't together, it was his face, his body that I cast in the role of my protector as I dreamed and sewed.

Our morning walk was always a bit hurried because I didn't want to be late for school—something Paolo made fun of me for.

"What's so important? You can read and write and do your

sums. What else is there to learn?"

I couldn't come up with any other answer than to parrot back what my mother said, about college being the only way to better myself in the world.

"And this thing you're writing. Haven't you finished it yet? What's taking so long?"

"It's an essay. I want it to be good, so I have to write it and rewrite it."

"Seems like a waste of time to me."

Did he really not understand? "It's the only way to win the prize. And the prize comes with a scholarship. A hundred dollars!"

"Now that's something I get! What will you spend it on?" His mischievous grin made me laugh.

"I can only 'spend' it on tuition at Teachers College. The money's not mine, it's just set aside for me."

He shrugged. "Then what's the point?"

"I'll be able to go to college and become a teacher." We'd slowed our pace as we approached the place where we usually parted.

He pulled me to a stop and turned me toward him. "Is that really what you want?"

If I could only tell him what I didn't dare tell another soul. Surely it wasn't wicked of me to wish I could be in the moving pictures? My mother never asked me what I really wanted, as if wanting were a sin, like sloth, or vanity. And in some ways, I did want to go to college. At least, I wanted it because she did. But always, in my heart, I clung to that other dream, to have a life so different from the one I had that I thought it must be better. At least, then, I would have done something exciting.

But I said none of that. "I'd better go before the bell."

The day before Christmas Eve, Paolo and I took a detour after school to Tompkins Square Park. He led me to one of the benches so we could sit down. I had never been so alone with

Paolo. A shiver of excitement passed through my body, so close to his, sitting on the bench. I didn't know what to say to him, why he'd brought me there.

"I don't know if I'll see you at Mass on Christmas Day."

I didn't expect him to say that, for sure.

He glanced around before reaching into his inside coat pocket. "I wanted to give you something. Something to make you think of me wherever you are." He handed me a small wooden box with a tiny brass hinge on one side and a latch on the other.

"What is it?" I asked, not sure if I should take it.

"Open it!" he said and swiveled a bit on the bench so he faced me directly.

My hands shook as I took off my glove to work the latch. I lifted the lid and gasped. The box held a simple pendant with a small pearl, or something that looked like a pearl anyway. "It's beautiful!" I said, and his face relaxed into the smile that always made me melt a little inside.

"Here, let's see how it looks on you." He lifted the pendant out of the box, had me turn away from him, threaded his fingers under my collar, and pushed my braid to the side to fasten the fine chain around my neck. I felt his hot breath as he concentrated on the clasp, and I shivered again, only in part from the cold. When he finished, his fingers lingered, touching the place where my hair stopped and the skin at the top of my spine began. I closed my eyes. "Thank you," I breathed.

He stood and reached down for my hand, pulling me up and turning me toward him. I opened my coat so he could see the pendant hanging against my shirtwaist. "It's not real gold," he said, "but the Chinaman said the pearl wasn't fake."

"It doesn't matter. I love it. I've never owned a necklace before."

He looked at me the way no one else in the world did, looking at all the parts of my face, not just into my eyes—the line of my chin, the curve of my cheek, the place where my forehead yielded to my hair. I wondered a little but didn't ask him how he had the money for a gift, even one as small as the necklace. All that mattered was that he had given me this, and that he liked me. The gift proved it beyond all doubt.

"Are you really going to hide yourself away in a classroom for the rest of your life in front of a bunch of kids who don't want to be there?" He lowered his voice, moving a little closer to me.

I tried to laugh, but couldn't, aware all the time of his body so close to mine.

"You said you liked the moving pictures. You're pretty enough to be in them yourself, you know." He took hold of my upper arm and rubbed it, slowly, warming me.

But how did he know? How could he have guessed at a dream I never shared with him? Perhaps he was just trying to flatter me. Yet no one had ever even tried to guess what it was I wanted, let alone hit on it so perfectly.

"You're just saying that." I was aware of how small my voice sounded, and of the faraway sounds of people passing along the streets in trolleys and cabs, children laughing, dogs barking.

"I wouldn't, unless I meant it." He stepped still closer and took hold of my chin, then turned my face this way and that. "*Si.* I have no doubt at all that you could even be a model in one of the magazines, *Harpers Bazaar*, or in the advertisements in *McClure's*."

"A model?" Suddenly us being there together felt dangerous. I tried to pull away, but he held me. Not hard—I could have broken away if I really wanted to—just enough.

"Hey, I have an idea. I know a photographer. He owes me a favor. Why don't you come with me, and he can take some pictures of you, see what he thinks. He's had photographs in the magazines. He'd know if you could do it."

I wanted—how I wanted!—to agree. But I couldn't. Could

I? How did I know if I could trust Paolo? All my mother's warnings swam in fragments in my mind. But they could not compete with the reality of him, there in front of me, touching me. Still...

"I can't. I have school, and when I'm not at school, I have to help my mother with the waists." My matter-of-fact words broke the spell.

"Well, if you change your mind, all you have to do is say." Paolo let go of my arm and I must have been pulling away more than I thought, because I lost my balance a little. He immediately reached out to stop me falling and drew me to him again. My pulse pounded in my ears. What was I doing?

Just as I felt the heat of his breath joining mine, I stepped back. He didn't stop me. I must have been red as a cherry. "I-I have to get home. My mother will wonder what's become of me, and it'll be dark soon."

He only smiled. That smile. Perfect, white teeth framed by full, moist lips. One night I dreamt about what it would be like to touch them with my own and awoke in a haze of pleasure. "*Andiam'!*" he cried, caught hold of my hand, and we set off running through the park.

When I walked through the door of our apartment, I was still breathing heavily. We hadn't run all the way, but we had to keep up a fast pace if I wasn't to make my mother suspicious.

"Are you well?" She put down her work and rushed over to me, laying the back of her hand on my forehead. "You look flushed. Are you *fièvreuse?*"

Before I could stop her, she reached under my coat collar to feel the back of my neck. I had thought to tuck the pendant down underneath my shirtwaist, but the clasp was still on top of my collar.

"*Qu'est-ce que c'est?*" she said, following the chain and pulling it until the pendant was revealed. "Where did you get this?"

What could I say? If I told her the truth, I would have to admit to more than two weeks of deception. I said the first thing that came to me. "It's only a penny trinket. A girl at school gave it to me today, for Christmas."

"Why would she do such a thing?"

In my mother's world, people did not spend money on gifts for other people that had no use or that they did not need. "I helped her with an assignment she couldn't understand. She was grateful." The lie tasted like ashes in my mouth.

"Well, as long as you are well. Come, we have work to finish."

I took off my coat and hat and put my satchel in the corner, then sat down and threaded a needle, unable to stop thinking of how it felt to have Paolo hold me.

CHAPTER
FOUR

Sylvie

Paolo and I spent as much time as we could in each other's company. I started getting to school late, I told them my mother wasn't well and I had to take care of her. My record of punctuality and fine work smoothed the way, and I got sympathy and offers of help from my teacher, Miss Potter. I had more than a pang of guilt for lying about my mother's health, and thought that God might strike me down, or make my mother really ill, just to teach me a lesson.

On our walks every day, Paolo tried over and over to convince me that I should go with him to have my picture taken. "Don't you want to at least see what it's like?" he said. "Everyone gets their picture taken. I bet some of your friends at school have done it." He brought his lips close to my ear. "And I bet none of 'em are as pretty as you."

A little shiver went down my spine.

"Come on, it'll only take an hour. We could go at lunch-time!"

"I...suppose." Would it work? Could I really do it?

"Day after tomorrow. I'll wait for you out here."

We were a block away from the school. I looked up and down the avenue, thinking, weighing the past against the future. "You promise it will only be an hour?"

Two days later I told Miss Phillips I had to go home for lunch and make sure my mother drank the broth I made for her. I met Paolo, and we practically ran all the way to his photographer friend's studio. It was a Mr. Angelotti, on Fourteenth Street.

Although I'd seen a fair bit of Manhattan on my detours to school and back, I hadn't gone north beyond Twelfth Street since the day I went to the Nickelodeon. Just two blocks farther felt like traveling to another world. Instead of ground floor grocers and tailors topped by stacks of tiny apartments, on Fourteenth Street, businesses climbed over each other to second, third, and fourth floors. Brightly painted boards fixed somehow to the building exteriors shouted, *Scissors Sharpened Here, Gents' Haberdashers, Leatheroid Trunks and Cases, Newcome's Detective Agency.* I paused at the delicious smell of coffee emanating from a café, wishing I had had time to eat my lunch.

"We can come back here afterwards," Paolo said, pulling me along west.

Just before Sixth Avenue he stopped and led me into a building and up three flights of stairs. On the fourth-floor landing, he knocked on a door with a sign that said, *Richard Angelotti, Photogravures.* I confess, I was a little relieved. Not that I thought Paolo would do me harm, but I knew so little about him. Whenever I asked about him, he always steered the conversation back to me. The only thing I could be certain of was that he lived on Delancey Street.

A muffled voice called out, "Come in!"

We entered a long, narrow room with a painted board at one end from floor to ceiling. A large camera with its bellows extended sat atop a wooden tripod, pointing toward the board. I had only ever seen a picture of a camera like that. A picture of something that took pictures. I smiled. Light flooded in from two large, widely spaced windows looking out over the street. On the opposite side of the room stretched a long table with electric lights above it, none of them lit, and at one end of the table, a heavy black curtain hung, hiding part of it. Beyond the table, a door led to another room, and in between the table and the backboard stood a plain canvas three-paneled screen. I thought I heard something behind it, like a rat scratching in a corner.

"*Eh! Ricardo! Come stai?*" Paolo walked to the curtained area at the end of the table and knocked on the soft fabric as if it was a door.

"*Momento,*" said the same muffled voice that had called out to us to enter.

I wanted to laugh. Of course that's where the photographer was! I knew enough about the process to understand that the images had to be fixed to paper in the dark. Miss Philips had explained it in a science lesson, after she confiscated a *carte de visite* of the Vitagraph girl from one of the other girls. I confess I found it fascinating.

"Dickie dear, where did I put my stockings?" I jumped as a woman with jet black hair tumbling down her back in loose curls, wearing only a silk robe and corset, emerged from around the paneled screen at the end of the room. She stopped and jerked her chin in my direction. At first, she pulled the robe closer around her, then drew one side of it wider and held it open behind the hand she rested on her hip. There she was, in her undergarments in front of strangers, one of them a man. I didn't know where to look and tried to stop the heat rising into my cheeks. "Well, if it isn't the gorgeous Paolo

Bonnano! Who's the girl?"

"Eh! Maddalena! Got some work?" Paolo approached her and they kissed on both cheeks. It was a gesture of affection such as family members give, but I still felt a little stab of jealousy.

"Aw, you know. Just some cheesecake. Keeps me in whisky."

A short man with a flushed and sweaty face emerged from beneath the cloth at the end of the table. "I think this one's worth keeping," he said, holding up a sheet of paper with an image on it. He angled it in Maddalena's direction so I couldn't quite see it, but I caught a glimpse of a woman's bare leg. So, these were the kind of photographs Angelotti took.

"Tommy! I need you!" Angelotti yelled in the direction of the door next to the screen, and as if he had anticipated the call a young man bustled through.

"Give me the plate." He held out his hand and waited for the photographer to retrieve something wrapped up in a square of black cloth, flashing a quick smile as he turned to go back where he came from.

"Goodness! Time has flown. I really need to get home," I said. This was a bad idea. I wanted to have a chance to get into the movies, but not if it meant being so uncomfortable. Embarrassed and afraid at the same time. I had to find a way to back out of the plan.

In an instant, Paolo was by me and had hold of my arm. "Don't go! Dickie's a great photographer, but even the best got to make a living. You'll see."

"Go get dressed, *cara*," Dickie said to his model.

With a rough-edged laugh, Maddalena strolled back to the screen, hips swaying, and disappeared behind it.

Dickie put the photograph face down on the table then approached me, his expression open and appraising. "Richard Angelotti, at your service. You can call me Dickie, like everybody else does." His crooked-toothed smile was so unlike

Paolo's. He stared at me as though he could see right through my clothes and into my body. I couldn't look at him.

"Miss Button wants a photograph taken. She's thinking of trying to break into modeling. Or acting. With what you know about the business, I mean, I thought you'd be the best." Paolo shoved his hands in his pockets and took a step back.

Dickie continued to look me up and down, from the very top of my hat to my worn-down heels. He circled slowly around me. I turned. "Stand still!" he commanded. I could feel his gaze burning into me as he continued his orbit. "Take your gloves, coat, and hat off." He was obviously used to being obeyed. A moment later he added, "If you please."

I unbuttoned my jacket, removed my dingy gloves and shapeless hat, and held them all out to Paolo. Dickie pulled me over to stand just in front of the painted board opposite the camera, and walked back and forth in front of me, lips pursed, arms folded across his chest. "She's a pretty one, I'll give you that," he said, tossing the comment over his shoulder to Paolo. "Takes something else, though. Something special. Could be the hair. But photographs don't show color." Dickie kicked a cushioned stool over to me. "Sit."

I did as he commanded. He took hold of my chin and turned my face this way and that, the way Paolo had done the other day, and stopped when he had positioned my head at an awkward angle that made my neck ache. "Hold that. Don't move."

I wished I could see what he was doing, but my line of sight was limited to where I could move my eyes without changing position. The quiet young man emerged from the room again, bearing an apparatus attached by an electric cord to the wall. He fiddled with it a bit, filling a cavity with black powder from a vial. "Keep holding!" Dickie barked at me. "Eyes straight to the camera!"

The room erupted in a flash of light so piercing it almost knocked me backward. "Stay there!" Dickie yelled, pulling a plate out of the back of the camera and handing it off to his assistant.

I rubbed my neck and twisted my head this way and that. All I could see was a black spot in front of my eyes. I blinked hard, but the spot remained, only very slowly subsiding.

Paolo chuckled. "It wears off," he said.

A short while later, the boy emerged from beneath the black cloth holding a printed photograph up so we could all see it. Dickie smiled. "You're a natural!"

He brought the photograph closer, and I tried to look at it but the black spot in front of my eyes made it difficult. Still, I came over all peculiar at the sight. Attractive girl gazing out from that flat piece of paper, looking a little surprised, but still lovely. Was that me? Not the me I thought was real, the one who stared back at me from the cracked bathroom mirror, or who I caught sight of sometimes in shop windows. It didn't even match my made-up image of myself when I was trying to be the Vitagraph girl. I was different, but I wasn't ugly.

"What's the matter? Don't you like it?" Paolo asked.

"I'm just...astonished. Is that really what I look like?" I held the photo up for Paolo to see. He came closer.

"No," he said, "you're much prettier. But it's a fine photo, Dickie!"

"So, what's it to be?" Dickie asked. "A single gelatin print? Or are we making a plate?"

I wasn't sure what he meant. My knowledge of photography only went so far.

"Just this for now," Paolo said.

"We can work out the details later," said Dickie. "Could be we might help each other out." He turned to me. "You can get up now."

It must be obvious that I was naive about all this. I looked toward Paolo for reassurance and just caught him shaking his head and frowning in Dickie's direction before he turned his beautiful smile on me. "What'd I tell ya? There's a future in that face."

On our way back, we stopped in the cafe as promised. My empty stomach growled. I had twenty-five cents in my pocket—my mother insisted I carry just a little money in case it was ever necessary to take a trolley or an omnibus home—and I pulled out my coins to pay for the roll and coffee. I would find some way to explain the expenditure to my mother later.

"Don't," Paolo said. He raised my hand to his lips. The warmth of his breath penetrated right through my threadbare gloves. "Your life is gonna change. Starting today. I know some people could help you out."

Change. It was something I wanted so badly but never allowed myself to believe in. Could this really be the beginning of everything? Could that single, unmoving picture possibly lead to the life I wanted more than anything?

The thought scared and thrilled me. It was time for me to decide if I had the courage to defy my mother, to act, to grab at my dreams.

The next morning, I decided to try out telling Paolo about my ambition before broaching it with my mother. "There's something you should know..."

Paolo pulled me to a stop, a wary look behind his eyes.

"It's nothing serious, except that I don't really want to be a teacher. What I want most of all is to be an actress. In the moving pictures."

There it was again. That beguiling smile. "I knew it! I knew you couldn't want to hole yourself up in a dull schoolroom. Now we got to take more photographs. The magazines and movie folks want to see how you look in different clothes, with different expressions," Paolo said, "Least, that's what I hear."

"I have to go back?" I hadn't thought of that. How did Paolo know so much? "These are the only—" I suddenly felt ashamed that I owned only one winter skirt and two waists.

"Dickie's got stuff. You can borrow some."

I couldn't help remembering the barely decent clothes that model wore when we were at the studio and hoped he didn't mean I was to dress like that. Besides, I had no idea how I could manage it without my mother knowing. I had already decided not to tell her anything until I could make a real plan, so she could see it was possible. She had a way of cutting things down, of seeing only the bad in them, and I wanted to be prepared to answer every objection. When Paolo told me next time the session would take several hours, my hopes evaporated like a puddle on a hot sidewalk. "That'll never work. I can't do it."

"Course you can," Paolo said. "You been setting it up all these weeks. You tell the school you have to stay home with your mama, and you tell your mama that you have to go to school."

It sounded so simple. I wondered how often Paolo did things he had to hide from his parents. Perhaps meeting me was one of them. He hadn't suggested I be introduced to them or invited me to his home. Then again, neither had I.

"I don't know..." The luster of the whole idea faded the more I heard about what it would take. The essay prize would be announced the next day, and after all, I'd worked for years to prepare myself for college. Perhaps my mother was right. There was no certainty in a dream. And how could I know everything would go as Paolo said?

"Dickie said he'd have time tomorrow. Otherwise, it won't be for a while, maybe never."

"Oh no! That's impossible."

Paolo's smile faded. "He had someone else lined up to come in if I said no, and I thought I'd take a chance."

"I don't know..." The school would certainly believe that I had a legitimate reason not to be there if I was skipping what could be the announcement of a prestigious honor for me. And my mother didn't know which day the prize was going to be presented. I could just as easily tell her the outcome the day after. I might never have this chance again. Before I could think anymore, I said, "I'll do it."

I shrieked when Paolo picked me up off the ground and spun me around until I was dizzy.

CHAPTER
FIVE

Justine

Half an hour of my time, once a month, I told myself, and Sylvie will never find out. It was always in the same place, a room in a house on Twenty-Second Street. But it wasn't always Alfonse. His plan for me was more degrading than that.

I would find the key under the mat in front of the door and let myself in, and wonder who it would be each time, making myself into a pillar of ice, pretending I had no feelings. That was most difficult when it was Alfonse himself. Easier when he would send proxies. Sometimes the men he sent in his place were more generous. More often, they didn't pay at all, seeing me as some kind of *gratuité* Alfonse owed them. Bile rose into my throat whenever I imagined how he would put it to one of them. *Please, she is mine, use her* comme vous voulez.

"Ah, there you are."

"Bonjour," I said as always, hoping the foreign word would

discourage conversation. That time it was someone I'd never seen before and he sat with his legs splayed in an upholstered chair in the corner of the room—balding, fat, and sweating like a horse already. He stood and took off his belt, I assumed so that he could remove his trousers. Instead, he strode over to me, grabbed my arm, and threw me face down on the bed. Before I could scramble away, he lifted up my skirt, tore down my drawers, and brought the belt down on my naked behind, time and time again until my tears soaked the silk coverlet. "Stop! Stop!" I cried, no longer able to bite back the words.

"You've been a very bad girl, I hear. You must be chastised, you harlot! Show me your naughty!"

He turned me over, pinning me with one hand while he opened the front of his trousers so he could ram himself into me, so hard I thought he would rip me in half. I cried out.

He smiled.

Monster. Bête.

He finished quickly and gazed down at me with disgust. Before I could roll out of the way, he hawked up a great globule of spit, hitting me in the face.

I retched as I wiped it off with my sleeve and jumped to my feet, raising my arm to slap him, but he caught it and howled with laughter. The hand that gripped my arm wore a wedding ring.

He threw a bag of coins into the corner of the room and left me, shaken and bruised. I would have to bathe completely before I returned home. Worse, he'd ripped my drawers beyond repair. I had only one other pair and I'd have to change into them quickly before Sylvie got home. She must never suspect anything.

At least the room Alfonse rented had a private bathroom. I filled the tub with the hottest water I could stand and lowered myself in, gritting my teeth as the water stung where the belt had pierced my skin. Hate flooded my entire being. If that man dared return and I could find a weapon, I had no doubt that I would commit murder.

My bath was short, of necessity. As I pinned my hair back into place with my shaking hands, I saw that I had bitten right through my lower lip. That was one injury I would not be able to hide from Sylvie. All the way home, I spent thinking up something to say to her.

Sylvie came home late that day, fortunately, so I had extra time to compose myself.

"Maman, what happened!" She dropped her satchel in the middle of the floor and rushed over to me.

I could hardly speak for the flood of fierce love that gripped my heart. This remarkable child, this young woman, was so much better than I. "It's nothing! I tripped and hit my lip on the stove."

She accepted it. Why wouldn't she? She had no reason not to believe me.

"Tell me about your day," I said, "Don't bother about me, *ce n'est rien.*" I smiled, although it hurt, and soon we were sitting together as always, stitching, concentrating, each in our own worlds.

All the time, my mind bubbled and churned with anger. *How dare he.* I blamed Alfonse. Never, never again would I submit to such degradation.

My lip healed, and also the wounds on my buttocks. As the memory of that horrible afternoon faded, I tried to pay more attention to Sylvie. She continued to come home late from school, always with the excuse that she had had to take the long way to avoid the leering groups of men who teased and tormented her. I believed her, knowing what men thought of a pretty girl, that she existed for their pleasure alone. Yet that did not entirely account for the change I sensed in her. She was distracted. When I asked her a question, sometimes it took her a little too long to respond, as though she had to pull her mind back from some great distance. Worry about school and the coming exams before graduation, I thought, not wanting to delve any deeper.

Spring held back that year, as if nature wanted to play a cruel trick on us all. The money put aside for coal disappeared, and by the day when the school would announce the winner of the essay competition, the coats and gloves we'd tried to make last just one more winter had worn through. My mind was on such things when Mrs. Cooper stopped me as I was on my way back from the shared lavatory to see Sylvie off.

"I don't suppose you have a dollar to spare so we can buy another blanket or two?"

She had chosen a vulnerable moment, when normally the people on our floor who shared the toilet turned our eyes away and pretended we hadn't noticed that someone had just finished the most private ablutions. She must have been desperate. But what could I do? The times affected us all. "I'm sorry. Work has been slow lately." It was a lie, but not for myself. I had put by some small savings solely so that Sylvie could go to college and be lifted out of this depressing corner of the world. We were so close. I feared I was not as neighborly as I ought to have been, but I could not risk it, and I feared that Mr. Cooper took a great deal of comfort in strong spirits they could not afford. "Have you asked at the Settlement House on Henry Street? I understand they sometimes give such things to those in need."

She lowered her eyes. We were of an age, I judged, but the lines in her face and the pallor of her skin betrayed great hardship. "I can't leave the apartment. The twins are poorly."

Merde, I thought. She had the same concerns as I did. Just a mother, wanting to protect her children. "Wait here," I said. A dollar was four waists, about 2 hours' work for me. But I gave it to her. On that day when I hoped to see Sylvie be celebrated in front of her whole school, I felt generous.

Sylvie was just putting a book into her satchel when I returned. I said, "Do you think you won the prize?"

Her expression registered confusion at first, then cleared. "Oh! No, that's not today. I think it's tomorrow."

At the time I assumed she didn't want to raise my expectations. But I knew otherwise: the school had sent me a letter saying that I should attend the prize-giving ceremony on that very day, as Sylvie's essay was among the highest placed, although they could not tell me at that time whether she was the winner. The prize came with a handsome dictionary and the $100 scholarship—money that would ensure Sylvie could fulfill my fondest dreams for her. My one worry was that the day was a Thursday, and the very day I was expected at Alfonse's apartment. I comforted myself that he didn't know where I lived, and I could explain my absence to him by saying I'd been ill.

I worked fast that morning, knowing that I would lose more than two hours' sewing time walking to and from the school and sitting through the presentation. At eleven, I took off my apron and tidied my hair, put on my coat, and left the apartment.

"Going out on a day like this?" Unlike Mrs. Cooper, who kept to herself and only emerged from the apartment next door to mine when she needed something, Mrs. Murphy, who lived on the floor below, never let an opportunity to be nosy slip by.

"I have an appointment I cannot change," I said. I wondered how much she saw, at home all day with her three youngest children, always looking for something to take her mind off the fact that her husband could not support them and he beat her because of it.

"Your Sylvie gets prettier every day. She'll be finding a husband soon."

"I hope not!" I said, causing Mrs. Murphy to purse her lips in disapproval.

"Surely you'll be wantin' grandchildren," she said, shaking

her head and stepping back inside her apartment. She left her door ajar as usual, always watching for something to happen that never did.

Of course, none of us locked our doors. Usually someone was home, so it hardly mattered. If not, leaving the door unlocked ensured that in case of a fire, if your apartment proved to be the only way out for everyone else, you could save all your neighbors. It had happened somewhere, so everyone said, although no one seemed to know the details. None of us had anything worth stealing anyway, except the tools of our various trades, and those were sacrosanct to anyone who lived in the building. Thieves from outside would never bother with a building such as ours. The meager takings would not be worth the risk.

I pulled my gloves on as I continued down the worn stone steps. It was always dark in the corridors during the daytime, with only a skylight up above to give any light until sundown when the gas lamps came on. But that day the space seemed darker than usual. When I opened the heavy front door, I saw why. Outside the sky had become gray and low, as if a spring thunderstorm threatened, but it was too cold for that. I gave it no more thought, though. I was bent on my purpose, to go and see Sylvie achieve the culmination of all my dreams for her. I had no doubt she won the prize.

All around me people scurried along the street, muffled in raised coat collars and thick scarves, hurrying to get wherever they were going as the bitter wind picked up and made the cold even harsher. But I didn't notice. I flew to the school, elated with the prospect of the recognition my daughter was about to receive. By the end of that school year, once she was safely enrolled at Teachers College, she would be safe. She would be untainted by the vice and corruption that had marred my early life and still followed me into my middle years.

I had been to the school only once before, when I enrolled

Sylvie at the age of fourteen. It had been newly built, and still smelled of fresh paint and sawdust. Now, as I approached the entrance, I thought it looked as though it had been there for a century, so solid, so secure it seemed. Knowing that Sylvie spent her days there when I could not look after her comforted me. I followed the other parents into the building toward the auditorium.

A woman who might have been a teacher handed each guest a printed program as we filed in. The smell of books, and chalk, and young girls eager to learn filled my senses. I sat among the other hopeful mothers in the last few rows of the auditorium, craning for a sight of their own daughters. I didn't see Sylvie's blond head among those seated at the front. I assumed someone taller must have been seated behind her and blocked my view.

All around me, the other mothers had divided themselves into little groups of acquaintances mirroring the local neighborhoods—German, Jewish, Italian, and a few others I couldn't put in any category. There were few French immigrants in New York, and none that I knew of so far south, so I sat cloaked in stillness, soaking in the atmosphere of education and innocence that reminded me a little of my convent days so long ago, when I still hoped there would be more to life than degradation and endless sewing.

"Good morning, students and parents. It is my pleasure to award the essay prizes to talented members of our senior class." The principal went on after that for a long time, not satisfied with simply announcing the business of the day. I wished he would come to the matter at hand in my impatience to get the ceremony over with so I could return to work. He droned on about the virtues of hard work and application, about the importance to the city and the nation of an educated populace, capable of making informed, rational, and moral decisions, so they could in their turn bring up future well-educated generations. This was nothing I didn't well understand. Hadn't I always made that choice for Sylvie? As the minutes ticked by, I sensed the weight of the sewing piled high on the table in my apartment.

After half an hour, the moment finally came. The principal announced the third-place winner first, a girl with a German name and brown hair crowning her head in circles of tight plaits. After that, an Italian girl walked up on the stage to claim her second-place certificate. I held my breath.

"The winner of this year's senior essay prize is Miss Sylvie Button." The principal beamed. I thought my heart would burst as I waited for Sylvie to mount the steps to the stage and say a few words of humble gratitude. The applause continued, but nothing happened. The principal raised his hand to quiet the room and scanned the first row of students, and a teacher rose and approached the front of the stage. The principal bent over to hear what she had to say, then straightened and returned to the podium. "It appears that Miss Button is not present to accept her prize. We understand her mother has been poorly of late and only assume that she was unavoidably required to stay home to attend her."

What did he say? The world closed in on me as I barely heard the murmurs of, "Shame!" and "Oh dear!" all around me. I rose, my legs weak, not meeting anyone's eyes, and stumbled over the other mothers' feet in my haste to reach the door and run out onto the cold winter street.

What just happened? Where was Sylvie?

My mind was so full of questions that I watched the first few flakes of snow land on my sleeve and melt without any sense of what they were. When I lost my footing and slipped on the sidewalk, I at last looked up. The snow started to fall faster and faster, already piling up on railings and window ledges. Not the fluffy, lazy snow that coats the streets for an hour and then melts into muddy slush, but fierce, small flakes that whipped down the streets and sent people scurrying indoors. I watched it as if from a great distance. My world, the one I had been so careful to create, in which Sylvie was protected from all bad influences, had suddenly been slashed wide open.

I don't recall how I reached our apartment building and was still in a daze as I climbed the steps in the dark hallway to the third floor.

The door was ajar. Relief surged through my veins. "Sylvie! There you are!"

I rushed into the parlor, ready with questions I should have asked weeks ago.

But it wasn't Sylvie. Instead it was the very last person I ever expected or wanted to see beyond that door.

Alfonse d'Antigny, wealthy businessman and investor, sat on my work chair, a peacock in an ugly cage, not smiling. "Who is Sylvie?"

For the moment I could not frame a sentence. I, who was always so careful in my speech, sputtered. "*Saloppe!* You must leave! You must not be here! You promised! How did you—" My voice rose. Alfonse approached me and I shrank back, but his physical strength had not diminished with the passing years. He reached out and grabbed hold of me, his fingers digging into my upper arms so that I felt the imprint of his fingernails through my coat and blouse.

He pressed his lips close to my ear. "It was a simple matter to find you. One question to a shopkeeper about the French woman, and that was enough. I had my driver follow you to this neighborhood after we first met so that I might be able to find you if I found it necessary to remind you of our arrangement. This Sylvie, I imagine, is your daughter. Or should I say, our daughter?"

I tried to shake my head, to will him away, but he did not move.

"Don't dare deny it! Could it be that this daughter has been with you all along? That you stole that child in Paris and carried her across the ocean?"

Say something. Anything. Words swirled so fast in my mind I couldn't catch hold of them, and I finally blurted out, "How dare you come to my home! Get out this instant!"

He pushed me away from him and I staggered. "I could have you thrown in prison for the rest of your life!"

Once I regained my balance I lunged for the doorknob, thinking I would run out of the apartment into the street, call for help, or call for Mrs. Murphy to do it for me. But Alfonse reached me first and once more gripped me, dragging me through the kitchen toward the bedroom. The knowledge of what he was going to do made my stomach churn. Out of the corner of my eye I looked for something, a weapon, anything I could use to scare him away. I spied the tray of cutlery with the knife I always kept sharp to use in the kitchen. As I drew level with it, resisting his pull toward the bedroom with all my might, I grabbed it.

He was too quick. In one movement he wrested the knife out of my hand and turned me around so one arm was wrapped around my body, trapping my arms to my sides, and the other held the blade to my throat.

He laughed. A full-throated, unfettered roar, and before I knew it, he had thrown me onto the bed and then his full weight was on top of me.

His grunts of pleasure as he entered me with anger—and passion—grew louder and faster. His face contorted in pain and ecstasy as he finished, dropping on top of me and knocking the wind out of me. His heart pounded, the vein in his neck pulsing. I couldn't move. After a time, he rolled off me, his eyes still half closed.

I was bruised, inside and out, but I forced myself not to cry. I would not give him that satisfaction.

Alfonse sat up, swung his feet over the edge of the bed, and stood. He barely fit in the small space between the bed and the window to the kitchen. Like a surveyor taking the measure of a piece of undesirable property, he stared down at me. "How old are you now? You must be over thirty. Not as fresh as you were at seventeen, but still *un morceau délice*. I wonder, have you passed on your secrets to your daughter?"

I sprang up and flew at him, but he caught my wrists and stopped me. We were locked in immobile combat, neither of us willing to risk letting the other gain the advantage.

"Maman?"

Why hadn't I heard the door? My world was collapsing around me. The second before Alfonse turned to look in Sylvie's direction, in a desperate moment, I took hold of him and pulled him to me, kissing him hard on the lips and then keeping him in a fierce embrace. Over his shoulder, I saw my daughter, her eyes wide, mouth open. Explanations, justifications evaporated as soon as I thought them. I watched, helpless, as she threw her satchel down on the floor and ran out the door.

"Get out!" I screamed and pushed Alfonse away as suddenly and passionately as I had embraced him moments before. I didn't care if the neighbors heard, or what they thought. Let them come running and find this vile creature in my home.

He pulled himself up to his full height and straightened his clothing. He hadn't even paused to remove his overcoat, and within seconds he looked as if he had just walked in off the street. "I can only imagine who that was. Don't think for a moment you can hide her."

"No! Please!" I laid my trembling hands on his lapels. "Leave us alone. I beg you!"

He brushed my hands away and sniffed, looking around and not liking what he saw. "For the moment. My ship sails in a few hours. I return to France, but the next time I see you, I will come with the police, and reclaim what you stole from me. Every last *sou*, every last drop of blood."

The door slammed behind him so hard the plates on the shelves in the kitchen rattled. He was gone.

I had so much to do before he returned.

CHAPTER
SIX

Sylvie

A man. A stranger. In our bedroom. And my mother embracing him. I couldn't make sense of it. Unless everything she'd ever told me about herself, about the values of virtue and hard work, was a lie.

But I had been lying too. That very day the biggest lie of all, and only a few hours ago when my world was still normal, still what it had always been. I had agreed to the photo session, knowing I would risk missing the prize presentation. Knowing that if my mother found out, it would kill her. *Grab your opportunity!* I repeated to myself as Paolo led me along the streets to the studio. When we arrived, Paolo kept his coat and hat on.

"Aren't you going to stay here with me?" My heart sank. How could I do this alone?

He said a quiet word to Angelotti and nodded in my

direction. "Can't. Got work to do. Dickie'll take care of you, and I'll come back at..." he looked toward the photographer, who was lining up film plates for the camera.

"Two," he said. "That'll be enough time."

Nearly five hours! How could it take so long? I'd never make it in time for any of the presentation if I left there at two. Before I could call after Paolo and tell him I'd changed my mind, he was out the door, his footsteps fading as he ran down the stairs.

So there I was. Standing like a scared rabbit in the middle of the studio, alone with this stranger, no sign of his young assistant. I shivered.

"The heat'll come up in a minute." Angelotti didn't turn toward me as he spoke. He was still lining up his equipment, every now and then glancing in the direction of the backdrop. "There's clothes for you behind the screen. Go and put something on." Now that Paolo was gone, he snapped at me.

What am I doing? I didn't know what else to do but obey him. If none of the clothes there were decent, I decided I would leave. Paolo would have to understand.

The first garment that caught my eye was a shimmering silk robe, a lot like the one the model in the corset wore when we came here before. No. I wouldn't wear it. There were a few other scanty clothes hanging up, but in the middle of them I spotted a very smart lavender print cambric day dress with a high waist and a tiered skirt. I felt the fabric. Cheap, but the cut and style were not bad. I had never worn a dress like that, and I couldn't resist trying it. I took off my shirtwaist and skirt and stood in my chemise and stockings trying to figure out how to unfasten the dress.

"Come out and stand in front of the camera for me, Miss, so I can judge the light."

"I'm not ready yet," I said. My hands fumbled with the buttons. The more I hurried, the slower it went.

"There's a robe there. You can go back and finish when we're done with this."

That robe. It didn't even smell entirely clean. No man—or boy, even—had ever seen me without all my clothes on, even in a robe. I wanted to say no, to say he should wait for me to dress properly, but somehow the dress got all tangled up and I didn't know how long that would take. So I put on the robe, holding it tight around me. I searched for a belt or tie to keep it closed but there was nothing.

"Come on then!" Angelotti said, then muttered, "*Mamma mia, che bambina.*"

I tried not to look at Angelotti when I stepped out from behind the screen, my arms squeezed across my chest to keep the robe from slipping open.

"Over there, *vai.*" He waved his hand impatiently toward the backdrop. The fact that he didn't appear to be looking at me gave me courage, and I stood where he asked, facing three cameras, all pointing toward me at different angles.

"I just need to take a couple to see if the light's right," Angelotti said. "Relax, smile, don't be shy!"

Just as I was about to say something, the flash went, once again burning a black spot in front of my eyes. I let go of the robe and put the back of my hand up to shield them. Then there was another flash, and as soon as I took my hand away from my eyes and started to turn, the third flash went off.

"Good!" Angelotti said. "I'll just develop these and you can finish putting on that dress."

I went back behind the screen and, calmer now, managed to get the dress unfastened and step into it. But there was another difficulty: the dress buttoned at the back. Only ladies with servants or husbands wore dresses like that. The shirt-waists Maman and I sewed all buttoned up the front.

Maman. The thought of her brought a wave of heat into my face. I couldn't imagine what she would say if she saw me now, in a studio alone with an unknown man in a dress that fell open at the back. And what if Angelotti had some motive of his own, now that Paolo had left me here alone?

When I thought about it, that seemed unlikely. I was under Paolo's protection, and Angelotti respected Paolo.

"I haven't got all day!" Angelotti called.

Here I go, I thought. It was time for me to take a step toward the future, the one Paolo had encouraged me to reach for. It was time for me to see if I had "what it takes," as he put it, to be someone whose face would be adored like the Vitagraph girl. A moving picture began playing in my head. I was a fashionable young lady going to a society party where a handsome suitor—who looked just like Paolo but wore a dinner jacket—greeted me by kissing my hand. I walked out from behind the screen. "I need help getting it fastened."

You've got a natural talent, Miss Button.

I kept hearing Angelotti's words as I stood on the sidewalk on Fourteenth Street waiting for Paolo to meet me. I could almost taste the new life waiting for me in Brooklyn—that's where Vitagraph Studios was, I'd learned. How would my mother react when I told her that I wasn't going to college? I couldn't even imagine what she'd say. I'd have to be brave.

In the hours that passed while I was in the studio, it had begun to snow, and as I waited there, flakes whipped and eddied down the street from the east, sending pedestrians scurrying for shelter. But I felt so alive! I didn't mind the cold.

I kept standing there as the snow fell harder, and still no Paolo. I knew the way home from there, but never thought I'd have to go alone. My glow of confidence began to wear off. I felt every threadbare spot in my coat and shivered. Everyone else out in the storm rushed to find shelter. The snow, already inches deep, had made it all but impossible for automobiles to drive down Fourteenth Street, and the trolley tracks were buried too. A block or so down, a horse pulling a cab slipped and fell to its knees. The cabbie helped the horse up and led it away.

That's when I began to panic. This was no little snow shower. If I waited much longer for Paolo, I might not make it home at all. The snow was a blessing, though, the more I thought about it: my mother would not question why I was late.

I somehow managed to stay on my feet, but don't remember exactly what route I took to get back to Mulberry Street. Despite the weather, I was still thinking of all the possibilities, figuring that there was now a real chance I wouldn't have to keep walking down the path my mother had paved for me over the years. To be a teacher, I now believed, was her ambition, not mine. I would stay in school and graduate. That would be enough. If I waited until after I went to college, I would be old, and the opportunity might no longer exist. I thought maybe, if everything didn't work out as I hoped, I could maybe go to college then.

My spirits soared as I took the stairs in our building two at a time. I didn't care if anyone saw me. I burst through the door, ready to get to work sewing with the secret of my changed plans for the future to keep me company.

As soon as I stepped in, I could tell something was wrong. Maman wasn't seated where I expected to find her, behind a mound of snowy cotton cambric, forehead creased in concentration as she whipped swift stitches into the neat folds she made with her fingers. She wasn't in the kitchen either.

The bedroom. There I saw her through the kitchen window, or at least I saw her eyes, looking over the shoulder of a broad man. The earth beneath me started to spin out of control. I turned away. I didn't want to see the man's face, and I didn't want him to see mine. This stranger and my mother must have been in our bed. I thought I would be sick. I couldn't stay there a moment longer. I couldn't face my mother right then. She would have to lie to me. Or tell me a truth I didn't want to hear.

I dropped my satchel and ran back down the stairs, out into the blizzard.

Paolo. I must find Paolo.

CHAPTER
SEVEN

Justine

As soon as Alfonse left, as soon as I was certain he could not be waiting out in the storm, I grabbed my coat and flew down the stairs, throwing the door open only to be met by a wall of blinding white. I could just see the outline of the buildings on the other side of the street, but not a soul was abroad other than me. I thought I'd be able to follow Sylvie's footprints to where she had gone and explain everything, bring her back to safety. But even the traces of Alfonse's automobile had been swept away by the wind and snow. I stood, helpless, looking up and down the empty street, willing Sylvie into view. Tears burned down my cheeks.

It was the first time I'd wept since Paris, since the day Alphonse stole our baby girl from me and assumed there was nothing I could do about it. No one would ever have allowed me to take her back from him, from the luxury and ease of his aristocratic wife's care. My claim—I was only a mother and a whore—would never be recognized. My body bore her, yet she was her father's property.

But Alfonse failed to understand that no law could keep me from reclaiming what was mine. He had underestimated the power of a mother's love, perhaps not believing that someone like me was capable of such a thing, thinking that all I cared about were jewels and gowns. He must have been so surprised when I took Sylvie away from her nursemaid that day in the park. I had planned it all so carefully, and by the time he informed the police, we were on board a ship to America with new names and twenty-five dollars. We were safe, and now Sylvie had blossomed into a beautiful, smart young woman, educated enough to do something good with her life. I had lifted her up, high above myself.

Alphonse! I wanted to scream his name, curse him aloud. It was his fault. His alone. He had driven Sylvie away.

Two more inches of snow had fallen by the time I felt the cold penetrating through my inadequate coat and into my bones. With no hope of success at that moment, all I could do was return to the apartment.

I no sooner stepped through the door than I heard, "Mrs. Button!" It was Mrs. Evans, who lived with her husband and four children in one of the first-floor apartments. She stood hugging herself in her open doorway.

I dashed away my tears. "It's so cold outdoors my eyes are watering. I just wanted to see if Sylvie was coming home."

"They sent the children home early from the schools, right after the snow started. She should be here by now."

From higher up the stairwell came another voice. "I thought I heard her just a little ago. Perhaps not. Maybe she stopped in at a friend's." Mrs. Cooper peered down over the railing on the second floor. Several more of my neighbors had come out onto the stairwell and into the hallway and followed my progress up to my apartment with curious gazes.

I came level with Mrs. Murphy standing in the doorway of the apartment directly below us. "She's not home yet, then?"

I shook my head.

Like a collection of dark-haired dolls, all the Winkelstein children stared down at me through the railings on the fifth floor as I trudged up the last flight of stairs to our fourth-floor apartment, all the strength drained from my limbs. What had they all heard? What had drawn so many of them out like that? The walls were thin. I had no doubt Alphonse's angry words had pierced them. But we spoke French. They wouldn't have understood anything.

"I expect Sylvie will be here soon," I said as I reached my own apartment and turned, encompassing all the neighbors in the sweep of my eyes.

When I closed the door behind me, I leaned my back against it and slumped to the floor, my legs no longer able to support me. Sylvie would return before I knew it, I told myself, and we would talk, and I would explain things I should have explained so very many years ago. She had just been startled by what she saw. She couldn't stay away for long. And she can't have gone far in that weather. No one could.

The unfinished pile of waists sat on the worktable, inert, unconcerned. The work waited for me, and I had to do it. I struggled to my feet, took off my wet coat, and hung it on the hook by the door. Work would soothe me. The familiar action of my fingers would help me think and plan. But my fingers were like ice, and it took me fully ten minutes to thread a needle before I could start in on the waists. There were too many for me to finish alone.

Alfonse was gone, but his threat rang in my head, swiftly followed by the words I wished I had had the presence of mind to fling back at him. I clenched my teeth as an argument raged within me. I told a mute Alfonse that I had only reclaimed what was mine, that he had no right to take an infant from her mother, that everything I did in those three years before I finally took matters into my own hands and repossessed my flesh and blood was because I had received a near-mortal wound, and had to withdraw from combat until I was strong enough to battle him. In that time, I simply did anything necessary just to stay alive. It was close enough to the truth, and it was what I told myself to excuse the fact that I had so easily gone back to the wicked ways that had gotten me in trouble before.

But then I hear Alfonse's answer. *I will have you thrown in prison. You could be hanged for your crime. I have powerful friends who will see you are returned to France to answer for your deed.* I knew too well that not just the law but also the power of wealth and position was all on his side.

The faster I tried to sew, the less progress I made. The pile of waists seemed to grow rather than shrink. I thought perhaps it was the light and rose to turn on the gas lamps. I glanced out the parlor window. Our only view was of the back of the row of brick tenements on the next street. Those buildings had disappeared. The wall of swirling white still descending from the heavens, both bright and dense at the same time, obscured everything normally in view. I put my hand out to feel the cold windowpane. When I took it away, my handprint was still there, as if a ghost on the outside was trying to get in.

Sylvie. Where was she? I had given up too easily. This weather was not just foul, it was dangerous. If she was out in it, I must try to find her.

Without another thought, I flew to where my still-damp coat hung on the peg by the door and shoved my arms through the sleeves. I had just grasped the doorknob when I heard two familiar knocks. Mr. Silverstein? But it wasn't yet six o'clock, the hour he normally arrived to collect our work until the calendar called it Spring, no matter the weather.

When I opened the door, there he stood, his hat and shoulders covered with snow.

"Where are you going?" he asked, then cast his eye around the apartment, spying the unfinished pile of waists. "I had to come early. Soon it will be impossible to go anywhere, even by foot."

He stamped the snow off his boots on the mat and entered, rubbing his hands together for warmth. "Where is Miss Button?"

I opened my mouth to speak, but my throat closed against the words so tightly I couldn't breathe.

Without hesitation, Mr. Silverstein took hold of my arms and steered me to a chair. "Let me get you some water. Then we will talk."

By then, I couldn't stop the tears I'd been fighting ever since I came indoors. When he returned with a glass of water from the kitchen sink, he gave me his own handkerchief. I took it, burying my face in it and letting my harsh sobs scrape into the air.

Mr. Silverstein brought the other chair over and sat directly in front of me, his knees almost touching mine. When the pressure in my chest relented so that I could breathe normally, I spoke. "Sylvie...she hasn't come home."

I couldn't tell him everything. I couldn't explain that she had seen me with the devil and her world had shattered around her at the same time, that she had come home and run away again.

"The weather is terrible. Most likely, she has stopped somewhere to seek shelter—in a shop perhaps, or with a friend."

I nodded, but I knew that wouldn't be true. Sylvie had no friends. She didn't have time to make them. Or did she? Why wasn't she at school on this of all days, when she was to receive an award that would go far toward securing her future? In the events of the afternoon, I had almost forgotten about her humiliating absence from the prize-giving and the questions it raised about what she had been doing these last weeks—perhaps months.

My eyes traveled involuntarily to Sylvie's satchel, still sitting on the floor where she dropped it before she fled. Mr. Silverstein followed my gaze. "Why didn't she take it this morning?" Now he looked alarmed as well. I scrambled to formulate a reason, anything but the truth.

"Mrs. Button—Justine, if I may—I have known you and your daughter these dozen years and more. I have watched her grow from a charming child to an eager and intelligent young lady. I have seen your struggles. I know how hard you work and the pride you take in your daughter's accomplishments. Something is wrong. Please trust me. I would like to help you if you are in trouble."

He offered me kindness, yet I could return nothing but suspicion. What interest could he have in helping us? Men did not give help without exacting a price, I knew full well. Yet Mr. Silverstein had never given me any cause not to trust him. I looked hard at this man whom I'd seen twice a day, six days a week, for such a long time. He wore the cap the Jewish men wore beneath his black Trilby. His coat was simple but of the finest cloth. He had a thin, tall frame and moved quietly through the world. I was ashamed of myself for never before remarking on the fact that he must have to stoop a little when he came through our door. And his dark eyes, half-hidden behind wire-rimmed spectacles whose lenses still had drops of water on them from the melting snow, held concern enough to thaw the iciest heart.

I realized then that Mr. Silverstein was the closest thing to a friend I had ever had in my life. "I don't want to keep you." I cringed at the inadequacy of such a response.

"I have time. No one is expecting me. I live alone. I go to my mother's for the Sabbath, but that is tomorrow. Please."

He settled as comfortably as he could into the straight-backed wooden chair, and I told him about the day, about the prize giving and Sylvie not being there. I didn't tell him she'd come home and run away again.

"That's very odd of her, to be sure. I don't understand why she didn't take her satchel, however, if she meant to deceive you in some way."

If I told him the rest, I had no doubt the good will I had earned from him over the years would vanish in an instant. "We had harsh words this morning. I refused to allow her..." I searched my mind for anything that would be believable, and then I remembered something she once asked me about, "...to go to the nickelodeon with her friends. She dropped her satchel and ran out the door, and that was the last I saw her."

He smiled. "In that case, surely she will return later, or if the snow is too deep and difficult, tomorrow morning, and all will be well. It is but the whim of a moment and will blow over quickly."

I wanted so desperately to believe his words. But I knew they were founded on an incomplete knowledge of the facts. "Thank you, Mr. Silverstein," I said, and stood and put out my hand for him to shake.

"Please, call me Aaron. Mr. Silverstein was my father." He smiled and enveloped my hand in both of his. "I am certain she will be here before long. I will return tomorrow, as normal."

His gaze fell once more on the unfinished waists. "A pity the weather prevented me coming here this evening to collect your work. I'll do it tomorrow evening instead."

Yet another kind gesture. Perhaps the kindest of all. "Thank you, Aaron."

He walked out the door and closed it gently behind him.

Sylvie did not return that night. I paced across and back in my tiny parlor until Mr. Murphy downstairs pounded on the ceiling with a broomstick.

I don't know why I hadn't thought of it before, but at about midnight my gaze fell again on Sylvie's satchel where she had dropped it next to the front door. It was never my habit to look in her things. Before that day, I had no need to.

Or so I thought. The fact of Sylvie's running away, the intrusion of my former lover into our private world—together they had crowded out the shock of going to Sylvie's prize-giving ceremony and discovering she wasn't there, and that she hadn't been in school at all. I wondered if that was the first time she'd left the apartment and not gone to school, just returned at the usual time knowing that I would not question where she'd been. What was it the principal had said: they knew her mother had been ill of late. Sylvie had not only been lying to me—perhaps more than once, perhaps many times— but also to her teachers, using my health as an excuse. I was more worried and confused than angry, though.

I brought Sylvie's satchel to the worktable, pushing the waists I had not finished that day to one side, and tipped the contents out.

A geography book, a notebook filled with mathematical problems, *The Last Days of Pompeii* by an English author, a book called *The High School Word Book*, and a composition book landed with a series of thuds on the worktable. I opened the composition book. It was neatly arranged with notes and dates for each class. I turned to the furthest page and was relieved to see that she had written notes the previous day and all the days before that, so yesterday must have been the first time she had missed an entire day of school. But why that particular one of all others, a day when she must have known she had a good chance of receiving a much-coveted prize? She can't have realized that the school made certain I would be there. Had she mistaken the date herself?

I started paging through the geography book. I wasn't really looking at what was there, only using it to focus on something, anything that would give me some reassurance that Sylvie would soon walk through the door, an explanation that made perfect sense on her lips.

Then I found it. Just inside the back cover of the textbook. A photograph. At first, I didn't even realize it was Sylvie. Looking out at me was a young woman in full possession of her beauty and ready to use it to conquer the world. For the first time, I could see Alfonse in her. The shape of her eyes. Her chin. I think I had deliberately ignored those traits before. Somehow, in that photograph it was all I could see. No amount of hiding her from him could change the fact that Sylvie was Alfonse's daughter. The photograph itself, with its muted grays and starched stillness, brought back scenes of photo exhibitions in Paris. Alfonse would take me with him, pointing out the ones he thought the best. He mingled with the photographers, fascinated by the process and the magic of photography. *These images are saved forever.*

Saved forever. *Oh Sylvie.* She was in much more danger than I thought.

CHAPTER
EIGHT

Sylvie

What did I just see? It was too much to figure out, too foreign
to everything I knew of my mother. I had run back outside so
fast that the snow on my shoulders and hat didn't have time
to melt before I was engulfed by the storm once more.

Paolo. I had no one else to turn to, no one with the slightest
idea who I was and what I'd just done, hoping to change my
life, to go forward. My mother only knew one way, I thought.

And yet, the man. The only other man who had ever been
inside our apartment was Mr. Silverstein. Where did that man
come from? Did Maman really spend all her time sewing while
I was off at school? My thoughts scattered like the snowflakes
that danced and whirled around me, and the only person I
wanted to talk to was an Italian boy I'd met at church who'd
seen something in me I hardly dared see in myself.

I could never go back to who I was, not now, not when I

knew my mother had been lying to me, possibly for years.

But where next? I looked back at the closed door of our building, the stoop now covered by at least six inches of snow, the fierce wind piling even more up as I watched. What if my mother came out looking for me? I didn't want to see her. I couldn't face her, not yet. I just started walking as fast as I could, kicking a path through the snow in the direction of the church. If I knew where Paolo lived, I'd have gone there. But he was the one who came to find me on my way to school. He said he lived on Delancey Street, but where? I thought I might see someone and be able to ask if they knew where the Bonnano family lived, but the shopkeepers had already pulled their wares indoors and closed their shutters against the storm, and anyone with any sense was rushing to get inside. Soon I was the only soul wandering through the neighborhood during a blizzard like I'd never seen before.

My shoes soaked through almost immediately, and my skirt was wet up to my knees and so caked with snow I could hardly walk. I was in a waking nightmare, colder and more alone than I had ever felt. I knew I should just go home, but I couldn't. I wasn't ready for explanations, for confessions. Nothing made any sense anymore.

My mother was a stranger.

I had worked my way south, beyond the Church of the Most Precious Blood, and thought I might be nearing the Italian neighborhood. My hopes were vanishing about the possibility of finding Paolo when, through the whistling wind, I heard a higher-pitched sound that I recognized after a moment as a policeman's whistle. Someone I could ask! Perhaps he would know of the Bonnanos, how to find their apartment. "Officer!" I called out, but the muffling snow deadened my voice, the way a scream in a nightmare doesn't carry no matter how hard you try. So I pressed on, following the direction of the repeated whistles, which as far as I could tell came from south and west of where I was, leading me out of the Italian neighborhood into Chinatown. Here one or two brave souls kept their shops open, taking advantage of the need of those caught in the storm to find shelter. An older Chinese woman saw me and beckoned me to come inside, but I remembered something my mother had warned me about, that sometimes people pretended to be kind in order to lure young girls into slavery. I shook my head no and continued toward the raw screech of whistles, now at least three of them.

A great gust of wind took my breath away just as I reached the wide expanse of Canal Street. The snow was so thick and fierce I couldn't see the other side, and it threw the sounds of the whistles around so that they were farther away one minute, then right by me the next.

In the rushing wind, I almost didn't hear it.

"Sylvie!"

I turned in a full circle. "Is someone there?"

"Over here!"

It was Paolo! But where was he?

Before I knew what was happening, two hands grabbed me from behind and pulled me into a narrow passage between two buildings. I shrieked.

"Shhh!"

I threw my arms around Paolo's neck. I thought I would be relieved to find him, but instead something broke inside me. All at once, I realized that someone I had only known for a few months was all the family I could claim for the future now that I felt I had lost my mother. She would never forgive me for running away. I started to cry. "It's awful!" My sobs swallowed up the words.

"Shhh, you got to be quiet!" His harsh whisper sounded both angry and frightened. He covered my mouth with one cold hand and put a finger to his lips.

He might just as well have slapped my face, my tears

stopped so fast. Something was wrong. This wasn't the Paolo I knew.

The police whistles grew very close. Paolo held me tight so that I couldn't move and backed further into the alley.

My heart pounded. Of course. The police I had heard were searching for Paolo. I stifled a gasp and looked up at his stony face. He didn't blink. He hardly breathed. If I couldn't have made out the curl of his lashes and the sensuous bow of his mouth, I wouldn't have recognized him.

"He's gone," one of the officers said. I heard it so distinctly he must have been standing very near the entrance to the alley.

"What's that down there?" another officer said, and I heard steps crunching through the snow, growing closer.

Paolo turned me toward him and kissed me hard on the mouth so that I could hardly breathe, bending me backwards with the ferocity of it. Soon the kiss softened, and the warmth of his lips and his tongue melted something inside me. I kissed him back. He made a little sound of pleasure and darted his tongue inside my mouth. I gasped.

"Better find shelter, you two! This ain't the weather for a clandestine meetin' outside!"

The two officers laughed and moved on. If they were looking for Paolo, they would be looking for one man, not a couple. That was why Paolo had kissed me. Not because he loved me. I pulled away, still feeling the press of his lips against mine, the imprint of his straight teeth, his hot breath. He had used me for his own protection, and still gripped my arms so hard it hurt. Yet my knees felt as if they might buckle, and all I wanted was for him to kiss me again.

Once the two officers' footsteps had faded down Canal Street, Paolo's whole body relaxed, and he let go of me.

"What's going on?" "Why are you here?" We both started talking at once.

"It's complicated. Too much to explain," I said. The glow

of the kiss had worn off and I started to shiver.

"Me too," he said, and at last turned his attention to me instead of his surroundings. I could sense he was still alert, ready to spring, like a hunted animal. "I have to get out of Manhattan for a while. Can you make it home in this weather?"

His eyes. Those eyes. Now the Paolo I knew was back. "Take me with you!" The words flew out before I could stop them. "I can't go home. Not now."

"You have to! You don't want to get mixed up with this, with me. Besides..." He traced the curve of my cheek with his index finger.

Paolo didn't finish his thought, and I didn't ask him *besides what?* All I wanted was to go with him. It was the answer to everything. I had no other choice. "My life, my mother—she's not who I thought. I can't go back, I just can't." The tears I'd swallowed back while we were hiding started again.

"Hey, now, it's all right." He reached into his pocket for a handkerchief but couldn't find one. "I want you to come. It'd be swell! But I have to walk a long way and fast as I can."

I wiped my tears away with the back of my gloved hand. "I'm all right. I can keep up. I have nothing to go back for." He couldn't leave me there. He just couldn't.

This boy I met in the safety of church, who had drawn me out of myself and awakened me to possibilities I'd only dreamed of, shook his head, drew in a deep breath, then blew it out through his mouth. "Come on then." He strode to the end of the alley and poked his head out, scanning for trouble.

Yet still I hung back. "Are you sure you really want me?"

Paolo's silhouetted frame almost completely blocked the entrance to the alleyway, beyond which was nothing but a white wall of swirling snow. I couldn't see his expression, so I had to trust his words. "Of course I do. I just have to change my plans a little. But that's all right. Let's go."

Forward, I thought, and ran to him. The snow was now

almost a foot deep and still coming down fast. "I got the same problem as you, in a way," he said. "Just follow me and do as I say. It's not gonna be easy."

He pulled me along and I trusted him. I pictured myself in a film, stepping outside of what was happening and watching it from a distance. Right now, we were in the middle of the crisis, the point where everything seems bleak and hopeless. But a happy ending was just around the corner. Whatever had happened, whatever Paolo had done to have the police looking for him, now that I'd taken this step, I felt safe. It made no sense, but I did. We started out west, the opposite direction the police had gone, against a wind that fought to push us back where we came from.

I don't know how long it took us to get there, but I soon found myself following Paolo up the slippery iron steps that led to the walkway on the East River Bridge. A sign posted across the roadway said, "Danger: High winds." The trains had all stopped, and even the guards had gone home to get out of the blizzard. We pushed on anyway, heads bowed against the wind, now roaring out of the east. I couldn't see the water below or any farther than a few yards along the bridge. We might as well have been stepping off the edge of the world. I supposed in a way that's what I was doing, leaving everything I knew behind and going toward a future I couldn't yet imagine.

I was sure we'd be the only people crazy enough to be on the bridge in this weather, until we reached the first tower that stretched up into the sky to support massive cables now caked with snow. But to my surprise, a lone photographer had set up a camera, the feet of the tripod buried, the black cloth that shielded the plate flapping in the wind. All I saw of the man were flailing arms as he tried to keep the cloth from letting in even a little bit of light. I glanced in his direction as we passed, slowing a little out of curiosity, but Paolo pulled me along harder. "We have to keep going!"

To where? The pause gave me just enough time to wonder. As we reached the middle of the bridge, my resolve faltered. "Exactly where are we going?"

"Friends," he said, "in Brooklyn."

Brooklyn. I'd never been there before, but I knew something about it, something Paolo probably didn't. Vitagraph Film Company was in Brooklyn. Somewhere. The girls at school talked about it, wondering if the Vitagraph girl might be spotted on the streets there, wondering if she ever went to Coney Island, or shopped in the busy town center. It wasn't much, but I chose to see it as a sign that I was heading in the right direction.

When we finally got to the end of the bridge, Paolo said, "We have to go this way, toward the docks. There's a place we can find some shelter. Maybe even get some food. Not far now."

I nodded. By that time, I was so cold I didn't trust my teeth not to chatter if I tried to speak. I had no choice but to do whatever he said.

I admit I was relieved to find that Paolo was true to his word. About fifteen minutes later, we reached a large warehouse near one of the Brooklyn docks. He pounded on a heavy metal door, and in a moment, it was opened not by a burly dockworker but by a boy about half Paolo's size. "Eh! Paolo! We thought you'd never get here!"

"Would I let you down, Tony?" he asked and they both started laughing. Paolo opened the door wider so we could get inside. The boy stopped halfway through a laugh when he saw me.

"Who's that?"

"She's a friend. She's with me. And we're froze through." Paolo clapped Tony on the back, but it didn't stop the young boy glaring over his shoulder at me as I followed them deeper into the building.

The sudden relief from the howling wind and snow made

my ears ring, and the silence magnified every little sound in the huge, empty space. I heard a fire crackling before we turned a corner, and I saw it, two more young boys seated near it on upturned barrels, hands extended toward the flames. Now I shivered in earnest as the snow that was stuck to my clothes started to melt.

Paolo brought two stools over from a pile of discarded furniture that leaned against a wall. "Take off your coat. It's wet. You'll warm up faster." I nodded.

Every time one of the boys started to ask Paolo a question, he shushed them. I had the distinct sense they needed to discuss something Paolo didn't want me to hear. By that time, I was too tired to care much, and it wasn't long before my eyes started to close as the fire warmed me through. Yet every time I began to slip into unconscious sleep, the image of my mother's horrified face jolted me awake again. I knew in my heart she had secrets she was too ashamed to tell me but never suspected something like that. The only part of her past she ever talked about was the convent, an English order, where she learned to speak the language. That, and being apprenticed to a horrible dressmaker when she left the convent. There were no men in that past she fed to me. Not even my father.

It didn't make sense. I wanted to know more, yet at the same time, I didn't want to know anything. Soon I was too tired to think at all. I was only vaguely aware that someone lifted me up and carried me to a place where I could lie down and sleep.

CHAPTER
NINE

Justine

When Aaron arrived the next morning, I had already been up for hours working on the waists left over from the day before, the full horror of what had happened flooding me with fear and sadness. I felt as if I had not slept at all, but I must have because I remembered a terrible dream where Alfonse and Sylvie ran away together, laughing at me, and I was in chains being led off to prison and was forced to watch them go.

I awoke with the certainty that whatever else happened, Alfonse must never find Sylvie. And that meant that he must never find me again. I would have to leave this apartment, find somewhere else to live. How I prayed that Sylvie would come home that day! Alfonse had said he was sailing for France yesterday and would come back—did he say in a few months? Why could I not remember?

The snow had stopped, but I could tell by looking down

into the yard behind the building that it was very deep. I would not have blamed Aaron if he chose to stay at home in such terrible conditions. I was relieved when I heard his familiar knock.

"Is Sylvie home?" were the first words out of his mouth.

I shook my head. The hopeful look drained from his eyes. He took off his hat and knocked the snow off it onto the mat inside the door. "I stopped at Leiserson's as usual. Half the girls are not there, the roads are still very bad, and no trolleys are running yet, although crews are out plowing and shoveling now and making good progress. And it's warmer today, so the snow will soon melt. It still could be that Sylvie got stuck somewhere and couldn't come home last night but will this morning."

"She'll miss another day of school."

"The schools are closed today, so at least there is that." Aaron continued to stand on the mat by the door, waiting for me to say something more.

"I'm sorry. Would you like a cup of tea?" I hadn't yet made any for myself. I had no idea if he would accept my invitation. It wasn't how we were with each other.

"I would, yes, but..." His voice trailed off as he looked toward my kitchen. "Perhaps just a glass of water."

I didn't understand at that time what made him hesitate, thinking that perhaps my kitchen wasn't clean enough for his taste. I had more pressing worries that morning than to feel offended, so I put the kettle on and fetched him a glass of water. He opened his mouth to speak, then closed it again. "What are you not telling me?" I asked.

"Only that, at the factory, there was talk of a terrible trolley accident, on Houston Street."

I put my hand over my mouth. Until then, I had thought it was only anger that could have kept Sylvie away.

"Apparently, a trolley's brakes wouldn't work on the icy

rails, and the driver lost control. Instead of curving around to go down Bowery, the trolley came off the rails and tipped over. There weren't many passengers because of the weather. Two people in the street were killed."

"What time?" My voice came out in a strangled whisper.

"Apparently, about a quarter past three in the afternoon."

I let out the breath I had been holding. "Thank God she was nowhere near there then." She had been in the apartment and already seen me with Alfonse at a half-past three. She would have missed the accident. It wasn't until I saw the puzzled look on Aaron's face that I realized I had revealed something I had kept from him the day before, about Sylvie coming home before running off for good.

"If I am to help you, Justine, you need to be honest with me. What really happened yesterday?"

I searched his face for some clue, some reason why he would care to take so much time to help me in this way. "There are things...I'm too ashamed to tell you."

"All you need to tell me is what is immediately pertinent to Sylvie's disappearance. Nothing more."

I rose and fetched the photograph from where I'd put it, underneath a plate on the shelf in the kitchen.

"Sylvie came home yesterday at her usual time, even though I knew she hadn't been in school. I confronted her about it, and she showed me this." It was as close to the truth as I dared go. I gave him the photograph. His face registered confusion at first, then as he looked longer, recognition dawned. I said, "Yes, it's Sylvie. I don't know how or when exactly, or where, but she went somewhere to be photographed."

"It's a fine one." He turned it over and examined the back. "Angelotti, it says. There's no address." He handed it back to me and I, too, examined the stamp on the reverse. Italian. How would she have known about such a photographer, or how to make an appointment with him for a portrait? Portraits cost money. Where would she have gotten that? And those clothes. I could see even in the picture they were cheaply made, although of a very modern style.

"So she showed you this photograph, and you were angry. Perhaps said some things that upset her, and she ran away. It seems a small thing to take so drastic a step over. But young people take everything to heart." He sipped his water. "If she doesn't return today, tomorrow we can go to this photographer. I will make inquiries and see if I can find out where he is. He must not be very far away."

"So I am simply to wait here, patiently, while my daughter may be lying in a gutter somewhere?" My voice rose at the end, and I stood. Aaron did likewise.

"Sylvie is an intelligent girl. She will have found shelter, and she will be trying to think of a way to come home and ask your forgiveness. I am certain she will tell you everything. Surely there is some innocent explanation."

If what I had told him truly were everything, perhaps he would be proven right. But I knew more and knew that there was more to fear from Sylvie's reaction and from the man who caused it. "You don't have children, do you, Aaron."

He shrugged. "Much to my mother's consternation. I have never wanted to marry."

"Then how do you claim to know so much about young people?"

"I was young once. I'm not so old that I can't remember those days." He put on his hat and inclined his head toward me. "I'll return later to collect the waists."

I, too, could remember those days, when I was Sylvie's age and even younger. They were as clear and present to my mind as if they had just happened the week before. Only I did not run away from a loving mother but from an abusive employer, who decided that when I bought my apprenticeship, she gained a slave.

I was vulnerable and unhappy, and a handsome man showed me a life that seemed to wipe all my cares away. I knew so little of the world, and when the man—Victor—told me I was beautiful, dressed me and fed me and took me to be photographed, I allowed myself to be led by him into a life of sin and dissipation.

I regretted so much of it in later years. I thought I had left it all behind me by putting an ocean between myself and my past. *Mais ça n'était possible.* It was not to be. That life had led me to Alfonse. And without Alfonse, there would be no Sylvie. He had found me again, but before that terrible day, I had kept him away from our daughter. In my false sense of security, I learned to accept my one blessing and pray for forgiveness for everything else.

Now, it seemed forgiveness was a promise that came with unacceptable conditions.

CHAPTER
TEN

Sylvie

I woke the next morning stiff, tired, and confused. It took fully five minutes for me to piece together the events of the day before, all the unanswered questions—and the shame. I don't know why I felt shame. Shame for my mother, I guess, and since it was just the two of us, somehow the shame attached itself to me as well. And here I was with a man, too. Or, not yet a man. A boy. And he'd kissed me, just as that strange man in our apartment had been kissing my mother. Had Paolo really meant his kiss, or was he just using me to hide from the police? Had my mother meant her kiss, or was she just using it to hide that man from me?

All these things circled in my mind as I watched Paolo pour hot coffee into two mismatched tin cups. Where did he get the coffee? Come to that, where exactly were we? Somewhere in Brooklyn was all I knew. The events of the day before had merged into one another, indistinct and shifting. All I could picture was the whirling snow, stinging and whipping, erasing every landmark ahead of us and all trace of where we'd walked behind us. It was a miracle that I'd managed to find Paolo without knowing where he lived or what he normally did during the daytime when he wasn't by my side, escorting me to school and back. I couldn't say even now, looking back, what had guided me, other than the merest suggestion that if I continued south, I would find Delancey Street.

The winds that howled around the outside of the empty warehouse and rattled the loose window frames had eased. The boys had gone, too. "Where are the others?" I asked, my voice sounding loud and echoey as I took the cup he handed me.

"Gone home. That's what you should do now, too." He lifted his own cup to his lips and blew across it, the hot steam mingling with his breath, and sat next to me on the bench that had served as my bed.

Home. Where was that? If home was my mother, it was no longer safe. The image I had held of her for as long as I could remember—glassy perfection, quiet reserve, judging me from a height that I thought put her on the same level as the angels—had shattered into millions of pieces. She had dissolved, scattered, like the blinding snow.

I ran away, but she forced me. She lied to me. She didn't deserve me anymore.

"What's wrong?" Paolo said, putting his arm around my shoulders.

I wiped the tears off my face and said, "Nothing," and then drank my coffee all the way to the bottom. It somehow managed to be both bitter and flavorless. "Where are we?" I asked.

"Brooklyn. Remember, we crossed the bridge in the snow."

"Yes, I know. But where?"

"Near the docks."

It came back to me now. And then, it struck me. Brooklyn.

Brooklyn! I had somehow managed to land in Brooklyn. That's where Vitagraph Studios was. Maybe nearby somewhere. Would it hurt to go there? I had nowhere else to go. I didn't know if it was the right thing to do. What was the right thing? I used to know. Everything used to be so clear. Now, I had nothing to cling to except Paolo, and I wasn't so sure about that either. He was physically there, but after yesterday, everything I thought I knew about him got all mixed up. He shouldn't have been out in the blizzard either. "What were you doing on Canal Street yesterday?"

Paolo took a long gulp of coffee before answering. I watched his Adam's apple rise and fall, noticing the shadow of stubble on his neck. "I was trying to help a friend." The steam from his coffee flushed his face.

He, too, was hiding something. First my mother, and now Paolo. "Why?" I asked.

"Let's get you home. I bet the trains are running again," Paolo said.

"I'm not going home. I can't."

"Why not?"

"My mother doesn't want me." It was the closest I could get to anything resembling the truth.

Again, Paolo paused, staring at me until I had to turn away. "So what are you gonna do?" he asked, fixing me with his deep eyes. "You can't stay with me." He'd softened his voice, but the words still stung.

I shrugged. I didn't need him to take care of me. I didn't need anyone to take care of me. "I'll think of something. There must be a dressmaker who needs an assistant, or I could mend clothes in a ladies' store. Or...you could take me to Vitagraph."

"Vitagraph?"

"You know, the picture studio I told you about. It's in Brooklyn."

"Brooklyn's a big place," he said. "What about going to

college, like your mother wants?"

Why was he suddenly so keen that I do what my mother wanted? I searched his face for some sign that he wasn't sorry I'd found him, that I hadn't really given him a choice to let me go with him. "Because it's what my mother wants, not me."

There, I thought. *I said it.* What had happened the day before gave me license to say whatever I wanted to say about my mother. I was my own self now. I would go on, go forward, because that's what you have to do if you want something badly enough. You have to go after it. I didn't want what my mother wanted for me.

"So, where to?"

"I'm going to go to Vitagraph Studios to ask them for a job. Any job."

Paolo stood, took his cap off, and ran his fingers through his hair before pulling me to my feet. Once he'd settled the cap on his head again, he stared at me hard. The fire in the barrel had burned down, taking away the illusion of warmth, and I began to shiver. Paolo took his own jacket off and draped it around my shoulders, standing very close to me, and leaned forward, almost touching me. "One thing's sure. You can't stay here." He murmured the words into the hair above my ear, and his warm breath raised goosebumps that tickled down my neck. Taking hold of my shoulders and pushing me gently away from him, he said, "If you're really sure you won't go home, I guess we should go find this Vitagraph place."

#

We set out away from the harbor and walked deeper into Brooklyn, putting Manhattan farther and farther behind us. Crews everywhere had been at work since early in the morning, sweeping the snow off the trolley tracks and shoveling it into piles at the curbs. A smooth coating of snow, like sugar icing, softened the contours of roofs and railings. It wouldn't last long, though, not at that time of year. The sun had come out, and already I could hear the drops of water plopping from trees, and my shoes and skirt were soon soaked again as we tried to step around huge puddles.

We turned down a busy street lined with shops, and I caught sight of myself in a store window. "Oh no!"

"What's the matter?"

"I can't go to Vitagraph looking like this." I spread my arms out wide. My vision of turning up and charming whoever owned the studio into giving me a role in his next picture faded as fast as it had blossomed. I looked like a bedraggled street urchin.

Paolo put his hands on his hips and angled his head to look me up and down. "You look fine," he said. "But maybe a little rough."

I shook my head.

"Cheer up! You can get something new. We're in the right place." He nodded toward the row of smart-looking shops

My heart sank. "I can't. I don't have any money at all. Not even a penny." I had left my satchel at home when I ran out, but even that only held the quarter I always carried for emergencies.

Paolo steered me to a quieter part of the sidewalk. "Look, I can't tell you anything about yesterday, but you got to trust me. It's nothing bad." He looked right and left to make sure no one was watching and reached into his pocket. He pulled his hand out, closed around a fistful of banknotes, and pushed them toward me. "Go into that store over there and buy something new to wear."

I stared at the money. Five-dollar notes, a lot of them, at least ten. It was more than I'd ever seen in one place before. "Where did you get this?"

"I earned it."

Earned it how, I wanted to ask, but didn't dare. "I couldn't!" I tried to push his hand away, but he took hold of mine and thrust the bills into it.

"Go on! You can pay me back sometime. I trust you."

I hesitated and looked up at the sign above the door. *Abraham and Straus.* It looked as elegant as the stores on the Ladies' Mile in Manhattan, where I'd only been once with my mother a long time ago. "Come in with me," I said.

"Naw, I'll be right here when you're done." He lowered his voice. "Better put the money away."

I'd been standing there like a fool with my hand full of bank notes, so I stuffed them in my pocket just to get them out of sight. He was right. I looked like a waif, an orphan. Like the orphan I thought I was now. If I expected to get a job, I had to look like I didn't need one. "You promise to wait?" I wasn't quite brave enough to be alone just yet.

Paolo tipped my chin up and kissed me so fast I didn't even have time to close my mouth. "I promise," he said.

When I stepped through the door of that department store, I entered a world I'd only imagined until that moment. People brushed past me, some of them—mostly women—wandering, picking up things, and putting them down again, looking as if they would purchase but never selecting anything. Others headed with great purpose toward whatever they were looking for—which, judging by what I saw as soon as I walked in, could have been just about anything. Posters and signs directed customers to upper and lower floors for furniture, clothing, tools, linens, flowers, jewelry...Shop girls stood behind counters looking busy but ready to stop whenever someone walked up to them and showed the slightest interest in anything. I didn't know where to start, and if no one had been waiting for me outside expecting me to come out with new clothes, I might have been tempted just to turn around and leave.

"May I help you?" A girl who couldn't have been much older than I was walked up and stood in front of me, looking down at me from arched eyebrows. Who could blame her? I looked as if I'd been dragged through a puddle.

I smiled and gestured toward my feet. "I need new shoes, a skirt, and a coat."

"You'll want ladies' wear. Next floor up. But I don't know if you'll be able to afford all that," she said, lifting her chin and turning away before I had a chance to say, "Thank you."

I headed to the staircase in the middle of the store, brushing off the insult, feeling the bills in my pocket.

On the upper floor, everyone was calmer. Up here was only ladies' wear, so not so many people would be interested. The familiar sight of skirts and shirtwaists, sensible coats, and modest hats made me feel more comfortable. Here was something I knew about. I headed toward the display of waists, curious to peek at them. A quick look and I could see that most of them were of inferior quality, probably finished in Leiserson's factory, or Triangle. Except for one, that is, carefully displayed on a dress form. I knew in an instant that it had to be a waist sewn by my mother, perhaps partly even by me. I reached out my hand and touched the smooth fabric, traced the perfectly uniform narrow tucks, the buttonholes neatly sewn. It was as perfect as I used to think my mother was.

"You have good taste. That's one of our most expensive waists. Two dollars and fifty cents. Perhaps you'd be more interested in these."

The shop assistant, her expression not unkind, patiently gestured toward a different counter. I wanted to ask her how it came to be that waists we were paid twenty-five cents to finish ended up costing ten times as much, but I thought she probably wouldn't know. So I nodded and let her lead me to a display of some others, all machine sewn with no handwork. I didn't want to waste any money on them. "I really only need a skirt, coat, and shoes," I said. My waist was still clean enough and dry.

"This way." She led me to another part of the floor.

Half an hour later, I stepped out on the street wearing a new, light-gray coat lined with darker gray that showed on the collar and the sleeves, a black skirt cut fashionably slim, new gloves that actually made my hands feel warm, and a hat that didn't droop in all the wrong places. I'd spent only seven dollars and a quarter, and Paolo had given me more than fifty. I started to hand him the change.

"Keep it," he said, once again looking around him as if he thought someone was watching us. "You might as well. I have more."

It would have taken my mother and me more than two weeks of grueling piecework to earn that much money. I didn't want to accept it, but I couldn't very well argue about it out on the street. And I had something I needed to do. "Where do we start?" I asked. "How do we find out where Vitagraph is?"

"You don't know?"

I blushed. "All I know is Brooklyn."

"Well," Paolo pushed his fingers under his cap and scratched. "I guess looking in the newspaper is the best idea."

We walked over to a kiosk on the corner near the store. The front pages of the Tribune and the Times were stuck to the outside walls. As I always did, I started reading the headlines. Of course they were all about the weather. I already knew all about that, so I moved closer to read the other articles. Before I could start, Paolo yanked me away and I nearly lost my balance. "Wait over there," he said, pointing across the road. "I'll go ask."

I was too astonished to ask him why I couldn't simply inquire for myself. He circled around the back of the kiosk to approach it from another direction. This was odd behavior, almost as if he was afraid of something, but I didn't see anything unusual, just people trying to go about their business in spite of the rapidly melting snow. But then, a policeman rounded the corner to my left and stood there, scanning the crowd, any view of Paolo blocked by the kiosk. So that was it. He didn't want the police to see him. And he wouldn't tell me why.

"Psst!" Paolo motioned me over to his side of the kiosk. I waited for a trolley to pass by and crossed to him. In his hands he held not an entire paper, but just a few pages from the center section. "Here's the notices about the moving pictures, what's on at the nickelodeons."

He handed me the paper. I scanned the headlines and illustrations, wishing I could go and see all the pictures. There was Biograph, and Essanay, and Pathé, and most of the others I'd never heard of. But no Vitagraph. I sighed.

"Here, there's some on the back too," Paolo said, taking the paper from me and turning it around.

"I don't see it there either." My hopes were fading fast. Here I stood in all new clothes, and I didn't know where to start looking for the only place I wanted to find. I certainly couldn't go home now, not with clothes I had paid for with someone else's money.

My stomach churned in a combination of hunger and despair. Paolo stood by, silent but watchful, shifting his weight from one foot to the other.

The clock in the façade of Abraham and Straus struck eleven.

Paolo glanced in its direction, then turned back to me quickly. "Listen, I promised I'd meet someone near here. Wouldn't be a good idea for you to come with me. I'm sure someone'll be able to tell you where that place is."

My spirits sank. Of course Paolo couldn't spend time sorting out my problems. He had his own. He'd already helped more than I had a right to expect. I felt tears prick behind my eyes, and I opened the paper again to hide them. I scanned the advertisements, this time looking at the small ones that I'd hardly noticed before.

Then I saw it. At the bottom of the page. So small I almost missed it. The advertisement said, *COSTUMER wanted, good dressmaking skills, willing to work weekends and nights. Must work a machine and do hand sewing. VG Studios, Midwood. Call after noon weekdays.* VG Studios. Could it be? "Where is Midwood?" I asked Paolo.

"What? I don't know." He was barely paying attention to me, looking around nervously, just like he had on Canal Street during the blizzard.

"I'll ask that officer," I said, pointing to the policeman who had left his corner and now approached the kiosk.

When I turned back, Paolo was gone. I was alone. The money in my pocket suddenly felt dangerous. I wish I'd been able to give it back to him. But then, how would I get to Midwood? What had I gotten myself involved in? And here I was, completely alone in a strange neighborhood. I might as well have been a foreigner just off Ellis Island. At least here almost everyone was speaking English. I folded the paper section and came around to the front of the kiosk to return it. I asked the newspaper seller, "Excuse me, but do you know how I might get to Midwood?"

"Midwood? What you want there? It's quite a ways." He leaned out over the display of papers and magazines so he could look me up and down. I stepped back and glared at him. He straightened up and said, "Walk over to Flatbush for the trolley. Might take more than an hour. Or you could take the Brighton Beach line, underground. The entrance is a block north on Fulton Street."

I thanked him and walked away, trying to look as if I knew what I was doing and where I was going. Fortunately, Flatbush was easy enough to find, and I spotted a small clump of people standing at a trolley stop a little way down.

I strode up to join them, my chin up and my shoulders back. No sense looking timid. I had taken charge of my own life. At least, I needed to pretend I had. Paolo might have played a role in getting me to Brooklyn, but I was the one who decided to push on. It was up to me to make something of myself. If I was right about the advertisement, I had stumbled onto a way to work my way into the one place I had been dreaming of for at least a year. *It was meant to be.* My mother would have said that God was rewarding me. I preferred to think of it as fate. If I wasn't right...well then, I could just be a seamstress for now. I would not starve. My mother had at least done that for me, trained me in a skill that could always get me work.

At the trolley stop, I felt in my pocket for a nickel, meeting the wad of banknotes Paolo had given me. I'd have to find some way to get the money back to him. But perhaps it was just as well I still had it. There was enough money to buy a meal and a room for the night, or so I hoped. I'd figure out how to pay him back later.

I stood at the back of the group of men and women who looked down the street, impatient for the next trolley. Some of them held young children by the hand, others clutched rolled up newspapers and leather folders. They all looked cold and now and again glanced up at the cloudy sky. A few flakes of snow had started to fall. I wasn't afraid of the weather after what I'd just been through. Nothing could deter me now. I tried to chase the image of my mother's worried face out of my mind. By now, she must be frantic. I hadn't just run away; I'd done it in the middle of a dangerous storm. I wanted her to know I wasn't hurt. I took a step away. I should go home. Paolo was right.

At that moment, the trolley came, and before I could change my mind, I stepped aboard and asked the driver to let me know when we got to Midwood, then took a seat at the back where I could gaze out the window. I wanted to take everything in, remember every detail about this moment. Someday I would tell my story to the newspapers, or Mc-Clure's, someday when I was an actress in the moving pictures, and everyone wanted to know me. Someday.

CHAPTER
ELEVEN

Sylvie

"Miss...Miss..."

At first, I had no idea where I was. My neck was sore, and something hard had been pressing into my shoulder. I sat up. I was in a trolley. Outside, leafless trees dripped with melting snow and the sun made brief, blinding appearances whenever clouds scudded apart.

"We're at the end of the line, Miss. You got to get off."

Everything flooded back to me. I must have been exhausted after yesterday's trudge and a bad night in a drafty, uncomfortable warehouse. I'd fallen asleep! I stood so fast the blood drained to my feet, and I staggered. The conductor steadied me.

"Easy, Miss! You know where you're going?"

"I-Yes- I mean..." I didn't want to seem ignorant, but as I looked around, all I saw were handsome houses with fenced-in yards and a few larger brick buildings that looked as though they could hold apartments. Nothing more business-like, not a sign or anything. "This is Midwood, right?"

"Yes, we're on the edge. Center's down that way, just walk along Avenue M, where the stores and businesses are. Are you looking for a particular address?"

"Fourteenth Street," I said, the address mentioned in the advertisement. "I'll just be going." I noticed that no one had taken much trouble to shovel the snow away here, and the slush was ankle deep at least. I would ruin my new boots. I started walking.

"It's the other direction!" the conductor called out to me.

I waved and turned to go the opposite way, feeling about as foolish as ever I had.

It must have been about half a mile later, when I could just see evidence of commercial activity up ahead, that my stomach started growling. I hadn't had anything to eat since the day before. I'd been too busy buying new clothes to feel hungry, and then Paolo left me there, and I had to concentrate on getting to Midwood. I spied what looked like it could be a cafe or restaurant and headed towards it. The welcome aroma of coffee and fresh bread lured me on.

I opened the door to a wave of warmth and cigarette smoke and chattering voices. I smiled. The place was bursting with life.

I found an empty seat at the counter and ordered a chicken sandwich and coffee.

"Two bits," the waiter said without looking up from the pad he was scribbling on.

I reached into my pocket for a quarter.

Nothing. All the money was gone. A ball of lead dropped into my stomach, which now not only felt empty, but sick. Someone must have stolen it while I was sleeping on the trolley. What would I tell Paolo? How could I have been so stupid. The waiter tapped his foot on the floor as he waited. "I-I'm sorry, I forgot I have an appointment," I said, and stood. No food for me. I wanted to run out of there, but I forced myself to walk slowly to the door and into the raw day. A dark gray blanket of clouds had spread over the sky. The chill my excitement had kept at bay until that point now penetrated my bones. I hugged myself and started shaking, partly from cold, partly from hunger. Another second and tears would start in earnest.

"You there!"

I forced myself to put a pleasant expression on my face and turned toward the voice. A girl, maybe a little older than I was, stood in the open door of the cafe and beckoned me to come back inside. I shook my head.

"Come on! You look hungry and cold. Join us!"

I said, "No, thank you. I'm fine," not feeling at all fine.

"Don't be a ninny! We won't bite!" Her big smile made her eyes wrinkle up, and I gave in. When I reached her, she looped her arm through mine and led me inside. She pulled a chair out for me at the table she shared with three other girls, two of them smoking cigarettes. "Name's Annabel Moore. And you?"

My name. If I gave it, I would be easy to find. I hadn't thought about that! "Sarah Potter," I said, grasping the first name that came to mind aside from my own: my teacher's.

"It was a chicken sandwich and coffee, right?" She snapped her fingers for the waiter, winking at him as he came over, gave the order, then put her elbows on the table and rested her chin atop her knitted fingers. "So, what brings you to Midwood?" The other girls at the table snickered.

I hesitated, then thought, *why not?* "I'm answering an advertisement for a job. As a costumer. VG Company?"

This brought forth peals of laughter and all the girls started chattering at once. "I told you!" "Had to be!" "Another one!"

If the sandwich and coffee hadn't arrived at that very moment, I think I would have run out of there and gotten straight back on the trolley going north. Only of course I couldn't. I didn't even have a penny in my pocket.

"Spent your last nickel to get here, I reckon," Annabel said. Her golden-brown eyes danced. She wasn't exactly pretty, more what most people would call handsome. Her nose was a little too long, and her jaw just a little on the strong side, but when she smiled, everything somehow harmonized. I didn't answer. My mouth was too full of food. "Well, you're in luck. You can come along with us, and we'll take you to Mr. Blackton, who's hiring someone to take over from Florence. You better really be able to sew, though. Not like the last three who only came because they thought they could get a role in a picture. Besides," Annabel leaned back in her chair. "I want my quarter back."

This provoked another outburst of hilarity. But I was too hungry and grateful to be offended that the joke was at my expense, or to spend much time wondering why this girl called Annabel would have gone to such trouble for me.

True to her word, as soon as we'd all finished eating, Annabel brought me along with them to the Vitagraph studios, which turned out to be a very short walk away, and so dominated that part of Midwood that if I hadn't been distracted by my cold and hunger, I would have seen it myself from Avenue M. The studios occupied an entire city block of four-story brick buildings beside a giant smokestack emblazoned with VITAGRAPH CO. in large, vertical letters, on Fourteenth Street and Locust Avenue. We entered a courtyard full of activity where at least a dozen men were trying to clear the snow and slush away completely.

"I'll take you to see—"

A commotion from across the courtyard stopped her midsentence.

"Until we have a replacement, you're going to have to keep mending costumes! You were hired as a seamstress as well, don't forget!"

Annabel lowered her voice and spoke to me, barely moving her lips. "Don't look now, but here comes Mrs. Costello. She thinks because she's married to Maurice, she can get away with anything."

"Maurice?"

"Don't tell me you don't know who he is! Only the handsomest actor on the screen, even if he is a little older. We call him Dimples. And he's got two little girls who hang around too. Rumor is they'll be in Mr. Blackton's flick of *A Midsummer Night's Dream*. Shooting this summer."

I wanted to ask who Mrs. Costello had been yelling at, but my own eyes answered the question a moment later. A young woman whose face was stamped on my memory steamed out the door the older woman had just slammed behind her, a gown balled up in her hands and a look of thunder on her face. "You can't order me around anymore! I earn twenty-two dollars a week! Mend your own damn dress!"

It was the Vitagraph girl, whose face was on postcards all over New York and probably the world. A nudge in my side from Annabel broke the spell.

"Let's go see Mr. Blackton before the afternoon shooting starts," Annabel said, pulling me in the opposite direction toward a door that said OFFICE. "I have to go get ready. Just tell them you're a friend of mine. Oh, but first—can you sew?"

"Like a professional," I said, at least confident in that.

Annabel held the door open for me and I stepped alone into an anteroom occupied by a typist seated at a small desk. The Remington machine and black telephone in front of her almost hid her from view. She picked up the earpiece of the phone and worked the crank on the side of the box. "Get me the exchange. Mr. Blackton wants to talk to Mr. Edison." Hardly pausing, she put her free hand over the mouthpiece and asked, "Who are you, and what do you want?"

More than anything, I wished Annabel was with me. I

didn't know what to say to this stern-faced lady. "Annabel sent me to see Mr. Blackton." Mentioning her name gave me a small measure of courage and postponed the need to answer the lady's question directly.

"Hah! Myrtle, is Mr. Edison available for Mr. Blackton? Something about a camera repair...Sure...I'll get him on the line."

But before she could do anything else, the door to the main office opened and a man of about forty in shirtsleeves, with hair that might once have been blond but now grayed at the temples and had started its retreat from his forehead, burst out with a sheaf of papers in his hand. "Have you got Edison?" He rolled up the papers and tapped them against the palm of his hand.

She nodded.

"Who's she?" he asked, jerking his head in my direction.

"Another of Annabel's strays."

He took no more than a moment to look me up and down, then said, "Can you sew?"

His question surprised me so much I didn't answer.

"If you can sew, there's a job for you. Otherwise, we've got all the girls we need, although you can sit on the extra bench and see what comes of it. Put Edison through." Mr. Blackton—I assumed that's who it was—tossed the papers he'd been holding onto the secretary's desk and disappeared back into the office. I heard him say, "Hello? That you, Tom?" before the door quite closed.

"Well?" The secretary stood. "You should go elsewhere if you're looking for work."

"But I can," I said. "Sew. Very well."

She frowned. "You better not just be saying that."

"Honest."

She spent a second peering at me and drumming her fingers on the desk, then sighed. "Come with me."

I was still so tired I wondered if I was dreaming. I followed the secretary through the warren of offices to a small room that seemed about a mile away from where we'd just been. When she opened the door, I don't know whether I was relieved or disappointed. A sewing machine, a cutting table, bolts of fabric leaning against the walls, and all the other accoutrements of a seamstress's workroom—the sight of it brought me down to earth pretty quick. "I'll get Florence to explain everything to you. Pay's seven dollars a week, and if you don't like it, you can always leave."

I sat in front of the sewing machine and wondered what had just happened.

I didn't have to wonder long. I'd just taken off my hat when the door to the sewing room burst open to admit four people: two men, a girl who looked about ten years old, and Annabel. They were in the middle of a conversation and at first didn't notice me.

"The important thing is to make sure she looks like a little sprite. All flimsy, gauzy stuff, and short."

"Mama doesn't like it when I show my legs that way."

"What's to see? You still look like a boy."

The young girl raised her fist up to hit the man who'd spoken to her, but Annabel moved fast and grabbed hold of her wrist. When she did, she saw me.

"Well! If it isn't Sarah!"

She looked so surprised that I realized she probably hadn't expected me to have any luck getting hired.

They all stopped in mid-gesture, like a tableau vivant.

"Mr...Mr. Blackton just hired me." I took my coat off and hung it on a peg. "What would you like me to sew?"

"Has to be light-colored," "Not that see-through stuff!" "She should look magical."

"One at a time!" one of the men bellowed. "I'm directing. I know what I want." He marched over to the bolts of fabric and unwound a length of smoky gray chiffon. "This. She needs a costume." He pointed to the young girl, who now stood with her arms folded over her chest and a pout that made her look even younger than I suspected she was.

The two men left, arguing at full pitch about how to make the scenes look real. "They've got to look like they're a few inches tall, climb in and out of a cigar box."

"The transition. It's all about the transition."

Their voices faded, and I started unwrapping the chiffon from the bolt.

"I won't wear it!" The girl stamped her foot and turned her back.

"Gladys, allow me to introduce you to Sarah, who is apparently our new seamstress." Annabel raised one eyebrow at me as she took Gladys by the shoulders and turned her around to face me.

I nodded. "How do you do?"

"Where's Florence?"

"Miss Turner to you!" Annabel snapped.

"She's Miss Turner when she's acting, and Florence when she's sewing."

Gladys's impudence shocked me. Was this the way everyone in the pictures behaved? I felt like a sparrow set among hawks. And Florence, or Miss Turner...that must be the name of the Vitagraph girl. I still hadn't quite recovered from seeing her like that, in the flesh. "I can make you look like a sprite by piling up layers and layers, like foam," I said, and bunched the material up to demonstrate.

"You'll have to help me a little with my costume," Annabel said, "but I'm much easier to please." She flicked Gladys's earlobe, and the young actress yelped. "I'll just go to the costume shop and find something you can alter."

Annabel left me alone with Gladys, whose face still looked thunderous.

In my exhaustion, I didn't have the energy to let it bother me, though. "I suppose we'd better get started," I said and rooted around in the sewing supplies for a tape measure. I figured measuring her was as good a place as any to start. But then what? An inspiration struck me. "Why don't you tell me about your character?" I asked, figuring she might say enough that I'd be able to get an idea of what the men were looking for.

It took a few minutes to break through the ice, but before long, Gladys Hulette—that was her name, and although she looked like a child of ten, I found out she was nearly fourteen—chattered away about Princess Nicotine, the Smoke Fairy. It sounded kind of crazy to me, and I couldn't imagine how they'd manage to make it look like two tiny fairies hid in the bowl of a pipe while a life-size man tried to light it. "How can they do it?" I asked.

Gladys said, "It's easy with film. You could never do it on stage."

I wanted to ask her more, but she didn't seem very patient, so I sprang into action, measuring and making a sketch with a pencil on a scrap of paper. She'd be back for a fitting later, and maybe I could pump her for more information. Something told me this little girl could teach me a lot without even realizing it, could be enough to help me get out from behind the scenes and in front of the camera.

For the rest of the afternoon, I snipped and sewed, wrestling with the flimsy material to create something I hoped was what the director imagined. The familiarity of needle and thread and sewing machine calmed my racing heart. I still couldn't believe I was actually there. Was this real? Had being able to sew made it possible for me to stumble into employment at Vitagraph Studios? Just twenty-four hours ago. A day, and a lifetime since I'd seen my mother with that man. Then, all I wanted was to get away. I couldn't have said for how long. I might even have gone back that morning. It would have been the sensible, safe choice. Paolo wanted me to. But something stopped me. And now here I was.

Paolo. What would he say when he found out I'd lost his money? I know he told me to keep it, but so much...He must have meant keep it for now.

And, of course, Maman. Yes, I was angry and confused. But why hadn't I given her a chance to explain? She certainly didn't look happy, staring at me over his shoulder. In fact, she looked scared. Was the man an intruder, someone who meant her harm, and I had gotten it all wrong? My feet pumped the pedals on the sewing machine more slowly. What if that had been the case, and she needed me to protect her?

I don't know what I could have done, and it was too late by then anyway. I had work to do. Whatever else my mother had taught me and planned for me, she taught me to work hard. So I would. Seven dollars a week. Twenty-eight shirt-waists' worth. It wasn't a lot, but probably enough to support myself in a shared apartment. I'd have to think about that later. For that night, I figured I could make some kind of bed in a corner of the sewing room, if they'd let me.

At five-thirty, Gladys came back so I could fit her costume.

"It's perfect!" She said, twirling and flouncing in the little room until I thought she'd topple the bolts of fabric leaning against the walls. Annabel had come with her; I don't know whether out of curiosity to find out if I had been lying about my skills or to protect me from any possible bad reaction from Gladys. I pinned the costume where I needed to make adjustments and sent Gladys away.

"So, you really can sew!" Annabel said, crossing her arms over her breasts and twisting her mouth up in a wry smile.

I laughed and continued tidying the scissors, thread, and scraps away. I was so tired my hands shook. Annabel caught my arm as I swept bits of thread off the table and into a waste bin. "Let's go eat with the crew," she said. "And you have to tell me more about how you pitched up here just when you did."

Food! My stomach growled, and we both laughed. Annabel led me through the compound, out of the area where the offices were located, and through rooms full of what I guessed must be filming equipment. We ended up in a large room with a long wooden table in the middle. The table had been set with plates and knives and forks. Ten stools stood empty on each side. Annabel and I sat next to each other at one end as boisterous voices approached from another direction, and about eight men, four or five women, and a couple of children tumbled in and took their places around the table. An instant later, another door opened, and four women brought trays mounded high with hot food—pot roast, boiled potatoes, and beans. I was so tired I could barely take it all in.

"Food's not fancy, but good," Annabel said, helping herself to meat and potatoes from the passed platter. I did the same.

"After dinner, then what?" She dabbed at the corner of her mouth with her handkerchief. "Got somewhere to stay, or are you going back into town for the night? Some of us girls share a few rooms near the park, if you're interested." She wrote an address down on a scrap of paper. "You can be a guest until Sunday, then you'll have to pay rent."

I wondered if I would have done the same if our positions had been reversed, or if my distrust of strangers would have kept me aloof.

That was something else to think about when I wasn't so tired. For the moment, I was just grateful to have a place to lay my head.

CHAPTER
TWELVE

Justine

When Sylvie did not return after three days, Aaron suggested getting the police involved. I sputtered out some irrational excuse not to do that, at least not yet.

He looked a little surprised but moved on. "I have some good news. I have found the photographer."

I stood, spilling my work on the floor. Aaron stepped forward to help me pick it up, and our hands touched. I flinched. He stood. "Did you see him?" I asked.

He shook his head. "I didn't want to go to him on my own. I thought it might seem strange for a Jewish man to inquire after a young girl who is obviously not Jewish."

"Of course." If I hadn't known it before, I knew it then, that Aaron was an honorable man, that his motives were simply kindness. I knew it, but who else would believe him in such a case? I offered him a cup of tea. He had relented the day before and taken the tea but without milk. I did the same, not knowing why other than that it seemed the courteous gesture.

After a long sip, he said, "Have you been to the school to see if Sylvie had any particular friends who might know where she would have gone?"

His question was reasonable, and I had considered it but soon rejected that course of action. The school might insist on getting the authorities involved, and I wanted to avoid that for as long as possible. "I sent a note, saying she was ill and would return when she was better. I didn't want them to award her prize to someone else." Even to my ears, it sounded feeble.

"Why would you say that? It's possible they could help you, perhaps give you information about the friends she had, who might have influenced her, or somewhere she might have gone."

"I don't want them to know she ran away, not yet, when she may return at any moment, and everything can go back to the way it was." I found it increasingly difficult to dole out information to Aaron without giving too much away. "Besides, she didn't have friends at the school. At least, none she ever named."

Aaron drained his teacup. "Perhaps there are other things you don't know about Sylvie. Sometimes a parent has to ask in order to find out what a child is thinking or doing."

He said it gently, but I felt the rebuke. I had lived so long with the fear of being questioned myself, with the desperate need to keep so much of my past hidden, that I never made inquiries of my daughter, at least none that probed much beyond the surface. Then I remembered something. "She did say that a friend at school gave her a necklace, a little pendant with a paste pearl in it."

"Did she mention a name?"

"No." And I hadn't asked. Foolish! My mind wandered back to that day. What exactly had Sylvie said? I recalled that she looked flushed and a bit distracted. What if she had come by the pendant some other way? We owned so few items that were not absolutely necessary. She might have been tempted to steal it—from another girl or even from a shop—having seen others in her school wearing jewelry.

"No," I repeated, answering my own unspoken question. I had at least accomplished that. Sylvie understood the difference between right and wrong. But I knew from my own experience that sometimes the one blended with the other, that what seems right can end up wrong.

"...So I think we should visit the photographer today. Justine?"

I snapped myself back to the present. "*Eh bien*, yes, all right. Just as soon as I finish these." I pointed to the pile of waists. It had grown over the last few days rather than disappearing each evening and starting afresh each morning. Aaron had only brought a few new pieces the day before. That day, he brought me nothing at all.

"I cannot continue to supply you with work you are unable to finish," he said. "My employers, the Leisersons, have been insisting for a long time that the girls in the factory can do the work you do and for less money. I tell them that none can do it as well or as quickly."

I always knew in my heart that Aaron had been making a special case by bringing us the waists—work that I knew no one else in the neighborhood still had. They all were required now to send their daughters out to spend long hours at noisy sewing machines in the dark, unwholesome factories instead of being able to keep them in school or at home, where they could share the work and make a decent living. I nodded. "I understand."

"I have plenty of money and no family to spend it on. I could give you a loan, just so you can pay your rent, while we look for Sylvie." He leaned across the table toward me.

I sat up straight. "No!" He sat back, his eyes sad and hurt. "I'm sorry, I didn't mean to..." Taking money from a man meant only one thing to me. "I have some money put by. I will be all right. But thank you for your kind offer."

"If you think a loan would put you under any obligation to me, you are mistaken."

Could he mean it? I saw nothing in his expression that rang false or carried a hint of hidden motives. "I'm not worried about an obligation," I said. "It's just that she is my daughter, and I need to be the one who makes everything right. She has come to this because of me. If I must spend all my savings to find her, so be it." My savings, the money I'd earned in a shameful way ever since Alfonse found me in New York five years earlier, was supposed to pay for Sylvie to go to Teachers College. Perhaps God was punishing me for thinking I could turn the wages of sin into gold for my Sylvie. Nothing was certain now, except that nothing would ever be the same again.

Aaron insisted on paying for a cab to take us to the photographer's studio on Fourteenth Street. We arrived at a building with several lopsided signs on the street-level door. A tailor, a bookkeeper, and one that said, *R. Angelotti, Photogravures, Fourth Floor*. Aaron held the door open for me to pass through and followed me up the stairs to the photographer's studio.

A small man with a long, straight nose and large brown eyes opened the door to our knock. "Do you have an appointment?" he asked.

Aaron said, "No, but we're looking for someone, and we believe she came to your studio recently to have her photograph taken."

He shrugged. "*Avanti.*"

We entered the studio. Angelotti didn't invite us to sit down, and we'd clearly interrupted him in the middle of something. The large space was littered with the paraphernalia of photography, and the smell of chemicals made my eyes water.

"Ten more, Tommy!" Angelotti shouted in the direction of

a young man I hadn't noticed at first, bent over a long table, peering at photographs through a magnifying glass.

Aaron cleared his throat. I reached into my purse, drew out the photograph of Sylvie that bore the photographer's stamp on the back, and showed it to Mr. Angelotti. He angled his head this way and that and pursed his lips. "No, I have never seen this girl," he said.

"But your name is on the reverse!" Aaron took the picture out of my hand and turned it over so he could point to it.

The photographer shrugged and curved his mouth in an insolent smile. "Perhaps there is another Angelotti. Or someone who wishes he were as great a photographer as I am."

I looked up at Aaron. His expression had turned so dark and angry that I hardly recognized the gentle man I knew. Before he could say or do something that would cause a scene, I said, "Thank you, we won't trouble you any longer."

I had to pull on Aaron's arm to make him turn and walk out with me.

"The devil was lying!" Aaron exploded as soon as we reached the street. "There is no other Angelotti photographer. And do you see—" He pointed to the backdrop behind Sylvie in the photograph. "That is the board that was on the far wall of his studio."

I hadn't noticed that, but now I saw it was true. "Why would he lie? What difference can it make to him?"

We had started walking down the sidewalk intent on our conversation when I heard running footsteps behind me and a breathless, "Excuse me!"

It was the young man, the one we'd seen bending over the table. He stopped when he was near enough to speak in a normal voice. "I recognize that girl," he said. "And I saw her afterwards, too."

I exchanged a look with Aaron. "You must explain yourself."

"It's kind of a story," he said, glancing back over his shoulder as if he was afraid someone followed him.

"Let's go in there," Aaron said, pointing to a cafe just ahead.

The boy hesitated and looked back again toward the photographer's studio. "I told him I was going out to buy a newspaper. I can't be long."

Once we had settled ourselves at a table with steaming cups of coffee in front of us, the boy—Tommy Morgan, he told us—started talking. "That girl came in this past Monday and had that picture taken." He took a gulp of coffee. "She was with Bonnano."

"Who is Bonnano?" Aaron and I asked at the same time.

"You maybe don't wanna know."

I held my breath, waiting for him to continue.

"He's the oldest son of a family a lot of folks—mostly businesses—have dealings with that aren't always on the up and up."

Tommy's vernacular was a little hard to follow. I looked at Aaron.

"He means illegal."

"How? My own daughter, how?" I could hardly speak.

"She's your daughter?" Tommy said, cocked his head on the side, and peered at me. "Yeah, I can see it now. She has your eyes. She came back for another session, couple days later, but I wasn't there. I see to the lunch crowd at the nickelodeon up the street on Thursdays."

"That was the day of the snowstorm."

Tommy nodded. "I saw her."

"But you said you weren't at the photographer's studio." Aaron hadn't touched his coffee or taken his eyes off the boy.

"On the same day, but later in the afternoon, almost evening. The nickelodeon closed early because of the weather, and I wanted to try to get something really original. So I borrowed one of Dickie's cameras—he skedaddled home as well with the snow and all—and lugged it down to the East

River Bridge. Got the last trolley running down Tenth, and it had to stop a quarter-mile short." He grinned.

"I don't understand," I said.

He paused to drain his cup. "It was fierce up there. The wind nearly knocked me over a few times. I was mainly concentrating on trying to keep the camera steady so I could get a shot. Just as I got the focus right, two people walked in front of my lens. A man and a girl. The girl turned and looked straight at me. Your daughter. I didn't recognize her until I made the print."

I tried to grasp what he was saying. Why would Sylvie have been on the East River Bridge during a snowstorm? And who was she with?

"I took the picture. It came out odd but interesting."

"Could we see it?" It was Aaron. I was still stunned into silence. Aaron turned to me. "If it is Sylvie, perhaps we can find the person she was with...Did you happen to recognize him?"

Tommy looked all around the cafe, even over his shoulder. "You didn't hear this from me." Tommy lowered his voice so that I could barely make out his words. "She was with Bonnano again. Paolo."

I started to perspire. My face felt hot. Sylvie had hidden a friendship with a boy. Perhaps even more. And a boy I most certainly would not have approved. "Where might we find this 'Bonnano'?" I asked.

"That'd be tough. The folks in that family usually find you, if you know what I mean."

"But find him we will." Aaron's voice was solid and sure.

"Suit yourself," Tommy said. "All I know is there's a bakery, somewhere down south near the Italian neighborhood. It's a front."

All at once, everything fit together. How stupid I had been! It had been staring me in the face, right in front of me plain as a stain, since before Christmas. This young fellow, this Paolo

Bonnano, must have been the boy Sylvie talked to after Mass. So much about her had changed after that day, now that I thought about it. She started coming home from school late and probably arriving late as well, using my supposed illness as an excuse. He was meeting her on the street. How much time had they spent together? What ideas had he put into her head? Getting her photograph taken was one, and by someone he knew. How else would she have found the photographer? I wondered, too, whose money paid for it.

And of course, it must have been Bonnano who gave her the necklace she said came from a girl at school and that she never took off. *Quelle folie.* I wasn't just stupid, I was blind. "Thank you," I said to Tommy. "We've troubled you *assez*."

I wanted to hurry away, but Aaron gave Tommy a card and said, "If you should hear anything or see anything that might help us find Miss Button, please send a message."

We shook hands and went our separate ways.

CHAPTER
THIRTEEN

Justine

"He saw her."

"We haven't seen the photograph yet. We can't be certain it was she."

I said nothing, but I knew. Just as I knew she had somehow found that boy, Bonnano, and he had taken her away. "We must go and look for her."

"She could be anywhere by now," Aaron said. "Brooklyn is a very large place."

"Very well, I shall go alone."

He shook his head and sighed. "You don't think I would let you do that, do you?"

"But surely you have to work. I, as you know, do not work at present." I tried to make it a joke, but I feared my smile appeared more rueful than amused.

"I have business that takes me to Brooklyn on Monday, if

you can wait until then," he said.

I confess to feeling relieved that Aaron was to accompany me, although I would rather we were to go sooner. Two days of doing nothing except worry and think and plan.

I could not tell Aaron exactly what it was I had to plan for. The plain fact was that I had only until Alfonse returned from Paris to find Sylvie, and I had no idea how long that would be. After that, Sylvie and I must disappear again. Now that he knew where I lived, Alfonse was unlikely to leave me alone, especially if it meant he could reclaim his daughter. Running away this time would be harder, though. I would be leaving so much more behind.

The day of our excursion to Brooklyn was unseasonably fine. A rare warm spell had set in ever since the storm and melted all the snow and slush away. Sidewalks were crowded with pedestrians grateful for any excuse to be outside. I took a chance and brought along a picnic, not certain if Aaron would be able to eat any of it. He had explained to me the dietary laws—no pork, no shellfish, no milk and meat at the same meal or even with the same dishes—I didn't eat much meat myself, not having the luxury of money to pay for it, so I packed bread and cheese and apples, and wrapped them in cloth napkins rather than bringing along plates, which in any case would have been heavy.

From Mulberry Street, Brooklyn seemed as far away as France to me, although from what little I'd heard, it was very like Manhattan, only less crowded. Some of my neighbors chatted about saving a few pennies to go to Coney Island in the summer, where there was an outdoor circus and sea bathing. The idea of doing something so frivolous was foreign to me, and I dismissed their chatter as I did everything else they said, keeping to myself, focusing on the one thing that mattered: Sylvie.

It was an odd feeling to spend so much time with Aaron. Our meetings before had been limited to a few minutes at the beginning and end of each day. Since Sylvie disappeared, we had been hours in each other's company every day. When he finished his deliveries, he would come to my apartment, and we would drink tea together and make plans to try to find Sylvie. He continued to press me to go to the police. I couldn't tell him why I would never do such a thing, and I was running out of excuses. We'd thought about putting an advertisement in the newspaper, but what to say? Which paper?

We took the trolley south to the Manhattan side of the bridge. We both decided we should walk across, as Sylvie had done, thinking perhaps it would reveal where she and her friend might have gone after they reached Brooklyn. "We'll go to Fulton Street first. It's as likely she would have at least passed through there as anywhere. It's the busiest part of Brooklyn, with many shops and businesses," Aaron explained.

It was the second time Aaron had gone over what we would do. I sensed he felt as awkward as I did. There was something *intime*, personal, about taking this small journey together. Our friendship—for it was that—had been predicated on certain boundaries of time and space, and without saying it, we had agreed not to pry too closely into each other's thoughts or feelings. Yet here we were, arm-in-arm like a couple out for an excursion of pleasure, except that he was clearly a Jew and I clearly was not.

As we started on the path that ran next to the railroad tracks, something about the unfamiliarity, about daring to come all this way, made me break our unspoken agreement. "Tell me about your family." I said it suddenly, ungraciously. "I mean, *si vous voulez,* if you want." I didn't dare look at him, worried that he might be cross.

But he shrugged and patted my hand. "There isn't much to tell. We are very like most of the other families we know. Except that I have never married. Much to my mother's sorrow."

I wondered why not but didn't dare ask. "Do you have

brothers and sisters? Nieces and nephews?" I always thought of Aaron as a solitary man, considering him to be the male equivalent of me, even though I was aware he must not be.

"A brother and a sister. They both live in New York and have given my mother much joy. My brother is a professor at New York University. My sister's husband is a pharmacist who makes a good living. They both have children. And we have many cousins and aunts and uncles, all from Germany. It's not so very interesting, you see," Aaron said.

"Oh, yes, it is! It has always been just me, and then just me and Sylvie. It must be such a comfort to have family."

He nodded. "Yes, it can be a comfort. But also a burden."

And yet here he was, taking on the burden of my difficulties. "Shall we rest here?" The walk across the bridge was much longer than I imagined it might be and quite chilly out over the water. I saw a bench up ahead, at the base of the first of the stone arches that held the great cables from which the bridge was suspended.

Aaron let go of my arm and took his pocket watch out to look at it. "We can stop for a few minutes. But if we're to go through even a bit of Brooklyn before I have to get back to the factory—the Heights, perhaps down to the park, and I must first stop in at Abraham and Straus to meet with their buyer—we'll have to move as quickly as we can."

A few other people were strolling on the bridge, and still more scurried across, carrying packages, bent on some business or other. Despite that, I felt as if I'd never been so alone with Aaron. Somehow, in my apartment, surrounded by my few things, everything was easier.

Once we were seated with the lunch basket between us and I had given him his wrapped roll and an apple, I said, "What do you do when you're not helping me? How do you spend your days?"

He sat in silence for a few moments. I could see thoughts

pass across his face like clouds over the sun. "I go to the factory for a few hours and do the accounts," he said. "I visit my mother most days at around lunchtime." He paused. "But lately, I spend a lot of time thinking about you...and Sylvie, of course." I watched the faintest warming, a slightly ruddy glow, spread over his face. "We should be getting on." He dusted the breadcrumbs off his hands and hastily put his half-eaten roll and apple back in the basket.

We didn't speak the rest of the way across the bridge until we set foot in Brooklyn. "Fulton Street is in this direction," Aaron said, guiding me along. "We can make some inquiries and then decide where to go from there."

I kept my hand in the crook of his elbow, partly so that I wouldn't lose him while I was so distracted looking around at everything, partly because it felt warm and reassuring. The handsome townhouses and imposing buildings in this neighborhood revealed much more affluence than was to be found on Mulberry Street or any of the streets in that part of town. People here seemed less hurried, nodded and greeted each other as if they were acquainted. Could Sylvie be among them? I searched each face as if I'd find the answer there.

In about twenty minutes, we reached Fulton Street, which was as busy as any avenue in Manhattan. There were shops of all kinds and crowds of people going every which way. I noticed several dressmakers' shops and haberdashers. They would be fortunate to have Sylvie's skills to call upon. In spite of myself and my ambitions for her, out of necessity, I had taught her well.

"What's wrong?" Aaron turned me toward him. I lifted my gloved hand to my face and found tears.

"Nothing. I think a bit of dust in my eyes." I couldn't bear to start talking about it out there, in public, about the deep pain it gave me to picture Sylvie as a menial seamstress. I had worked so hard to prevent her ever being in a place like the one I had been in after I left the convent. Her safety and comfort were all that mattered. I had planned her life carefully so she would not find herself forced to make the same mistakes I had made.

"Here is where my business takes me. Come in with me; you'll enjoy seeing the clothes."

Aaron held the door of the bustling department store open so I could pass. Of course, I'd been in many stores in Paris, but few in New York. I had little money to spend, and what I spent was mostly on the necessities of work and life. I had forgotten what a pleasure it was to see fine goods laid out for inspection, to smell the lingering perfume and watch elegant ladies of leisure select from the available wares as if they cared little whether they purchased them or not. I could not deny that I envied them.

I followed Aaron to an upper floor and to the counter displaying shirtwaists. I could tell even from a distance that they were poorly made. The ones Sylvie and I sewed were superior in every way, and the material used by Leiserson's was of good, solid quality, if not luxurious. Aaron struck up a conversation with the girl behind the counter, who went away and soon returned with a very dapper gentleman. I wandered off while they discussed business.

"Excuse me, don't I know you?"

The girl from behind the counter, now displaced by her superior, approached me. "No, I'm afraid I have never been here before," I said.

She drew her eyebrows together in puzzlement. "I could swear...You were here, a few days ago, the day after the blizzard. That's a day I'll always remember!" She smiled charmingly, and I was about to nod and walk away when all at once it occurred to me that she hadn't seen me; she'd seen Sylvie.

"You say you saw someone who looked like me?"

She blushed. "I...I see now that I was mistaken."

The girl turned to go, but I grabbed hold of her arm. She

looked alarmed, and I let go of her. "I'm sorry, I did not mean...
It's just that I think you may have seen my daughter."

"I suppose I might have. Good day." Clearly, she was
embarrassed.

"Wait, please. Could you tell me more about this person
you saw?"

At that moment, Aaron rejoined me. "What's all this?"

"Sylvie was here!" I was so excited I could hardly speak.
"This young lady saw her!"

The girl's eyes were round with alarm.

"Please excuse us. My friend meant no disrespect," Aaron said.

He didn't believe me! "Tell him, please, *Mademoiselle*." I
turned to Aaron. "She thought it was me. The day after the
blizzard. Don't you understand? It must have been Sylvie. She
was probably tired and worn down, and..." I couldn't go on.
Aaron helped me to a chair.

"Stay here. I'll look into this."

I didn't enjoy being treated like someone who had taken
leave of her senses, but without causing a scene and possibly
being ushered out of the store like a thief, I had no choice but
to do as Aaron said. When he returned, he silenced me with a
look, and we went outside.

"Well?" A note of irritation found its way into my voice.

Aaron sighed. "I know it's frustrating. It is true that a girl
who looked very like Sylvie came into the store on that day.
But she bought a coat, skirt, and boots, all of quite good
quality, according to the shop girl. I don't see how Sylvie
would have had the money to do so." He took my elbow and
steered me toward the entrance to the subway. "Let's go for a
walk in the park. They say it's beautiful at this time of year.
The spring flowers are just beginning."

My friend, this man who had become a companion in my
desperation these past weeks, couldn't know how what he said
had shocked me to my core. I knew in my heart that the girl

that shopgirl had seen had to be Sylvie. The coincidences were too many—the timing and the fact that the girl had mistaken me for her. But now, it seemed that Sylvie had money. What could explain such a thing? It made me sick to imagine. "I'd rather just go home. I'm quite tired."

Without a word, Aaron steered me to the other side of the street, and we took the subway back across the East River Bridge to Manhattan, each lost in our own thoughts.

CHAPTER
FOURTEEN

Sylvie

It was an odd feeling, plucking myself out of the only world I had ever known and stepping into a place so wildly strange and different. I went from sheltered schoolgirl to runaway to employed adult, all in the space of a little more than twenty-four hours. It made my head spin. I pushed thoughts of my mother away. I didn't want to imagine how she must feel, what she must be doing. I didn't want to think of anything that could make me turn back, not now. However much I had that itchy feeling I should tell my mother where I was, I pushed it down. She would make me go home, I knew. And in that place, I was so close to achieving my dream!

Well, close physically anyway. Shut in the sewing room, I hardly noticed I was in a picture studio. I could have been in a dressmaker's shop, spending twelve hours a day sewing—but a dressmaker who made the most outlandish clothes. The bolts of fabric that lined the walls were like a silent carnival, all flowered and striped and polka-dotted, like they could leap off the wall and start twirling and doing tricks. Of course, the stuff was cheap. It all reminded me of my mother's tales of the dressmaker she worked for in Paris. I could almost hear her voice and see the sneer on her face, talking about the material that snagged and frayed but that she had to turn into clothes that looked expensive—until someone wore them for a while. Mother said she was virtually a slave then. My situation in the studio couldn't have been more different. I chose to be there. In fact, I lived in fear not of being beaten or starved but of being turned out to make my way with my needle somewhere else. I swore I'd give them no excuse to find my work lacking.

That's what raced through my mind as I did my best with the cheap fabric, fingers fumbling and fighting with the slippery chiffon for Gladys's costume, which refused to stay under the foot of the sewing machine. I almost longed for the starchy certainty of white cotton shirtwaists. I pricked my finger so many times it became numb. But the drops of blood rinsed out easily from the badly woven fabric, and I soon learned not to care.

Gladys arrived for her final fitting later in the afternoon the day after I started working at Vitagraph. I found a folding screen in a corner and figured it would do to give her a little privacy. But before I could set it up, Gladys breezed in and stripped down to her underclothes, not even shutting the door behind her. As fast as I could, I pulled the costume over her head and knelt down to mark the hem.

"So, where did you come from?" she said.

My mouth was full of pins, which gave me a moment to think up an answer. "Connecticut," I said, after I'd marked where to sew flowers on the bodice, the final, fairy-like touch. I lifted the costume off over Gladys's head.

She didn't dress right away, though, just stood there

looking at me. "Where in Connecticut? Mother's folks are from New Haven."

Damn. "Not there," I said. "Out in the country, on a farm..."

"What about your mother and father?"

"They're dead," I said. This put an end to the conversation. "Here, try this on now."

I watched Gladys twirl and flounce in the costume—which I considered a success and hoped the director, Mr. Kent, would too. "That'll do, I guess," she said, flicking the skirt and not looking at me.

"What about you?" I asked. "Where do you come from?" I wasn't used to asking people questions about themselves, and it felt bold and dangerous to do it.

"Oh, I've been in Manhattan mostly, except when I was touring in the Midwest."

"Touring?"

She grimaced. "I hated it. Every night the same thing, city after city. A song and a dance, and reciting poetry, until I got too old."

Too old? "When was that?"

"Couple years ago. I was ready to quit anyway. Mama had me out there singing when I was three!"

To be on the stage so young! I couldn't imagine it. "The dress is finished, but what will you wear on your legs?" I thought for sure she must need bloomers or stockings or something.

"Mr. Blackton says my legs are to be bare. I don't care as long as it's warm in the studio." With that, she skipped out of the sewing room, kicking her heels up in a way I later learned was typical for her.

It had taken me only two days to make Gladys's costume. After that, for the moment at least, I had nothing to do. I tidied up the sewing room—the "stitchery," as the sign on the door said—and set about organizing the supplies. I discovered every tool I might ever need, but they were so scattered about in boxes and cubbies that if I'd been looking for something in particular, it would have taken me hours to find it.

A while later that afternoon, when I was sure the workday must be soon over, Annabel poked her head in the door. "Aren't you going to come and watch?"

"Watch what?" I asked. I assumed I was supposed to remain in my fabric-filled fortress all day to earn my dollar and fifteen cents.

"Don't be a ninny!"

She grabbed hold of my hand and pulled me along to what I later learned was the main studio. "She's here in case the costumes rip," Annabel said to no one in particular, then pointed me to a stool in the corner of the studio, out of the way.

We had entered a space unlike anything I'd ever seen. The walls and high ceiling were glass, which, I learned later, was to let in as much light as possible. A raised wooden platform occupied the middle of the floor, and a bank of lights did their best to enhance the feeble winter sunlight.

On the platform stood a barrel stuffed with straw with a pole jutting out from its bottom, a big wooden chest painted to look like a cigar box, and a smaller wooden box with the word MATCHES stamped on it. I watched, mesmerized, as Mr. Kent had Gladys and Annabel rehearse what they would do for one scene, which mostly consisted of Gladys pulling the straw out of the barrel and then climbing in, after which Annabel piled the straw back in around her.

"More animation! I want people to see that you're scheming, making up a trick to play on the smoker." Mr. Kent paced back and forth as he shouted instructions.

It took several hours to get that scene rehearsed so Mr. Kent was happy with it, and then they filmed it three or four times. By then, my back ached, and my behind was sore from sitting on a hard chair, but I didn't dare move and call attention to myself in case they told me to leave.

"Tomorrow we'll do the cigar box and the matches," Mr. Kent said, clapping his hands. "Good work, everyone."

Gladys made a beeline for me, stripping off her costume right there in front of all the camera operators and other people whose jobs I didn't know. "I tore the skirt climbing in and out. You better fix it tonight." She tossed it to me and called over her shoulder as she skipped off wearing only her underclothes, "I'll collect it in the morning." More than one pair of eyes ogled her slim legs. I wondered if she knew it and made such a spectacle of herself on purpose.

I balled up the mass of tulle that was Gladys's skirt and stood, preparing to go back to the sewing room.

"Where are you going?" Annabel stopped me.

"Miss Hulette says I'm to mend this for tomorrow."

"Don't be silly! She never gets up before noon herself. You'll have plenty of time in the morning. Come and have some dinner out with the girls."

It sounded so tempting. But I couldn't. "I won't be paid until Saturday." At that moment, my stomach churned aloud.

"I'll put it on account," she said and laughed.

It took two weeks to finish filming the moving picture called "Princess Nicotine." By the time everything was wrapped up (that's what they called it) and the sets in the studio broken down, my former life had begun to feel like someone else's dream, as if Sylvie Button never existed, or as if she still existed in some parallel life, going to school, sewing waists, attending Mass every Sunday and confession once a month. Sarah Potter was a little fragment of that girl sliced off like a cutting from a tree and somehow picked up by a bird and dropped into new soil miles and miles away.

The work was hard, but I didn't complain. I was glad enough not to be one of the would-be actors who sat day after day on the extra bench outside the studio, hoping they'd be picked to be in one of Mr. Blackton's pictures. I was so busy sewing I hardly had time to talk with the women in the costume shop, a much bigger room filled with racks and racks of musty garments right next to my hovel. The costumers and dressers were kind enough, but mostly they handed me work to do and told me it was needed in an hour, or five minutes, or tomorrow.

Every day, I thought about going home. And every day, the more I settled into life with Annabel and her friends and with everyone at Vitagraph, the more I pushed the thought away. From eight in the morning often until eight in the evening, I sewed, mended, watched rehearsals, took notes. We had Sundays off, but the trains and trolleys barely ran then, and it was the only day I had time to wash my clothes and my hair and get some rest.

I should at least write a letter, I thought, not tell her where I was, just let her know I was still alive and unharmed. But somehow the letter didn't get written. And the idea of going home faded as I became busier and busier and learned more and more.

Of course, being a seamstress made me invisible to most of the people at Vitagraph, except when they needed my services. I didn't mind because I could wander around where I pleased on the rare occasions when I didn't have anything else to do. I'd watch the men building sets and figuring out lighting, the Cooper Hewitts, as they were known. And I'd listen to Mr. Blackton and Mr. Kent scenarize stories from books or history or speak about the comic pictures they were planning to make.

"The gimmicks, the effects—that's what people want to see. That's the magic of this medium. I could do so much more! Ghosts, fairies, witches—when I finish making a picture, people will believe in them," Mr. Kent said one morning. He and Mr. Blackton were strolling in the same direction I was, and I held back just far enough that they wouldn't notice me, but so I could hear everything they said.

"That's all well and good," Mr. Blackton said, "but the story—that's what's important. Think of it: We can bring versions of the greatest literature in all humanity to the screen so that everyone with a spare nickel can experience them!"

"Yes, but there's nothing original in that."

"It's original to people who haven't seen or read Shakespeare or Hugo or Tennyson before. And the rest will glean some pleasure from the interpretation."

I was trying to decide which of them I agreed with more when Mr. Blackton entered an office, and Mr. Kent continued to the concrete editing room—where I was headed. I had talked one of the camera operators into showing me some footage of Florence Turner—the Vitagraph girl—in her most recent picture. She wasn't cast in Princess Nicotine; none of the roles suited her. But she was going to act in a different picture they hadn't started rehearsing yet, something very ambitious, a pet project of Mr. Kent's. This left Miss Turner with a break in her schedule, and she had gone away somewhere. Visiting her family, if you asked some people. Others—like Annabel—said she was meeting up with one of the actors at the studio, who was also away.

Whatever was true, she would return in a few days, and I had to have her costume ready for her by then. I still couldn't believe that she'd been the seamstress before me. The most famous face in moving pictures had been hired not just to be an actress but also to sew. A few of the men who played minor roles doubled as carpenters or painters, but none of them were as famous as Miss Turner.

I followed Mr. Kent into the cold, dark editing room. He bustled up to the editor, who sat at a hand-cranked machine feeding a reel of film through it, peered over his shoulder, and pointed. "Cut it just here. I think that will make the illusion more realistic." I couldn't see what he meant because nothing was being projected. A light pointed up through a glass panel underneath where they placed the film, which allowed them to see each tiny image. I held my breath as I watched the editor slice through the celluloid with a razor blade, then carefully butt it up to another piece and fix them together with a transparent bit of tape and glue. He had to be very careful. Mistakes in editing showed on the screen.

The floor was littered with scraps of celluloid that had been cut out and discarded that day. Annabel explained that every scrap of film had to be carefully treated so that it would not catch fire, and there was an incinerator out in the back lot of the studio where, every month or so, they intentionally burned the edited-out bits and pieces to reduce the chance of an accidental blaze. A celluloid fire couldn't be doused with water. It just burned and burned until all the fuel was gone. I cleared my throat. Mr. Kent looked up. "Oh, Miss Potter. I need you to create something very special for Miss Turner for my next film, *Launcelot and Elaine*."

He briefly explained the story, based on a poem by Tennyson. Florence would be the lovely maid Elaine who guards Launcelot's shield for him, nurses him back to health when he is mortally wounded and falls in love with him, but when he doesn't return her love, she dies of grief.

"I want something medieval but not elaborate."

Before I could ask him anything more, he rushed off. Medieval. How was I supposed to know what that was?

"Sarah? It's Sarah, right?"

I looked up from the table where I had unrolled a bolt of cream-colored linen that I thought might do for Elaine's gown, deciding that simple would work and I could always make changes later, to see Florence Turner herself silhouetted in the doorway of the sewing room, one hand high up on the door frame, her body making an elegant S-curve for a perfect pose. "Yes, Miss Turner," I said. Without taking my eyes off her, I reached for the scissors and ended up stabbing the palm of my hand in the process. I squeaked in pain, and Miss Turner rushed in from the door and grasped my hand.

"You poor thing! You cut yourself. And look how your fingers are all torn up from the needle. That's what always happened to me until I finally persuaded these men that sewing and acting didn't mix."

"It's all right. I just forget to use a thimble sometimes." Honestly, I felt stupid. It was a mistake a child would make.

"I couldn't help noticing that you're really an exceptionally good seamstress," she said, standing but not walking away so that I had to crane my neck to look up into her large, expressive eyes. "Much better than I was. I hope we can be friends. Will you come to all my rehearsals and be there to mend anything that tears, and so you understand what the costumes must be like to achieve the best effect? The men just don't have the vocabulary to explain things to you. I know you'll help me look my best." She smiled and placed her perfect, white hand on my shoulder.

"Of course, Miss Turner," I said, wondering if she really had the right to command me like this and whether Mr. Blackton would mind. Right or not, I knew I'd do whatever she asked of me. She was the reason I was here, really. I looked down at my hands to break the spell and tried to sound light and casual. "Mr. Kent said he wanted something medieval for Elaine. I don't suppose you know what he meant." I glanced back up at her, but she'd already turned away and had started strolling around the room, touching the bolts of fabric with the tips of her tapered fingers.

"Oh, like something in the fairy-tale books, I think," she said, flashing me a quick smile over her shoulder.

I nodded. I'd never read a fairy-tale book. Maman thought they were a foolish waste of time. She thought I was so educated, but how much knowledge had she kept from me in her way?

"Good! In ten minutes, we rehearse Titania. In the small studio. After that, it's Elaine, in the large studio. Of course, both of these pictures will be shot outside once the weather improves."

She paused in the doorway, again posing before turning and blowing me a kiss, then sweeping out of the door so smoothly and quietly she might really have been the queen of the fairies. I sighed.

The story of Titania I did know. We learned about Shakespeare in school. In a month, we'd be shooting in Mr. Blackton's enormous garden near the studio for *A Midsummer Night's Dream*—so Annabel had told me. I wasn't certain of the schedule for Elaine. The Tennyson had a cast of only three, that I knew, which made it easier to manage. But Mr. Blackton wouldn't skimp on the fairies and townspeople for *A Midsummer Night's Dream*, which would mean hiring some of those hopefuls who sat on the benches, day after day. If one of them, why not me? I'd been secretly working up the courage to speak to Mr. Blackton about it. But now that I was supposed to devote myself to making sure Miss Turner looked her best at all times, how would I manage that?

These thoughts swirled around in my head as I stood at the trolley stop alone that evening. Annabel had a late rehearsal and said I shouldn't wait for her. It was the first time I'd taken the ride up Flatbush to our apartment on my own. I was a little frightened. Something about it brought to mind Paolo walking me to school every day. Where was he now? What was he doing? And why hadn't he come to look for me? I was running out of excuses to make for him. I'd already been through: *he's busy, he had to go out of town for a few days,* even *he caught cold the day of the blizzard and is sick in bed.* He left me alone before I knew I'd actually get myself to Vitagraph, but he knew that's where I wanted to go. If he remembered, I hoped it would be the first place he'd look for me.

The days were getting longer, and the west still glowed with leftover sun. Soon it would be summer. My first summer as an independent woman. Why wasn't my heart leaping up and down with joy? I wasn't just independent: I'd wormed my way into the very place I'd been dreaming of ever since I first went to the nickelodeon.

The trolley came and I climbed aboard, taking a seat next to an older woman reading a book. I hadn't read anything since I came to Vitagraph, except the occasional page or two of a script. It didn't matter. I wasn't Sylvie Button, the model student, anymore. From now on, I was Sarah Potter, responsible working woman, poised to make her dreams come true.

My heart sank.

CHAPTER
FIFTEEN

Justine

Our excursion to Brooklyn frustrated me. I felt certain Sylvie was there somewhere, not from any actual evidence—after all, she might have come back after crossing the bridge—but I had such a strong instinct about it. Yet, other than the shop girl possibly having seen her, we had no information to lead us to her. As Aaron said, we might as well be trying to find a single thread in a mountain of scraps.

The very next day, we met Tommy outside the nickelodeon, and he showed us the photo he took that night of the storm. I instantly recognized Sylvie's frank, lovely gaze, her brow furrowed in sadness. Sadness that I had caused. Oh, how I yearned to embrace her and tell her everything! She would forgive me once she knew, I was certain. The young man she was with held her elbow, I saw, but the view of him was blocked, and his face partly turned away. All I could see was the hint of a profile. He might have been the same boy Sylvie spoke to in church that day, but how could I say for sure? He was tall, and I remembered that boy being tall, and what I could see of his hair curling out beneath his cap was dark, something else I vaguely remembered. It wasn't enough, though, to be certain the boy Tommy recognized as Paolo Bonnano was also the boy who had attended Mass on the first Sunday in Advent at Church of the Most Precious Blood.

After staring at the photo for a long time, I said, "Thank you," and held it back out to Tommy, reluctant to give the picture back to him.

"Don't mention it. It'd be all right if you want to hang onto that photo. I have the plate; it's easy as pie to make another one."

"You're too kind." I was so grateful. Grateful and sad at the same time. What if this was all I ever had of Sylvie for the rest of my days? The warm spring sun went behind a cloud, and I shivered.

"Are you cold? Would you like my coat?" Aaron's voice startled me. I had almost forgotten he was there. He'd stepped back to let me talk to Tommy quietly, allowing me the courtesy of seeing the photograph first, and when I turned to go home, he fell into step with me.

"Perhaps we should go to the police after all," I said.

"We should check all the hospitals again," he added, without contradicting my suggestion. I knew the idea had been at the back of his mind during the past weeks since Sylvie left. My reluctance was selfish, I knew. It pained me that I would have to admit to the police that Sylvie had gone willingly, that she had run away. I didn't even know if they'd bother looking for her since she wasn't a child anymore and hadn't been abducted.

I stopped.

"What's wrong?" Aaron asked.

I turned to him. "Do we really know that she went willing-ly?" I took the photograph out of my pocket and scrutinized it

again, searching for something. "Do you see, here, he is gripping her arm, I think pulling her along. And she looks...*inquiet,*
worried." It was just possible. Just possible that Sylvie had
dashed out of the house in anger and confusion and would
have returned a few hours later when the weather had cleared,
but that she had been under the power of this young Bonnano
fellow. His family members were criminals, so Tommy
implied. Why wouldn't he be one as well?

"If that were the case, why have they not contacted you for
money?"

"There are other reasons for abducting a pretty young
girl," I said. I shuddered.

Aaron looked more closely at the photograph. "It appears
to me that he is simply supporting her arm and helping her
make her way through the snow and wind." He patted my
hand. "I don't think it's possible to tell just from this photograph what was really happening that day."

In my heart, I knew he was right. I knew too that, by waiting
so long to go to the police, I had probably spoiled any chance
they might have of finding Sylvie—if she wanted to be found.

There was nothing more to do except one thing. "We must
find the boy."

"Is that wise, given all that Tommy has told us?"

"If nothing else, I would know right away if Sylvie met him
before, at church. And if he is a good Catholic boy, whatever
else his family does, I can talk to his mother, and perhaps she
will help me." I could not imagine a mother who wouldn't be
moved by my story.

Aaron and I crossed Houston and plunged into the crowded cacophony of that part of New York where streets narrowed, and shops and stalls made passing down the sidewalk
difficult. With so much noise around—merchants hawking
their wares, neighbors shouting out greetings, children yelling
and crying—we could not continue our conversation. No

trolleys ran down Mulberry Street, only the occasional horse-drawn cab, so we, like most other pedestrians, made our way down the middle of the road.

We reached the stoop, and I invited Aaron to have a cup of tea with me, as had become our custom of late. He looked up at the building. My eyes followed his, and I saw what he did. Faces, nosily watching through dirty windows, in all probability judging their unfriendly neighbor and this man from a world so different from theirs. "Hah!" I said. "They mean nothing to me."

"Neighbors are not always to be shunned, even those with whom you have little in common. Have you asked any of them what they saw that day?"

I considered lying to him, for just a moment. How could I explain why that was the last thing I would do? If they had seen Sylvie, they had no doubt seen Alfonse. No wonder they stared at us with such scorn. "No, and I don't intend to. Please, I ask you, do not inquire of your own accord. I don't want them to know Sylvie ran away." It was the only excuse I could think of.

Aaron nodded, but he didn't come in for tea that day.

In the past, work had prevented me from attending the daily morning Mass at the Church of the Most Precious Blood. Now that I was no longer doing piecework—at least for a while—I decided to adopt that habit, and not simply for the sake of my soul. From snatches of conversations I'd overheard on Sundays over the years, I knew that many of the Italian matrons whose households were clustered down at that southern end of Mulberry and Baxter Streets used the daily ritual of morning Mass as a convenient excuse to share news and gossip. What better way to discover the whereabouts of one particular Italian family?

Of course, my habit of staying aloof from almost everyone would not serve me well in this endeavor. I would have to break the habit of nearly fifteen years and extend a hand of friendship to strangers. What gave me courage was that the Italian enclave was unlikely to be acquainted with anything French. They kept themselves to themselves. They might easily shun me, be suspicious of allowing an outsider to speak to them at all.

I decided, therefore, that I should spend a few mornings simply attending the service, nod to some of the women, perhaps say hello, until they grew accustomed to seeing me there.

The early weekday Mass was very quick, and in between the responses and the Eucharist, I didn't have time to observe much. Afterwards, most of the women rushed off as soon as possible—the younger ones especially, who no doubt still had children to prepare for school, husbands to send off to work. Yet on the very first day, I noticed a group of about five older Italian women who took their time walking down the steps at the front of the church, chatting in Italian, lingering at the bottom before a distant bell from another church tolled out the eight o'clock hour. These women might be able to help me. I knew it. Every fiber of me wanted to scream to them, to shake information out of them, to beg them to assist me so that I could find my daughter. But I forced myself to be patient.

The fourth day that I attended early Mass, instead of just walking past the group and nodding politely, I stopped, standing just a little outside their circle. I could discern a few of the Italian words that were something like the Latin in church: *madre, Dio, pane.*

Pane. Pain. Bread. Of course. Tommy had said something about a bakery.

"Excuse me, *pardon,*" I said when a pause gave me the opportunity. "*Pane.* Bread. Would you be so kind as to tell me if there is a good bakery nearby? The only ones where I live are the Jewish bakeries, and their bread isn't to my taste." I had no idea if there was any difference at all between Jewish bread and French bread. I baked rolls in my own oven, using a recipe I learned at the convent. At first, the women all stared at me, uncomprehending. Surely one of them spoke English! I could not have survived more than a week when I came to New York without at least the rudiments of English—I had learned enough of the language from the Sisters of Sion. Then again, I was alone, not surrounded by a whole community of other French immigrants who could live their lives speaking only to each other.

The women drew closer to one another and murmured so that I could not hear. I was about to turn away, berating myself for possibly spoiling an opportunity by acting in haste, when one of the younger ones detached herself from the group and stepped toward me. "You want a bakery? Italian? But you are not Italian."

"No, but your bread is not so very different from ours, and I don't have time to bake every day." I hoped it sounded plausible.

She nodded. "Most of us bake our own. But there is a bakery; on Delancey Street."

"Is it far from here?"

She shook her head. "Turn right on Delancey. It's just there." She pointed north. "The Bonnano bakery. They only open in the early morning. It's already too late for today."

I sputtered my thanks and said a silent prayer to the *Sainte Vierge*. She had been watching over me. She knew that at heart I was not a sinner, that my love for my daughter atoned for my past deeds. And to prove it, she had dropped the very information I needed directly into my hands.

I walked toward home thinking about what the woman had said: a bakery that wasn't open all day, or at least until noon like others in the neighborhood. It fit with what Tommy had told us.

As I crossed Delancey Street on my way home, I decided to alter my route so I could pass by the bakery. Even if it was closed, there might be people around, and I might learn something that would lead me to the young man who spoke to Sylvie after Mass and could well be the same boy who took her to Brooklyn in a blizzard.

I wondered for the first time if he had also disappeared. If his own mother was suffering through the agony of trying to find her boy. I hoped, perhaps, to find an ally.

After I turned down Delancey Street, I kept my eyes forward. I didn't want to appear lost or too curious. A sign above the only likely shopfront said *Panetteria*. But just as the woman at the church had said, it looked closed up, abandoned even. In fact, it stood out from the rest of the businesses on that busy street for its singular lack of activity. I pretended to examine the apples on display at a greengrocer a few stores down and waited to see if anyone emerged from the building. After a few minutes, a man in an overcoat and bowler hat walked out from the alley next to it, looked up and down the street, then fished in his pockets for a cigarette and some matches.

The women were right. I would have to come back another day.

Aaron and I continued to meet each day in the afternoon. He came to me for tea and to collect whatever of the remaining waists I had managed to finish. I continued to sew them both because I needed the money and because I needed to keep my hands busy. He also brought me news.

"You know about the robbery on Canal Street on the day of the storm?" he asked, handing me a newspaper folded to the item.

"No, I have not heard of it." With so many other matters on my mind, I paid little attention to what else was happening in New York. I couldn't imagine why Aaron thought I would be interested in a robbery. But I took the paper from him and read.

When I finished, I looked up at him in horror and saw that he had made the same connection. The police had tied the robbery to the Bonnano family and were searching for the oldest son, who had not been seen since that day.

"Sylvie," I murmured. "She had money. She was the girl who bought clothes at Abraham and Straus!" I stood and paced around my tiny parlor, my blood boiling in my veins.

"We can't be certain..."

It was a feeble protest. Aaron knew as well as I did that if Sylvie was with this Bonnano boy, she must have accidentally been caught up in the robbery. The pieces fit together too perfectly.

"I will go to the bakery tomorrow. I know where it is."

"Let me go with you."

"No," I said. "You know we make an odd pair. The two of us together would attract notice. I need to be discreet. Especially now, à cause de ça." I held up the newspaper.

He nodded. "I'll wait for you somewhere so that if something happens, I may sound the alarm."

I agreed, and we made our plan to meet early the next morning.

When Aaron left, I was once more alone with my thoughts. Without the daily routine that revolved around working and caring for Sylvie, I tortured myself going over and over my life, wondering if I could have turned a different corner and prevented what had happened. I retraced each step, reexamining my choices, trying to see if there was a particular moment when I could have done something different, and always ended at the point where the choice had not been mine to make, when my own mother disappeared, and a well-meaning gendarme took me to the convent. It was a kindness, to be sure. The sisters taught me a skill that has fed and clothed Sylvie and me for fifteen years, and I learned to read and write in French and English and do sums. They, too, were kind, thinking they were giving me a good start in life by apprenticing me to a seamstress. No one would have expected her to be such a tyrant. No, try as I might, I could find not one instance where, without being able to see into the future, I would have chosen differently. I became a courtesan to escape a life of drudgery as a low-class seamstress. Young, pretty, naive, I could never have resisted the clothes, the jewels, and the admiring glances of the men and envy of the women. I even persuaded myself, once, that I was in love.

Love. Why had I not warned Sylvie about it?

CHAPTER SIXTEEN

Sylvie

I'd begun to settle into a busy routine at the studio. Florence found a way to command my every waking hour, demanding my presence at rehearsals and when the cameras whirred as they captured the scenes on celluloid. I didn't know why. It really was hardly necessary. When I was watching her, I couldn't be sewing, and my work would pile up and keep me there late almost every night. And yet...she was the Vitagraph girl. In a way, I was living in my dream. Although I did not have her notoriety or talent, I was part of her life.

Annabel took pains to warn me about her. "She'll eat you alive, just you see. Her face is all sweetness, but she's as calculating as any general on a battlefield."

Deep inside, I suspected Annabel was right. But watching Florence, being there while she rehearsed and filmed, taught me so much I would never have been able to learn, at least not so quickly.

Before I knew it, more than a month had passed. It must have been nine o'clock that night in April, after *Princess Nicotine* was finished and before filming for *Launcelot and Elaine* had begun. I waited outside the studios for the trolley that would take me up to the apartment that I shared with Annabel and two other girls when I heard a voice that startled me.

"Sylvie!"

I looked behind me. No one. I turned in a complete circle. It must have been my imagination playing tricks on me. I was tired, hearing things. Countless times I had imagined that voice, had pictured a scene where Paolo would come to me, and I could tell him that I didn't need his help, that I had managed not only to find work on my own but that I had landed in the very place where all my most cherished dreams might come true. And he would admire me and not see me as a helpless girl—which, of course, would fascinate him.

"Sylvie!"

This time, I knew it was real. I whirled around again.

"Over here!"

He stepped out of the shadows across the street, next to a building, looking up and down the street and beckoning me when the traffic cleared. I ran across, right into his arms. He held me so tight I couldn't breathe. "Where have you been? Why didn't you come before?"

"No one found you. Good," he said, releasing me and holding me a little away. Not *I missed you,* or *Sorry I didn't come before.*

"I work for Vitagraph, changed my name." I had so much more to tell him, but he seemed breathless, in a hurry.

"That's good it worked out. Smart to change your name." He poked his head around the corner of the building and looked up and down the avenue. "Is there somewhere we can talk?"

"There's a cafe nearby."

"No, somewhere private." Again, he glanced around and

over his shoulder.

The only place I could think of was the sewing room. Many people worked late into the night at Vitagraph; the doors would still be open. "Come with me."

He stooped and picked up a valise. I hadn't noticed it before; I couldn't take my eyes off his face, trying to read everything I could in it—why he was there, why he hadn't come sooner, what he thought of me. But to go to the studio, I had to peel them away, and I led him across the street and back to the studio entrance at a near run. I was breathless by the time we got there, and the doorman gave me a suspicious look as we passed. I said over my shoulder, "New actor, he'll be five minutes." So many hopeful actors came and went each day that no one would question it.

I led him on a roundabout route that would avoid the rehearsal rooms and the people who camped out on the extra bench, finally arriving at the stuffy little chamber that had been my domain ever since I last saw him.

"What's this place?" he asked, looking it all up and down as if he expected someone to leap out from between the tightly packed bolts of fabric.

"It's part of the costume shop," I said. "I do the sewing." It hurt a little to admit that to him.

"I thought you were gonna be in the pictures." He smiled and reached out to tap me under the chin, but I turned my head away. He didn't have the right to an opinion after leaving me to fend for myself.

"That will come. What did you have to talk to me about?" My scrutiny of his face hadn't revealed what I wanted it to. I didn't see a boy who missed me and who felt bad about not coming to see me before. "Why did you leave me like that—so suddenly? I might have ended up sleeping on the street and dying of the cold."

He finally focused on me, and his searing gaze nearly

melted away my irritation. "I can't tell you. Not right now. You got to trust me. Someday you'll understand everything, but for now, I got to ask you a favor. Besides," he came close to me, taking hold of my hands, his eyes beseeching and kind, just a warm breath away from a kiss. "I figured you had enough cash for an emergency if it came to it."

Of course. I still owed him the fifty dollars I no longer had. "About that money…"

"Aw, forget it. I can get more. It's not important. What is important is that I need you to do this one thing for me. It's just for a while, maybe a couple of weeks. You've got it all set up perfect. I need you to look after this, keep it safe and secret." He let go of my hands and picked up the valise.

What? Was that all he wanted of me, a service? "What is it?" I asked, trying to keep the bitter edge out of my voice.

"It's money. I…I've been saving up, working odd jobs, to start a business of my own, and I'm afraid someone will steal it from me."

It didn't add up. And he didn't look into my eyes when he said it. "If they'll steal it from you, won't they steal it from me?"

"They won't know you have it. They won't even know there's any connection between us." He glanced behind him again as if someone might be there.

"Who are 'they?'" I didn't like it, not one little bit. But he was there, so close. Every once in a while, that look came back into his eyes, and I could smell him—slightly acrid sweat, smoke, and something else, something that suggested cooking, something yeasty.

He moved closer and put his arms around my waist, pulling me to him. I could feel his wiry strength, protective and dangerous at the same time. He nuzzled into the hair just above my ear. A shiver went right through me. "You're a smart girl," he murmured, "and you're gonna be something, I can tell. It'll all turn out all right, I promise. I need you to keep this money safe for me. I'll be back for it, and then we can maybe step out together, you know, like a proper couple."

I imagined for an instant what it would be like to go to a dance hall on Paolo's arm. All the girls would envy me, and the boys would keep their distance. I would be under his protection. How could I refuse him? He'd taken a risk for me, too, helping me run away. "I'll keep it safe. You can count on me."

"I know I can."

His kiss was warm and gentle at first, just touching my lips with his, then his tongue darted in, and I felt his teeth against mine and soon I forgot about the money and worrying about where it came from, and I kissed him back, squeezing him so close it seemed as if our clothes, our skin, everything that separated our two bodies would disintegrate, and we would become one person.

I don't know how long we kissed, but when our lips parted, I heard the tiniest sound and noticed that the door to the sewing room was open just a crack. Someone had been standing there, looking in, listening. "You'd better go. I have to meet Annabel." I pushed Paolo away.

He caught me again and kissed me once more, quickly, breathlessly. "I'll come back for you," he said.

Before I knew it, he'd run off, making hardly a sound, leaving behind only his vague, tobacco-tinged scent and the valise full of money.

I found a cubby in the corner of the sewing room that was hidden behind several bolts of fabric and stowed the valise as far back in it as I could. I thought about looking inside to see how much money was there, but something made me think it would be a bad idea. I didn't want to know exactly how much there was because if it was a lot, I would have to wonder what Paolo had done to get it. I suspected this money was somehow tied to the fifty dollars he gave me on the day of the storm, and if I probed too deeply, I might find out something I didn't really want to know.

I soon became so busy I barely had time to eat and sleep, let alone worry over something I couldn't do anything about. The release of *King Lear* at the end of March had been a huge success. Mr. Blackton and Mr. Kent were now busy planning out more and more pictures for the coming year. They would have to shoot most of them in the next few months—even if they wouldn't be shown in the nickelodeons until late fall or winter—because they needed the strong sunlight. Even with a studio made almost entirely of glass, there wasn't enough light to make pictures during the winter months, and bad weather was always a danger.

Every day it seemed the studios got busier and busier. All around me was a frenzy of activity, all the time, from early in the morning until after dark. One day, I counted eight different moving pictures being rehearsed or shot, some right there, others in Mr. Blackton's garden, which was not far away. Rehearsals for *Launcelot and Elaine* had started, but they were in one of the smaller studios. The big glass studio was reserved for an enormous production of *The Life of Moses*. This ambitious project was a boon for many of the extras who'd been waiting for their chance on the benches, and it would fill five reels instead of just one.

"I can't believe it will work," Annabel said one afternoon when we met in a hallway. She was on the way to rehearse *The Seven Plagues of Egypt*, the third scene, and I had my arms laden with scraps of material I was supposed to help the wardrobe mistresses figure out how to turn into costumes for the large cast. "People are willing to pay a nickel for twenty minutes of entertainment they can fit in during a lunch hour or on the way home from work," she said as we hurried along together. "But something that takes more than an hour and a half? And where would it be shown? No one wants to sit on one of those hard benches in a nickelodeon for that much time!"

"They'll release the parts separately, I hear."

"But they believe it's all one picture and should be seen all at once."

I had heard that too, and I agreed with her that it might not work, but Mr. Blackton and Mr. Smith—who everyone but me called A.E.—were apparently determined. The whole studio was buzzing about it.

The noise got louder as we approached the studio and spilled out in a roar when we opened the door. I'd gotten used to that, everyone talking and working at once. They all went quiet during shooting, though. Not because it made any difference, but because Mr. Blackton said he needed to concentrate.

I headed to the side, where those not immediately involved in the scene stood, shifting my bundle to ease one arm.

"How are they going to make the Red Sea part?" one of the extras standing nearby asked no one in particular.

"They'll do that and perform a few other miracles too." It was Roy, one of the grips. "How you doing, Stitches?" he asked me with a wink.

But the Red Sea parting wasn't being filmed that day. It was Moses turning his staff into a serpent. I'd seen tricks on film before, mostly in editing, but I'd heard they were going to do this one in the filming, which was why I'd stopped in on my way to the wardrobe room. As the extras went to their places, I found a quiet spot behind a long bank of Cooper Hewitts where I wouldn't be in the way. Chaos reigned as about twenty actors of different ages moved here and there, no one quite certain where to go, with Mr. Kent himself dressed up as Pharaoh trying to arrange them in groups and tell them how to act.

"Perhaps they should seem a little more frightened." A man wearing a priest's dog collar rose from the chair he sat in. I hadn't noticed him before, but Annabel told me that they'd hired a minister to write the story and help make sure it didn't offend the religious folks. I watched him mixing with the motley cast, the only one not in costume because he always wore one, and strained to hear what he was saying over the din of set builders hammering, cameramen shouting, "Don't stand there!" and the constant creak of the floor as dozens of feet scurried across it, all bent on some business or other.

"Why aren't you in costume?" It was Mr. Blackton. He must have slipped into the space I was in to check something.

"Oh, I'm not in the picture! I'm the seamstress."

He looked at me from my head to my toes and said, "Huh, so you are," then walked away.

My heart was pounding. Why did I say that? I could have pretended, and I would have acted in my first moving picture. Too bad it wasn't possible to do a retake of a real-life moment, for me to go back and redo the scene like they did when something went wrong in the filming!

A second later, a shriek pierced the air. It was Edith Storey, an actress with an innocent face and sweet expression that was perfect to portray a woman in biblical times. She pointed down into a box that a young man had brought over in preparation for filming.

"It's a harmless snake!" Mr. Blackton strode over, reached into the box, and pulled out a long black serpent. It writhed and wriggled in his hands. "You're a beauty, you are." He let the snake twine itself around his arms and spoke soothingly to it, as one would to a child.

The young man who brought the box came over and took the snake from him. It was on loan, apparently, from the Brooklyn Zoo.

I couldn't stay to watch all the shooting, because unlike some of the other scenes, this one took a very long time. Mr. Blackton insisted on using stop-motion photography. I could tell the man playing Aaron was uncomfortable with the snake, and it would be torture for him to have to go through the motions step by step, slowly, as that technique required.

Later that day, I met Annabel for dinner at the cafeteria table. It had been an exhausting day of shooting, and everyone was subdued. My back ached from sewing for five hours straight without a break, making Florence's "medieval" gown, and running back and forth to the costume shop as they handed me things to mend for Moses.

"That damned snake!" Annabel said. "One time, it got loose and slithered away right out the door of the studio. Mr. Blackton found it and coaxed it out. Good thing he likes reptiles."

I laughed. It felt good to laugh. I hadn't really noticed it until then. Something about me had changed in those weeks, and it was more than being independent. The place suited me, even though I wasn't acting. Yet. It bubbled with joy, everyone working hard at something they loved, doing whatever small part was theirs to achieve that miraculous finished product: a moving picture.

I looked up from eating my potato to see one of the actors from Moses sitting opposite me, scooping soup out of a bowl with one hand, reading a newspaper with the other. I absently scanned the headlines. I hadn't paid much attention to anything outside the studio before then.

But the headline I read pierced through my deliberate ignorance: *Canal Street Blizzard Robbery Still a Mystery.* Then a subhead said, *No Sign of Stolen Money.* I stopped breathing, my heart flipping over in my breast.

"Are you all right?" Annabel put her hand on my arm.

"Yes. Only, I think I'm tired. Let's go home." The last thing I wanted was to explain it all to her.

That night, I tossed and turned on my side of the bed I shared with Annabel. I would have to do something now. Obviously, the money Paolo left with me had been stolen. It had to be. I could no longer ignore the truth. How foolish of me to think my life was getting better. I had stepped right into a trap. Now, even if I wanted to, I couldn't go home, not with a valise full of stolen money in my hands. What if Paolo came back for it? If I gave it to him, I'd be helping him get away with a crime. Perhaps I already had. I could be arrested. I could go to jail.

There was nothing to do for now but wait and think and try to make sense of it all.

CHAPTER
SEVENTEEN

Justine

I smelled the bread baking as I turned the corner onto
Delancey Street, slowing my brisk pace, not wanting to look
too eager when I reached the door. Aaron had gone to a
restaurant on Mulberry Street where I was to meet him after
I accomplished my task. When I spied the line of women
outside the door with their shopping bags at the ready, I knew
I'd made the right decision to do this without Aaron. A couple
would have attracted unwanted notice.

I took my place at the end of the line. One or two of the
women stared openly at me, then turned to each other and
said things in low voices so that I could not hear. I sensed some
tension among them and wondered if it stemmed from my
being there, someone they didn't know, an interloper.

The line moved slowly. The women went into the bakery
one at a time, emerging with loaves of bread and looks of relief

on their faces. When the door opened to let the lady directly in front of me inside, I tried to look in, but the person on the other side of the door closed it too fast for me to see much of anything.

After a few minutes, the last woman emerged, looking the same as the others with her loaf of bread wrapped in paper in her shopping bag, and her face eased of some worry or other. I stepped forward for my turn, and the door slammed in my face. A hand inserted a placard that said CLOSED between the blind and the glass on the top of the door. Without thinking, I pounded. Nothing happened. I pummeled the door again and again, ready to cry with frustration, when at last it opened a crack, and someone looked out at me. "We're closed! Can't you read the sign?"

"Yes, but I've been waiting in line to buy bread. The ladies at Most Precious Blood said that I could buy good bread here before eight in the morning, and now you say you're closed."

"We have no more bread today. We only bake for people who order the day before."

The woman was about to shut the door again, but I inserted the toe of my boot in the opening just enough to make it impossible. "Please, I would like to order, but more than that, I need to talk to Mrs. Bonnano."

I heard a sharp intake of breath. After a moment's hesitation, the woman said, "One moment," and walked away, leaving the door slightly ajar. I took the opportunity to slip inside and close it behind me.

It was the strangest bakery I had ever seen. I could see no sign of an oven, only a rack for displaying baked goods, yet the aroma of warm bread lingered. The room was dimly lit by a single electric bulb hanging from the middle of the ceiling. The only other feature was a door leading to the back of the building.

I had to remind myself to breathe as I waited there what seemed forever but was doubtless only a minute or two. Footsteps approached the door I'd noticed, and a key turned in a lock. A woman entered, closing the door behind her before advancing toward me.

"I am Signora Bonnano. What do you want?"

"I am Justine Button, and I would like to speak with your son, if he is here." My heart raced. I could not imagine how she might react.

"What do you know about my son?" she asked, drawing her eyebrows together.

"I know nothing, except that he was seen with my daughter after she disappeared."

The word "disappeared" caused her eyes to narrow. "Who saw my son with your daughter?"

My mouth was dry, and my hands began to perspire inside my gloves. "They were photographed. On the bridge to Brooklyn, the day of the blizzard."

"That's impossible," she said, her face growing darker, her gaze more intense. "My son was here all day. What mother would allow a child out in such weather as that was? Where is this photograph you speak of?"

With each succeeding question, her voice became louder. She was trying to frighten me. Yet behind her aggressive tone, I sensed discomfort, worry. I couldn't guess what she was thinking, but her ready lie told me that she was accustomed to being the family's gatekeeper. "I don't have it with me," I said. I did have it in my purse, but I had encountered such a different tone from the one I imagined that I thought better of letting her see it. I wasn't certain I wanted her to know what Sylvie looked like.

"I don't know what makes you think my son would have anything at all to do with your daughter. He's a good boy."

A boy currently being sought by the police for his potential connection to a robbery, I thought but didn't say. "Surely there would be no harm in my speaking to him, then."

"He's not here. He has gone away."

So, had he disappeared too, or was he hiding and she knew where? "Perhaps when he returns..." I tried to make the inquiry sound casual.

"We expect him to be away for some time," she said. "He has unfinished business in another part of the country."

"Mrs. Bonnano." I took a breath and calmed myself before continuing. I needed to find a way to break through her defensive posture. I had intended to confront her mother to mother. But clearly, something else was at stake here. And I was certain it had to do with the robbery I'd read about. So I gambled on a different approach. "It would seem to me that if we could prove that your son and my daughter were together the day of the snowstorm, it might be useful to you." I didn't dare say anything more specific in case I was entirely wrong.

"There is no we! Your daughter must be a very wicked girl to run away, but my son is not involved."

Her vehemence, even in the face of my offer to help, closed a door. Far from sharing my feelings or sympathizing with me, she stood in front of me like an armored guard before a fortress. I would get nothing more that day.

"I won't trouble you any longer," I said.

I let myself out and heard the bolt scrape into place behind me.

As I slowly walked back to meet Aaron and tell him what I hadn't discovered, I let my mind wander. My search for Sylvie really began fifteen years ago. Then, I knew where she was but lacked the resources to find her, until chance worked in my favor. The infant who had been torn from my arms in a pension by the sea was, by the time I started trying to get her back, three years old and a stranger to me. Did I really know her any better now? The Sylvie I thought I knew would never have run away, or if she did, she certainly wouldn't have stayed away. In these past few weeks since she left, I was already losing little pieces of her—her expressions, the color of her eyes, the sound of her voice, her light tread on the stairs. I knew all those things intimately, but they had become less vivid. I wished I had taken more care to look at Sylvie and listen to her. I never suspected that I would not have her near me until I died. Now, perhaps I risked losing her all over again. Perhaps she was gone from the earth, and I would never know.

I shook the thought away. Sylvie was alive somewhere; of that I was certain. And Mrs. Bonnano knew more about her than she was willing to tell me. If any harm had come to Sylvie, I sensed that Mrs. Bonnano would not have been so frightened of me, of what Sylvie's reappearance could mean for her son. I wondered if she actually knew where my daughter was and simply refused to say. Aaron and I had traced Sylvie to Brooklyn, but she could have gone anywhere from there.

That night, I could not sleep. I paced back and forth across my tiny parlor until I forced myself to go to bed, where I tossed and turned, falling into a fitful sleep and waking with a start as soon as the light in the apartment showed the slightest hint of dawn. Time is elastic, and that day it stretched until I thought the evening would never come.

When it did, bringing with it Aaron's reassuring knock and calm presence, I said, "Bring me more work. If I do nothing but worry all day, I will go mad."

And so, since I had long since caught up with the backlog of work from the day of the snowstorm, Aaron once again started bringing me waists to finish. Not as many as before—I could not work as fast without Sylvie. And I was still distracted. Sometimes I would find myself staring at nothing, needle poised above the fabric, and not even be able to recall what I had been thinking about. I was anchorless, adrift, without Sylvie's future to think about and to give me purpose. What else mattered in the life I had created for us than that she should be well and become someone better than I was?

I began to have terrible thoughts, ideas no sane person would have. I saw everything in my apartment as an instrument of harm. My scissors, the kitchen knives, even the needles

I sewed with. I began to imagine someone was following me on the few occasions I went out to the grocer or to purchase sewing supplies. One day, I would think it was the police, who not only suspected Sylvie of wrongdoing but who also had somehow connected me to her abduction fifteen years before on another continent. Then the next day, I'd imagine an Italian man was keeping pace with me a few steps behind, waiting for me to lead him to Sylvie, and thence to the boy, who would hand over all the money stolen on that day.

I was caught. I went over and over it in my mind and eventually had to accept the conclusion that if I were able to find Sylvie, it could put her in danger.

I could hardly explain to Aaron all the reasons why I decided to suspend my active search for my precious daughter. I saw the questions in his eyes when he came morning and night to bring to me and pick up the work he so generously found for me. When he suggested some new avenue of inquiry, I would shake my head, unable to put into words my dire suspicions.

Two agonizing months passed in that way. The neighbors had begun looking at me with a combination of suspicion and worry.

"Your Sylvie still hasn't come home? Have you checked the hospitals?" It was Mrs. Murphy, peeking out her door as I went past down the stairs to buy some food. I thought I had managed to time my comings and goings to avoid encountering any of the other people in the building, or at least to see them only when they were too busy to stop and chat. But apparently not.

"Sylvie is fine. She did return, but only very briefly. She won a scholarship, you know, and has gone to Albany to study." I had rehearsed the explanation, changing details until I was certain there was enough truth that those who knew us a little would believe me.

Mrs. Murphy's mouth formed an O, and just as she drew

breath to ask more questions, I said, "I'm sorry, but I am late for an appointment," and hurried away.

Since then, I had relied on Aaron to bring me all the supplies I needed for sewing, and of his own accord, he started bringing me groceries. I tried to pay for them, but he would not let me.

I had remained in the apartment in case Sylvie returned. As time went on, the suspicions of the neighbors, and the possibility that Alfonse might return any day, made me decide that soon I would have to move elsewhere.

One balmy early June evening, Aaron took hold of my wrist as I handed him the finished waists to put into his bag and said, "Will you walk out with me? It's lovely outside, and I'm sure the air would do you good. I fear staying indoors like this will make you ill. You must take care of yourself, for Sylvie's sake."

I tried to summon up a smile. I was sorry to have caused Aaron worry. "Perhaps tomorrow."

But I didn't go out with him. Day after day, I sat in my dark parlor, taking advantage of the small bit of sunlight that managed to filter in from the backyard my window faced. Assailing me with their cruelty, thoughts of the times Sylvie had sat across from me after school, quietly pushing the needle in and out of starchy fabric that reddened our fingers, disrupted my peace.

The cruelest memories of all, though, were from that moment in the seaside rooming house where I spent my confinement. I relived over and over the exquisite joy of giving birth to Sylvie, seeing her tiny, scrunched-up self for the first time, watching her hunt for my nipple, and feeling her strong sucking, drawing nourishment from my body.

If I could have stopped the memory at that point, it might have comforted me. But I couldn't. I relived over and over again the horror of having her wrenched out of my arms when she was only a few hours old, my complete confusion and sense of loss, and watching the needle full of drugs being pumped into my arm. Then the moment when I awoke, being told my Sylvie had died at birth, that I had only imagined seeing her alive and must now do my best to forget.

That was all Alfonse's doing. I hoped he'd suffered these fifteen years even half as much as I suffered in those few moments. He deserved it. I would never forgive him.

CHAPTER
EIGHTEEN

Sylvie

"Places, everyone! Let's make some magic!"

Mr. Blackton's face was serious, but his eyes glistened with excitement. He was always happy when the shooting started for a moving picture after weeks of practice. In this case, it had been more than two months. Two months where I went through my days smiling, laughing, sewing, while all the time a knot of dread sat in my gut like a tumor. I had gone over and over it, thinking about how I could get rid of the money Paolo left with me without being seen as a criminal or without getting Paolo into more trouble than he already was in. So far, I had thought of nothing.

And here we were, in Mr. Blackton's garden, everyone dressed in the costumes I'd either made or altered for the purpose. Not a stitch was out of place. I had worked extra hard on this picture. I didn't want to be sitting in a dark room sewing at a time when I might finally get my chance to act.

"Let's have Titania and Penelope talking. You girls know how to make it look like you've had it with men."

This made everyone laugh. Even funnier was what Florence and Miss Kimball were actually saying to each other. They made sure it had something to do with the story, or their gestures and actions would look insincere, but some of their words made me blush. They weren't suitable for me, and even less so for the children who were acting as sprites and fairies.

"Remember what I told you." Annabel strolled over, looking as if she was trying to fix her hair, and spoke so that only I could hear it. "Just be in the right place at the right time."

For the past few nights, I'd been making an extra costume for a fairy at Annabel's insistence. "He as much as said there weren't enough people in the scene at the end; that he needed a few more bodies, but there wasn't time to hire any more actors," Annabel had said.

I had made the mistake of telling her about my failure to seize the opportunity during the filming of Moses, and she'd been scheming on my behalf ever since. "You'd be better than most of the people who clutter up the extra bench," she said. "And I wouldn't mind seeing the look on Florence's face when you step out of the little box she's put you in."

Annabel and the two other girls we shared the apartment with, who also worked for Vitagraph as secretaries, sat me down after dinner about a week before filming was to begin. "Didn't I warn you not to get too friendly with Florence?" Annabel said.

"But she got me a raise, and I didn't even ask for it." I wanted to close my ears to anything bad about Florence, who still had only been kind to me.

"Fifty cents more per week! She can give that to you out of her own pocket money."

"She must be. I haven't seen anything on the books that looks like you're paid more than seven dollars a week." It was

Judith, a girl from Brooklyn who helped with the bookkeeping.

I had to admit Florence kept me more and more busy for no particularly good reason most of the time. She would send me to fetch something she'd left in her dressing room whenever Mr. Blackton or Mr. Kent came in to talk about her roles. And half the time when I returned with whatever object it was—a compact, a comb, a handkerchief—she'd forgotten about it and moved on to the next thing. By that time, of course, the two directors who made all the decisions about casting were with the men operating the cameras, focusing on the technical things of getting the images onto celluloid in what were often stories that depended on some special effects, to be created later in the editing stage.

I guess I saw what she was doing, but I didn't want to believe it. On top of that, I suppose I should have asked myself why Annabel was going out of her way to help me. She was ambitious too, I saw. Yet, I was so blind then! It makes me laugh to think how innocent and trusting I was. Daily I bumped up against something that showed just how successfully my mother had kept me ignorant of the ways of the world. I'd seen the petty jealousies of the girls at school, the elbowing their way into favor with the teachers and trying to outdo each other with fashion, but my reputation as the smartest girl there earned me the privilege of ignoring them. Now I saw things from the other direction, from someone not yet where she wanted to be, overlooked and looking for opportunity.

Motivating me wasn't just my desire to be in the pictures. I was preparing for the inevitable day when I must go back to my mother. I knew that day would come eventually, but if I remained a seamstress, even in such a glamorous business as the moving pictures, I would have proven her to be right all along. I realized I was wasting my talents, not rising to what I knew I was capable of. I couldn't wait for luck. I'd used that up by getting the seamstress job in the first place. If I wanted to be in front of the cameras, I would have to force the issue.

So, every day of that hot July shoot, I did as Annabel suggested and wore my waist and skirt over the costume I'd made. I was on hand eight hours a day to make repairs and fetch and carry, and for two more hours at least back at the studio after filming was finished for the day, all the time wearing two layers of clothing.

"You all right?" We were nearing the end of filming. Mr. Costello, cast as Oberon, was taking advantage of not being in a scene to smoke a pipe and had wandered behind the same tree where I was trying to find some cooling shade from the baking sun on the hottest day so far.

I stood quickly and pasted a smile on my face. "I'm fine, I just..."

I've never been one to faint. I'd never fainted before and haven't since. It must have been the heat. Dots of light danced in front of my eyes and blotted out everything, and suddenly the world disappeared.

I came to just a few minutes later to see three faces staring down at me: Mr. Costello, Mr. Blackton, and Florence. The men looked genuinely concerned. Florence's expression was harder to interpret. I sat up, mortified.

"I'm so sorry! Please don't mind me." I went to stand, and Mr. Blackton took hold of both my hands and pulled me upright.

"Now that, Titania. That's how asleep you should look when Puck casts his spell on you!"

At Mr. Blackton's words, Mr. Costello lifted his chin and guffawed to the sky. Florence smiled and laughed, but not with her eyes.

"The heat must have overcome you. You're dressed like it's winter." Mr. Blackton looked concerned.

"I'm fine now, really." By now, the entire cast and the men running the cameras had gathered in a circle around us, including Annabel.

"I told you not to do it!" Annabel said, her voice cross.

I stared at her. What was she doing? Wearing all these clothes had been her idea.

She marched up to me and, before I could stop her, ripped my shirtwaist open—the one I'd been working so hard to preserve because my mother had sewn it—and tore it down the middle, sending little buttons flying to the ground. Everyone gasped. "She made herself a costume. Been wearing it underneath for weeks, thinking she could act in the film."

By now, my face must have been redder than the roses in the nearby flower bed. My eyes stung, and I willed myself not to cry. Why was she being so mean?

Then Annabel leaned forward and whispered in my ear. "Do it! Ask him!"

Of course. This was the moment. "That's right," I heard myself say. "You need more fairies for the final scene. I've been watching for months. I know what to do." As I spoke, I took the rest of my clothes off to reveal my gauzy costume. After being excessively hot for so long, I almost got used to it. I shivered.

I could feel the men looking at me differently.

"I have to admit, there's something fairy-like about you, with your fair hair and slender figure. Not to mention those enormous blue eyes."

"Pity there's so much for you to do! I tore my costume just now, and it needs to be mended. I was just coming to find you when you fainted." Florence placed herself between me and Mr. Blackton, holding up her skirt where I could see the tiniest rent in the fabric, concealed in a fold.

Mr. Blackton gently moved her aside. "That won't show on camera. Come on, Miss..."

"Potter," I said.

"You may as well have a try. We can always edit you out." Mr. Blackton took hold of my arm and pulled me out of the shadows and into the blinding sunlight where the next scene would be shot.

I would have to deal with the consequences later.

#

My spirits were higher than they'd ever been by the time we finished filming *A Midsummer Night's Dream*. I was only in a couple of the scenes at the end, and it was difficult sometimes because Florence would damage her costume—sometimes I thought on purpose—or lose a flower from her hair at the most inconvenient moments. Once, Mr. Blackton told me to ignore her. I didn't dare look at her to see how she reacted.

It wasn't until the shoot ended and we were back in the studio, and I was once again in my sewing room ripping apart and remaking the costumes for another picture that I felt the full weight of what I had done in putting myself forward like that.

"Knock knock!"

As usual, Florence didn't wait for me to answer but walked right in. I was in the middle of fixing a torn buttonhole, a very fiddly job, and didn't look up.

"So, now you think you're going to get more chances to act, is that it?"

That made me put my work down and pay attention to her. In front of others, she kept up the air of sweetness that was her biggest appeal on screen. I had heard this acid tone of voice only once before and not directed at me. "I'm sorry?"

She started strolling around the room, touching the bolts of fabric as if testing how they felt had been her purpose in coming there. "It's not a life for an innocent young girl, you know."

"You've done all right," I said.

She whirled around and fixed me with a hard stare. "You have no idea of the cost. I will not have an upstart seamstress interfering in my future. You know I could have you fired at any moment."

I gave a short laugh. How could she? I did my work well—Mr. Blackton and Mr. Kent and all the actors said how superior my workmanship was. "Who would sew the costumes? You?"

She waved her hand dismissively. "Seamstresses are a dime a dozen. You only got the job because of that bitch Annabel. That and your pretty face. Oh, don't look all shocked! You know how to use it. Fainting. Honestly. Do you think I fell for that for a single second?"

Her voice grew louder and louder. I glanced anxiously at the partly open door. Like a fury, she strode over, slammed it shut, then came and stood so close to me I could see the pulse in her neck. "I know something that could have you out on the street. I know you're hiding something in this very room. Would you prefer to take your chances at another studio after being fired from here, probably end up exploiting your looks in a much less savory way, or stay here where you can earn a decent wage and be safe?"

My blood turned to ice. What did she know and how? My mind raced, trying to figure out how I could prevent her from using whatever it was against me.

Florence reached into her pocket and pulled out a scrap of something that looked like newsprint. "Read it." She slammed the paper down on the sewing table, folded her arms across her chest, and tapped her foot impatiently.

My fingers trembled as I took the scrap and smoothed it so that I could decipher the faded image and text. There was a drawing of a young man, a familiar young man, with a caption that said, *Robbery suspect in custody. Won't reveal whereabouts of stolen money.* I read the short article. It followed up on the article whose headline I had seen during the filming of *Moses*, about the robbery of a jewelry store on Canal Street the day of the blizzard in March. It was plain as could be. I could no longer hold out any hope that my belief was mistaken. Paolo was a thief. He lied to me.

"This young man came to see you and gave you something to hide."

I remembered, then, about the door creaking. Florence must have been watching. I was too shocked to say anything. I looked down to see that I'd been gripping the needle so hard it had impressed a groove into the pad of my thumb.

"Don't tell me you didn't know." She snatched up the paper again. "I'll keep this for now. Just as I'll keep your secret. So long as you go today and tell Mr. Blackton that you're no longer interested in becoming an actress, that you're happy doing the job you're really good at: sewing."

I was too weak to stand or do anything except stare at the door after Florence shut it so violently behind her that dust rose from the floor and tiny threads of fabric shook free from the bolts of material.

That day everything seemed very far away, coated with mist. I didn't know what to do, what I could tell anyone. Any step seemed destined for disaster. Was Florence the only person who had seen something or guessed at it anyway? More than anything, I wanted to talk to Annabel. But perhaps she wasn't the person I thought she was either. How did I know I could trust her? This dust-up with Florence happened because Annabel had pushed me to do something I was afraid to do. Yet I wasn't sorry. It's what I wanted more than anything, and now I'd done it.

"I said, please step aside!"

I was distracted and didn't hear the men coming. I flattened myself against the wall of the corridor as Mr. Blackton and a cameraman struggled past, carting a heavy piece of furniture toward one of the studios. "Let me help," I said, scurrying after them. Perhaps I'd have an opportunity to talk to Mr. Blackton because I had no doubt that I must do as Florence said. Even if I were to go straight to the police with the money, they would draw the worst conclusion. They would think I had helped

Paolo steal it. And in a way, I had. Without me there, Paolo probably would have been caught that very night.

"You did a good job in the film, you know." At first, I didn't realize Mr. Blackton was talking to me. He and the cameraman rearranged three pieces of furniture in the otherwise empty room whose walls were painted black. The only illumination was a harsh work light dangling from the crisscrossing metal beams suspended below the glass ceiling. The sun had set, so there would be no filming until tomorrow.

"I-I wanted to talk to you about that," I said.

"Oh, no need. I've seen what you can do. We've got other roles for you. Crowd scenes are difficult because your face draws the eye. So I've got you in mind for a featured role."

One day ago, my heart would have leapt and done a somersault hearing the director of Vitagraph say those things to me. Now it just made me want to cry. "Well, you see..."

I didn't know how to go on. If I said what Florence wanted me to say, I would sound ungrateful, and I knew Mr. Blackton was thick with everyone throughout the movie industry in New York, especially with Mr. Edison, whom everyone respected. Saying no to him would mean saying no to the career I so desperately wanted.

"Rehearsals start tomorrow for *Les Misérables*. I was going to use Gladys for Cosette, but you have more of the quality of a waif. She's better in comic roles." He turned and faced me now. "You don't look happy. Isn't this what you wanted?"

I forced a smile. "Yes. Yes, it very much is. I just can't believe it, I guess."

"Good! I've told Judith we'll start paying you ten dollars a week."

It was too much to refuse. I had until tomorrow, I figured, to sort something out about the money. The first thing would be to move it somewhere, hide it where Florence couldn't find it. Other than her word that she'd seen me with Paolo and the existence of the valise, what proof was there, after all?

Paolo. He complicated everything. If he told the police I had the money, it would be the end of all my hopes.

The irony was, I was certain that if she'd been in my shoes, my mother would know what to do. After all, she'd apparently kept something immoral hidden from me, perhaps for my entire life.

For the first time ever, I understood what true loneliness felt like. It wasn't the lack of people around or having no friends. It was not being able to tell anyone about something that frightened you or that was so big, so momentous, it could change the course of your life.

CHAPTER
NINETEEN

Sylvie

"Where's Florence?" I asked Annabel as we sat in the courtyard and ate lunch together. It was a fine August day, and I hadn't set eyes on Florence since she had threatened me a week earlier. Every day since then, I braced myself for her to fly at me in anger when she discovered not only had I not told Mr. Blackton I didn't want to act in any more films but that I had accepted a featured role in an important picture, one that would be a bit like *Moses*, telling a longer, more complex story over four different reels. But she was nowhere to be seen. I knew she wasn't cast in *Les Misérables*, yet there were plenty of other pictures in production that she might have featured in.

Annabel glanced around to make sure no one was near, then lowered her voice. "Mr. Blackton loaned her out, apparently."

"Loaned her out? Where?"

"Some French cinema company. Over here to see the new

technical advances and make some pictures to take back to France."

I tried to understand this unexpected turn of events. Florence was the most popular actress at Vitagraph. She was known everywhere in New York, and with nickelodeons and picture palaces cropping up all over the country, her fame must have spread well beyond. Why would Mr. Blackton have sent her to a company that might steal her away?

"I could have predicted it. You were off in your little sewing cave, but everyone else could hear her ranting and raving behind Mr. Blackton's office door."

"What did she say?" I tried to sound uninterested.

"Some rubbish about you, about you being a thief or something. Then Mr. Blackton said, 'I'd understand if you were just angry I've given her a big role in my next picture, but this is stooping too low.'"

"Why is she so threatened by me?" Anything to steer the conversation away from what Annabel had heard Florence say about stealing.

"Either you're dumber than you seem, or you're just play-ing a game. Anyone with eyes can see that you could do what Florence does. She's right to feel threatened."

Her words embarrassed and pleased me, but I still didn't understand it all. "Then, why don't you feel threatened by me?"

Annabel shook her head. "We're not the same, you and me. The roles they give me wouldn't work for you. I'm not old, but I look more mature, and comedy comes naturally to me. You, on the other hand, look even younger than I suspect you are. So does Florence. She depends on her innocent, naive, and open quality. People feel sorry for her and weep when she's in peril on camera."

What she said made some sense. But still, I couldn't shake the feeling that Annabel wasn't telling me something. Some-thing important.

And then, as if the clouds had parted on a rainy day for the sun to shine through in dramatic fashion, I knew what it was. "You want to be the main actress. The main attraction. And, as long as Florence is around, you won't be."

Annabel sat up straighter and glared at me. "I don't know what gave you that idea! It's ungrateful. After all I've done for you."

"I-I'm sorry." I was, in a sense. But also glad to have some understanding of what was really going on in this strange, magical world I had inched my way into. Annabel's interest in me had always been puzzling, from the very first day when I saw her in the cafe. Had she already seen then what has now come to pass, that there was a chance I could take the place of her biggest rival? I was grateful, of course. Without her, I would never have gotten into Vitagraph so easily. And if by some miracle I had, sewing would only have taken me so far. Her nudge pushed me in the direction of acting. "I think it's time for rehearsal." I stood and put out my hand to help Annabel up.

She either didn't notice—or didn't choose to notice—and pushed herself up from her spot on the dry grass, smoothed her skirt down, and arranged her face in the expression I was most familiar with—a smile with a wry twist in the corners. "See you after!" She waved and walked off as if nothing much had happened.

But for me, the world had changed. It wasn't so noticeable at first, yet in a way, it affected everything about my life. Little pieces of the puzzle chinked into place, like melting crystals of snow that melded into each other, blending into a solid strip of ice. I had passed over a threshold I would never be able to re-cross, from innocence to knowing. From now on, whatever I did would be underlined by what I now knew about the way the world worked. Or the way this particular world worked, in any case.

Now that I knew Florence wasn't lurking around every corner waiting to pounce, everything became easier for me. No one expected me to stop in the middle of a rehearsal to mend a seam or sew on a button. I'm not sure I could have done it otherwise. It was one thing to jump in at the last minute to fill out a crowd. Something else to have to perform a role that was central to the story.

Nowhere was this more obvious than in rehearsals for *Les Misérables.*

"Your mother has left you in the clutches of Thenardier, who treats you like a slave in his home. He extorts money from her for your care, and she has been forced to become a woman of the streets after selling her hair and her teeth to meet his demands for money. In Paris, she would have been called a *demimondaine.* A woman of the world, but a world of shadows and lies." Mr. Blackton ran through a speech like that to me before each scene, trying to make me understand who I was so that I could convey the character without any words.

"I suppose you haven't read the novel." Mr. Blackton had been trying to get me to stand a certain way so that I would look like a downtrodden child. He tried to explain it to me a dozen different times, tried to show me with his own body what he was looking for. But everything I did felt wrong, artificial. Not that I really knew anything about acting, but he had an image in his head, and I knew that somehow I wasn't creating it for him. For the third time that afternoon, he walked away, rubbing the side of his face. "Maybe this was a mistake," I heard him say under his breath.

I was failing. I had never failed at anything in my life before. I had to do something drastic if I didn't want to lose this opportunity. "Make my hair wet," I said on a sudden inspiration.

He cocked his head on the side and thought for a moment, then said, "All right. Hey Hank, bring that bucket of water over for Miss Potter."

Hank, the cameraman, approached with a two-gallon bucket full of water, always on set in case of fire. I intended to dip my hands in and pat my hair to make it straggly and wet. But before I could move away, Hank upended it over me, drenching not just my hair but my clothes as well. Everyone laughed as I sputtered and wiped the water out of my eyes. "That wasn't exactly what I meant," I said, mortified to be standing there dripping. I hunched my shoulders forward and shivered.

"That's it! That's what I want!"

Ahh. I had been finding it difficult, when I was so elated about my unexpected elevation to an important role in a Vitagraph film, to appear unhappy. I didn't know how to make myself look downtrodden, but cold I could certainly manage. We finished shooting the scene, and I finally understood that acting was about more than just putting yourself in a character's place and understanding the story. Sometimes it was about finding whatever way worked to make it *seem* like you were doing that.

"A good day's work, everyone!" Mr. Blackton rubbed his hands together in that way he had when things had gone to his liking.

Maurice Costello, who played the main part of Jean Valjean, approached me then, his face still painted with the dark lines that appeared as normal facial creases when seen through the lens of the camera. Ever since I started working with him, I began to understand why everyone thought he was so handsome. He had a way of looking at me that made me feel as if he could see right inside me. It wasn't the same as the feeling I'd experienced when Paolo gazed into my eyes. I was in no danger of falling in love with Mr. Costello—he was old enough to be my father, after all. But perhaps that was why when he said, "Good job, Stitches!" and clapped me on the shoulder, I felt unaccountably pleased.

The first part of *Les Misérables* was nearly finished by that time in late August and would be shown in the nickelodeons in early September. They'd been working on it all summer, filming bits on the days when the weather wasn't good enough for *Midsummer* outdoors. I wasn't in that first part because it concerned the story with Jean Valjean and the policeman who chased him for stealing a loaf of bread for his starving children. I sometimes watched and helped with the costumes. They still needed my skills as a seamstress, and I found the work anchored me. Everything except the feel of a needle and thread pushing through fabric was strange and new.

But when I was sewing, I couldn't help thinking about my mother and imagining what she would think of my life now. My dream was really the opposite of hers. But here, as I got used to being away from the pressure of her desires for me, I began to understand that what she did, how she treated me, came from love. Not the soft, moving-picture love Mr. Blackton sometimes tried to evoke, but something fierce and hard, a wild animal protecting its young, because survival depended on it.

And I also knew, deep down, that I had been partly to blame, too. I was cowardly. Rather than trying to make her understand what I wanted and risk displeasing her, I simply went along with everything. It was easier to keep my real desires to myself and let the days pass unruffled, as orderly and clean as the waists we sewed.

From time to time, I considered finding a way to tell her what I was doing now, to explain why I had run away and then stayed away. I imagined myself taking the Brighton line to the bridge and then transferring to the IRT to Houston Street. I pictured myself walking up the stoop on Mulberry Street, the Murphy children stopping in the middle of their game of hopscotch, or jump rope, or whatever they were playing and locking their eyes on me as I passed by. What would they have heard about why I hadn't been there for so long? *Sylvie Button disappeared/ran away/was kidnapped*. In a way, all three things were true. Then, in my mind, I climbed the stairs inside; four flights up, in the daytime darker than at night because the gas lamps weren't lit yet. Would I knock or just enter the apartment?

That was the moment when I would catch my breath, and nausea would rise in me. I didn't want to picture my mother's horrified face looking at me over the shoulder of that strange man.

My fantasy about returning home would end almost as soon as it began, and I resumed my thoughts about the present, about my life, and about acting. I was a good actress. Hadn't I proven it, not just in front of the camera, but in every detail of my life every day? Everything I did was a lie. The money Paolo left with me weighed me down as much as if I had stolen it myself. Now, according to that clipping Florence had shown me, he was in custody. How long before he relented and told the police where they could go to find the money? That would end my career, officers marching into the studio and taking me away in handcuffs.

I shivered. I couldn't let that happen. I would find a way to get rid of the money. The trouble was that Florence had taken the clipping she showed me away with her, and I didn't recall the name of the jewelry store that had been robbed, only that it was on Canal Street.

Working seven days a week until filming for *Les Misérables* was over, there would be no time for a jaunt into Manhattan anyway. I could only hope Mr. Blackton would give us a day to rest sometime soon and that I could think of an excuse for not going along with whatever plans Annabel and the others would make by way of diversion.

CHAPTER
TWENTY

Justine

I opened the door of my apartment to Aaron's knock. He stood on the other side of it and reached his hand in to take mine. I hung back.

"You spend every day in this one small place. I don't remember the last time you went out. It must have been months ago since you said you would walk with me! Staying here won't bring you closer to Sylvie. Going out into the world might."

"But to Coney Island?" That was what he had suggested. The idea was absurd to me, yet nonetheless, I let him pull me toward the door. I stopped just before stepping into the hallway. I was all dressed to go and still torturing myself with doubts. How could I tell him seeing Sylvie was in part what I was afraid of? As long as I stayed at home, I wouldn't have to bear witness to her possible descent into sin. What I didn't see wouldn't hurt me. I knew in my heart it was wrong of me, that ignoring what might have happened would not make it any less true, or me any the less to blame for who and what she had become.

My greater fear, though, was that I risked encountering Alfonse again. At home, I could at least lock the door. Enough time had passed since that terrible day that I feared by now his voyage to France was over, and he had returned to New York as he threatened he would, and I—despite my first thought of moving so he couldn't find me—had remained in this apartment, in this building, on this street, with the sole purpose of making it possible for Sylvie to find me should she come home.

It was foolish. But the thought of going out, of venturing on the subway and then a train, felt perilous. I swallowed. My mouth was dry. I reminded myself that I owed it to Aaron to indulge him this once. Aaron, who had been my friend, coming day after day not just to bring work but to sit with me over cups of tea.

"We'll miss the train if we don't go soon," Aaron said. The note of disappointment in his voice nearly broke my heart. He wanted to give me this day. It would be generous of me to let him.

"Very well," I said and put my foot outside my door with the intention of leaving the building for the first time in nearly three months, letting him follow me down the stairs and out into the street.

"It's too bad we have to take the subway. It's so nice out here," Aaron said as he took my elbow and propelled me toward the station. I assumed he was afraid I would break free and run back to the sanctuary of my tiny apartment, but now that I was out, I wanted to go on. To get away. Every now and then, I caught a whiff of rich, decaying leaves, perhaps blown across the river from New Jersey, or caught up and wafted from Central Park. I breathed deeply and lifted my chin. "Thank you," I said, releasing his hand from my elbow so I could take his arm.

"There's an outdoor circus, and we can go to one of the amusement parks. Steeplechase, all rebuilt after the fire, or Luna, or Dreamland." Aaron had been selling this idea to me for days, and now that he realized I had decided to embrace it, I could hear the excitement in his voice. He sounded younger. Happy.

"Won't it be very crowded?" I asked.

"Don't worry," Aaron said. "I'll be right there with you. You don't have to do anything you don't want to. I would like to ride the Ferris wheel, though." He squeezed my hand against his side.

We took the IRT down to the Brooklyn Bridge and changed to the Coney Island Railway, which took us above ground through Brooklyn. We sped past rows and rows of houses, some with small gardens, through fields that were still farmlands, and past cemeteries.

Aaron stood up suddenly and pointed. "Look! Isn't it extraordinary!"

I followed his gaze, and rising up above the houses and trees, I saw the curve of the Ferris wheel amid turrets and lights that sparkled even in the daytime. I had never seen anything like it.

We lost sight of the amusement parks when the train drew into the station and the crowded carriages emptied out onto the platform. I held onto Aaron as we followed the river of people out to the streets.

Soon we were promenading on Surf Avenue along with thousands of people of all ages and descriptions. A cacophony of languages flooded into my ears, and bright colors everywhere assaulted my eyes. There were jugglers and card tricksters; men wearing sandwich boards that advertised the most fantastic spectacles, promising to astound and amaze and frighten; a strong odor of grease and burnt sugar. I gripped Aaron's arm more tightly. He put his other hand over mine and squeezed. "I won't let go of you. Perhaps we should see some of the attractions. It's probably less crowded where people have to pay to get in."

I scanned the brightly painted signs. We had a choice of ogling a bearded lady, watching acrobatic midgets, glimpsing a horse with two heads...None of them appealed to me. I couldn't help thinking that if we were lured into such attractions, someone would be waiting to pick our pockets.

And then, I saw a sign that wasn't like the rest but elegantly painted with flourishes and flowers. It read *Theatrical Presentation by the Famous Actors of the Screen.* A theater. It would be dark and quiet and cool. "Shall we go there?" I pointed.

It took Aaron a moment to see the sign because it didn't shout and claim attention like the others. "A play? Wouldn't you rather go for a ride or see the outdoor circus?"

I knew those were things he would prefer because he talked about them so much. But I wasn't quite ready for that. "Let's do this first. It will give me a chance to rest a moment before we are in the midst of the *raffut.*" I didn't know an English word that meant the same thing, but I trusted Aaron to understand.

Aaron paid our admission—he wouldn't let me contribute anything at all—and we entered a small theater hardly large enough to own the name. The seating accommodated no more than twenty, and the stage was raised up only a foot with one velvet curtain drawn across it. We were the first to take our seats, but soon others joined us and the theater filled. An expectant hush fell as the lights above us dimmed. I found the twilit room soothing and was prepared to lose myself in thought when a man came out on the thin strip of stage in front of the curtain to address us.

"*Mesdames et Messieurs,*" he said.

His French accent was flawless. I hadn't heard such an accent since...Alfonse's face swam into my mind, and I shuddered.

"It is my great pleasure to introduce to you the artistes of American and French film in this brief tableau. I am Monsieur Gaumont, filmmaker from Paris, visiting your fair shores for inspiration. I have discovered the most marvelous delights here, which I soon hope to bring back to my studio in France. The photographic arts have been so superbly advanced as to make moving pictures almost commonplace. But today, by combining the living and the timeless, I hope to introduce you to the possibilities of this superb art and to invite you to join me in supporting such endeavors in the future."

So, the man was genuinely French, not pretending. How odd, I thought, to find such a fellow in Coney Island. It was a peculiar event altogether, if I understood what was to come. What had attracted me to it? Aaron was right. We should have gone to the circus.

All at once, the back of my neck started to prickle. I thought it was the closeness of the atmosphere, that I was starting to perspire. The small, crowded space had warmed up fast, and one or two people began to fan themselves with pieces of paper. But when I reached around to feel my neck, it was dry. Something else then. I shifted my eyes to look at the other people who had come in to see the show. Everyone gazed straight forward, focusing on the stage as the man continued to speak.

All, that is, except one. He sat off to the side, away from the door. He must have come in after the lights had dimmed. He did not look at the stage but instead scrutinized the audience. I didn't think he could see me from that angle, but I could see him well enough to know exactly who it was. "I...I must leave. Right away," I whispered to Aaron and tried to rise, but he held me in place.

"Shhh!" He patted my hand. "Whatever it is, you must face your fears. Let us stay and see the program. I am here with you. I will let no harm come to you."

My heart fluttered in my breast. I felt the walls closing in on me. Aaron did not know that a monster sat only a few feet away from us. We had to get out, while the lights were low. Alfonse would not expect to see me there, especially not on the arm of a Jewish man. I wouldn't have to look in his direction or pass him to leave. "You don't understand." I squeezed Aaron's hand hard. "I am in great danger here. You have to believe me."

"All right," he said, perhaps finally hearing the quiet panic in my voice.

We slipped out as quickly as we could. I kept my face averted and held my breath until we were once again out in the blinding sunlight.

"I think you must explain to me what all this was for," Aaron said. He didn't sound angry—he was never angry with me—but an unmistakable note of annoyance edged his voice.

I nodded. I could keep it from him no longer. "You may as well know the worst of me."

Instead of enjoying the diversions and amusements of a sunny day in Coney Island, Aaron and I went down to the beach to walk. The shore was littered with families and couples. We had to stroll half a mile away from the center of things to be alone enough that we wouldn't be overheard.

"So, you were going to explain?"

He'd waited until all was calm around us to say anything. It was so like Aaron not to press me. I smiled at him. "The last time I was on a beach was the day before Sylvie was born," I began.

And then I told him, as plainly as I could, who I had been, what I had done. I told him about Sylvie's birth and what happened afterwards, and how I vowed to reclaim her no matter what I had to do.

When I finished my tale, I looked up to see Aaron gazing out over the water. Small waves lapped the shore while freighters and liners inched along the horizon. The tang of salt air and the slightly sticky feel of the humid breeze took me back to those days in Normandy before my confinement. Alfonse had sent me there, to be out of sight when my belly swelled with life. I did not guess then what he intended to do. "The man I saw, in that little theater. He was Sylvie's father."

Aaron stiffened. "How do you know?"

"His is a face I shall never forget. He has returned."

"Returned?"

Of course, I hadn't yet told Aaron about Alfonse finding me in New York years ago and about our arrangement since then—or that he himself had been the cause of Sylvie's flight during the blizzard in March. "I mean, he has returned to my life, as I always suspected he would one day. I can't say more now. Except that now I know I must leave my home and move elsewhere, somewhere that man cannot find me."

"A man as wealthy and important as you say he is would hardly be likely to go nosing about in the tenements to find a former lover."

Something in Aaron's tone made me look up at him. He still stared out to sea. More softly, he said, "Surely you don't want to leave a place you call home, and where Sylvie can find her way back to you?"

"If it means Sylvie would never have to know that man, it would be a sacrifice I am willing to make."

We stood in silence for a while, listening to the waves, occasional laughter, and shrieks of delight wafting over from the amusement parks. I could not imagine feeling such abandon, such freedom as those people seemed to feel. My actions all those years ago had doomed me to solitude and secrecy, to avoiding friendships and love outside the limited confines of a mother and her daughter. I was suddenly weary of it all, exhausted from fighting with every breath, day after day after day.

"Shall we wade?"

Aaron's question surprised me. I expected probing, remonstration, lecturing after all I had just told him, although he still did not know the worst of it, my shameful behavior in the last five years. "I'm wearing shoes and stockings," I said.

He shrugged, sat in the sand, unlaced his shoes, and removed his socks, revealing feet so pale I wondered if they'd ever seen the light of day before, and rolled his trousers up about six inches. Before I could comment, he stood and marched toward the wet sand and strode into the shallow water. He reached his arms out wide and swung them up and down. I couldn't help smiling, and I quickly shed my own shoes and stockings and crept forward, my skirt lifted just enough to avoid getting wet. We did not speak but wandered slowly back and forth. The cool water and the rough sand tickled my feet. The constant of the world. There would always be sea and sand and air. We mortals mattered not in the slightest to that great beyond. For the briefest moment, I felt my heart expand and peace descend into my body. And I had Aaron to thank for it.

But it could not last. Who was I to think I could escape my sins and all their consequences? "I think it's time to go home."

The two of us trudged slowly through the sucking sand until we reached the dry place where we had left our shoes. Aaron gave me his handkerchief. "To wipe the sand off your feet," he said.

I didn't deserve his thoughtfulness. He didn't use a handkerchief on his own feet, just knocked what sand he could off them before pulling his socks on again.

"Now that we have come this far, next time will be easier," he said.

"Next time," I said. But I knew there would be no next

time. Even during this one adventure, I had exposed myself to danger. Yet, strangely, I felt calmer that I had let go of one secret, that I had shared something of my past with Aaron. He knew now that Alfonse was Sylvie's father, and I think he understood why I wanted to keep her from him.

Aaron. My friend. Did he regret becoming involved? I was afraid things would only complicate themselves from now on.

"I would like to move tomorrow," I said.

I hadn't asked him, but Aaron said, "I can help you find a new apartment and vouch for your good name."

More kindness. Only the fact that Sylvie wouldn't know where I was cast a shadow over the plan. But I could overcome that difficulty. I would make sure Sylvie could find me, one way or another.

CHAPTER
TWENTY-ONE

Sylvie

Florence came back in mid-September.

"Remember, she can't touch you now. You're too deep in with Mr. Blackton," Annabel tried to reassure me as we took the trolley to the studios one morning, but she still didn't know about the money.

"I think I need to take a trip myself, just for a day or two," I said.

"Don't be stupid!" She grabbed my upper arm and dug her fingers in. "You could jeopardize everything."

Of course. Annabel's future was closely tied to mine. Even if I truly wanted to run home, I'd have a guilty conscience about spoiling her chances when she'd done so much to help me. But I had to get rid of the money—or at least find a better place to hide it—before Florence could start making trouble again. If there was nothing to be found, how would they ever connect me to the robbery?

Unless Paolo had already told the police. So my thoughts circled around again and again with no end in sight.

I was so preoccupied I hardly noticed we'd reached the sewing room, and without thinking, I had set up everything for the day so I could come back and get right to work between rehearsals. I heard quick steps heading toward the door, and I knew exactly who it was.

"There you are! Just the person I was looking for!" Florence breezed into the room. She cast her eyes about, examining every corner, just to make sure I realized she hadn't forgotten about her threat.

Annabel took my arm and led me out the door past her, propelling us both quickly down the hallway. "Excuse us, we have a rehearsal to attend."

"Would that be the rehearsal for *Les Misérables?*"

I looked back and saw Florence keeping pace with us a few steps behind.

"Yes," I said and kept walking.

"Because it's been canceled. Instead, we're all going to Coney Island to do some promotional work for Vitagraph and the Gaumont Company. But you probably don't know what the Gaumont Company is."

We stopped dead in our tracks. Florence smiled, putting on that innocent expression that was so effective on camera but so obviously insincere off. How could I ever have been taken in by her? "We'll just check with Mr. Blackton," I said. For all I knew, she could have been lying to make us miss a rehearsal.

"He's already on his way, with Monsieur Gaumont and his investor friend. They went by automobile. We're to take the train. I would have gone with them, but they wanted me to make sure everyone else came along. Oh, and bring your bathing costume. He said we could take a dip in the ocean after if we wanted to."

I started to walk back toward the sewing room with

Annabel when Florence called after me. "I almost forgot! You're to bring the costumes for the two films. *Les Misérables* and *Midsummer*."

Annabel rolled her eyes and murmured, "Look who's back in fine form."

I smiled. "It's all right," I said. "I'll manage."

Florence hadn't moved, instead holding her hand out as if waiting for one of us to take it. "Come along, Annabel. Let's get the others. I've got money for train tickets."

"I'll just be five minutes," I said, forcing myself to adopt a breezy tone, quite the opposite of what I felt.

"Do you need help?" Annabel asked.

"No! I mean, it's nothing. You go, and I'll catch up to you. Wait for me at the station!"

Once I was sure they had both turned away and were headed in the other direction, I broke into a run back to the sewing room. My mind was racing, trying to figure out how I would carry all the costumes. They weren't so much heavy as voluminous. And then, I hit upon it. I had a bag, a case, that would fit them all nicely. The valise Paolo had left with me. Using it might help me throw Florence off about the money if she'd seen Paolo give it to me, and then I would have more time to figure out what to do next.

I didn't waste a moment. I made sure the door was tightly shut behind me and gathered up the costumes as soon as I got back inside the sewing room. For *Les Misérables,* they were mostly rags, so not much to speak of, and the costumes for the Shakespeare, although somewhat bulky, were made of such flimsy fabric they could be squashed down quite small. Still, I wasn't certain everything would fit.

The bag, of course, was still where I'd hidden it, only now covered in dust. I blew the dust off, provoking a fit of coughing, then set to work on the clasp.

It was locked. Of course, it would be. And I had no key.

My mind flitted through various possibilities. I could carry the costumes over my arm. Or perhaps fashion a bag out of some plain stuff.

Or, maybe better, I could use a seam ripper and get the lock to open.

Quickly, before I had time to think it through, I grabbed the seam ripper and some scissors and set to work.

The lock was not very secure. It yielded to my efforts surprisingly easily. I paused before opening the valise, afraid of what I'd find. *Courage,* I told myself and lifted the lid.

Five stacks of bills with paper seals stamped with $100 around each bundle lay scattered in the bottom of the valise. Five-hundred dollars. Such a lot of money. And it was the exact amount that had been stolen from a jewelry store on Canal Street the day of the blizzard. So, it was true, then. I think I'd still been trying to persuade myself that it had all been a misunderstanding. As long as I didn't know for certain how much money he had left me with, I could continue to believe in Paolo's innocence and believe that I had not been so foolish as to be taken in by him. Now, plain as could be, I was looking at the evidence of who he really was. My stomach churned.

I could do nothing about it at that moment with everyone waiting for me, so I stuffed the bills into the corner of the cupboard and covered them with a piece of black cloth. Anyone looking in quickly wouldn't even notice anything was there. I'd think of a more secure hiding place later. For now, I must pack up the costumes and meet the others at the train station. I had to sit on the case to get it to close again, and for a moment, I worried that I'd broken the latch altogether. But no, it was fine. The costumes were heavier than I thought they'd be given how flimsy they were, and I struggled the half mile to the station where the Coney Island train stopped.

By the time I joined the others on the platform, I was perspiring heavily. I stopped to catch my breath before climbing the stairs to the platform and saw the girls I knew—Florence, Annabel, Gladys, and Elita, an older actress who often played the mothers and aunts. They looked like a bunch of exotic flowers in the middle of a vegetable patch in their colorful dresses and stylish hats. The dowdy mothers and children and down-at-heel men carrying racing forms couldn't take their eyes away from this vivid display.

"I wondered how you'd manage it," Annabel said when she saw me. "Where'd you get the case?"

I smiled at Florence, whose expression revealed a combination of surprise and admiration. "I found it in the prop closet," I said. Everything you could imagine was in the prop closet, so she had no reason not to believe me.

The train steamed up to the platform, and we clambered aboard. It was quite full already, having come from Brooklyn Heights where passengers from Manhattan would have boarded, and at first, I thought we'd have to stand. But the only three men in the compartment relinquished their seats for us. Florence claimed one right away, then Elita. "You sit," Annabel said to me. "You're carrying the costumes."

"I can take the bag," Florence reached out for it. "You should sit, Annabel. Age before...you know!" a smile intended to appear sweet and accommodating masked her real motive, I knew.

I gave the valise to Florence and hung onto the railing with Gladys next to me. I was happy to be standing. I could look out the windows on both sides and see the neighborhoods we passed through. "Coney Island's a bore," Gladys said, but her eyes said otherwise. "I've been there lots."

"I've never been," I said. The girls in my class at school often talked about it, the amusement parks with the rides and exhibits, the outdoor circus with its tigers and acrobats. I never paid much attention, assuming I was unlikely to ever see them. Today, I doubted we'd have time to enjoy any of the attractions, though, since, according to Florence, we were supposed to be drumming up excitement for the coming pictures, the next installments of *Les Misérables,* and the release of *A Midsummer Night's Dream* on Christmas Eve. We traveled the rest of the way in silence.

Mr. Kent met us as we got off the train.

"Come with me. Got the costumes?" I held out the valise, which he mercifully took from me. "It's just down Surf Avenue. We'll have an hour of work, then you ladies can have some fun."

I fell in step with Annabel, a little behind the others. "Do they do this sort of thing much?"

"I've never heard of it," she said. "Can't imagine what this is about, to be honest."

I hardly had time to notice the people and take in all the garish sights and sounds before we were ushered down an alley and into the back door of what turned out to be a small theater. "What will we have to do?" I whispered to Annabel as we crowded into a room barely bigger than a closet to slip quickly into whatever costumes we were told to.

Mr. Blackton opened the door when we were nearly dressed. "I'm going to describe a few scenes, and you'll do tableaus. No speaking, just a pose. Here's what I want."

He took a piece of paper out of his pocket and read the instructions we were to follow. In between each tableau, we would rearrange ourselves in a pose that illustrated the next part of the story. He said there would be three shows of twenty minutes each, then we could go off and do what we liked, meeting back there to catch the five o'clock train.

It all went well, to my surprise. The *oohs* and *ahs* of the people in the audience and actual applause after each tableau surprised me. And it pleased me, I had to admit. I had never seen how anyone reacted to my performance on film. That seemed out of time, separate from the world, except for Mr.

Kent and Mr. Blackton and the cameramen. Then, it was only a *good job* or *well done* when it was all over. I understood why someone might be tempted to go on stage, to feel this appreciation right at the moment, for every performance.

When we were finished and had gone back outside, Monsieur Gaumont and his investor friend came out to greet us.

"You are as lovely and talented as Stuart told me!" Monsieur Gaumont stressed the second syllable of Stuart and left off the T at the end. With a pang, I recognized the inflection of my mother's much-less-obvious accent. "Allow me to introduce Monsieur d'Antigny, who is helping me raise the funds to make some moving pictures together with Vitagraph."

An older man who had remained behind him stepped forward and bowed low, sweeping his hat nearly to the ground.

"Charming to see you again, Alfonse," Florence said, putting herself in front of the rest of us. She reached out her hand not to shake his, but palm down, and he took it and brushed a light kiss on her fingers. "So good of you to assure me that I would play a prominent role in your first film!" Florence glanced back at us as she said it.

"Good. Maybe she'll leave us then," Annabel muttered. I suppressed a laugh.

"I would like to be introduced to the rest of the ladies." The man Florence had called Alfonse stepped around her and approached us. Mr. Blackton said our names, and Alfonse bowed to each of us in turn.

"And last but not least is Miss Sarah Potter, our newest find," Mr. Blackton said.

Alfonse looked at me with the oddest expression. "Have we met before?"

"N-no, I don't think so." I could feel everyone staring at me.

"Eh," he said. "I must be mistaken. But perhaps you would walk with me and show me the marvels of this extraordinary place?"

He had an easy smile that revealed straight, white teeth and grey eyes flecked with blue and gold. I had never seen eyes like his. Although he must have been at least twice my age, he was still a very handsome man. As I was about to take the arm he offered, Florence bustled up and took his other arm. "I don't believe Sarah knows anything about Coney Island. She's never been here before."

"Well, perhaps the two of us may discover it together." Alfonse gently released himself from Florence's grasp and put my hand in the crook of his elbow. "I believe there is an amusement park just down the street, called The Steeplechase?"

I had not actually agreed to accompany him but found myself unable to refuse. I cast a nervous glance back at Annabel.

"Come on Gladys, let's go along!" She grabbed Gladys without giving her a chance to respond, and they fell in step behind us. I didn't turn around, but I could feel Florence's angry gaze. She would make me pay for this later, I was certain. But what had I done?

I didn't know exactly how old Monsieur d'Antigny was, yet in his zeal to try everything, he seemed younger than he looked. We hurried from spectacle to spectacle, ride to ride, losing Annabel and Gladys somewhere along the way. When I was fearful about getting on the Ferris wheel, he grasped my hand. "You will be safe with me."

As we went up, up, up, the mechanism beneath us juddering as if at any moment it would fail, the bottom fell out of my stomach and my breath caught in my throat. I closed my eyes tight. Monsieur d'Antigny put his arm around me. It felt comforting, friendly, not like Paolo's embrace. "Don't be afraid. Don't look down. Look out and around. See how much you can see, what the world looks like from up here!"

I opened my eyes just as we reached the top of the circle.

There before me lay the universe as I knew it. Little people grasping what enjoyment they could to escape from a hard life. Among them, pickpockets and thieves, no doubt, ready to spoil their day. Rooftops with families beneath them, squabbling, loving, growing, and lying to each other. And among it all, the earth, pushing trees up in unlikely places, with the ocean serenely teasing the shoreline, a promise and a threat. I felt tears spill out of my eyes and roll down my cheeks.

"Are you still afraid? Here." Monsieur d'Antigny gave me his handkerchief. The softest silk, with an embroidered crest. I dabbed away the tears.

"Sorry, foolish of me. I've just never seen anything like this. I'm not afraid. Not now." My small worries were nothing. At least, not while I was on the Ferris wheel.

We stayed on for two more rides. He told me about how he'd always been fascinated by photography, and when moving pictures began to be perfected, he wanted to be a part of that world. "Of course, I couldn't really work. My family is too proud for that. So I call it investing. My money does something useful, something beautiful. Something that makes the world a happier place. *Comprenez?*"

I nodded, not realizing that in doing so I revealed my own familiarity with his native language.

"You speak French!"

"No! I mean, I studied it a little in school."

"I could teach you more, if you like." He inched closer to me on the seat.

I moved away, and he immediately returned to his original place. "No, I'm afraid I'm too busy at Vitagraph. You see, I'm not just an actress. I'm the studio seamstress, so I'm always busy."

At that moment, the ride ended. "Again?" he said.

I looked at the clock on the tower of the amusement park. It was a quarter to five. "No, I must go back. I have to fetch the costumes before I meet everyone at the train."

"*Eh bien*," he said and reached into his pocket. "Here is my card, where I can be reached in New York. I will return to France in a few days, then come back for Christmas to see *Midsummer Night's Dream*, or perhaps earlier, for *Les Misérables*. After that, Léon has promised to let me help him write and produce a movie here in New York to take back to France."

I smiled. "It was lovely meeting you. Thank you for the rides." I put out my hand to shake his. He bowed over it and kissed it, not the dismissive brush he'd given Florence, but an imprint that felt warm and sincere.

"There is something about you. I don't know what it is. You are familiar. Perhaps we knew each other in a former life, as the Buddhists would have it!" He laughed and shook his head. "It would please me if you would be in the picture I am investing in. I know Stuart would lend you to the Gaumont company if I asked him."

"I-I don't think it's a decision I'm allowed to make." My heart beat very fast. I wasn't sure what I wanted to do. Monsieur d'Antigny frightened me a little.

"I shall see to it. *Au revoir*." He bowed to me, and I turned away, rushing back to fetch the costumes before going to the train station.

When I reached the little theater, the man who ran it greeted me at the door. "I need to take the costumes. I left them in a case in the back room."

He scratched his head. "There's nothing there—Oh! The gentleman, Mr. Blackton, took them away with him in the auto."

I thanked him and walked to the station in a daze. I must get the case back. I hoped it wouldn't be too difficult. The last thing I wanted to do was raise any questions.

"So, what were you off doing with that attractive Frenchman?" Annabel asked. There were plenty of seats in the train carriage in this direction, so we sat together.

"Attractive? He's so old! We rode the Ferris wheel," I said.

"Old and rich. Put Florence in a real snit you did!" She was positively gleeful. "No matter. I went into the funhouse, and Gladys and I walked down to the beach and put our toes in the water. It was grand."

Soon Annabel, Gladys, and Elita nodded off to the rocking of the train. I stayed wide awake, gazing out the window, wondering and worrying. I wasn't certain what exactly had happened. It was all too much to think about. I shook my head and looked away from the dizzying scenery, only to meet Florence's gaze, fixed on me with such hatred it made my stomach lurch. Within a second, she changed her expression and gave me a superficial smile. I would have to watch out for her even more than before.

CHAPTER
TWENTY-TWO

Justine

The apartment Aaron helped me find was very much like the one I had just left. With so few possessions, it only required a tinker's cart to move my and Sylvie's belongings to a second-floor tenement on Hester Street, east of the Bowery. The distance was not great, but the neighborhood was different enough that no one would know me. Here, mostly Polish Jews made their homes. I would have felt as if I'd moved to a different country if my new apartment had not been so similar to the old one. I couldn't read any of the signs above the shops; I only guessed what they were by the display of wares spilling out onto the sidewalk. And here, instead of Irish accents and Italian phrases, exotic Polish and Romanian mixed with the more guttural Yiddish in what was to me an incomprehensible soup of a language.

"You'll get used to it," Aaron said as he helped me pound

nails into the wall so I could hang up my pots.

"I have put you to such a great deal of trouble." I couldn't imagine why a man would want to help me as Aaron had, with no suggestion of recompense.

Aaron stood and stretched his arms over his head. "At least here you look out over the street."

The light was indeed much better. I faced south, and the street was a little wider than Mulberry. It was Friday evening. I watched as devout Jews, heads covered with scarves if they were women and top hats if they were men, walked companionably toward the east on their way to synagogue.

"It will soon be sundown, so I must leave you, I'm afraid."

"Is there a church nearby? Oh, perhaps you would not know that."

"St. Mary's. On Grand Street."

"Thank you. You surprise me."

He shrugged. "I thought you might want to find one."

Aaron had thought of everything. Even though I could easily walk to the Church of the Most Precious Blood from my new dwelling, I had already decided it would be better to sever all ties to that neighborhood if I was to be safe. Quite apart from Alfonse, I worried about Mrs. Bonnano. She knew who I was and what I looked like. "You're sure Mrs. Murphy understood? And she didn't ask too many questions?"

He nodded as he put on his hat. "If Sylvie returns, she is to tell her to find me, and I will lead her to you. I have given her my address. This information must on no account be imparted to a man, no matter how gentlemanly."

We'd gone over it again and again and decided this was the only way. Mrs. Murphy had already asked questions I could no longer evade. I told her as little as I could, explaining my reticence by saying I had received threats—which was also why I must move.

As to Aaron, I knew I asked a great deal of him. He had to

trust me without knowing the entire story. But he had proven again and again that he was my friend. This gesture of his, the way he helped me without asking questions, was yet more proof.

The landlord was at first disinclined to rent to anyone who wasn't Jewish, but Aaron knew him and vouched for me. The rent, so Aaron said, was the same as the rent I'd been paying on Mulberry Street, but it hardly seemed possible. I feared that Aaron contributed to my upkeep without telling me. But then, what could he gain by it?

My suspicions were aroused when, a few days after my move, Aaron arrived without any waists for me to sew. Instead, he held a magazine in his hand. "You realize, of course, that you have a remarkable talent. I never have to explain how the pieces should go together, even when I bring you a new model. And the work you do is superb, every stitch." He paused to sip his tea, then carefully placed the cup back on its saucer and picked up the open magazine. "Do you think, for example, you could duplicate a dress like this?" He pointed to a photograph of a model wearing a lovely evening gown, silk with beads and embroidery, a high waist, and cascades of skirts of different lengths dipping down to her ankles.

I studied the photograph. When I was finished, I looked up at him. "Of course. But I would make some changes."

He nodded, encouraging me to say more.

"The dress looks pretty in the photograph, but I don't think it would be very comfortable to wear." I pointed out how tight it was around the underarms and that the skirt would hamper walking. "If one cut the fabric on the bias, there would be room for movement," I said.

Aaron nodded. "What if I brought you enough material to make that dress you imagine? How long would it take?"

"Sewing by hand, with those long seams...a week."

"If you used a sewing machine, what then?"

Aaron had taken back the machine we'd been lent when

Sylvie was there to help with the waists. The work he'd brought me was only the fine finishing, only the work I could do with excellence. "I cannot afford a sewing machine, you know that."

"You could borrow it again. Shall we try?"

How could I refuse him when he had done so much for me? "A day, maybe two," I said, "with a machine."

"Such a dress would sell for twenty-five dollars," he said and stood, signaling that it was time for him to leave, leaving the pouch of coins for the work I had done that day on the mantel above the stove in the kitchen.

"Until tomorrow," he said and went on his way.

The next day he brought material.

"This is so very fine! Where did you get it?" I couldn't stop stroking the beautiful mauve crepe de Chine. He'd also brought buttons and thread and some contrasting materials with which to face the sleeves and hem, and the promised sewing machine had been delivered early that morning. I had already tried it on some scraps of material. The stitches were not as good as by hand, but people were not so fastidious about those things now.

"I have good relationships with several fabric sellers, of course. These were the end of a bolt, so not as costly as you would think."

I knew full well the silk had not been cut from the end of a bolt. It was perfect. "I'll make a beautiful gown from this," I said as Aaron left.

Two days later, I finished the dress. I had forgotten how satisfying it was to create something other than a stiff, practical shirtwaist. Aaron examined it, a smile spreading across his face. "Will you put it on? I'd like to see how it drapes."

Strange that I hadn't thought of trying on the dress myself. Aaron's request was faintly embarrassing, but he had an eye, that was certain, and I supposed he would want to make sure

I had done my best with the fine stuff he provided. I went into the bedroom, drew the curtains across the window into the kitchen, and closed the door.

The silk felt like a caress on my arms. My plain chemise and stockings didn't do it justice. It hung perfectly and moved like liquid when I walked. It had been more than fifteen years since I'd worn anything but a waist and skirt, and I was instantly transported back to my days in Paris. I had a curious sensation of shame mixed with elegance, high spirits, and a sort of camaraderie I never had in New York. I patted my hair, squared my shoulders, and walked out into the parlor.

"Well?" I turned in a circle slowly so Aaron could judge my work.

"Exquisite."

When I came fully around to face him again, his expression caught me by surprise. Aaron's eyes shimmered with tears. I instantly put my hand up to my cheek as he stepped toward me. I knew his admiration was not solely for the dress I had made. Was this the recompense he expected after all? I lowered my eyes, half resigned to what must come next.

"Would you do me the honor of walking out with me this fine evening?"

I looked up again. Aaron's eyes still brimmed, and I could feel desire bridging the space between us. But he maintained a respectful distance, instead taking my coat off the hook by the door and holding it so I could slip my arms into the sleeves. "But the dress," I said, "will you still be able to sell it?"

"There will be more for you to make."

I understood that he was making it a gift to me. I hardly knew what to say or do, so I simply nodded.

It was a lovely early Autumn evening. The air was almost fresh out on the street. Goods from the stores and merchants' carts spilled over onto the sidewalks and impeded the progress of many others who had the same idea as Aaron. The crowds were so thick that at one point, I risked losing all track of him. If he hadn't been so tall, I never would have seen him over the four or five people who managed to get between us. It took him a minute or two to realize I was no longer next to him, and he turned. I saw a look of panic cross his face as he scanned the pedestrians and raised my arm up high to signal where I was. He stopped and waited for me to reach him, then took my hand and tucked it firmly in the crook of his elbow. "Don't let go until we cross Houston."

I was happy to do as he said, until Houston and beyond. The sun had dipped down behind the buildings, taking much of the air's warmth with it. "Where are we going?" I asked.

"I thought we'd visit the nickelodeon. There are some new pictures everyone's talking about. The second part of *Les Misérables*, actually. I thought you'd enjoy it, because of the French story. We missed the first part, but I'm sure they'll explain it in the beginning."

I didn't say anything and continued to walk holding onto his arm, but my previous feeling of lightness and joy vanished into the evening, and each step forward felt suddenly effortful.

"Are you feeling unwell?"

"No, I'm quite well, thank you." I smiled up at him, but I knew there was little genuine cheer in my face.

We walked along in silence for a while. "Don't give up hope," Aaron said, squeezing my hand into his side. I couldn't say anything. I couldn't tell him that I was too sad to cry anymore and that actively thinking and hoping for Sylvie to return caused me so much pain that I sometimes couldn't breathe. Part of my body, my mind, my soul was somewhere in the world, and until I knew where, I would feel incomplete.

We arrived at the nickelodeon and stood in line for the next show. "It's new today. That's why so many people are waiting," Aaron said.

Up ahead, we saw Tommy chatting to the couple at the front.

A nice, respectful boy. I waited for him to look up, then waved.

Instead of smiling and waving back, Tommy went white, then turned away. "I'll just go to the front and say a word to Tommy," I said to Aaron, freeing my hand from his grip. I began to walk forward, but the people ahead of us in line started calling out, "Hey! Wait your turn! We've been here longer than you!" One woman actually took hold of my arm and pulled me back. It seemed we'd have to wait to find out the reason for Tommy's reaction. My heart raced. Somehow, I knew it must have to do with Sylvie.

In twenty minutes that felt much longer, we reached Tommy. Aaron gave him a dime. I leaned in and said, "What is it?"

"Not here," he whispered back. "I'm done at ten."

How could I be expected to wait two hours to hear something about my daughter! I wanted to demand he stop what he was doing and talk to me, right there. Perhaps sensing I might do something like that, Aaron took firm hold of my hand and pulled me away into the little theater. "He knows something. He has some information. Why can't he just tell us?" I whispered.

"There must be a reason."

And why, too, hadn't he gotten in touch with Aaron about it before, if it was something important?

I was so distracted that I missed the start of the picture, the caption that gave the story so far.

After a minute or two, I recognized the familiar tale anyway, although the film had begun in the middle of it. Hugo's evil Thenardier congratulated himself on striking a bargain that would get him a young girl as a slave and destroy her mother. Women have no more power now, I thought, than they had then. So long as we are willing to sacrifice everything for the sake of our children, we are vulnerable.

The pianist changed his tune, and I knew we were about

to see the innocent, young Cosette enter the scene, watch her be abused and nearly starved by the man who had ruined her mother. It was my nightmare, one I was living through every day, and now I had to sit and watch it play out in silence. "I don't want to stay," I whispered to Aaron, who was so wholly involved in the picture that his lips were parted, and he leaned slightly forward.

"It's not long." He patted my hand without looking at me.

After all, he had paid my nickel. It would be ungrateful of me to spoil his kind gesture. In an effort to take my mind off the impending fate of poor Cosette, I sat back and examined what I could see of our fellow audience members. Without exception, they were so caught up in the story unfolding in front of them that they appeared absorbed into another dimension of time and place. Unlike me, they were not sitting in a crowded, smelly theater, thrown together with strangers, but walking the streets of the Paris of long ago, feeling the pain of people who were worse off than they were. I noticed a tear escape a young woman's eye before she quickly wiped it away and looked up to see what had provoked her.

There was Cosette, hunched over, her hair in filthy strands, with Thenardier towering over her and gesturing angrily. I didn't want to watch, but then the camera shifted to show Cosette's face, large and in the center of the screen.

I grabbed Aaron's arm and shrieked, "Sylvie!"

A chorus of "Shh!" erupted.

"We must go and find her, right now!" I whispered.

"Are you certain it's she?"

"Look!" I pointed at the screen. Although the close image was gone, now her face was visible, and with every movement, every gesture, I was more and more certain it was my daughter.

"Yes. Yes, I think you're right."

"Come!" I stood and tried to pull Aaron up with me, but he forced me to sit again.

"There's nothing to be gained by leaving now. Perhaps there will be some information at the end, on the caption." He spoke as quietly as he could, but still, people turned and glared at us.

I sat, tense and anxious, drinking in every glimpse of Sylvie's face, trying to imagine how she could have ended up in a moving picture. It must have been this that Tommy wanted to talk to us about, and the picture was new that day, which explained why he hadn't tried to contact us.

At the end, the caption named the company who made the film as Vitagraph Studios, Brooklyn, New York, and the director J. Stuart Blackton, but none of the actors. When we emerged from the theater, Tommy was busy taking money and managing the crowd, which had grown in the thirty minutes we'd been inside. I tried to get his attention. "He said he'd talk to us after his work was finished," Aaron said. "Let's go get supper." I nodded, although the thought of food turned my stomach. I was impatient, keyed up to a fever pitch, but I could do nothing at that moment.

We arrived back at the nickelodeon just as Tommy was closing up. "I'll walk with you," he said when he joined us. "I have to get back to my rooming house before they lock the door at ten-thirty."

I barely heard what he said, I was so bursting with desire to know more. "Tell me," I said, "How do we find this Vitagraph Company, and will they tell us where Sylvie is?"

Tommy stopped walking. "What are you talking about?"

Aaron spoke. "We saw her, this evening, in the picture."

"Really? The flick is new today, and we were so busy I didn't have a chance to watch it."

If that wasn't what he had to tell us, then what?

"Well, at least she's got an honest job," Tommy said.

"What does that mean?" I said, my mind instantly jumping to a series of unsavory thoughts

My tone must have revealed my indignation because Aaron swiftly intervened. "I think you should just tell us what information you have."

Tommy reached into his pocket and pulled out a postcard. "I found this."

Although Aaron reached out for it, Tommy gave the postcard to me, the photograph side facing downward. I turned away from them and moved closer to a streetlamp to look at it, and the blood drained from my limbs until I thought I might collapse.

"What is it?" Aaron asked. I sensed him moving closer and soon felt the weight of his hand on my shoulder.

All I could do was shake my head. I saw in that photograph my lovely daughter in her underclothes, lips parted in an expression more of curiosity than amusement or passion, one strap falling off her shoulder in a provocative fashion. Although not exactly pornographic, the photograph was clearly meant to titillate. "It's Sylvie," I said, my mouth dry as dust. "Not as I would like to see her."

I turned to face Aaron. The light from the streetlamp cast a yellowish glow, but I nonetheless saw his cheeks redden. I looked away from him and toward Tommy. "Where did you get this?" I struggled to keep the anger out of my voice. I didn't want to discourage Tommy from telling us everything he knew.

"It was in a box, at Angelotti's studio." He murmured the words, his eyes not meeting mine.

"In a box?" Aaron asked.

"I'm afraid...there were hundreds of them."

He sounded as if he might cry, and I knew then that he had had nothing to do with this. That didn't change things, though. I staggered, and Aaron steadied me.

"I'm sorry. So sorry." Now Tommy came over to me and gazed into my eyes. "I'm going to try to find a way to destroy them, but unless I find the plate, he can make more."

I still hadn't shown Aaron the photograph, and he didn't ask to see it.

"I kind of suspected something was going on, with other models, not with your daughter. Suspected for a long time, but I had a good thing with Angelotti. I could borrow his equipment, develop my film and print. And I figured the girls knew what they was getting into. Except your daughter. A couple of magazines have bought some of my street scenes." Tommy babbled on, and I felt sorry for him.

"It's very brave of you to show this to me," I said, wondering if he would have come to us with this information if we hadn't happened to be there that evening and how long he'd known of the postcard's existence.

"Trouble is," he continued, "the Bonnano family is involved. They're the ones who got the contacts, and they know how to get these things into the right hands and steer clear of the wrong ones, if you know what I mean."

At that moment, all became utterly silent and deafeningly loud at the same time, and everything around me disappeared and yet suffocated me in one almost unbearable blow. I caught myself with the fleeting, barely coherent thought that it would be better for Sylvie to have died than to face such humiliation, and at the hands of the boy's family—a boy she trusted enough to let him take her to Brooklyn in the middle of a snowstorm.

I forced myself to look at Tommy, whose face had lost all its youthful liveliness. He was just a boy, really, but he had seen so much. I softened my voice, not letting the panic I felt deep inside make it shrill and hard. "If you could discover for us who we might talk to, where we might go to find out how Sylvie came to be in that film by—what was the company?"

"Vitagraph." The word came out of Tommy's mouth as a strangled whisper, but I put it together with what I had read on the screen. He cleared his throat and continued. "They probably won't be shooting this time of year. The sunlight's not good enough, see, even with electric lights to help. Most of the actors have to find other work for the winter."

"What sort of work?" I asked, my hope of finding Sylvie fading.

He shrugged. "Music halls, theaters, I dunno know really. I don't go out to music halls."

Manhattan bristled with such places, more than I could count. Doubtless, they were to be found in Brooklyn too. I could surely gain some information about Sylvie's whereabouts from the company that made *Les Misérables*. But what then? The photograph still existed. As long as it did, Sylvie was in danger of being exploited. I couldn't bear the thought that she might be forced into a life not so very far removed from the one I had led in Paris. Someone who saw the picture she was in and managed to obtain one of those postcards would recognize her as the same girl, and perhaps seek her out. That person could threaten to expose her. From there, her life could be ruined, and it would be my own doing. I had brought her up to be even more innocent and naive than I was at her age, and I had easily enough been led down a disreputable path.

Tommy's shoulders drooped as he left us to go back to his rooming house. Aaron and I walked home in silence, all thoughts of having a pleasant evening driven away. My mind was in a fever of activity. Now I knew for certain that Mrs. Bonnano could tell me more about Sylvie, and now I had something I could use to persuade her that helping me was in her interest as well. Just that morning, the papers said that her boy was released from jail for lack of evidence. He must have gone home. I would find a way to reach him and talk to him.

CHAPTER
TWENTY-THREE

Sylvie

This time, Florence left the newspaper clipping beneath the presser foot of the sewing machine.

Bonnano Released after Four-Month Detention. The brief article went on to say that the case against him had fallen apart, largely because they could not find the money that was stolen. And because the robbery had occurred during a blizzard when no one was out on the street, they found only one witness, who turned out to be partially blind.

If I wasn't so certain he had committed the crime, I would have been incensed that he'd been jailed for nothing. As it was, I just went cold, all my delight at my recent success evaporating as if it had never happened. I was caught, even if Paolo wasn't. Before, the threat of the law catching up to me and my unwitting part in the robbery was real enough, but the longer nothing happened, the more secure and immune I had started to feel. Now Paolo was certain to come looking for me—or more likely, the money. I no longer fooled myself by imagining he would seek me out for my own sake. He hinted that others had some kind of stake in the money he left with me too, that his "business" had "partners," and if so, they would no doubt demand their share now that he was free to move about the world. Like Cosette, I was being buffeted around by forces I could not control.

"Sarah! You missed your cue!"

We were filming part three of *Les Misérables*. I appeared in one scene only, and it should have been easy to play my role, but I found myself unable to concentrate, the words of the newspaper clipping driving everything else out of my head. "I'm sorry, something distracted me."

We reset to the beginning of the scene while Mr. Blackton went to talk to Monsieur Gaumont, who had come to watch the filming. Things had gotten off to a slow start as it was. We were trying out Gaumont's new cameras, which the camera-man explained were far superior to the Edison machines we had been using, but the men who operated them had a hard time getting used to their quirks. Annabel told me the previous night that a deal was being struck where Mr. Blackton could purchase the cameras at a lower price and permit Florence—and perhaps one other actor—to appear in Gaumont's next film. That day was really important, and I had messed it up already.

I forced thoughts of Paolo out of my mind and tried my hardest to imagine myself in the world of the beleaguered Cosette, who, in this scene, gradually realizes she has been saved by the handsome stranger who purchased her from Thenardier.

Mr. Blackton clapped his hands, signaling for us to stop just as Maurice reached for my hand to take me away. "We've got to figure out a way he could hide you when Thenardier comes after him, regretting his decision to part with you."

I suppose he meant "we" in a general sense, but I took it as a direct challenge because it was obvious to me that the solution had to do with a costume. "Jean needs a bigger coat," I said. "Lots of fabric, and he can tuck me under his arm so I'm not in view. The camera angle can make it work."

Mr. Blackton, Mr. Kent, Monsieur Gaumont, the two cameramen, Maurice, and Mr. Ranous (Thenardier) all turned to face me at once, eyes open in astonishment and mouths agape. Monsieur Gaumont broke the silence. "Eh, you remind me of Alice. She is always putting her nose in and coming up with the best solutions."

Everyone laughed. I didn't know who Alice was, but in that moment, I was grateful to her.

"Yes, I see it, and it will balance out his other hand carrying the valise," Mr. Blackton said.

There it was. The prop master appeared carrying my valise. Or rather, Paolo's. Of course it had gone to the property shop; Florence would have made certain of it. No getting it back now.

But my idea for the scene put an idea into my head about the money. I'd have to do it stealthily, when no one was likely to come into the sewing room—and do it soon as well. It wouldn't be easy to deal with all the bills, and it would involve hand sewing. Each one would take...about ten minutes, I thought. Ten minutes without interruptions. One-thousand minutes. About seventeen hours. Two nearly full workdays. No, I had to find a way to do it faster.

"Can you put something together before tomorrow?" Mr. Blackton asked.

I'd forgotten that. Suggesting a new costume meant sewing work for me. "Yes, of course," I said. It would be a late night and no hope of getting started on my other project.

In the end, it took a week. A week of anxiously looking over my shoulder wherever I went, expecting I don't know what. Paolo? Florence? The police? I turned the sewing machine table so that I faced the door at all times, watching out of the corner of my eye in case someone tried to open it quietly and peek in. But Florence stayed out of my way that week. She was busy with the Gaumont company and enjoying her celebrity. Monsieur d'Antigny had not returned.

It was late, so I didn't expect a knock on the door of the sewing room. I had just finished hiding all the money in a place no one would think to look and testing out my deception. The door burst open, but now I wasn't afraid of discovery.

"Ah, so you finally took my advice and made yourself something new to wear!" It was Annabel.

"You're still here?" I didn't know whether to be surprised or relieved.

She shrugged. "Thought I'd wait for you, then got bored of it and decided to come and drag you away from your work. You've been looking tired and anxious lately. Is something wrong?"

"I'm fine, just a lot to do." Annabel had gotten to know me well enough to read my moods, so it had been tricky to keep her from digging in to find out what was going on.

She came to me and touched the outfit I was wearing, a new skirt with piping in the seams and a matching jacket— also piped. I'd found some gabardine in the corner, enough for the two garments, and the piping took very little extra material. "Pretty, but it looks heavy. All right for winter. I thought you might make yourself something more frivolous to go out in."

"This suits my purpose more than a gown would." *Yes,* I thought, *I needed the thick seams to hide one hundred tightly rolled five-dollar bills.*

"Well, I've come with an invitation. I know it's an invitation because I got one too."

She handed me a smooth envelope addressed with an

elegant hand to Miss Sarah Potter. I untucked the flap and slid out a pasteboard card edged with silver. It said we were invited to a reception honoring the Gaumont Film Company at The Colony Club. Our hostess was Miss Elsie de Wolfe. Aside from the quality of the paper, I didn't know enough to be impressed. "Will you go?"

Annabel threw her hands up in the air in the kind of gesture that would have been hilarious on film, but that just seemed out of place in real life. "Of course, I'll go! You can bet it's the only chance the likes of you and me will get to see the inside of that exclusive place."

I looked at the address. Madison Avenue and Thirtieth Street. Not so very far away from the school, and my mother. But too far to the east for my mother to pass by on one of her rare trips to the garment district.

"What's wrong? You look as though someone just said you had to go to prison."

I shook myself out of my reverie. "I was just thinking. I haven't been across the bridge for a long time." Not since I ran away from home, but Annabel didn't know that.

"That outfit won't do, though. Isn't there a costume you could borrow?"

She started raking through the odd assortment of garments and fragments of fabric hanging on racks, then opening cupboards. Before I could stop her, she found the hidden place where the valise and then just the money had been stored. I thanked my stars that all this hadn't happened a day earlier.

I was just about to feel relaxed and confident when Annabel said, "Aha! Look what I found. Good luck, I think!" Joy and mischief lit up her eyes as she waved a five-dollar bill in the air and started dancing around the small space, almost toppling one rack until finally collapsing into the chair I sat in to sew.

I felt sick. I missed one of the banknotes. It must have slipped out when I undid the bundles. I hadn't bothered to count each one and add it all up. There wasn't time. "Where was it?" I asked, knowing the answer.

"Over by that rack, just inside the cupboard. Someone must have put it in a pocket and forgotten about it."

The idea of being able to forget about that much money was foreign to me, but not to Annabel, so her explanation must have seemed logical to her.

"Finders keepers, losers weepers! What shall we spend it on? I know: let's go to Abraham and Straus and get you an evening gown."

"Five dollars won't buy much of a gown!" She was joking. I was relieved.

"Don't you know about their basement? They have damaged goods down there on sale for cheap. I bet we'll find something you can fix up with your talented fingers."

"I'll think about it," I said as I put away the scissors and other sewing implements. My dress felt heavy with its weight of currency. I wanted to take it off, but it would be harder to carry than to wear. I wrapped the clothes I'd worn that morning in paper and tied string around the package. "Let's go home."

In the end, I couldn't dissuade Annabel from making me buy a dress for the reception. And as the next day was Sunday and our day off, I went with her on the subway up to Brooklyn Heights to Abraham and Straus, the very place I'd bought the clothes I wore every day when I wasn't in costume—aside from the skirt and coat my mother made me, they were all I had. I prayed that enough time had passed so that no one would recognize me from the last time.

Instead of going upstairs to the ladies' garments floor as I had last time, I followed Annabel down to what looked like pure chaos—people and material and odds and ends, a sleeve sticking out here, a strap of a chemise there, silks and cottons and linens all mixed together, and everyone talking all at once. The large, open room teemed with girls and women like us, looking for something they could make over, something that would be more stylish than the clothes we all wore day after day. I don't know why, but I ached with sadness. Something about the piles of fabrics in different colors and weights made me think of my mother, not as the woman I hadn't recognized the day I ran away, but as someone whose hard, selfless work had given me everything I had for seventeen years.

"This is perfect! The blue will set your eyes off beautifully." Annabel held up a dress with beaded trim that had come loose and threatened to drop the glass tubes everywhere. I took it from her and carefully rolled it up to protect the beading. It was pretty. I saw that I could probably fix it and that she was right: it would be a good color for me. Annabel pointed to a sign on a stand that said all the items on that table were six dollars. "Do you have any money on you?"

I felt like laughing out loud. I had so much money on me, literally, that we could have purchased an entire expensive wardrobe. But of course, only I knew that. "I brought seven dollars. Everything I've saved. I'll pay for it."

"No, I wanted to use the lucky five dollars for you. For us. I just have this feeling about the reception, as if something big will happen there for our careers." She put her arm around my waist and squeezed. Even if Annabel was ambitious and scheming, she'd never done me any harm. I was grateful for her friendship.

We made the purchase and were walking through the main floor on our way to the door that led to the street when I heard someone behind me say, "You there! Do I know you?"

I kept walking.

"Miss! Miss!" Steps hurried behind us and soon, someone tapped me on the shoulder.

"I'm sorry?" I said as I turned and recognized the girl who had helped me on the day of the blizzard.

"Glad to see you've dried off!" she said, open and friendly.

I smiled. "I'm sure you're mistaken."

"No, how could I be? Of course I remember someone as pretty as you, with hair that color."

I felt Annabel's gaze boring into me. "Still, it must have been someone who looked just like me. I've never been here before."

Annabel spoke up. "You probably saw her in a film at the nickelodeon. We're actresses, with Vitagraph."

"I suppose." The girl stepped back and gave an apologetic smile. I felt a little sorry for her. She was only trying to be friendly, and she was right.

On the subway on the way home, Annabel said, "Get used to that. The more pictures you're in, the more people will think they know you and come up to you on the street. They won't know your name, though. That's a big to-do with Florence. I think she's using this Gaumont thing to persuade Mr. Blackton to list her by name in the credits."

Even I knew what a dramatic change that would be. Actors like Maurice were already known, and sometimes Mr. Blackton used that to get newspapers to write about the pictures he made, to whip up some publicity and excitement. But naming all the cast members so the public could write letters to them and swoon over them—that was something they resisted. For now, the pictures belonged only to the men who made them. "I don't want my name to be known," I said with a shudder.

She turned me toward her. "Well, I do. I hope Florence succeeds, for all our sakes."

If such a thing was on the horizon, and there was a chance my false name could work its way into public knowledge, I had to act, and quickly. I had a few ideas about how to translate my sewing project into returning the money to where it came from, but so far, nothing seemed foolproof.

The perspiration dripped down my back in spite of the cool weather all the way back to our rooms.

CHAPTER
TWENTY-FOUR

Justine

The first time I went to talk to Mrs. Bonnano, I had learned nothing. My vague suspicions based on circumstance were not enough to prove to her that she should believe me and help me. But now, I knew something that could directly implicate the Bonnanos in illegal activities if I chose to inform the police. The question remained whether she would agree or whether her desire to hinder me was stronger than her desire for self-preservation.

On a chilly October morning, I once again took my place in line behind the Italian women waiting to get their loaves and whatever else it was they went to this odd bakery for. A cruel wind carrying a hint of winter to come blew across the island from the west, and every one of us was wrapped up in woolen scarves and heavy coats, a parade of gray and black. Perhaps it had always been the same in Paris, although I didn't

213

really remember, but in New York, people turned in on themselves in the bad weather. We hid our bodies, of course, but along with that, we hid our souls in protective layers, closing everyone off from those around us to guard our individual warmth. In the cold, we were like rocks tumbling down a slope, separate, impervious.

But I was glad of it. I wanted to be as sharp as flint when I confronted Mrs. Bonnano again.

As the line inched along, I allowed myself to wonder what Sylvie might be doing that morning. I tried to picture her walking briskly along the sidewalk toward a job, one of the legions of secretaries and shopgirls who would work twelve hours and then return to their boarding houses to share stories and gossip. She needn't have become a showgirl in the off-season, as Tommy suggested. She was too smart for that. But perhaps performing in front of a camera had given her a taste for it, and she had chosen that path. The music halls in New York were unknown to me, but I was once intimately familiar with the ones in Paris, and I knew what kind of girls danced and simpered and sang their bawdy songs to men who leered up at them from the audience. I shook my head to dispel the image of Sylvie's honest, pretty face caked with makeup and winking and smiling at the lewd crowd.

A woman standing behind me nudged me in the back. I was about to turn around and glare at her but saw that I had reached the door and it was my turn to enter.

Mrs. Bonnano had her back to me, reaching for a loaf and wrapping it in paper. A multitude of footprints disturbed the flour on the floor around her. The shop smelled good and wholesome. Something inside me sank. Has it all come to this? Were truth and lies so seamlessly interwoven as to be indistinguishable from one another? I put my hand into my pocket to retrieve the offensive picture postcard. When she turned to me and held out the loaf, recognition flickered into her eyes.

"My daughter has not come home." I let the words hang in the air.

"I am sorry for you, but that has nothing to do with me or my family."

"I would like to speak to your son. I understand he has now been released from jail."

"He was wrongly accused of a crime."

I took a step toward her. She did not move. "I have evidence that he may have been involved in another crime."

Her eyes widened momentarily, then her expression hardened. "You had better not be accusing my son of something you could not possibly prove. He is soon to be married to a girl from a respectable Italian family."

"My daughter may not have an opportunity to marry respectably, thanks to your son."

She gave a short, hard laugh. I thought I detected relief in her eyes, which surprised me. "I suppose she's pregnant and claims my son to be the father? It would only be her word against his."

So that was what she thought! I wanted to slap her. How dare she! And yet...my own history weighed on me. So I drew the postcard out of my pocket and held it up to her face. She glanced at it and turned her eyes away. "Disgusting. Is that your daughter? You should be ashamed of her."

The angry words bubbled up inside me, but I bit my tongue. It would have done no good to let them. I would match Mrs. Bonnano's calm strength with the power of my own convictions. "I believe your son—or your family—had a great deal to do with this photograph, which has been illegally distributed God knows where and to whom."

"Who told you that?"

"Never mind who. But it could easily be traced back to this very place, of that I am certain." Of course, I was never more uncertain. But I didn't let my voice or my gaze falter.

"What do you want?"

Ah, so that worked, at least a little. "I want to speak to your son."

"Paolo had nothing to do with this! Speaking to him won't reveal anything—even if what you say is true, which it is not."

I now knew that she would claim anything to defend her son, true or not, so I simply ignored her and continued. "And I want every last one of these filthy postcards destroyed, or I will take the one in my possession to the police." She couldn't know that was an empty threat, and the briefest flicker of concern leapt into her eyes. "I also want to know if your son has any idea of where Sylvie may have gone."

Mrs. Bonnano took a few breaths before answering as if calculating what to say. "I assure you my son knows nothing of your daughter. And this picture—no one in my family would sully themselves with such a thing. Good day."

I stood my ground a little longer, only then noticing that the door to the back of the bakery was slightly ajar. A floorboard creaked just beyond it.

"Go away from here and do not come back!" Mrs. Bonnano gripped my arm and propelled me toward the door. As I stumbled out into the cold, the woman next in line made a move as if to enter. Mrs. Bonnano stopped her, said, "We're closed!" and shut the door in her face.

I walked away with my chin high, certain that what I had just seen and heard confirmed everything I believed. It did not bring me any closer to knowing exactly what happened to Sylvie, though. But I felt sure that, thanks to Tommy, I had stumbled on a way to get to the truth.

By the time I reached Orchard Street, I knew someone was following me. I continued walking but took a turn away from my direction home. Whoever it was, whatever the purpose, I didn't want him to know where I lived. That had already resulted in disaster. I quickened my pace just a little. Ahead of me, a crowded café offered refuge. If I went in, my follower would either have to confront me or leave.

Just as I reached for the door handle, someone touched my arm gently. I turned.

"Mrs. Button? I'm Paolo."

#

We talked over coffees we barely sipped. After a while, I believed Paolo when he said he meant Sylvie no harm and, in fact, had tried to protect her from his mother, who was the only one who had figured out the truth. But there was something behind his words, something I could tell he was trying to hide from me.

"Did you rob the jeweler?"

"They dropped the case," he said, not answering. He ground his teeth and looked down at the floor.

"Was Sylvie with you that day? Did she help you? Not to steal, but perhaps after?" I whispered so no one else could hear. I knew it was risky confronting him like that, but I needed to know. I couldn't plan anything without a sense of whether Sylvie had gotten mixed up in something illegal, and it was only fear of discovery that kept her from returning home.

When Paolo looked up, I saw a different expression in his eyes, not the apologetic youth who had inadvertently brought harm to an innocent young girl, but the look of someone making a calculation, figuring out an angle. "Do you know where she is?"

"Do you?"

Paolo was the first to look down. "No."

The way he glanced at me quickly but would not hold my gaze awakened some hope in me. He knew something he wasn't saying. I would have to draw him out. "When I find my daughter, I intend to bring her home and make sure she is not made to suffer for whatever she inadvertently became involved in. If that means taking her to the police to tell her story, so be it." I took the postcard out of my purse, put it face down on the table, and slid it halfway across toward Paolo. "Have you seen this? I showed it to your mother." I didn't know how much he had heard of my conversation with Mrs. Bonnano or whether he already knew about the postcard. I gambled on the chance that seeing Sylvie so compromised might awaken a protective instinct in him.

He picked up the edge of the postcard and peered at the photo without turning it over, then slammed it down and shoved it back toward me. "God damned Angelotti!" He said the words with a quiet intensity that frightened me. I would not want to be that photographer.

Paolo gripped the edge of the table so hard his fingertips turned white. "I think you better back off, Mrs. Button. Not meaning no offense, but you finding Sylvie will not be a good thing. Not yet. Now that my mother knows what she looks like, she's in a heap of danger. That's why I got to get to her first."

"Someone, the person who gave me that postcard, thinks your family is distributing it illegally. I thought...mother to mother...."

He stood so fast his stool fell over. The café went silent, and all eyes turned toward us. A vein in Paolo's temple throbbed. He turned the full force of his dark gaze on me, and I instantly understood how Sylvie could have been beguiled by him. Although his eyes revealed nothing but fury at that moment, their deep expressiveness spelled danger. He reminded me of a man I once knew in Paris, who so easily manipulated my naiveté with the power of his attraction. Paolo leaned his hands on the table and bent toward me. "Don't go looking for Sylvie until I say it's fine. You got to promise."

A man from another table came over. "Is everything all right here?"

I stood. "Yes, sorry. We were just having a bit of a dis-
agreement." I smiled at Paolo. "Perhaps you're right after all.
We'll see how everything arranges itself."

I nodded to him and the stranger who had intervened and
walked out of the cafe, barely able to hide my trembling hands.

Paolo caught up with me outside and gave me a scrap of
paper. "Sorry, Mrs. Button. Here's a way to find me if you hear
anything or if you find out Sylvie's in danger. My parents can't
read English. There's things I can do."

I shuddered to imagine what those things were and prayed
I would have no cause to contact him.

Later, I sat for a long time at the table in my parlor, hands
cupped around a tisane. What was I to do next? It seemed
whatever step I took could result in disaster for Sylvie. I tried
to picture her going innocently about her day at the movie
studio, if she was still there. I had no idea what went on, how
she did what she did. All I could use from my experience were
the theaters and music halls I'd frequented in Paris so long
ago. The women on the stages were no better than I and my
fellow courtesans, and perhaps worse. Was it the same for
cinema actresses?

Aaron's gentle knock pulled me out of my thoughts. I let
him in.

"Justine?"

Something about the sight of his kind, familiar face broke
me open. I threw my arms around his neck and wept against
his shoulder.

He pushed the door shut with his foot and wrapped me in
a tight embrace. I could feel the beating of his heart, and it
comforted me and frightened me at the same time. After a few
minutes, when I had regained control of myself, he held me a
little away and said, "What happened since we last spoke?"

"It is so much worse than we thought. I don't know what
to do."

It was then I decided that, even if it meant he would abandon me and the search for Sylvie, I would have to tell Aaron everything.

CHAPTER
TWENTY-FIVE

Sylvie

As I might have predicted, Florence had made herself the center of attention in the Strangers' Room at the Colony Club, even though we were celebrating the release of part three of *Les Misérables*, a film she had no role in.

"Better help yourself to champagne early, in case it runs out." Annabel stopped a woman with a tray of filled glasses and took two, handing one to me. "Nice job on the dress."

I was very pleased with the way my new frock came out after I fixed it and added a few touches of my own. "At least I have a skill for when I'm finished with the pictures," I said.

"Ladies and gentlemen! May I have your attention, please!" Mr. Kent stood on a dais at one end of the room where a white sheet had been stretched over a frame to make a screen. Monsieur Gaumont stood next to him. The projector sat on one of the tables about fifteen feet away. Chairs had been arranged to face the screen, and everyone moved toward them and took their seats. "For the first time ever, a Vitagraph moving picture has been filmed on Gaumont cameras."

Then Monsieur Gaumont stepped forward and spoke. "And for the first time ever, a Gaumont company moving picture has been graced by the talents of Miss Florence Turner, the Vitagraph Girl. It is our hope to produce pictures with synchronized sound at our plant in Queens. We invite you to visit us when you are able."

Everyone applauded. Now I understood Florence's look of false modesty, her expectation of accolades. I looked over and saw her flutter her eyelashes in theatrical bashfulness.

"Please. I'm going outside to smoke." Annabel stood and turned her back in a way that no one could miss and walked out the door. She may have expected me to follow her, but I didn't want to. I wanted to see the picture I was in—even if my part was small—and I was curious about the other one. The cameramen had been talking about Gaumont films, and how sometimes they tried to do more than just entertain, that they were often more serious, and Léon Gaumont risked putting stories on screen that would never be acceptable here. The thought intrigued me.

The French picture, called *La possession de l'enfant,* was to be shown first. The title cards were all in French, and of course, I could read them. I pretended not to understand, though, and listened as Monsieur Gaumont translated them aloud in English. Starting with the first caption, which, remarkably, held the names of all the cast members along with the role each was playing. A list of technical participants and other collaborators followed. Among them was Alfonse d'Antigny, *dramaturgie.* He had told me that day in Coney Island that he was an investor. Perhaps his skills went beyond merely being rich.

I watched, fascinated, as a story about divorce unfolded on

the screen. No one I knew ever spoke about divorce other than in hushed tones. Of course, Mr. Blackton was divorced and had remarried—that was something everyone knew. We just didn't mention it.

The couple in the picture have a little boy, and fight over who would get to raise him after the divorce. The court awards the child to his father. The boy becomes unhappy, despite his wealthy surroundings. He visits his grandmother, who helps his mother to abscond with him. But the mother lives in terrible poverty, taking in laundry to earn a few pennies so they can eat.

The father goes to the police when he discovers his son has been stolen.

"The mother of my child stole her from me, sixteen years ago," a voice with a French accent whispered behind me.

I turned my head. It was Monsieur d'Antigny, who must have come in after the film started and taken a seat behind me. He smiled but said nothing more. I went back to watching the film, but I wasn't paying attention anymore.

The film ended to polite applause and murmurs. I wondered if everyone was as stunned as I was by its audacity. Florence had performed a bit over-dramatically, in my opinion. But who was I to judge her? She stood, and everyone clapped more enthusiastically. I thought it was a little embarrassing.

The room quieted again for the showing of Les Misérables, Part Three. Although I had seen most of the film in bits and pieces, this would be the first time I watched it as a true audience member would, and I suddenly wanted to become invisible. How had I gotten to this place? Such strange twists and turns had led me here, but if I hadn't been brave and taken the chances, I would never be at Vitagraph. I could just as easily have gone home the very next day after the blizzard, or even the same day. It would have been the safe thing to do. I still don't entirely understand what made me act so crazy then. The Sylvie Button that was would have obediently gone back to the lies and silence, graduated first in her class at the High School for Girls, and gone to Teachers College. But Sylvie Button died the day Sarah Potter was born. And that person there, in the black-and-white representation of moving life, acting out a part that she hoped was believable—that was me. I did it. I was Cosette.

"Bravo!" Everyone in the room stood and clapped as the screen irised to black, startling me out of my thoughts. Before I knew it, Mr. Blackton called out my name to come and stand at the front with Maurice and Elita. I shrank back.

"You should take your bow. It's not like the theater. You won't get another chance to do it." It was Monsieur d'Antigny who put his hand on the small of my back and gently pushed me forward. As I walked to the front to stand with Mr. Blackton and the others, I caught sight of Florence. She clapped as well, but I could tell that behind her theatrical smile lurked anger and spite.

We all bowed, then waitresses put the chairs back around tables and came out with platters of tea sandwiches and cakes. I was too nervous to think about eating. Annabel was off to the side talking to someone, and when I caught her eye, she came over and stood with me.

"You have to tell me again who everyone is," I whispered to her.

Before the showing, Mr. Blackton had introduced me to many people whose names I recognized from the broadsheets and the society columns in the newspapers. I paid them no mind, but Annabel liked to read bits aloud to us sometimes when there was something scandalous to hear.

"Let's see..." she said and scanned the crowd. "There's at least one Vanderbilt, as well as a Schermerhorn, but of course no Astors. The really old money doesn't have anything to do with the moving pictures, but a few of the millionaires realize there's a fortune to be made in them."

Three women detached themselves from a knot that included Monsieur Gaumont and headed in our direction. I thought they were coming toward the table laden with food and expected them to pass by, but they stopped and made a semicircle in front of me. One of them, an attractive older woman with kind, brown, half-moon eyes, put her hand out to me. I sensed Annabel back away and leave us and wanted to turn and beg her to stay but didn't know how to do it without being rude.

"I'm Elsie de Wolfe, and these are my great friends, Bessie Marbury and Anne Morgan. We were very impressed with your performance. Have you made many moving pictures?"

"No-no," I said, "This was only my second one."

"You must have appeared on stage before, then. You were very convincing as a French waif. In fact, your features could well be French." Miss Marbury examined me as if appraising a sculpture.

"My mother—taught me to love all things French." Just in time, I avoided spilling a truth.

"You should come to France and stay with us, at Versailles. We have a charming villa there. You could appear in some French moving pictures, if Mr. Blackton will allow it," Miss de Wolfe said.

"You really ought to meet Alice. I hear she is coming to America, now that she is married and has a child," said Anne Morgan, who appeared somewhat younger than the others.

"Forgive me, but who is Alice? This is the second time someone has mentioned her to me."

Miss de Wolfe took my arm and steered me toward the tables laden with food as she talked. "Alice Guy. She is a pioneer, truly. Her films are legendary in France, although they haven't been seen much here yet."

"Is she an actress?"

This made all three of them laugh. "No! She writes and directs her own pictures, along with her partners at Gaumont."

Before I knew it, we were all sitting at a table with plates of food and cups of tea in front of us. They spoke glowingly of France and of moving pictures and how wonderful it was to be a free woman with a career. "You are fortunate indeed not to be one of the girls in the shirtwaist factories. There are so few ways a woman can support herself with honor. Your mother and father must be very proud of you."

"There you are!" Annabel appeared out of nowhere. "Excuse me, but Sarah needs to speak to someone." She pulled me up from the table before I'd had a chance to take a single bite of food and dragged me away.

"It was lovely talking to you," I said over my shoulder.

"Think about France!" Miss de Wolfe called after me. I was afraid they would be offended by my hasty departure, but they all smiled.

Annabel took me out into a corridor that led to the ladies' powder room. "Do you know who you were talking to in there?"

"Miss de Wolfe, Miss Marbury, and Miss Morgan. Why?"

She lowered her voice. "It's said that they live in...you know...together, but they're all ladies."

I had no idea what she meant.

"You really are a child, aren't you? Let's get out of here. Some of us are going to a club uptown. Your Mr. D'Antigny is coming. And he's paying."

I had had enough excitement for one day. "I think I'll just go home," I said. "Besides, he's not *my* Monsieur d'Antigny. Is Florence going?"

"We're trying to sneak away so she doesn't notice. And don't be a ninny! This is a once-in-a-lifetime opportunity! I insist you come with us."

"With us where?" We both turned at the same time to see

Florence just closing the powder-room door behind her. "Oh, do you mean to the Alhambra? Alfonse and Léon already asked me to come. I think I shall."

After her reaction to the reception my performance got a while earlier, I didn't trust Florence one little bit. Who knew what she might say about me? And when did she start calling Monsieur d'Antigny 'Alfonse?'

"I'll just get my wrap. Are we taking a trolley?" I said, patting my hair and turning toward the entrance of the club, where our coats and shawls had been carefully put away in a cloakroom.

Annabel suppressed a satisfied smirk. "We're to ride in Monsieur d'Antigny's auto. How are you getting there, Florence?"

It turned out there was enough room for the four of us, and Mr. Blackton, Mr. Kent, Maurice, and Monsieur Gaumont took Mr. Blackton's automobile.

"See you there!" Mr. Blackton said as he drove away.

#

We sat in uncomfortable silence all the way up to 125th Street. By then, it was already nine o'clock, and I was dead tired after that exciting day. I was sorry for my impulsive decision to go along. Not to mention how uncomfortable I felt—physically and otherwise—with about two hundred dollars hidden in the seams of the piped jacket I had made. My old coat was too threadbare to wear to such a fancy event, and it was too cold not to wear a jacket. I had been uneasy about giving my jacket to the coat check at the Colony Club, and I was determined not to part with it at a music hall.

Florence's familiar face guaranteed us a prime table at the front of the large ballroom, near the stage where performers came and went, one act after another. We were close enough to see the perspiration on their faces. I knew enough about performing to guess how hard it must have been for them. "This is what actors in most studios have to do in the off-season," Florence whispered to me. "You'll probably have to, as well. I'm contracted to do publicity. I'll make appearances to conjure up excitement for the pictures releasing this winter." She flashed another of her insincere smiles at me.

Monsieur d'Antigny ordered champagne for the table. I tried to refuse because I hadn't eaten, but everyone kept making toasts, and I had to drink until I felt quite unlike myself.

"Annabel." She was sitting across the table from me, so it was hard to get her attention without causing a fuss. But she noticed and came around to me. "I'm not feeling well. Let's go home." I had no idea what time it was or how we would get all the way back to Brooklyn from Harlem. But I knew I couldn't stay there any longer. I stood and staggered a little, but Annabel held onto me as I made my excuses to the host. "Monsieur d'Anti...d'Anti...gny..." My lips were numb, and I could not make my mouth form his name.

"Please, you must call me Alfonse, *comme tout le monde!*" He didn't seem to notice, and his eyes were glassed over anyway.

"Alfonse, then, I need to go home now."

Florence laughed. Her cheeks were as bright as polished apples, and I thought mine must be even redder. I turned and instantly regretted it. The room spun around me. I gripped Annabel's arm.

"Oh dear, looks like someone is unused to champagne." Florence lifted her glass toward me, and it separated into two glasses for a moment.

"Allow me." Alfonse stood and took my other arm, and together, he and Annabel steered me out of the crowded ballroom to the sidewalk. The cold air hit me, and I went to the curb, doubled over, and vomited.

"I can take care of her," Annabel said, pushing Alfonse away.

"Please. My motorcar is at your disposal. This will purchase a new dress for Sarah, since the one she's wearing is now spoiled."

I remember little of what happened after that. I awoke the next morning at eight, my head throbbing. The light streaming in from the tall windows cut into my eyes. Annabel stood next to the bed, a cup of hot coffee in her hand. "Drink this."

My mouth felt as if it was coated in velvet—thick and soft and dry. It was hard to swallow that first sip, but gradually I let the hot liquid bring me back to myself.

"The others have gone to work. I didn't have the heart to wake you up too early. We'll just be late."

I stood, slowly, and when I was certain I wouldn't keel over, I went to the wardrobe to get my heavy skirt and jacket and my old waist. "It's gone!"

"What? Your coat? Oh, I expect someone brought it back. It's probably at the studio. Anyway, with this," she pulled a banknote out of her pocket, "you can buy something new."

I panicked, thinking she had discovered my secret, until I noticed that it was a twenty-dollar bill. I stared at her. "Where did that come from?"

"Your friend Alfonse. He was so embarrassed."

Not more than I, I thought. "I feel like such a fool. And in front of everyone, too."

"Come along. Get dressed, and we'll face the ribbing together."

"Could we get a sandwich on the way? I haven't eaten since breakfast yesterday."

She stopped halfway to the sink with my now empty coffee cup. "Ah-ha! That's why the champagne hit you so hard. Of course we can."

I didn't remind her that she was the one who took me away from my food at the Colony Club and rushed me out the door.

Everyone was busy at the studio that day getting ready to

film *King Lear.* Both Annabel and Florence were in it—two of the daughters—but I was just making costumes. They were more elaborate than for *Les Misérables.* It suited me not to be hanging around Florence after making such a fool of myself the night before. And I was still a bit giddy from both the champagne and the way everyone admired me for my role as Cosette. Apparently, today people were standing in lines that went around blocks waiting to get into the nickelodeons to see it, and there was already talk about Part Four—which was "in the can," as the cameramen said, and just needed some final editing.

I would have been happy but for one thing: my jacket. Someone must have it here, I thought, but I didn't dare interrupt the work to ask about it. Instead, I headed to the sewing room to get started on King Lear's cloak.

I opened the door and stopped in my tracks. In the middle of the floor sat an enormous arrangement of flowers—roses, lilies, daisies, and many I couldn't name. The stuffy room smelled cloyingly sweet. There were too many flowers for such a small space. I coughed and approached the bouquet slowly, spying a card nestled in between two roses. The front of it simply said, *Miss Sarah Potter.* I teased it out, careful to avoid thorns. When I turned it over, I saw the note, written in an elegant, curving hand.

Dear Miss Potter,

I am sorry you became ill last night and had to leave. I have your wrap, which you left behind in your haste. I would be happy to bring it to you at your convenience, or perhaps you would come retrieve it yourself? You will find me at the Hotel Astor.

Avec amitié, Alfonse d'Antigny

My heart banged against the walls of my chest. Alfonse, I hoped unknowingly, held my guilty secret hostage. At least I knew where the jacket was and would be able to retrieve it. I would have to write to him and make arrangements, and fast. I needed the jacket, not simply for what was hidden in the seams, but because, at least for the moment, it was the only warm garment I possessed. My coat from the previous year was too short in the sleeves, and the fabric was so thin I could feel wind right through it. Besides, I couldn't wear such a shabby thing now. So I didn't want to wait until Alfonse—it still felt odd to call him that—was coming to Brooklyn again. I scribbled a note to him to give to the postman who came to collect the mail at midday. Of course, Annabel would think I was making an excuse to see him again. I supposed I would have to suffer some teasing about it. I knew from my own eyes and from Annabel's talk that one way actresses tried to get ahead was to get friendly with the right men, whether they had any real romantic interest in them or not. And making pictures cost money too, money that wasn't always made up from the thousands of nickels people paid to see them. Gaumont and Vitagraph were courting Alfonse as an investor and trying to use the beautiful Florence Turner to do it. Florence was happy enough to play along, no doubt thinking she'd get a few baubles out of it. Annabel would have no trouble believing those were my motives as well, to have Alfonse make sure I got the leading role in a big movie and maybe treat me well. I would deny it, of course, but it was enough so that if I went to see him—especially after the flowers—it would make her wonder.

Then I thought, what if that's what happened? What if he decided to convince Mr. Blackton to put me in more and more pictures? People would notice me and wonder who I was. That was the last thing I wanted right now. It wouldn't be long before someone from my old neighborhood or my school recognized me. What then?

For the first time since that March snowstorm, I wished

with all my heart I could be back on Mulberry Street, doing schoolwork and sewing waists, with a dull but safe future laid out before me.

CHAPTER
TWENTY-SIX

Justine

Three weeks had passed since my conversation with Paolo. I swear that every waking moment of that time, and often in my dreams, I saw that shameful photograph. For right or wrong, the vision of it blotted out the thought that Sylvie might have gotten herself involved in a robbery, whether by intent or accident. That, for the moment, was conjecture. There was nothing ambiguous about the photograph. It was real. A stain. At all costs, I was determined to do what I could to wash it away. But what? Nothing I thought of was practical or would avoid bringing public notice to the photograph of my daughter in her underclothes.

Then, one day there came a moment when the exact course of action I had to take was suddenly so obvious, I couldn't understand how I had not thought of it before. It happened in the middle of a conversation on a day that was very much like all my other days. Aaron and I sat in companionable solitude, sipping tisane in my new parlor. It was just as tiny, furnished in exactly the same manner as my old parlor, except that Aaron said the hard wooden chairs bothered his back and brought over a comfortable upholstered chair one day. Clever of him to pretend that it was for his comfort, not mine.

"Do you think Tommy could find out where all the copies are and destroy them?" I said.

"If he were to do that, it might well put him in danger. I have heard that the underground trafficking in such things is highly lucrative and fiercely protected by those who engage in the business."

I could well believe it. "Mrs. Bonnano clearly did not like it when I showed her the postcard," I said. "I imagine she only thinks of the girls who pose for those pictures as half-human, deserving to be exploited that way." I had seen that attitude all too clearly in the way the men in New York treated prostitutes. There was nothing—at least, nothing obvious—that compared with the open patronage that courtesans in Paris enjoyed. Back then, Alfonse had been more than a customer. He kept me, making it possible for me to live in illicit splendor, and people accepted us as a couple wherever we went.

"I have been making inquiries about that family," Aaron said, placing his empty cup gently on the table. "Apparently, the police believe they are involved in several illegal enterprises—pornography, gambling, extortion—but whenever they are close to making the connection, the family somehow manages to evade capture. One of the officers I spoke to—"

"You spoke to the police?" My mouth went dry.

Aaron reached out his hand and took mine. Such physical contact between us had become frequent, and although at first it felt strange, I was becoming accustomed to the sensation of calm it gave me. "No, no, my dear! Please, do not think I would do such a thing without telling you first. I simply joined in a conversation on a street corner, where a few of my acquaintances were discussing the fact that the Bonnano boy had been let out of jail. Someone suggested that the police would watch him, perhaps make him feel safe so he would lead them to the stolen money. I mentioned that I'd heard the family was involved in other dubious enterprises."

I sat up straighter in my chair. Of course. Paolo. He could help me. He told me it would be dangerous to look for Sylvie and thereby reveal her whereabouts to his mother, but he did not say I had to do nothing. "Perhaps it is within our power to destroy the postcards without endangering Tommy. I have no fear for myself. I could do it. *J'en suis certain.*"

I stood and started to pull my hand out of Aaron's gentle grasp, but he clasped it more firmly, not letting me walk away. "What are you suggesting?"

I recognized his tone of voice. I suspected it was one he would use if he had children to care for and wanted to prevent them from doing something that would harm them. Clearly, I would have to reassure him. "I have no plan at present. I would simply like to speak to Tommy again, now that we have had some time to think things through. The situation has changed with Paolo out of jail and so clearly angry at the photographer who took the photograph."

"Promise me you won't do anything foolish?" His eyes were filled with a mixture of sternness and affection, an expression that was so different from anything I'd ever have expected from the gaze of a man.

I smiled. We finished our tea in silence. Despite Aaron's justified concern, I had already decided that I would go to Tommy on my own and somehow get a message to Paolo. I would say nothing about it to Aaron. I had no desire to put my good, kind friend at any risk.

Aaron had commissioned me to make another gown. This

one he promised he would take to the buyer at Lord and Taylor's, and if they purchased it, I would make more of the same or similar, and perhaps even have helpers to do the machine work.

It was while I transformed the luxurious fabric into a gown, stitch by stitch, that my plan took shape, too. By the time I finished, just a day and a half after my conversation with Aaron, I had everything decided down to the last detail, a map I could see in my mind. I snipped the last thread once I had sewn the final tiny, silk-covered button on the gown that was almost exactly like the one I had worn the night Tommy showed us the postcard. After a quick glance at myself in the polished bottom of the tin pot to make certain my hair had not come loose, I put on my coat and left my apartment. I would walk to the nickelodeon—it was against my principles to pay for transportation unless I was unfit or the distance was too great. How strange, I thought, to be going alone to a place I had previously never considered worth my regard.

As I passed through my neighborhood of Polish Jews and on through an Italian block, carefully skirting the environs of Mulberry Street, it all seemed so drab and unvarying. The same run-down storefronts, the same wares for sale, the same faces lined with care and want, no matter where they had come from to get here. And yet, deep in their eyes, not always obvious but always there, hope glimmered. Difficult as life was here, what they had left behind was infinitely worse. Here most people could afford some kind of dwelling and could put food on the table, and the ones who brought a skill with them and worked hard stood a real chance of doing better, as I had. Those would be the ones who would leave the tenements for the larger and safer apartments on the other side of Houston Street in the vicinity of Tompkins Square Park, where the Germans who had already been here for at least a generation clustered.

By the time I was at Fourteenth Street, the businesses were

closing up for the evening. As I reached Sixth Avenue and turned the corner, I saw young Tommy up ahead, leaning against the doorframe of the nickelodeon, smoking the last of a cigarette. When he had reduced it to the tiniest stub, he flicked the end from his fingers into a puddle in the gutter where it landed with a hiss and then sank. He had not yet seen me, and I watched him stare at a group of pretty, giggling girls as they passed, keeping his eyes on them until other pedestrians obstructed his view. I wondered if he had a sweetheart, and what it would have been like had Sylvie fallen in love with a Tommy instead of the dangerous Paolo Bonnano.

As Tommy turned to go inside, he caught sight of me and stopped, his hand on the door handle. "Mrs. Button!" He waved.

Without hesitating, I walked up to him. "I need your help. Where might we talk?"

It was early in the evening on a weekday, before tired workers had finished dinner and would walk out in search of companionship and whatever entertainment they could afford, so no one was waiting to see the next showing of what looked to be a cowboy picture. Tommy led me inside the small theater, and we sat at the back in the near-dark. "I want to destroy all the postcards of Sylvie and make it so that no more can be printed. Where are they? Where is the plate, I think you called it?"

Tommy leaned back and gave a short, skeptical laugh. "No offense, Mrs. Button, but I don't bet you could do what the others have failed at for a couple years."

"What others?"

"I hear things. There's the police, of course. They try and track down the men who take the photographs and print them, but I think there's probably an officer or two who's getting paid to turn a blind eye. Then there's the other operations, the ones who want in on the money with their own products."

I wanted to ask him how he happened to know so much

but was afraid of frightening him into silence. "How long have you known about Angelotti's involvement in this business?" I asked, and thought, *and why did you do nothing to stop him?*

Tommy shrugged. "I didn't know. I thought he just took a few publicity photos for actresses when things were slow in his portrait work. I have a sweet deal there. He lets me use his equipment when I want and even the chemicals. He taught me everything he knew. He's a great photographer, whatever you think of him. Then I overheard a conversation one day when I was in the back room making prints."

I nodded, encouraging him to continue.

"A man came into the studio, I thought maybe for a portrait, but instead, he told Angelotti that he needed him to work on something with him, that he'd be well paid. Angelotti said, 'I'm not sure that's the sort of work I want to do.' And then the man said, 'If you don't, we could make it so you never take another photograph.'"

My mind raced, trying to understand what that might mean. Destroy his equipment? Hurt his eyes, or his hands? I shuddered. "So, he was forced to do it."

"At first. But then I think he got to enjoying it in a way. And the money...he liked that, a lot. I said something to him once, real casual, and he told me to keep my nose out of it, or he'd fire me."

"But Sylvie wasn't one of those girls," I said, "the ones who want to flaunt themselves and make money like that. How did he photograph her in such a manner?"

Tommy shrugged. "I don't know. He must have caught her off guard while he was taking test shots. That makes the picture all the more valuable. Like peeping through a window blind."

It was just like that, I thought, an invasion of my daughter's private moment. "Tell me where the plate is. Where the postcards are stored. I will destroy them!" I stood.

"Now, hold on a minute. Don't do anything they could

trace back to me, and as far as I know, only me and Angelotti know where he keeps things."

Of course. So far, there was nothing to connect me to Tommy. I could have come across the postcard in myriad ways. I did not tell Mrs. Bonnano that I knew who had taken it. "What if it can be done in a manner that will not implicate you?"

He narrowed his eyes. "What are you thinking?"

"I just want to know if the plates and printed pictures are all stored at Angelotti's studio."

Tommy squirmed in his seat. "No. They're not there. Angelotti has a key to a warehouse. He sent me there once or twice to get chemicals and photographic paper. I didn't nose around, but there were boxes stacked up, some with girls' names on them."

"Where is this place? Can you get the key?"

I knew a struggle was raging in Tommy to decide whether or not he should tell me and risk someone finding out he had led me there, or if the fear of reprisal was too great to overcome his instinct to do good. I could not blame him for being cautious in such a circumstance.

"He'll only take more. Just destroying what's there won't stop him."

"*N'importe*," I said. "It doesn't matter to me if grown women engage in activities they know are immoral. I only want to protect Sylvie from any further harm." He wouldn't suspect my own past in such circles.

Still, he hesitated.

I put my hand on his arm. "No one will ever know you told me. I won't go to the police. I can't, for other reasons."

"There's just one problem. I know where it is, but I don't have the key."

I thought for a moment. "Is there only one key?"

"No, I think someone in the Bonnano family has one. They go there to get the pictures. It'd be too obvious to come to the studio."

That was all I needed to know. By the time I left the nickelodeon, I had the address etched into my memory. All that remained was to contact Paolo, and pray that he could get me the other key.

CHAPTER
TWENTY-SEVEN

Sylvie

When I told Annabel that I was going to the Hotel Astor to fetch my jacket, I said, "You must come with me." I had decided on reflection that I shouldn't go alone.

"Don't be stupid! It's you he wants to see."

I shook my head. "I can't explain it. I need you there. I need someone else there."

Annabel reached for my hand, and I let her take it. "You're really very young, aren't you?"

Her soft tone knocked me off balance. I wanted to cry, to confess everything to her, about running away, about Paolo, about the money. But instead, I took a deep breath and smiled. "That's why I need you to protect me."

Annabel looked away, but I caught the hint of something beyond her usual detached, cynical expression. How odd that I had found this friend quite by accident at the moment when

I most needed someone's help. Perhaps she, in her own way, needed me too.

We had a day off because they were filming scenes in *King Lear* that didn't involve Annabel, and I had finished all the costumes. We chose the subway as the fastest route. On the train, we kept up a light, bantering conversation that distracted me. But once we were on the crowded, noisy Manhattan streets, all my fears and anxieties flooded into my mind so that I hardly saw where we were going. This part of New York was so different from the small world I used to inhabit, the blocks between Mulberry Street and my school. I could have navigated those streets in my sleep. But here—if Annabel hadn't been there, I doubt I would have found my way to the hotel, even with the numbered streets and avenues.

The entrance, with its crimson canopy and scarlet-coated doorman, was on Fifty-Sixth Street. Just as we got to it, a long automobile pulled up, and before it quite came to a stop, the doorman stepped smartly forward and opened the passenger door. The lady who emerged wore ropes of pearls and a fur coat and entered the hotel without looking to either side, as if she was too exalted to notice the rabble. I shrank.

Annabel took my arm and propelled me forward. The doorman held it open for us, but I sensed him looking down his nose with disapproval.

"Go on, ask!" Annabel nudged me toward the concierge's desk. "Think of it as playing a role. Only with real words."

I couldn't help smiling at what she said as I approached the thin, sharp man also dressed in a scarlet uniform. "Excuse me." My voice came out sounding small and squeaky, as if I were about to ask for a crust of bread. I cleared my throat and pretended to cough. "We are meeting Monsieur d'Antigny. Could you let him know we are here?"

The concierge lifted his chin and peered down at me at the same time, a hawk sizing up his prey. "And who would 'we' be?"

His scrutiny made me acutely aware of how out of place I looked in this magnificent hotel lobby where the fabrics hanging at the windows and covering cushions were finer than any I had ever seen. The Colony Club, which previously appeared the height of luxury to me, paled beside the opulent interior of the Hotel Astor. Annabel nudged me again. *I'm playing a role,* I thought, and I just hadn't put on the costume yet. I cleared my throat and said, "Miss Potter and Miss Moore." I looked him straight in the eye, imagining I was projecting my gaze through the lens of the camera to an unseen audience. The man looked away quickly and made a great show of shuffling through some papers, and for a moment I thought perhaps Alfonse had not received the note that said I would come today at this time to collect my jacket.

After clearing his throat, he muttered, "You'll find him in the bar." He didn't look at me as he said it.

Annabel nudged me out of the way and went right up to the desk. "I suppose it would be too much trouble for someone to escort us there?"

Still pretending to pay attention to something very important on the surface in front of him, the concierge snapped his fingers, and a young bellhop came over. Unlike the concierge, this fellow was obviously well pleased to encounter two pretty young ladies who needed his help.

Soon, we stood just inside the entrance of this famous bar I had read of in the society columns. "I don't see him," I said. How embarrassed I would be if he wasn't there.

"There he is." Annabel took my arm and pointed.

I looked where she indicated and froze.

I saw a man, from the back, who looked for a moment like the very image of the man who was with my mother that day. Her face, peering over the shoulder of someone built exactly like Alfonse, was something I would never forget.

"He hasn't seen us yet." Annabel started walking toward

him, and he turned around.

Alfonse looked past Annabel to me. I shook myself out of my stupor and hastened to catch up with Annabel.

"You brought your friend?" He stood and bowed over each of our hands.

I expected he'd be surprised and had planned what to say. "Yes, it turned out we both had business in Manhattan, so we decided to make a day of it."

If he was disappointed, he hid it quickly. "Here is your wrap." He handed me a parcel tied up with string. "Quite a heavy garment for a lady as slight as you."

"I feel the cold. It keeps me warm," I said, hoping he hadn't noticed how threadbare the coat I was wearing that day had become.

He motioned us to sit, and a waiter came to the table almost immediately. "Champagne?"

I was about to demur, but Annabel said, "Yes, that would be lovely." I couldn't let her drink alone. This time, though, I'd be careful not to have too much.

"When I folded your jacket to wrap it up, I noticed how well made it is," Alfonse said. "Do you mind if I smoke?" We both shook our heads no. He reached into his breast pocket and pulled out a cigar case. By the time he had selected a cigar, clipped its end, and motioned to a waiter to light it for him, three glasses of champagne bubbled noiselessly in front of us.

The low hum of conversation all around was not cover enough for complete silence, so I spoke. "Thank you for helping me get my jacket back. I went to such a lot of trouble to make it."

"Not at all," he said and puffed on his cigar, looking at me with his head tilted slightly in the way he might examine a work of art, or something he was about to purchase. "I once knew a seamstress. In Paris. Although she had ceased that occupation by the time I met her. You remind me a little of her."

All at once, I felt completely alone in that room, as if I had fallen down from the sky and landed in a place where I could see people, but they could not see me. My eyes played tricks on me, reforming Alfonse's face into something alarmingly familiar. Perhaps he was that man, the one he so resembled from the back. Perhaps my mother was the seamstress he had known in Paris before I was born, and he had come to New York expressly to seek her out again. Could what I witnessed have been nothing more than the embrace of two old friends?

No. Even in that split second on the day of the snowstorm, I could sense the brittle tension of intimacy that went beyond friendship—but could also have been its opposite.

"So, are you and Monsieur Gaumont going to make another picture here while you're in New York?" Annabel initiated talk on a safe topic, and I silently thanked her for it.

Alfonse tore his gaze away from me to address Annabel's question. "We have not decided. Alice is here, in Queens. We plan to go there tomorrow and discuss it with her."

"Alice Guy?" I asked.

Annabel stared at me. "Who's she?"

I then remembered she hadn't been part of that conversation. "Miss de Wolfe and Miss Marbury talked about her at the Colony Club. She isn't an actress; she writes and directs films."

Alphonse smiled at me. "You are interested in the process? Not just in flaunting your undoubted beauty and talents in front of a camera?"

Heat rose into my face, no doubt turning it an embarrassing shade of scarlet. "Well, it seems like it would be more interesting."

"And what's wrong with acting?" Annabel pushed me playfully.

"Nothing! But don't you ever want to do something more, something that requires your whole effort, not just posing and strutting, but thinking, creating a story of your own?" Although I'd never said anything like that in so many words, as I spoke, I felt the truth of it.

"You have ambition. And I have an appointment across town in half an hour," Alfonse said and stood, and we did too. His expression had changed. He didn't exactly look angry, more confused. What had I said to change things so? "Please allow me to order my automobile to take you home."

I tried to refuse, but he insisted, saying he could easily get a cab to his appointment, which was not very far away.

As we sat ensconced in the comfortable backseat of Alfonse's auto, Annabel said, "That mouth of yours, with your ideas and dreams, it's gonna get you in real trouble someday."

I clutched the parcel containing my jacket and thought, *it already has.*

As soon as I walked into the sewing room the next day, Annabel burst through the door. "There you are! There's a special person here to see you."

I was still wearing my heavy outdoor jacket, but nonetheless, Annabel all but dragged me back out of the sewing room toward the large studio. I couldn't imagine who this person might be. The way things had been going, I didn't expect it to be anyone I particularly wanted to see.

In the middle of the studio, the cloak I'd made for King Lear was draped over a table, and three people stood around it fingering it, lifting up the edges, examining the seams. Thank heavens I'd finished them! No raw edges there. Two of them I recognized as Monsieur Gaumont and Miss Marbury. The third was a lady I had never seen before.

"Come, join us," Monsieur Gaumont said.

The unknown lady said, "We were admiring your handiwork. Where did you learn such skills?"

It was my mother's voice almost exactly, but with a stronger accent. I tried not to let on that I noticed.

"Allow me to introduce Madame Alice Guy—now Alice Guy Blaché," Monsieur Gaumont said with a polite little bow.

I opened and closed my mouth a few times, unsuccessfully trying to think of something appropriate to say, and so I dipped a strange little curtsey, so out of place in that setting.

"I won't eat you, you know!" Madame Blaché said and took a step nearer to me and smiled. She was shorter than me by a few inches, but her serene oval face, dark hair that matched her eyes, and a mouth whose slightly prominent upper lip made it seem as if she was always about to speak combined to give her an air of confidence that made her seem much taller. Who would have thought I would actually have a chance to meet this lady whose name I kept hearing, someone who had already accomplished so much?

"*Je suis ravie,*" I said, without realizing it slipping into the French my mother and I often spoke at home.

"You speak French! Delightful! Bessy, you did not tell me this."

Miss Marbury shrugged. "I didn't know. Miss Potter and I only met briefly at the Colony Club."

"Only a little," I lied.

"I have seen you in *Les Misérables,*" Alice said, continuing in English, although I sensed she would have preferred to speak French. "You have a talent. You look natural on camera, not like some, with their exaggerated actions and pulling faces." She arranged her features in a perfect parody of Florence Turner, and I laughed.

"*Mon amie,* that's unkind," Monsieur Gaumont said. "There are many great actors and actresses in the American films."

"Yes. Perhaps it is the ridiculous stories that make them behave so artificially."

She was fearless. I had never met a lady who spoke her mind so openly and artlessly.

"But not Stuart's," Gaumont said. "He is alone among

American cinema directors in creating moving pictures that tell a real story instead of simply making a spectacle."

"*Beh.*" Alice lifted her shoulders and her eyebrows at the same time, exactly as I had seen my mother do when she meant, *Perhaps you are right, but I still don't believe you.*

"We're here because Elsie wanted you two to meet." I had almost forgotten that Miss Marbury was there. "I don't represent actors or actresses in the moving pictures, or I would have made this a professional conference."

I had hardly been there at the Colony Club that day, so out of my world and uncertain. I had stayed on the surface, just watching. I didn't realize anyone was observing me that closely, especially not Miss Marbury. She had a bearing about her that made me understand her power, her way of commanding respect, but she still managed to remain reserved, holding something back. Miss Marbury spoke again. "We are sorry to be mysterious. Alice wants you for her next picture. Mr. Blackton has already given his permission."

"You won't have to sew for us," Alice said with a sly purse of her lips.

My eyes went from one face to another, all three new or almost new to me. How far I had come to even think of trusting any of them with my life, my future. I gazed longest at Alice, then had to look away. She was the only other French woman I had ever met besides my mother, and although they were not in the least alike physically, the way she formed her mouth when she spoke, her stance, her air of just tolerating the world and letting everyone know that she was, in fact, above it all—these things called my mother to mind so powerfully I was afraid I would break down. How would it be to work with her, to see her every day?

"Miss Potter?"

Monsieur Gaumont snapped me back to the present. They wanted an answer and expected a yes. "What is the movie about?" I asked, stalling for time to gather my thoughts.

"Does it matter? You will work with the famous Alice Guy!" Gaumont came over and took my arm, starting to lead me away, I thought possibly to scold me for not leaping at the opportunity.

"Let her be, Léon. She is right to ask. Not every actress would bother, only thinking of the fame and the money. It is important to do something good with a life, not just amass dollars and seek for safety." Alice came right up to me, took hold of both my hands, and looked me in the eye. "It will be a story worthy of your talents. A drama, about a family. An unhappy one, but it will all come right in the end."

I felt as if by gazing at me, she could peer into my soul. Tears burned behind my eyes, and before I could blink them away, one slipped down my cheek. I drew myself up to my full height. "I'd be honored to be in your picture, Miss Guy."

She rose on her tiptoes, leaned forward, and kissed me on both cheeks, just as my mother used to every day when she sent me off to school. One kiss, I noticed, landed on the teardrop and wiped it away.

"When do we start?" I said.

CHAPTER
TWENTY-EIGHT

Sylvie

I didn't realize that being in one of Alice Guy's pictures would involve moving for a while to another borough of New York. Queens. To a neighborhood called Flushing.

"You're only there for a few weeks, remember," Annabel said as she helped me stuff my few belongings into a cheap valise I bought at a local store.

So, this was what it felt like to leave and say goodbye, not run away and have to change my name and invent a new history—or be abandoned without a chance to say a word or decide whether it was what I wanted or not. The move made this person I had become all the more real, more permanent. I wondered if my mother thought I was dead. I blinked back tears.

"Gosh, I didn't know you felt like that!" Annabel took my chin and shook my head back and forth, making me laugh. "That's better. Write to me. I want to hear all about it, all the gossip and details."

I promised her, then went down to get in the automobile with Alice and her husband, Herbert.

The roads that threaded the boroughs were sometimes rough, and I had to hold onto the strap to avoid toppling into Alice. "Where are you from? Who are your people?" she asked.

A particularly bumpy part of the road rescued me from having to remember the story I'd made up for Annabel. By the time the road smoothed, I had thought of a way to change the subject.

"Tell me what you are doing here. I thought France was where all the best pictures are being made now."

She shrugged. "Some are quite good, yes. But your country is a bigger world. And we are making experiments here, with new machinery. Chronograph. To make pictures and sound work together."

Annabel had given me a bit of the background, something she had read in *The New York Dramatic Mirror*. Gaumont owned the studio, but Alice and Herbert ran it. They had already started to make more films for the American market. However, Annabel told me that so far, instead of doing everything here, they sent the raw footage back to Paris to be developed and edited and have the scene captions inserted—which made for some funny translations. It was clear that Alice wanted to change all that, to do something extraordinary, carve a path of her own.

The Queens studio—or plant, as they called it—was simply a smaller version of Vitagraph. One large building held rehearsal studios, an editing room, and a props and costumes studio. A yard out in the back had sets that suggested Westerns—a saloon, a general store, and the like. A small lake and a few outbuildings stood in the waste ground beyond. The large studio wasn't quite as big as the one at Vitagraph and had only a couple of Cooper Hewitts lined up, nowhere near the impressive array at Vitagraph.

"You should see the Gaumont studios in Paris!" Alice rolled her eyes and puffed out her breath. "We were the first with a glass-ceilinged studio in which to film, whatever the weather. Someday I will make the same thing here. Perhaps not right here, but somewhere."

I noticed she said *I* and not *we*.

A cameraman picked up my bag and led me to one of the rooms they kept for actors and actresses who were there just for the duration of filming. On the way, I heard singing coming from behind a closed door, with a sign on it that said, "Silence! Recording!"

"What are they doing in there?" I whispered.

"Oh, no need to keep your voice down. That's just Lois, singing over the recording she made yesterday, so she gets it exactly right when she's on camera."

That must be the Chronograph machine Annabel told me about.

"Get yourself settled, then come down to the main studio. We passed it on the way. Got to get to work, a long day of shooting the outdoor scene tomorrow."

I was the last one to enter the large studio that morning. Looking around at the others, I could have been back at Vitagraph. It was so easy to tell who operated the machinery, the lights, and cameras, who made the costumes and built the sets, who acted, and who made the decisions and directed everything. The only difference here was that this last person was a woman. Otherwise, the two worlds were identical, down to the motley sets placed around the walls to create artificial neighborhoods and interiors. It was all magic. Here, we could be wherever the director's imagination took us. I still sometimes created my own stories when I was standing around waiting for my cues, just as I had when I was living with my mother. I preferred it to letting my mind be drawn down avenues that led to danger and disgrace. Before, in the old neighborhood, I used my imagination to escape from a life that was gray and ordinary. Now, I let my mind wander on pleasant jaunts to escape from possibilities that were anything but ordinary, from the possibility of being sent to jail for committing a crime or being hunted down by thieves looking for their stolen loot. In this artificial world, I could almost be safe. No one would find me here, I thought, just as no one could have entered my dreams when I was younger, unless I wanted them to.

I shook myself out of my daydream just in time to learn that I would play the leading female role in Alice's picture. I tried not to act surprised, not wanting to call even more attention to that fact. But unlike Vitagraph, none of the others seemed the least put out by it. At least, not that I noticed then.

"We have just a few hours of good light tomorrow to shoot the outdoor scene for this picture," Alice said. "We'll go over to Fort Lee before dawn so we're there as soon as the sun comes up."

True to her word, we were all out hours before sunrise bumping over the bad roads in Queens. I sat in a truck between Alice and the driver that chilly November morning. A truck! My first time ever, but it wouldn't be the last. It was just like an automobile with an extended back that had a covered platform. It actually looked more like a wagon than a motor car. The back had been loaded up with crates of costumes and three cameras. The cameramen sat on the costume crates, somehow managing to remain seated as we jolted over cobblestones and rutted dirt roads. No bridge crossed the Hudson at that time, so we would have to take the ferry. It would be my first time on a boat of any kind. I tried to pretend I wasn't afraid.

"The best locations are in Fort Lee," one of the cameramen told me. "Looks wild and natural. Lots of companies film there, including Biograph. That's why we have to get there so early. It's a dash for the best positions."

In the course of my lightning-fast introduction to the making of motion pictures, Annabel had talked about the other companies, telling me all about Vitagraph's rivals and which ones to avoid if I ever found myself out of work at Vitagraph, so I knew about Biograph. Mr. Griffiths was just as well respected as Mr. Blackton, apparently. Not that I'd seen any of his pictures. I could tell Annabel admired them, though.

"When we get to the ferry landing, we must be hasty," Alice yelled into my ear over the roar of the engine.

"Fast is better," I said, "Or quick." The day before, I'd soon noticed that she didn't mind having her English corrected and, in fact, welcomed it.

"Our scene is not long. We have a house with a...veran-dah?"

"Porch," I said.

"And there is a, what is it, a piquet gate—"

"Picket fence."

Our conversations were like a school exercise where you fill in the blanks in a story. I didn't mind. I think Alice valued me all the more when she saw I could double as an English teacher.

Of course, I had so much to learn from her, too.

We made fast progress over the brand-new Queensboro Bridge and through a Manhattan that was just waking up. I imagined the thousands and thousands of people stretching, yawning, facing another day just like the one before, stoves being lit and kettles coming to the boil. We were too far north to be anywhere near my mother. That was a relief. Nothing familiar to tug at me and confuse me.

Once we reached the Hudson up around 125th Street, the crew members carried everything down to the ferry landing. I tried to hide my nervousness, but Alice, who had an uncanny sense about people, noticed.

"Don't worry, they go over and back several times a day. It's just a river. Not like crossing the ocean." Her voice, so like my mother's, reassured me, and soon we were plying the waters of the Hudson, heading west as the sun just started peeking up behind us.

"Moving pictures are not like the stage. You don't have to make big..." Alice waved her arms around, almost falling to the deck when we hit a particularly rough area in the middle of the river.

"Gestures," I said, reaching out to steady her.

"The camera brings you close to the audience. Everyone can see your *visage*, the expressions. The more you look natural, just like they—"

"Them."

"*Oui*. The more them...or is it they?...see themselves in you, it has all the more force."

"It's more powerful." I nodded. I could see her committing the phrase to memory. I'd only been there for one day and I had been unable to disguise that I understood her French. She'd soon become accustomed to depending on me to smooth out her English. I never had to tell her anything twice.

We reached the opposite shore just as I was starting to feel queasy.

"You, all you camera men, we're going up there." Alice pointed up a long flight of stairs that led to the town. "Then we will find a conveyance to our location."

The men didn't move very quickly, I noticed. If Mr. Blackton had told his men to do something, they'd hop to it. Yesterday when Herbert—Mr. Blaché—was in the studio, the cameramen paid more attention. I could see Alice's frustration as she glanced at the sky, and so I went over to the small crate of costumes, picked it up, and started climbing the stairs, not struggling, just acting as though I could easily do what they did.

The men soon got to work in earnest.

"I want to finish this filming before our investor, d'Antigny, returns to Paris. He sails in a week."

I had forgotten for the moment that Alfonse was friendly with Alice and Herbert. Our last conversation, only a few days before, still unsettled me. I tried to put it out of my mind, but things—like this—kept reminding me of it.

"That expression, it's perfect."

Alice stopped me when we reached the top of the stairs. A rickety wagon with a tired-looking horse hitched to it creaked as the men loaded all the crates onto it.

"I was afraid you would not be natural enough for anyone to believe you had cares and trouble. Whatever you were thinking of *à ce moment*, think of it again in front of the camera."

I smiled. If only she knew.

The weather cooperated, and the outdoor shoot was successful. We didn't get back to the Gaumont studios until after ten o'clock. I was exhausted. The guard at the gate into the compound stopped me as I trudged through, barely able to put one foot in front of the other. "This came for you while you were gone, Miss."

He handed me a note in a sealed envelope. It was addressed simply, "Miss Sarah Potter, Gaumont Studios, Queens." There was no stamp, so it hadn't come in the mail. The handwriting was unfamiliar, not Alfonse's, which I knew from the note about my jacket.

I tore the corner of the envelope, my hands too clumsy from fatigue to open it any other way, and slid out a folded piece of paper. I knew as soon as I read the greeting that it had come from Annabel.

Stitches,

I thought you should know that a VERY HANDSOME young man came looking for you here yesterday, not long after you left. I didn't know what to tell him. He said he was your cousin, but he looked about as much like you as I do, which is to say not at all. He said he'd left you his valise to watch over some belongings while he was traveling on business and had come to collect it. I know there's nothing in the apartment, so I nosed around the sewing room but didn't find anything there either. If I had, I wouldn't have given it to him. He asked where you'd gone, said he'd go and look for you there. I pretended I didn't know, claiming that you were shooting a picture on location somewhere. He never mentioned his name, just said he'd come back in a week or two when you returned. I didn't want to send him to you without talking to you first. Did I do wrong? Write back to me and tell me what I should do if he comes back before you do.

Toodle-oo!

Annabel

By the time I finished reading, I was perspiring through my shirtwaist. What could I do? He would come to claim the money. It was in my possession, but if I gave it to him, I would be aiding him in his crime, possibly even cause both of us to be arrested. The police were no doubt watching him closely, and now they knew to keep an eye on Vitagraph studios, where I would be returning in a little over a week.

I was too tired to think clearly about any solution that night, so I splashed water on my face, got into bed, and soon fell into a restless slumber. Such dreams! The world of the moving pictures and my real life mingled and swirled together. Faces from the past and present loomed above me, threatening. I tried to run but could barely lift my feet, and the dream ended with me cowering in a corner from which there was no escape, watching as a man who looked something like

Alfonse stepped toward me with a dagger held high over his head in a melodramatic pose.

When I awoke, I knew I had to let someone know what was happening with me. It was too much to bear alone. I dressed quickly and went to find Alice. I had thought of a way to tell her without telling her, and I didn't want to lose my nerve before I had the chance.

CHAPTER
TWENTY-NINE

Justine

I swore to myself I wouldn't tell Aaron what I planned to do. I wanted to protect him from any implication in my deed. I was going to commit a crime. After all, the crimes of my past already placed me beyond redemption, so what was one more? I did not fool myself into thinking that because I targeted a criminal rather than a scoundrel that what I was about to do wasn't still very much against the law.

Yet everything, all my sins—including this one—were done out of love. My heart guided me, showing me the way just like a beacon on a rocky shore. Still, the law would never consider me innocent. The woman Aaron knew as conscientious and upright was created only through a lie so artfully upheld throughout my years in New York that even I had begun to believe it. Once a month, though, I had been forced to face up to the person I truly was, and would always be, in a small apartment on Twenty-Second Street. Alfonse controlled me, forced me back to who I used to be. If I were honest with myself, though, I had to admit that Alfonse's control was not only based in fear of retribution. Much to my shame, I found myself disappointed somewhere deep inside me when the person I met in his apartment was a stranger. In my weaker moments, my body still yearned for his. I hated myself for it.

I knew that what I planned to do was likely to end my friendship with Aaron. He had been forgiving to a fault and had trusted me when he should not. I didn't deserve his good opinion, and he didn't deserve my continued deceit. So I decided it was time for him to learn the whole story, the full truth about me. Telling Aaron would mean that if anything happened to me because of what I was about to do, he would be able, in turn, to tell Sylvie all the truth if he ever found her.

When Aaron came to meet me the next day, I asked him to stay a while. He sat in the upholstered chair while I stood, pacing back and forth, not looking into his eyes, telling him things that I knew would sully me irreparably in his eyes. I explained the entire, sordid affair. I told him that in Paris, I had earned my living as a courtesan, that Alfonse had been my lover and that we bore a child, Sylvie. I told him how I waited three years to earn enough money and wait for an opportunity, when Alfonse and his wife brought Sylvie to Paris, then tricked her nursemaid into trusting me to care for her while she was alone with her beau. I told him everything about my desperate flight to Le Havre with the distraught little girl I barely knew, and the rough crossing to New York where we began to know each other. And I admitted my fear and distress as I walked the streets with no money, trying to find a way to support the two of us, fearful that I would have to resort to becoming what I had fled from in Paris once again.

When I finished the entire, sordid tale, he sat in silence. I gazed out the window, the view below distorted by my tears.

Without turning, I said, "I don't know what I would have done, were it not for you."

I hugged myself, trying to become as small as possible, a dense knot of unworthy, imperfect woman. I thought it would make it easy for him to leave me, now that he knew what I truly was.

When I felt the gentle pressure of his hands on my upper arms and could see the reflection of his face above mine in the window, I turned and looked up into his eyes. I half expected him to embrace me, to kiss me, to go through the usual awkward fumbling and undress me while I did not make it difficult but made no effort to help, believing that now that he knew all, he would treat me just as every other man I'd known had treated me.

Instead, he took my hands and just looked at me. In his eyes, I saw everything from sadness to wonder, empathy to anger. Mine wasn't a simple story, I realized. I was both criminal and victim. And Sylvie was the price I'd had to pay. I never would have expected another person to understand that, yet here he stood before me.

"Everyone who comes here from Europe is running away from something," Aaron said. "Poverty, sickness, hate, misdeeds. Here they are washed clean and start again, in a city where all things are possible."

If our friendship had been of a different nature, I might have threaded my arms around him and buried my face in his chest, breathing in the comforting, faint scent of mothballs and pipe smoke that hung around him. But we were not those people. We were not a comfortable couple. So I made an effort to smile.

"Tea?" I asked.

#

A city where all things are possible. Aaron's words soothed me as, later the next evening, I walked through the dark Manhattan streets, my coat wrapped tightly around me with a shawl covering my head. I kept my eyes down toward the pavement, hoping no one would notice anything unusual in a denizen of the night on her way to an assignation. For I knew only too well how to play that role. I had let my hair loose from my tight chignon and left the top few buttons of an old shirtwaist open. This I carefully concealed, though, to be revealed only if I was confronted by someone who suspected I was bent on some other criminal pursuit in this unsavory part of town near the cargo piers.

I felt the contours of the heavy key in my pocket. Paolo had received my message and met me at a cafe with the key earlier that day. I'd told him I had hired a man to get ahold of the pictures and destroy them. He didn't know that I myself planned to carry out the scheme. I agreed to meet him and give him back the key after the deed was accomplished.

As I walked, it started to rain, and I was glad of it. That meant fewer people on the streets, and those out would rush to their destinations to escape the rain. I pulled my shawl tight under my chin, concealing my face as much as possible. The farther west I went, the more deserted the streets. A large rat darted out of an alley and ran across my foot, and I stifled a cry. My heart beat so hard I felt it in my ears and thought anyone close enough to me would be able to hear it.

I had committed Tommy's instructions to memory, repeating them to myself like a litany. *The building is on Eleventh Avenue. You'll find the entrance near the corner of Forty-Ninth Street. No one will be there after eight o'clock, and the door will be locked.* Only one time in my life before had I felt such fear but also determination, knowing that my child's future depended on me. Then, I clutched not a key, but my Sylvie. Then, I was running away from all I knew to start again in a different city in a different country. Now, there would be no escaping. I would have to go back to my apartment and pray no one ever connected me with this crime—not the police, not the Bonnanos, not even Aaron if it could be helped. If I managed things correctly, the way Tommy instructed me, it would all look like an accident.

I was so intent on what lay ahead that I hardly noticed my surroundings, or that the number of people on the street increased as I approached the warehouses near the docks until I heard someone scream, "Watch out!" and felt myself suddenly lifted off the ground and carried back to the sidewalk. Seconds later, a freight train barreled down the avenue right where I had been crossing a moment before.

"Gotta pay attention crossing Eleventh."

The man sounded as shaken as I was. *"Merci,"* I said, in my panic slipping into French. "Thank you, I meant."

"Don't mention it." He lifted his cap up off his head and looked at me hard. "This ain't a place you oughta be at this hour. It's not safe."

"I'm quite all right, thank you. I have an appointment to keep. Again, thank you."

I turned away and this time glanced up and down the avenue before crossing. Only when I reached the other side and started looking for the entrance to the building did I realize I had dropped the key when the man lifted me out of danger. *"Merde!"* I muttered. No one was around to hear me curse, but I regretted it anyway. I started back across, searching the ground for a glint of metal. All manner of trash and tossed off bits of this and that littered the street. I might as well be trying to find a needle in a bowl of pins.

I was ready to scream in frustration, so angry at myself for not having anticipated such a possibility when I heard him. "Looking for this?"

In front of me stood the man who had rescued me. He

dangled the key from his two fingers.

"Yes, thank you, I need it to get into the building where my appointment will be." I walked over to him and reached out for it, but he jerked it just out of my grasp.

"I think you better tell me what you're up to."

To my surprise, I started to laugh. I couldn't help it. Something about the absurdity of where I was, what I was about to do, and this gentleman somehow getting in the way, undid me from within. Soon I was doubled over and hardly able to catch my breath. I struggled to explain, gasping out words. "You...don't...understand...my daughter..." But my hysterical laughter returned with a vengeance, and tears coursed down my cheeks. I wondered what I would have said to this stranger if I had had the power of coherent speech.

He waited for me to calm down, no sign of amusement on his face. "All right, lady. Here's your key. But you got to let me warn you it's no good trying to do something shady on your own over this part of town. There's rough characters you wouldn't want to meet in the shadows."

I took a deep breath and wiped the tears of laughter off my face. "It's all right. You don't need to worry about me." I put out my hand, palm up, and he dropped the key into it. "Thank you. You have been truly kind, more than I deserve. Now, if you'll excuse me."

He took off his cap, not just raising it this time but clutching it to his breast and bowing his head in a respectful salute. Then the man backed away. I wished he would just disappear, but he stood there and watched me cross again. No matter. I had no other choice than to go forward and continue with what I had set out to accomplish, whatever the circumstances.

My immediate panic dispelled for the moment; I found the door Tommy told me about. The padlock was heavy, and the chain twisted around the door handle. I could hardly turn the lock enough to see where to insert the key. But I managed eventually, and the lock yielded, letting the chain slip out and fall to the ground with a crash. I stood up straight and looked all around me to assure myself I was still alone. Slowly, carefully, I took hold of the door handle and pulled it toward me.

Inside, it was darker than night. The glow of the city street lamps did not penetrate here. I hadn't thought to bring so much as a candle. But I hadn't come this far to stop now. I stepped inside and pulled the door to, not closing it out of fear of being trapped in utter blackness.

Gradually my surroundings took shape. I was in a corridor, as Tommy said I would be. *It's mostly for storage, you know, cargo from the ships and all before it goes somewhere else,* Tommy told me. Angelotti rented a small part of it, through what Tommy described as "contacts." His room would be through the third door down on the left.

I kept one hand on the wall to guide me, steeling myself not to be repulsed when I felt the soft bodies of spiders and disturbed cockroaches at their nightly business. Every other step was accompanied by some creature—a mouse or a rat—scurrying away. I was glad at that moment that I couldn't see them.

I think I held my breath until I reached the door. It opened easily, as Tommy said it would. Angelotti had such confidence that no one would ever think to find anything of value in such a place that he didn't bother to secure it.

There's a light switch next to the door. The chemicals are stored in jugs along the far wall. Opposite, you'll find the cardboard boxes with the postcards inside. Plates are stacked up on a table.

I pushed in the button to turn on the light, and the naked bulb dangling from a cord in the ceiling dazzled me so that I had to cover my eyes. When I could blink them open again, I surveyed the room. It was exactly as Tommy had said it would be. I went to the jugs of chemicals first, releasing their stoppers one by one. They were unmarked, but Tommy described to me the smell of the one that would destroy the postcards, eradicating the pictures on them so they would be useless. The cartons by the wall were stacked one deep in the small room but five or six high—too high for me to reach with the undiluted acid that would accomplish my goal. Tommy said he didn't know how many boxes would be there because deliveries were made as and when, usually under cover of the busy daytime activities. I hoped there was enough acid in the one jug to destroy everything. I could do nothing about the postcards already in the hands of men, but at least I could stop their spread. I stepped forward, the uncorked jug in my arms, thinking carefully about how best to proceed. If I doused the cartons on the bottom, perhaps they would weaken and send the ones on the top tumbling down.

I swung the jug back, summoning all my strength.

"What are you doing, lady?"

I froze.

"Why don't you put that down, and we can talk."

I recognized the voice again. It was the man who stopped me from being crushed by the train. Of course, he had followed me. I had been too focused on my purpose to imagine that possibility. For one fleeting moment, I considered tossing the acid at him and running away, but then I would leave the postcards and the plate behind. And he had saved my life, after all. Reluctantly, I placed the jug of acid on the floor at my feet and turned.

He reached into his pocket and pulled out a metal badge. "I'm Detective Sergeant Harold Whitney. Now suppose you tell me who you are, and why you're here."

#

They were kind enough to bring me a cup of tea after the uncomfortable ride in the back of the police wagon to the headquarters on Mulberry Street. My hands shook as I lifted it to my lips, splashing a few drops onto my white waist. I was too exhausted and frightened to care, or to appreciate the irony of being in the one place I spent all my life avoiding for fear of being charged as Sylvie's abductor.

"You see our predicament, Mrs. Button." Detective Whitney sat across a wooden table from me, hands placed flat upon it. I noticed his eyes, hard yet deep at the same time, a color somewhere between blue and gray. His face was clean-shaven, and I judged him to be about thirty years old. "You were caught in a place you had no right to be, yet you did not break in. I discovered you trying to destroy private property, yet you did not succeed in destroying it. And now, thanks to you, we have uncovered the hiding place of a trove of pornographic material and have a potential connection—the photographer, Angelotti, whose storage space we already knew it was—to those who create and distribute it."

I looked down at my hands, gripping each other so hard they turned the tips of my fingers white.

"Who gave you this information, and how did you know to ask for it?"

"I have told you, I cannot say." I refused to mention Tommy, who had put himself at great risk to help me. I refused to reveal that one of the girls on the postcards was my own daughter, worried that she would be hunted down and prosecuted for participating—even unwittingly—in such an illegal activity. And I would not mention the name Bonnano. Paolo had acted in good faith, and Tommy was more afraid of them than the police. If he was that fearful, I feared for Sylvie as well.

"You leave me no choice. I'm sorry, but we'll have to detain you here until we get some answers."

A policewoman entered and pulled me out of the chair by my upper arm, a little roughly, I thought, considering I was half her size and hardly capable of running away. She led me down a corridor to a cell where four other women already waited for something; I didn't know what. I recognized two of them, or their type at least, as the streetwalkers who used to prowl my old neighborhood, just a few blocks away from where I was now. The others might be common thieves, I thought. Three women occupied the one bench in the cell, spreading themselves out so that no one else could sit down despite there being plenty of space. The fourth woman leaned against the corner and looked me up and down with amusement in her coal-black eyes.

So, this was what it felt like for my worst fear to come true. I was in the hands of the police, perhaps not for my original crime, but for a crime, nonetheless. My one consolation was that now the photograph of Sylvie would be destroyed along with all the others they found and no longer be seen by salacious men. The irony of it all was that because my escapade had gone so terribly wrong, if the full weight of the law was brought to bear upon me, I might never see my daughter again either.

The floor of the cell was filthy, and it smelled of urine and sweat. Nonetheless, I sat. My legs could not hold my weight any longer. I closed my eyes and tried to think of Sylvie. I fought to cling to the knowledge that all this was for her, and I could take whatever was ahead because of that. I pulled my knees up, wrapped my arms around them, and put my head down between them. *Dieu la protège,* I prayed.

CHAPTER
THIRTY

Sylvie

It was early, so I wasn't sure I'd find Alice in the studio. She and Herbert lived in an apartment a few blocks away with their baby and a maid. But, what was I thinking? Of course, she was at work already, poring over some typewritten pages, a cup of coffee sending up a lazy curl of steam at her elbow.

"Ah! Sarah! Up so early after such a day?"

"I'm not at all tired," I said.

"I am going over the script and the shots for today, interiors here in the studio. Would you like to see? Most is about you. I mean your character, *bien sûr.*"

She pushed a few props aside on the table and spread the pages out. I came over and scanned them, but I couldn't concentrate. I was so full of my idea, I had to tell her quickly before anyone else arrived.

"Alice, I wanted to ask you something. If I could possibly

do something. I have an idea, for a picture."

She turned her ever-curious eyes upon me and raised one eyebrow.

I launched into what I'd prepared, hoping I didn't sound too nervous. "It's about a girl who has become involved, without realizing it, in a crime, and she must think of a way to prevent herself from going to prison and at the same time protect the boy she loves." I continued to sketch out the story of this girl who runs away when she finds her mother with a man who isn't her father (of course, I made the setting a little more affluent), and meets the boy she's in love with on the way just after he has stolen a lot of money from a bank. I didn't want to make it too believable. I had the girl working for a cruel seamstress when the boy finds her and leaves her with the money before getting caught himself. "And because she is a good, moral girl, she finds a way to hide the money and get it back to the bank by sewing the banknotes into the seams of a skirt and jacket. She puts the clothes on over her other clothes, walks into the bank, takes her outer clothes off and leaves them behind, then walks away without being caught."

It sounded silly. There was no getting around it. I could feel my cheeks going red and immediately wished I hadn't said anything.

"That is a very imaginative tale you spin," Alice said. "I prefer something a little more easy to believe, less...not dramatic, *précisement*..."

"Melodramatic," I said, my hopes fading.

"But I think there is something to work upon in what you say. The innocent, corrupted by forces around her, who takes control and regains her character...Yes, it is a good story. Or there is some part that is good."

She stepped back and looked at me, her eyes taking in everything about me. I was wearing the very garments that were at the center of my supposed fiction. My heart sank.

What had possessed me to come to her like this? "I guess it's a silly idea," I said, turning to go back to my room and prepare for the day's shooting.

"Not silly at all," Alice said. She took hold of my arm and turned me to face her. "The best stories always have some *base de vérité.*"

I drew in my breath to protest, but she put her finger to her lips and pointed down at one of the piped seams in my skirt. It was coming undone just a little. Wearing the skirt day after day must have put some strain on the seams. It was tiny, but unmistakable. A hint of something green. I gasped.

Before she could say anything more, the door to the studio opened and two of the cameramen from yesterday's shoot in Fort Lee yawned into the studio, stretching their arms up in exaggerated expressions of fatigue.

"Speaking of melodrama," Alice said and squeezed my hand, whispering into my ear as she passed me to go and speak to the cameramen about the day's work, "I will help you if I can."

At the end of the day, Alice invited me to dinner. "To make this picture of yours, we must have finance. I know the gentleman to help us. You are acquainted with him as well, no?"

I realized she meant Alfonse, and I wanted to protest. Something about him disturbed me. I was probably being unfair to him, I thought, since he had never been anything but kind to me. Yet he had looked at me so strangely when I last saw him, and the story he told, about a French seamstress, was uncannily close to home. I told myself not to be so foolish. My imagination, once again, was getting the better of me. In my heightened state, I heard echoes of my own past everywhere.

"To make such a picture as you imagine, with outdoor and indoor scenes, and as you say, the final scene in a real bank, will cost approximately..." She counted on her fingers and made a mental calculation. "...three-thousand dollars American."

"I had no idea!" I felt foolish for not adding up in my head what the cast and crew would have to be paid, that the seamstresses and set builders would be called into action, and then there was the time in the studio and editing suite—oh yes, and the editor and someone to direct the film—it was impossible. Not that I actually expected my picture to be made, only perhaps rehearsed, so that I could dispose of the garments in a way that wouldn't make anyone suspicious.

I was still reeling from what Alice told me when Alfonse arrived in evening clothes. I owned only the dress I had worn to the reception at the Colony Club. It would have to do.

"We have just finished work for the day," Alice said after she let Alfonse kiss her hand. I stood far enough away that he would have to take several steps in order to reach for my hand and nodded to him, hoping he wouldn't bother. Alice saved me by taking his arm and walking away with him. "But we have another idea for a project that I think may interest you."

Alfonse opened his mouth wide and laughed. "Oh, *ma chère Alice!*" he said, once he had regained control of himself. "You know I promised myself only to back one of your New York pictures. I am already committed to Gaumont in Paris for three more."

"I will give you a much larger share than Léon." She smiled coquettishly, an expression I didn't expect from such a professional woman.

"We will discuss over dinner." Alfonse glanced back at me, and I saw him look me up and down in one quick appraisal, and it reminded me I had yet to change.

"I won't be a moment," I said and scurried away to my room.

#

Alice, Herbert, Alfonse, and I were all squashed into the backseat. I sat between Alfonse and Herbert, feeling like a sparrow between two vultures. The driver took us across the Queensboro Bridge, but instead of going north as we had the day we shot in Fort Lee, we turned south on Fifth Avenue.

"Where are you taking us?" Alice asked.

"I have been told of a private club—well, private in the sense that most people don't know of it even though it is right here, how to say it, under their noses."

"I hope there will be dinner and not just drinking. I'm rather hungry," Alice said.

I was glad she said it. After a long day of work and only a light lunch in the middle, I was hungry too. I hoped my nervousness over the situation I was in—seated in a motorcar with a famous cinema director and her husband and a wealthy investor whose interest in me was difficult to fathom— wouldn't make it impossible for me to eat.

Alice started explaining, in vague terms, the outline of the picture that she wanted Alfonse to put his money into. I held my breath, hoping she wouldn't mention that it had been my idea, that her grasp of the situation back at the studio would mean she understood that no one must know the connection the story had to my real life.

"Your imagination, your grasp of human frailty, knows no bounds, my dear Alice," Alfonse said, touching his two fingers to the brim of his hat in an admiring salute.

I breathed again. My secret was safe, at least for now. I looked out the window, only then noticing where we were going. First Avenue. And we'd just crossed Fourteenth Street. My stomach turned sour. In two blocks, we would pass my school. If we kept going south, my mother would be a stone's throw away.

A light tap on my arm sent a shock through me. I jumped. "So, you will take the leading role in this film Alice speaks so enthusiastically about?" Monsieur d'Antigny gazed at me as if he saw right through it all to the person I really was: a frightened girl who'd taken on more than she could manage.

"I...I suppose. I hadn't really thought..."

"If that is the case, then we will discuss the details in the morning." He reached across me and Herbert and shook Alice's hand. She smiled.

Herbert, who had been silent so far, changed the subject. "Will we be entertained at this club to which you are taking us?"

A look I couldn't read passed between the two men. "I am certain we shall all find it most entertaining. And the food is said to be simple but very good."

We continued south. Soon we would cross Houston.

Alice leaned across her husband and reached for me as if to tuck one of my stray hairs behind my ear and said, "Is something wrong?"

Was it so obvious? I was a better actress than that, I thought. I let my shoulders drop and flashed her a cheery smile. "Of course not!" I said, trying not to look out the window at the familiar sights.

We didn't stop near my old apartment, thank God, but went farther south, finally turning on Delancey Street.

Delancey Street. What was I thinking? It couldn't be worse. It was the one fact I knew about Paolo: he lived on Delancey Street with his family. If Alice knew where we were and what connection this street had with my life, I don't know whether she would laugh or be horrified.

By the time the driver let us out in front of a bakery that appeared deserted, I had to struggle not to shiver. Alice looked at me and shrugged. Alfonse stepped up to the door and knocked in a very particular way. The door opened a crack, and he spoke to someone beyond it hidden from our view. When the door closed again, Alfonse nodded to us to join him and opened the now apparently unlocked door to let us through.

The first room we entered was completely dark, but light glowed around a door at the back, and sounds of people talking and laughing filtered through. I took a deep breath, deciding there was nothing I could do but follow along, and pasted a smile on my face as we passed through into a room filled with blinding light from three chandeliers and perhaps a hundred people in evening clothes clustered around about a dozen tables, smoking and chattering and alternately moaning with disappointment and shrieking with joy. There were dice and cards and a wheel that a man spun around after people placed chips of different colors on a felt cloth with numbers. Roulette, I later learned.

"I didn't know gambling was on the menu this evening!" Herbert smiled and rubbed his hands together.

"*Nous faison des jeux* after dinner," Alfonse said, taking me by the elbow and steering me through the crowd toward yet another door in a far corner.

I looked back, but Alice and Herbert had stopped at the roulette table to watch. The only games of chance I'd seen before were old men playing dice on the sidewalk for pennies. "Isn't it illegal?" I whispered.

Alfonse laughed again and tapped my chin with his finger as we walked into another room that looked just like a normal restaurant, with people seated at the tables smoking and eating and laughing. An older, heavy-set woman who reminded me very much of the Italian matrons from the Church of the Most Precious Blood—except that she wore silk and had a pearl-encrusted brooch at her throat—showed us to a table for two. In fact, I was certain I had seen her before, no doubt at Mass.

"What about Alice and Herbert?" I asked.

"They no longer seem interested in eating. Champagne!" He called to the woman, who gestured to a mousy young girl. A few moments later, we had an unlabeled bottle of red wine and two tumblers in front of us. "I suppose that is what they have to offer," Alfonse said, pouring us each a glass. He took a gulp and then grimaced.

"Not as good as the wine in Paris?" I said. He smiled.

A quick glance around showed me that everyone at every table was eating the same thing: plates heaped with noodles and topped with a tomato sauce that looked as though it had meat in it. I guessed it was that or nothing and that most people came in here simply to fortify themselves before going back to lose money in the other room.

I was just about to say so and mention that I'd prefer to go back to Queens and get some rest before my busy day tomorrow when a man with six plates of food balanced on his two arms backed into the dining room through a swinging door. At first, I stared at him out of curiosity, just waiting for a disaster to happen. Then he turned and scanned the tables for diners with no food in front of them.

I quickly pretended I'd dropped something on the floor and bent down, hoping he hadn't seen my face. It was Paolo. "I have to leave. Right now," I said to Alfonse in a hoarse whisper.

"Are you ill? Waiter!"

To my horror, he gestured to Paolo.

Paolo saw me in that instant, and from his expression, he might as well have seen a ghost. He started, and I watched as one of the carefully balanced plates began to slide, causing a reaction that sent another and then another to the floor until all six of them had shattered into a mess of rapidly spreading red sauce and slippery noodles. A cry went up from the diners, and people stood and frantically wiped at red stains on their clothes.

In a panic, I stood and turned in a circle until I spotted a door opposite the one Paolo had come through. I took advantage of all the confusion and made a dash for it, slipping through it as quickly and quietly as I could.

On the other side of that door, I found myself in yet another completely different world. Here, the gas lamps were turned down low, and couples lounged on divans and deep, tufted armchairs, so absorbed in each other that I doubted anyone noticed me. So little light made it hard to see for a moment. A way out, I thought. Please let there be a way out! I had to avoid running into Paolo again. He would know enough to look for me at Vitagraph, but he wouldn't think of going to Gaumont. I needed the time my transfer there had given me to get rid of the stolen money.

And now, Alfonse. He would have questions I was in no mood to answer. Next time I saw him, I'd just say that the closeness in the room had made me feel faint, and I simply went out to get some fresh air. If I did see him again.

Heavy, velvet curtains hung from the ceiling to the floor along all the walls of the room, only parting at the door I'd entered by. I wanted to cry, but I knew I had no time for that. How did I ever get myself into this mess? If they had noticed me go, any moment, either Paolo or Alfonse would walk through into this room, and everything would be over.

Just then, one of the curtains swayed away from the wall as if someone had walked behind it. At least there might be space back there where I could hide for a while, I thought, until people stopped looking for me. I flew to the curtain and felt along it until I found a break and quickly slipped into the gap between it and the wall.

The curtain hung away from the wall by about three feet, marking off an area that was much colder than the rest of the room on the other side of the curtain. A short way down from where I stood, a broken windowpane let in just enough of a breeze to disturb the curtains from time to time. I hurried to the window. It wasn't locked. I had no idea what I'd find beyond it, but this escape route had fallen into my lap.

I managed to open the window wide enough so that I could crawl through and drop to the pavement on the other side. My dress tore as it caught on a splinter of wood.

Cold and terrified, I tried to get my bearings. My heart thumped so hard in my chest I thought it would burst out of me. *Don't panic*, I told myself and took a few slow, deep breaths. I had to be able to walk away without attracting any attention. But how? I quickly figured out that I was in an alley that led to a wide road, probably Delancey. It was early enough still that plenty of people were on the street. A passing stranger might help me if someone came after me. Or, on the other hand, they might notice I was alone outdoors in a torn dress with no coat and think the worst. At least the wrap I'd left behind was something I'd borrowed from Alice, not the jacket hiding the money.

And once I was away from there, where to go? I had left my purse behind, but Annabel had told me to keep a pouch sewn into my chemise with a few dollars in it in case I was ever parted from it. *Thank you, Annabel,* I thought. But I didn't know if the trolleys or trains were still running to Brooklyn, or even exactly what time it was.

I forced myself to walk at a normal pace to the end of the alley and turned what I hoped was west on what I assumed was Delancey Street. A few people cast curious glances in my direction, but no one followed me. Soon I crossed Bowery and continued on to where the street was no longer called Delancey.

When I reached the intersection with Mulberry Street, I stopped. Less than two blocks to my right was my mother's apartment. I was so near her then I could hear the sound of her voice in my mind, scolding me a little for running away, but oh so relieved to see me again. Whatever had happened that far-off day, before everything in my life had changed, I would be safe there—if she would have me.

Like a puff of smoke, my image of happy reconciliation vanished. Who was I fooling? I was no more ready to go home than my mother was probably ready to have me. Yet what else could I do? A girl alone on the street at this time of night was asking for trouble. My mother wouldn't turn me out. And this time, knowing what I knew of the world now, I would listen to her, give her a chance to explain what had happened and why she had kept so many secrets from me.

The shops, now all closed and shuttered, looked just the same as I remembered. There was the greengrocer, wilted greens decaying in the gutter in front of it. The tailor's sign squeaked as it swung in the breeze. The butcher had sloshed water over the sidewalk to wash away the blood and entrails he tossed out at the end of the day, but their sickly, fleshly smell lingered. I hurried past, getting colder by the minute. I imagined my mother wrapping me up in our one warm blanket and making me a hot tisane.

Soon I was at the bottom of the familiar stoop, ready to climb up and let myself in, take the stairs two at a time as I once had done every day after school. I caught my breath and mounted the concrete steps to the door of the building, which I knew would be unlocked until midnight, the time when the men who worked the second shift in the factories would return home.

I flew up the three flights of stairs to my mother's apartment, hardly stopping before pounding on the door with the side of my fist. *"Maman! Maman!"*

A moment later, the door opened a crack. A young woman I didn't recognize peered out at me. "Who do you want?" she said.

"I...I...I'm sorry." Where was my mother? Had something happened to her? Who was this stranger? Whatever the answer, she wasn't there.

I backed away from the door, sat on the steps, and wept.

CHAPTER
THIRTY-ONE

Justine

At some time in the night, I must have lain down on the hard floor of the holding cell and slept, dreamless, despite the discomfort. I awoke when someone pulled on my arm and dragged me to my feet. Gray morning light struggled in from a tiny, high-up window, and a quick glance around showed me that I was now alone.

"The others have all been seen by the magistrate and dealt with." It was the woman police officer who had led me to the cell after Detective Whitney gave up trying to make me give him names. "The detective says he'll let you go for now, if you've got a man to vouch for you."

"I'm not married, and I am an orphan." *But I have a daughter*, I thought, although I had no intention of telling them.

"Don't you have a friend, a neighbor? Someone who'd be willing to keep you out of trouble."

Why was it assumed that a man would keep me out of trouble? Men were the source of all the troubles in my world. All except for one. Aaron had never done me any harm. My intention had been to accomplish my deed and then go home, never telling him about it. He might guess, but I vowed not to burden him with a certainty. And if I involved him now? I would be so ashamed. Better to disappear from his life forever.

"No. There is no man I know well enough to call upon in this instance."

I sat back down on the bench in the cell, not knowing exactly what they would do with me. As the detective said, I hadn't broken in, nor had I had a chance to destroy any property. I don't know how long I waited there in that state of uncertainty. Several hours stretched out to seem an eternity. I clasped and unclasped my hands, fidgeted with my clothes, noticing every tiny snag and seam that needed resewing. It was the first time I had been idle since my long-ago days in Paris. I stood and walked all around the small cell. I hoped I would be let out soon, with or without a man to vouch for me. I suspected they would not be able to keep me indefinitely without some sort of charge: creating a disturbance, or perhaps a drunk and disorderly complaint, although I hadn't been drinking.

Late in the afternoon, the detective returned and brought me back to sit across the table from him.

"You are clearly adept at keeping secrets," he said. "I wonder if you realize how much danger you could be in."

My ears pricked up at the word danger. I never minded danger where it concerned only me. But Sylvie's involvement, whatever it was—that was a different matter. "Why am I in danger?"

He drummed his fingers on the table. "Your actions have led us to—if not the source, a key element in the pornography ring. We intend to follow it up. I have plans to go and talk to this Angelotti, whose photographs we found in that warehouse. If he gives us any information, it's quite possible that whoever pays him will link it all back to the breach of their storage place. And if he puts the pieces together, he may well find you. That…" He paused and leaned back in his chair until it creaked. "That might very well alert the Bonnano family that we apprehended an informer. From there…You tell me what connections they might make."

In my heart, I knew he was working upon me with all the techniques of an expert interrogator. He made me doubt myself, and think through to consequences that might never occur. I knew because it was precisely what I had done to myself for so many years. I had welded parts of my soul shut with lies and deceptions, locked them so far inside that even I had forgotten some of them.

"I am sorry I cannot help you."

The detective rose and opened the door, signaling to the same lady police officer to take me back to the cell. I stood and went ahead of her, not wishing her to take hold of me again.

The corridor that led in one direction to the holding cells led in the other direction to the front of the police station, where the public entered to make inquiries. Some disturbance was in progress there. "I tell you, she has disappeared. I would like to report her missing!"

I stopped suddenly, and the policewoman nearly walked into me. "Keep going!"

I listened hard. "She's a small French woman with light hair. Very attractive. She is not in her home, nor has she been there in the past twenty-four hours. We're friends, you see, and I look in on her every day, and it's simply not like her to be out for so long. She is a marvelous seamstress."

I smiled in spite of myself at the tone of voice I recognized so well, of Aaron becoming a little exasperated and starting to babble. I had wanted to protect Aaron from involvement in my illegal actions. I think I believed he would simply shrug and walk away, not feel my absence in his life if I were no longer in it. But the sound of his voice, his familiar, comforting expressions, broke my resolve.

And he had told the sergeant at the desk that I was attractive. I could hardly remember the last time I heard myself referred to in that way.

"I said, keep moving!"

"I beg your pardon, Madame, but the man currently at the desk speaking to your sergeant is my friend. I believe he is looking for me."

She took hold of my arm once again and began pushing me toward the cell.

"Let her go." It was the detective. "I said before she could leave with a male friend. Give the sergeant your address on your way out. We may want to talk to you again."

The policewoman let go of my arm, but not before giving it a malicious extra squeeze. I did not give her the satisfaction of thinking I noticed.

I walked unhurriedly to the front of the station, smoothing my hair down as best I could. It was not caught up in its usual chignon, and my clothes were dirty and rumpled from my night on the floor of the cell. Aaron would hardly recognize me and perhaps regret his generous description of me to the sergeant.

I paused when he came into sight. He hadn't looked in my direction yet. His black eyebrows were drawn down and together, an expression of worry very familiar to me. He passed the brim of his hat through his hands in a ceaseless circle. I had never seen him so agitated.

I cleared my throat. "*Bonjour*, Aaron."

He looked toward me, and before I had a chance to realize what he was doing, he took two big steps and reached me, threw his arms around me, and lifted me off the floor, squeezing me so hard I almost couldn't breathe. "I thought you were dead," he murmured into my ear.

He put me down gently, and before he could wipe them away, I saw tears pooled in his eyes, which brought answering tears to my own.

"Your address, ma'am." The sergeant held a pencil out to me, his expression blank, dispassionate. I obliged him by noting down where I lived. It occurred to me to lie, but it also occurred to me that if I did so, it might support their belief that I was somehow connected to the illegal enterprise I was trying to disrupt.

"Take me home," I said to Aaron as we stepped out onto the street, and I blinked my eyes against the glare of the late autumn sun. "I must bathe." I took his arm before he offered it.

He grabbed my hand and angrily uncoupled us, and started walking so fast I scrambled to keep up with him. We continued like that for a few minutes, heading east on Houston. I could not blame him for being angry. Perhaps I would lose his friendship because of what I had done. The thought sent my heart plummeting.

Just before we crossed to the other side of Houston, he stopped and turned toward me. "No more. I will not remain your friend unless you tell me everything. I know you have other secrets that you are keeping from me, or you would not have disappeared as you did. I know where you were and what you tried to do. I made Tommy tell me."

So he, too, had lied to the police. Perhaps that was why he sounded so nervous and unsure. "When I have washed myself and changed my clothes, and after I have had a cup of tea and some bread and butter."

He agreed. This time it was he who took my hand and put it in the crook of his elbow, and we walked the rest of the way back to my apartment.

I kept my promise. I told him everything—about Alfonse finding me in New York, and our arrangement. About the men who had used me and abused me. I was certain that after he knew all that, he would either never want to see me again or prove himself to be just like all the others and expect favors from me.

At the end of my confession, over a tisane in my new home, Aaron stood and held out his hand to me. I don't know what I expected, but all he did was bend over it and kiss it, as he had done on occasions before. Then he put on his coat and nodded to me. "I will return in the morning with material and a new picture for you to copy. That is, if you still wish to do so."

Relief washed over me like a cool waterfall. I wanted everything between us to remain just as it was, and it seemed that was what Aaron offered. "Of course."

That night, I slept more soundly than I had in perhaps ten years, having told someone the worst of me, and not having been judged for it.

CHAPTER
THIRTY-TWO

Sylvie

I wasn't sure how long I sat in the gaslit stairwell of the building I used to live in with my mother. Although I had stayed away mostly because I wanted to, because I was angry and hurt by her lies and secrecy, in the back of my mind, underneath all my wounds, I clung to the certainty that she would be there when I was ready to come home.

As I descended the stairs, one halting step at a time, I tried to think back before the day of the storm, before I met Paolo, to a simpler time. Right and wrong were so clear in those days. Stealing was wrong. Carrying on with men you weren't married to was wrong. Telling the truth was right. Staying pure and untouched was right. Black and white. Now I understood that as in photographs, as in moving pictures, gray—in all its subtle shades—was a much more common color.

Seeing Paolo like that had jolted me out of my false sense of safety. I thought his world and mine were so far removed from each other that there would never be any danger of them mingling unless I brought it about. Although the note from Annabel had raised an alarm, I was still far away from him, and it would take considerable effort and time for him to find me again. I had allowed myself to escape into the fantastical, make-believe world of the cinema as if it could cloak me from reality, from having to face what I had done, and what I must do.

I now knew that not only Paolo but his entire family were somehow involved in unlawful doings. That woman who had seated us in the restaurant—of course, she must be Paolo's mother. That's why I recognized her. She appeared not to know who I was, though. Perhaps Paolo hadn't told her anything and wouldn't still, and I could go back to my singular problem about the money, not have to worry that not only the police would come after me, but members of Paolo's family who might feel they had a right to the money he stole could pursue me as well.

I reached the second floor, and Mrs. Murphy's door creaked open. "Who's there?" she said.

"It's me, Sylvie."

At that, she flung the door open wide and rushed out, squashing me in a meaty embrace. "You're alive! Everyone was that worried about you. Your mama was beside herself, although heaven knows she tried hard not to show it. If it wasn't for that Jew, we'd never of known what was going on. Come in and get warm. You're froze through!"

I didn't have the strength to refuse. Her apartment was the exact image of my mother's, except the parlor was taken up with blankets on the floor where her six children slept. They hardly stirred when I came in, no doubt used to sleeping through all sorts of noise. Mrs. Murphy dragged a wooden chair with a broken back into the kitchen, told me to sit, and lowered herself onto a stool that looked too flimsy to support her weight.

"Now tell me where you been. What you been doing."

"It's a long story, and I'm very tired. I wanted to find my mother, but she's not there."

"Oh, lamb, I almost forgot. Just you wait." She stood and reached a cracked pottery jug down from a high shelf, up-ended it, and a folded scrap of paper tipped out into her hand. "This is for you."

I took it from her and nearly wept at the sight of my mother's familiar handwriting.

Ma chère! I will explain everything. Mr. Silverstein knows where to find me. Go to Leiserson's and ask for him. He has told them they are to give you his address. Je t'embrasse, ma jolie Sylvie.

She had obviously written the note in haste. She must be running away from something, or someone. Leiserson's factory wouldn't be open until seven the next morning. I would have to go back to Queens. "Thank you, Mrs. Murphy. You are a great friend." I stood and put out my hand to shake hers, but she once more engulfed me in her ample arms.

"Take care, young lady, and tell your mama I wish her well."

I didn't know whether to feel relieved or distressed. What had made my mother leave her apartment, and how was Mr. Silverstein involved? I was still puzzling over it all when I stepped back out into the cold, deciding that I would have to spend all my money on a cab to take me back to Queens.

"Sarah!"

There was Alfonse, leaning against his luxurious automobile, its motor still running. "How did you find me? What led you here?" I said.

"Please, it is too cold to stand and talk out here." He held the door to the backseat open for me, and I got in. "To Gaumont," he instructed the driver, who pulled away from the curb and headed north at a frighteningly fast clip. "At least, I presume that is where you would like to go."

I nodded and then said, "Well?" in a tone I hoped would convey that I expected an answer to my previous question.

Alfonse took a deep breath, held it for a moment, then exhaled as though letting go of all the air he'd ever breathed. "I have been to your mother's apartment before."

I was too stunned to say anything, instead letting the silence build between us until he had to break it. He knew my mother, knew that she was my mother.

"Your mother and I, we were lovers in Paris. Our acquaintance took place when she was the most celebrated courtesan in all of society."

I couldn't believe what he said. Indignant, I said, "My mother was a seamstress!"

"She was that too, although before I knew her. I knew her, as well, when she found herself...*enceinte*. I helped her get away to a place where she could bear her child in secret. And I thought I helped her by removing the infant from her before she could become attached and bringing that baby girl back as my wife's and my own. We had been unable to conceive at that time."

"Did my mother fall pregnant again?" I was confused.

"No, she had only one child. A daughter. We had every intention of giving her the very best life, my wife and I—the finest schools, clothes, introducing her to society—but when she was three years old, someone abducted that little girl from her nursemaid in the Luxembourg Gardens."

"Who?" I asked, barely able to form the word.

He shrugged. "I do not know for certain. But my daughter disappeared so completely that we guessed that she had been taken abroad. To New York, to be exact. But we had no indisputable proof."

Everything began to fall into place. My mother's secrecy. Her obsessive guilt, her devotion to the Virgin, to whom she prayed every night for my safety and protection. I had so many more questions, but I could barely form the words. "How did you find her? Find...us?"

Alfonse shifted uncomfortably in his seat and looked out the window. "It was...what do you say...happenstance."

I sensed he was unwilling to elaborate. Eventually, I would find out, but for now, I had only one question. "How long ago? Was it last March?" It had to be. His was the back I had seen that day, the man embracing my mother. He was not some stranger but an old friend. A lover. Perhaps she was happy to see him. No, she did not seem happy, and she would not have wanted to encounter the man who had taken me away from her as an infant. She must have been terrified of him. What would she have told me if I had stayed?

"I did not know you still lived until very recently. Your mother tried to make me believe you had died of diphtheria soon after you both arrived in New York."

"But how did you know I didn't? When did she tell you this? Why would she lie?" My questions tumbled out like stones down a hillside.

He turned to me. "For these answers, you must ask your mother. Now I have a question. Who was that young man to you?"

"Which young man?"

He didn't answer. Of course, I knew he referred to Paolo.

"That, too, is a long story," I said, deciding that it gained me nothing to lie. "It began close to a year ago."

We were already in Queens, nearing the Gaumont plant. "Will you tell me more about him?" he asked.

"I'm tired. I just want to go to sleep." I didn't know how much to trust this man. He knew my mother, but he had taken me from her when I was an infant, perhaps thinking he was doing her a favor. My imagination swirled with possibilities. The whole story sounded like the plot of one of Alice's pictures.

The trouble was that the happy ending had yet to take place, if indeed it would.

As Alfonse had said, only one person could answer all my questions. I would sleep, and then decide what to do.

Alice looked exhausted the next day, and Herbert was nowhere to be seen. I came into the studio wearing my suit with all the money hidden in its seams.

Alice looked me up and down. After I told her about the picture I wanted to make, and she guessed it wasn't based entirely on fiction, she knew what secret the jacket and skirt held. "Where did you disappear to? I assume, *évidemment,* that Alfonse drove you back here."

"Yes. I felt a bit faint. I think I was tired and I hadn't eaten enough. Do we have much shooting to do today? I have an errand I must run that cannot wait."

She looked at me, searching my face for something, letting her eyes trace the seams of my suit. "How long will this errand take?"

"I really don't know. Perhaps the entire day."

She shrugged in her usual way. "There is enough to do here without you. The weather is not good, too."

A thick layer of clouds had come over, and Gaumont did not have enough artificial lights to make up for such a lack of sunlight.

"Do you need some money? I have not paid you yet for this week."

"I haven't been here for a full week."

"Eh. I will make certain you work hard enough." She pursed her lips, her way of pretending not to smile. "*Et alors,* I won some money at the roulette table last night."

The ride on the train into Manhattan went quickly, and it took little time to get a trolley across town to Leiserson's, where Mrs. Murphy told me I would find Mr. Silverstein. But when I stepped off the trolley, I found myself in chaos. Crowds thronged the streets, distant policemen's whistles pierced the din of thousands of people shouting incoherent slogans. Everywhere women and the occasional man marched with placards demanding better working conditions. At one point, one of the marchers handed me a sign and told me to hold it up high.

"I'm sorry, you're mistaken!" I had to shout so she would hear me.

"Not one of the scabs, are you?" she said with a sneer.

"No! I'm just trying to find someone."

I couldn't get near the factory entrance. It was blocked by an impenetrable line of hard-faced women. I tried to talk to one of them and explain that I was just looking for a particular person, but she didn't budge from her position. All around me stood young girls, eyes ringed with red and pale, ashen skin. They were the textile workers whose conditions were the source of this protest. They were the girls in the airless factories where dust from the cotton they worked with twelve hours a day irritated their eyes and throats. This was the nightmare Mama did not want for me.

Desperate, I scanned the crowd. Almost all of the girls wore the same uniform clothes. But over to one side, I noticed three women standing higher than the rest on upturned crates, leading the chants of the crowd, and I recognized one of them. Anne Morgan, whom I had met at the Colony Club the day of the showing. Her face glowed. She looked completely different from the modest, quiet woman I spoke to briefly about Versailles and Paris.

I turned sideways so I could edge my way through the angry, noisy crowd shoulder first, and by the time I reached Miss Morgan, I was angry too, that exhausted, beleaguered girls and women should have to fight for so little. Their signs said they wanted nine-hour workdays and one and a half days off per week, and to be paid more than six dollars a week. Six dollars! For seventy-two hours of backbreaking work.

"Miss Morgan!" I yelled. "Miss Morgan!"

She couldn't hear me. I elbowed my way forward, excusing myself, and took hold of her skirt and tugged. She started to yank it out of my hand but quickly recognized me and turned to the woman next to her, put down her sign, and stepped off the box. I had to yell into her ear to tell her I was looking for someone at the factory who had an important message for me, about my mother, and that it was the man who had brought us piecework for years.

"No one is going into the factory today. Only the owners and some men they've hired to work in the girls' places. You say piecework? I thought that was all finished with."

I didn't have time to explain anything to her and was about to thank her and walk away, but she took hold of my arm and steered me to the edge of the crowd, where it was a little quieter. "There have to be thousands of girls here," I said.

"Tens of thousands down at the Triangle factory. It's criminal what these men do to the girls. They're treated like slave labor."

"I had no idea," I said. "And I'm sorry to be so concerned with something personal, but I need to find Mr. Silverstein." I still had to yell in order to be heard.

"You looking for Silverstein?" It was an older woman nearby who hadn't been shouting with the rest, just standing on the edge, watching and listening.

"Yes! Do you know where he is?"

She narrowed her eyes. "What's your name?"

"I must go back. Come and see me this evening, if you wish," Miss Morgan said, handing me a calling card. She looked toward the women in the center, one of whom had tented her hand over her eyes, and searched the crowd, probably looking for Miss Morgan.

"Yes, I won't keep you," I said. She smiled and edged her

way back through the throng.

I turned to the older woman, who had kept her distance while Miss Morgan was with me. "My name is Sarah—" I caught myself. "Sylvie Button."

She stepped forward and reached into her pocket. "Silverstein's all right. I told him to stay away today, didn't want him to get caught in all this." She handed me a folded bit of paper. "He told me if someone by your name came looking for him to give you this note."

"Who are you?" I asked.

"I sit at the door and stamp the girls' timecards when they come in."

From the south came a chorus of police whistles and clanging bells. The woman looked around. "If I was you, I'd get out of here quick, or you might get arrested."

I thanked her and headed away from the strike, relieved when it was quiet enough for me to hear myself think. What a strange day. I unfolded the note. All it contained was an address, in a part of the city even farther east than the club where I'd seen Paolo the night before. I would have to pass quite close by that place to reach the address if I took the direct route. So of course, I didn't.

My roundabout walk gave me plenty of time to doubt myself, to doubt that going to find my mother was the right thing to do. I had a vague idea that somehow she could help me solve the problem of the stolen money. I don't know why exactly. Perhaps I'd dredged the thought up from some far-off notion that she could solve anything, that as my mother, she held the answer to whatever troubled me.

Yet there was another side to my reasons for seeking her out now, if I were to be honest with myself. Pride. I was willing to go back to her, even looking for help from her, because I had something to show for the time I had been away. I had managed on my own. More than managed: I'd been able to earn a livelihood as an actress in the moving pictures, however modest it was. She could hardly now lecture me that school was the only route to prosperity and safety. Now I could show her that she had been wrong and tell her there were so many other possibilities for women now. Look at Alice! Yet still, there were the girls in the factories, like guilty consciences niggling at me for not understanding how my mother could have been so anxious on my behalf.

As I walked, the signs on the shops gradually changed from English to Yiddish, and then a language I couldn't tell but guessed to be Eastern European, perhaps Polish. Six-pointed stars adorned many of the shops' signs. Mr. Silverstein was Jewish, that much I knew, but I also knew he was German. And by the cut of his clothes and the quality of his hat, it was evident that he was much more prosperous than the people who lived here, on streets no more affluent than Mulberry Street and perhaps even poorer. The narrow buildings with their windows placed close together undoubtedly held the same sixteen tiny apartments. The families who lived in them were just like us, or the Murphys or the Coopers, doing their best to survive in the most cramped quarters, working hard for a dream they believed could only come from back-breaking labor and sacrifice. It made my heart sore to think of them all. How many of them had daughters who risked their livelihoods to strike from the factories in hopes of better treatment?

I was fortunate. I could walk through these streets knowing that I had found a way out. I had a card in my pocket from Anne Morgan, daughter of the wealthiest man in New York. Somehow, despite everything, I had landed on my feet. More than that, I thrived; my dreams were coming true. Why, then, did I feel so unrooted?

I stumbled upon rather than found Hester Street and started down it, looking for number 32. Mr. Silverstein lived here? Surely he had enough money to live farther uptown, in neighborhoods with larger apartments, perhaps near Tomp-kins Square Park where most of the German girls I knew from school lived, where they only had to share a bedroom with a sister, not five other siblings. No, this seemed not at all as I imagined Mr. Silverstein, if I had ever given him more than a passing thought. Odd, since he had been in our lives for so many years. In, but not of. He had always been respectful, shy almost, but apart. He was not so much a person to me as a symbol that meant hard, unrelenting work. He was a token of everything I wanted to escape.

Number two, number eight, number sixteen. The clock in the nearby square struck four. It was almost time for me to go back to Queens. My stomach growled. I hadn't eaten since breakfast. All at once, the thought of a hot meal prepared for me and the other women and men who worked at Gaumont was irresistible. I had done as I promised myself. I had tried to find my mother. Today I was not meant to succeed.

I was about to turn and head back to Fourteenth Street to catch a subway uptown toward the Queensboro Bridge when I stopped in my tracks. The sight was so familiar I almost failed to understand it. Up ahead, I saw my mother's tiny, fragile, upright frame, her way of walking unbowed, not giving any hint that she had seen hard times. Yet she was not alone. She leaned heavily on a man's arm, and in an instant, I knew it was Mr. Silverstein, as familiar a figure as anyone in that city to me. I stepped out of sight behind another stoop where I could watch them approach and wait to see what would happen.

In a few moments, Mr. Silverstein supported my mother up the stoop of a tenement building that could just as easily have been the one on Mulberry Street. When they reached the top, he opened the front door and, with the tenderest care, helped her inside.

Something about the sight of them left me deeply shocked. I'd come looking for my mother but didn't expect to find her, especially not in the company of a man who clearly regarded her with affection, even love. Seeing her like that, as she appeared to the outside world, turned everything around. Now all I wanted was to get away again. How could such a tiny package of blood and bones and flesh be so infuriatingly opaque and hide so many monumental secrets?

But, but, but. Alfonse had raised questions that demanded answers. Unless I knew the truth, I could never move forward. At some point, someone would discover that I wasn't Sarah Potter, but a runaway who let a boy she hardly knew involve her in a crime. The longer I waited to bring everything to some kind of resolution, the less and less likely it was to result in anything good. Even if my mother couldn't think of any way to solve the problem of the money, she was part of it all anyway. There was no leaving her behind.

I waited for Mr. Silverstein to come back out of the building and turn toward the south, then squared my shoulders, walked to number thirty-two Hester Street, and climbed the stoop. I would knock on doors until I found her. After that, I didn't know what.

CHAPTER
THIRTY-THREE

Justine

I had failed at everything. At protecting my daughter, at leaving my life of sin behind me in Paris, and at doing what I could to stop a criminal enterprise. What had possessed me to think I would be capable of a single one of those acts, let alone all of them? The only reason I was now free and not still behind the bars of a stinking cell was because Aaron came to look for me, somehow divining that I had taken matters into my own hands, as they say, and done something foolish that ended in disaster. Yes, I had failed. And as a woman, I was not permitted to face the consequences of that failure and find a way to reconcile myself to them. As a woman, I could not be trusted alone. I must have a man to vouch for me.

Did no man realize that he was the root of all the problems women faced? Why did men not suffer for their transgressions as we women did? *Sainte Vierge*, how could you have fooled me for so long, how could you have let me believe that praying to you would not only absolve me of my sins but ensure that all would be well for my daughter, for whom I wished nothing more than to avoid such a life as I had led and that shadowed me even as I thought I had escaped it?

I paced up and down, across and back. Aaron had been rightfully angry. The changing expression in his eyes still haunted me. One minute, they were full of sadness, the next anger, and then a look of such tenderness as I had never before seen. Aaron. My savior, my mentor, my friend. My employer as well. With each crossing of my parlor, I passed the enormous pile of white shirtwaists Aaron had brought that morning, and which I had only just started to work on before he arrived to take me to lunch, to ensure, he claimed, that I ate something to fortify myself for the day and night ahead. No elegant dresses for me to copy today. The factory girls were on strike. I must help him by doing twice the amount of work I used to do. For all his show of caring, all I was to him was a pair of skillful hands.

The knock was tentative, and I did not hear it at first. Whoever it was must have heard me pacing, though, because they did not give up, only knocked the louder. I hoped they would go away and leave me to wallow in my own disappointment. But the knocking continued.

Soon it was apparent that I would have to answer the door and send the intruder away. It was odd to have someone calling at this hour, but I was in a new neighborhood and did not yet understand all the customs. I patted my hair into place, lifted my chin, and went to the door.

"*Maman?*"

Only one other time in my life had I felt as I did at that moment. That was the instant I first laid eyes on Sylvie, when she was still wet and bloody from having been thrust out of my womb. This, though. This moment when I saw her again, having feared it was never to be, was at the very least equal to that other. For there in front of me stood my beautiful, my intelligent, my educated daughter. The pain and doubt of the past months evaporated in an instant when I beheld Sylvie's face, when I gazed into her blue eyes. They were just the same and yet different. They held depths that were not in them before she had run away and faced the world without me.

I could hardly move. At first, she backed away, perhaps disconcerted by my reception of her, which must have felt cold and distant. As soon as I collected myself, I reached out for her hands and pulled her into my apartment. Once she crossed the threshold, I squeezed her in an embrace that held all my hopes and fears, an embrace in which I hoped to make her understand that whatever had happened, I would welcome her.

"Oh, Sylvie," I finally said, holding her away from me but unwilling to let go of her entirely. "Where have you been?"

I saw a world of conflict and questions in her eyes. I knew enough to understand that she had somehow found her way into the moving pictures because I had seen her myself, but I had no idea what that meant. Had she lost her virtue there, as so many of the girls who mounted the stage in the clubs of Paris had done? Was she forced to perform to work off some debt or other that had kept her alive—just as I had been forced?

"I-I want you to tell me what happened in Paris. Who were you? Who are you?" she said.

Those words. In her voice. They sliced through my breast so that I could hardly breathe. I stepped backwards and sank into my work chair, blood pounding into my ears and streaming like ice through my veins. I opened my mouth to speak, but nothing came out. Sylvie turned and took two steps toward the door. "Don't go!" It came out as a whisper, like a nightmare scream that no one could hear. But she heard it and turned back to face me.

"I want you to tell me about Alfonse d'Antigny."

The mention of his name, a name I had worked all my life to prevent ever passing my daughter's lips, tore the veil away from my carefully constructed fiction of a life. First Aaron, and now Sylvie. My past had caught up with me in the most cruel way, and yet, I felt curiously lighter. There was no decision to make. She had made it for me. If she knew that much, it followed that I must tell her the rest.

"*Il est ton père.*"

CHAPTER
THIRTY-FOUR

Sylvie

At first, I thought my mother was spinning another lie. She said Alfonse was my father. If it was true, why wouldn't he have told me that with everything else? And yet, as I listened, her story fit with what Alfonse had said. It fit like a key in an ancient lock.

Somewhere soon after she had begun to narrate the true story of my life and hers, we both sat down at the worktable, and without thinking, I started helping her with the pieces. She spoke more freely when her hands were busy, and she could look down at her work instead of at me. At some point, she rose and lit the gas lamps so we could continue working. It occurred to me that I was breaking the strike those poor girls risked so much for. But all I cared about was that the past—my past—was unfolding in front of me at last. By turns, I hated and loved Alfonse, just as my mother had. One moment

I wanted to scream at his cruelty, the next at her selfish actions. And then I would be overcome with tenderness and want to rest my head in my mother's lap and comfort her, tell her that all she had sacrificed for me was not in vain.

I lost all sense of time and hardly breathed until the sound of someone climbing the stairs and then knocking softly at the door broke the spell. I looked up from my sewing, half blinded by staring at the stark, white fabric for so many hours. My mother rose and opened the door to Aaron Silverstein.

He had to duck a little coming through the door. I never noticed before how tall he was, or even the color of his eyes, which were a dark brown, almost black, and shimmering with life and expression. When he caught sight of me just after removing his hat, I thought he would start to cry. Only when I saw my mother's pain and sorrow reflected in his eyes did I realize how she must have suffered these past months.

To my surprise, once Mr. Silverstein had removed his hat and coat, he went into the kitchen, lit the stove, and put a kettle on to boil.

"Aaron is my friend. Nothing more," my mother said in response to my questioning glance. He looked up briefly when she spoke his name, and I thought I detected a slight sag in his shoulders when she said the words, *nothing more*.

While the kettle was on, Mr. Silverstein came back into the parlor and sat on the only upholstered chair, something that hadn't come from our days on Mulberry Street. "Why did you come back just now?" He had recovered from his initial emotional greeting, and now he sounded cautious, suspicious even.

And he was right to be. I had not returned for the joy of being reunited with my mother after nine months' separation. I had come because I wanted answers, yes, but more than that, I needed her help.

"She has met Alfonse." My mother's words dropped like a

stone into the room.

"Does she—"

"Know? Yes. I have told her everything."

Mr. Silverstein nodded his head slowly. "So, that is why you are here?"

I took a deep breath before answering his question, so unlike what he would have asked in the old days, just *how are you?* Or *is school going well?* "Only in part. I didn't know until Maman told me just now that he was my father. Some stories he told me, about a woman he knew in Paris, made me suspect he at least knew Maman. That he maybe knew more about her than I did, come to that."

Steam poured out of the kettle's mouth, and my mother started to rise to make the tisane, but Mr. Silverstein motioned her to sit and went himself. We were silent while he took the teapot and three cups off the shelf, spooned the mixture of aromatic herbs and spices into the pot, and poured the boiling water over them, releasing a fragrance that reminded me of the best times in my childhood. Not until we all sat with our full cups in front of us did I summon up the courage to tell them what had happened and how I found myself in such a predicament.

"I didn't know at the time who Paolo really was," I said. "I was so confused. He seemed more trustworthy at that moment than you did, Maman." I was still trying to come to terms with the fact that the man I had seen my mother with so briefly was my father. Alfonse d'Antigny, the wealthy investor in the cinema, married man, and Paris roué, who had stolen me away from my mother as a newborn and tried to pass me off as his legitimate daughter.

"He—this Paolo—was the one who stole the money, *n'est-ce pas?*"

I stared open-mouthed at my mother. "How...?"

She shrugged, reminding me in that instant of Alice. "At first, we guessed. Then other things happened, and the connection was too plain to ignore."

"What 'other things?'"

My mother stood slowly, as if it cost her great effort. She went into the bedroom. I heard her lifting one of the floorboards. A moment later, she returned with something in her hand, something small, no larger than a postcard, but she wasn't looking at it. She held it face down and didn't raise her eyes from the floor when she gave it to me.

Somehow, I was shocked but not surprised. Of course, I remembered how it must have happened. Those test shots, to check the lighting. Had Paolo known Angelotti would do it? Or was this something the photographer had thought of on his own? I felt vaguely sick, but this matter was out of my hands now.

"I tried to make certain no one else would see this image of you." My mother still hadn't looked at me.

"You must understand that I had no intention of having such a picture taken." I reached for her hand, but she stepped away. I placed the postcard picture side down on the half-empty worktable.

"No matter. At least now that enterprise is in the hands of the police."

"Something else needs to be placed in the hands of the police," I said. I stood and removed my jacket. I'd kept it on while sewing. The apartment was cold. "I learned my craft well from you, Maman. Please examine those beautiful piped seams."

Mr. Silverstein rose from his chair and came over to see what I could possibly mean. My mother pulled a seam so she could see the stitching. "You did this by hand."

"I want you to rip it open," I said.

"Such a pity," Mr. Silverstein said.

"Please." I picked up the seam ripper from the worktable and handed it to her. Reluctantly, she inserted the blade between the stitches and popped them open, one by one, then teased out one of the tightly curled five-dollar bills that had given the piping its stiffness and shape.

The silence in that apartment was so thick I could have sliced through it with a knife. "It's all there. In the jacket and my skirt. Nearly five-hundred dollars. Five-hundred stolen dollars."

"What will you do with it?" My mother's eyes were open wide. I didn't know if it was wonder or excitement.

"Of course, I want to return it, but I don't know how. How would I explain it? And Paolo...he could go to prison. And I could go to prison for helping him!"

Mr. Silverstein picked up the jacket and weighed it in his hands. "You have been carrying quite a burden."

My jaw tightened, I drew my lips together and held my breath, but it was no use. Tears streamed down my cheeks. Mr. Silverstein gave me his handkerchief, and I buried my face in it, too ashamed to look up.

"Who else knows?" I recognized that tone of voice in my mother. All business, tackling a problem, like the time I lost the money for groceries on the way to the store.

"Alice knows," I said, wiping my eyes and sitting up straight. "She saw a frayed seam."

"Who is Alice?" My mother said, peering at me with interest.

"I can't explain now. It's too much."

She held her hand out to me. "You must not wear those clothes any longer. If any of the Bonnanos found you, you would not be safe. Come with me."

My mother took me back to the bedroom and pulled aside the curtain that hid a small alcove with a few garments hanging in it. She pulled out a gray gabardine skirt and a pale pink linen shirtwaist. "Put these on."

Whose were they? The skirt was too long for my mother. I towered over her by at least four inches.

"I made it for you. I was saving it for your birthday, but then you...I knew you would come back...You always liked having new clothes, and your old skirt was getting too small." She blinked rapidly, as though fighting tears. My mother never cried. I couldn't bear it if she did, so I took the clothes and quickly changed.

"They're lovely!" I said, twirling around, trying to lighten the mood. "Now, I must go. They're expecting me back at Gaumont."

We walked arm-in-arm back into the parlor.

"Take my coat." My mother took her own coat off the hook by the door. It was too long to be a jacket and shorter than the skirt, but it would keep me warm.

"What happens next?" I asked, looking back and forth between my mother and her friend. Even though the money had yet to be returned, just knowing it would no longer be in my possession sent a flood of relief through me.

"Come back in three days. That will give us time to invent a plan." My mother smiled. I had a feeling that this problem to solve was a relief to her compared to trying to find me and worrying that I might be dead.

We embraced when we said goodbye, my mother clinging to me as she never had before. "I will come then, I promise," I said and kissed her on both cheeks.

Only Alice noticed something different about me when I returned, that I was wearing a skirt and waist she had never seen before. I assumed it was because she had spotted the money in the seams of my other clothes and was therefore more aware, and also because of the story I had spun about a movie script. She raised one eyebrow at me, and I decided I would have to find a time to speak to her privately. But for three days, we were so busy there was simply no opportunity. Each evening, she dashed away home the moment we finished shooting so she could see her daughter before bedtime. I couldn't help feeling that the little girl was fortunate to have Alice for a mother. She was so open and direct. I couldn't imagine her lying about anything or hiding great parts of herself from everyone, even from those she loved. And she proved, as many women could not, that the only way forward was not always the obvious one, the well-worn path through marriage and family, that a woman could have that and much more besides.

Partly out of relief, partly because I was still very anxious, I threw myself into the role Alice had cast me in so completely that it blotted out everything else. By the third day, when we had to shoot the poignant scene of reconciliation, I think even the cameramen had tears in their eyes. I was exhausted, drained of everything I had, by midday. All I wanted to do was sit somewhere in silence and think about what lay ahead, wondering how my mother and Mr. Silverstein could possibly find an answer to what to do about the stolen money.

But it was not to be.

Just as we were breaking for lunch, Alice said, "Ah, look who has come to see us! The man who holds the key to our prosperity in his hand! And he brings your friend as well." Alice advanced to the door of the studio with her hand outstretched, expecting someone to kiss it. Of course, I knew right away she meant Alfonse. What I didn't expect was to see Annabel with him.

Annabel rushed over to me while Alfonse went to talk to Alice.

"I just had to find out! Is it true?"

My blank look conveyed to her that I had no idea what she was talking about.

"Look!" She opened her purse and took out a much-folded page of a newspaper and gave it to me. I was afraid to open it up, right there in front of everyone, not knowing what I would find.

"I'll look at it later," I said.

She was about to protest, but Alfonse approached us. "You appear tired, my dear," he said, reaching his hand out to me and expecting me to take it. But I couldn't. Especially not knowing what I now knew. I tried to pretend everything was as it had been, but when I looked into his eyes, I could tell he knew something had changed. "Alice tells me you went to Manhattan a few days ago."

I nodded, not wanting to engage him in conversation at that moment. Annabel stood by, deliberately placing herself where she could hear every word.

"I wonder, did you happen to speak to our mutual acquaintance?" He said it so smoothly, as if it meant nothing to him. "I should simply like to warn you not to believe everything you hear of me."

I stared at him hard. I wanted to demand that he tell me what he meant, but with everyone around, I couldn't. "I'm sorry, I'm rather tired, and I have more scenes to shoot this afternoon. If you'll excuse me."

I stood and walked away, but not before noticing that his eyes were the same shape as mine, and I could see my own hands in the taper of his fingers.

Annabel stayed to watch for the afternoon. I knew she was waiting until I had a chance to read the article so she could quiz me about everything that was going on. I wasn't ready to talk to her about what had happened the other day, though. I would have to think of a way to put her off, to lie—again.

"I think Alfonse is sweet on you," she murmured as I changed into a different costume.

I blushed a deep crimson, but not for the reason she imagined. "He's old enough to be..." I couldn't finish the thought.

"Oh, that doesn't matter anymore! He's so rich, he'd make sure you had a great career. If I were you, I'd try to get him crazy about me."

"You are not me, and among the many other reasons I would not do such a thing is that he happens to be married."

She shrugged. "Ever hear of a thing called divorce?"

I wanted her to stop talking like that. I felt queasy imagining it. And the way she put it made it sound as if I would be behaving exactly as my mother had all those years ago. "Please, stop."

"Not until you look at that article. It's important!"

I sighed. Reluctantly, I took the paper she'd given me out of my pocket and smoothed it on the dressing table. In an instant, I understood why Annabel had come here to show it to me. I caught my breath and put my hand to my mouth.

"It's him, isn't it!" she said.

I nodded. The headline read, *Police Sting Operation Nets Bonnano Family in Gambling and Pornography Ring*. And there were three illustrations beneath the headline, of the elder Bonnano, his wife, and their son. Paolo. They had been arraigned and would appear in court the next day. "I have to go and help him. He's not guilty, not of that!"

"How can you possibly know?"

I felt the carefully constructed fabric of lies that I'd cloaked myself with begin to fray in one corner. All it needed to unravel completely was for me to pull on the thread Annabel had teased out through what she observed of me and the little I had revealed to her. Suddenly, the effort of resisting the temptation to do so felt monumental. I needed her help too.

"Come with me to Manhattan tomorrow. We're finished filming, and I was supposed to go back to Vitagraph anyway." I gripped her hand.

"Ouch! I suppose I could, just to keep you out of trouble."

"Stay here tonight. We'll take the train across first thing."

"All right, but you have to tell me what this is all about. You're being mysterious, and it frightens me."

"Not here. Not until tomorrow. You have to trust me about this." The ride in would give me ample time to explain everything, and I didn't want her to know about Alfonse until he was well out of sight.

"Promise you'll tell me everything tomorrow."

"Promise."

CHAPTER
THIRTY-FIVE

Sylvie

Annabel and I left the studio and walked to the train station early the next morning. I wore my old, threadbare coat and carried the one I'd borrowed from my mother the other night over my arm.

"*Un moment, s'il vous plait.*" The voice behind me made me stop in my tracks just before we were about to enter the station lobby. I turned. Somehow, Alfonse d'Antigny managed to be there at that early hour. He was leaning against his automobile, which was parked at the curb by the station. The driver was nowhere to be seen.

"I'll only be a moment. Here." I gave Annabel money. "You go buy the tickets, and I'll catch up."

She narrowed her eyes. I could see she didn't want to leave me.

"It's all right, I promise. I'll be right there." I pushed her gently toward the door, then walked over to stand near enough to hear what Alfonse had to say but far enough away so that he couldn't touch me. "What do you want?"

"I thought we might talk a little. About the possibility that you could come back to Paris with me."

"You want to steal me away from my mother again?" The words came out before I could think what they meant, that now he would know that I knew who he really was.

He nodded his head slowly. "So. You have seen your mother. I told you she might lie to you."

"The only lie she ever told me was that I had no father. And now I understand why."

He took a step toward me, and I backed away. "What? You think I will snatch you? As she did?" His voice had a bitter edge. "I want you to come to Paris so that you can be in the cinema there. I will make certain you are well paid. You will never live in a tiny hovel like your mother's apartment again."

"I don't think I want the kind of protection you offer," I said. "My mother is still suffering for it, for how you treated her." My words of defense sounded strange even to my ear, but it was the truth.

"So, you think so ill of me? Surely I do not deserve that from you. I have only ever tried to help you." His voice, normally smooth as the finest silk, had a hint of tears in it.

I didn't want to talk to him about it anymore; everything was a confused muddle in my mind. "I can't stay here any longer. Annabel is waiting for me."

"I would like, if you would permit me, to come to know you better. Would you allow me that, or has your mother turned you completely against me?"

I struggled to find the right thing to say. "She has only told me the truth."

"From her perspective."

My head felt near to bursting with the effort of sorting

through everything I'd absorbed in the past few days. He was right, though. I had only heard it from my mother's point of view. "All right. We can talk again, but not today, not while it's all so new, and I have something else very important that I must do in Manhattan."

He touched the brim of his hat and bowed a little. "That is all I ask of you. *Au revoir, ma fille.*"

I ran as fast as I could to the train, struggling against the urge to cry. *Ma fille.* That was what my mother called me.

Annabel was already on the platform, waving my ticket. "Hurry, or we'll miss it!"

I reached her just as the train pulled up and hardly had time to say anything to her until we were seated. I wiped a stray tear away with the back of my hand, hoping she hadn't noticed.

"What's wrong?"

"Nothing," I said, although I don't think she believed me. "Now, I have a lot to tell you before we reach the courthouse, so don't say anything. Just let me talk."

By the time we reached Hester Street, she knew the whole story.

"Goodness. Your life sounds just like the script of a picture. Except no one would believe it, so it wouldn't be very good."

I laughed, breaking the tension.

It was just eight o'clock. I hoped my mother would be up but not yet out anywhere—if she would go out at all when she had so much extra work because of the strike. I intended to ask her to come with us. I counted on her loyalty to me outweighing her need to help Mr. Silverstein. I didn't deserve it, but the plain truth was I needed her. She could back up my claim. When we spoke the other day, she told me that Paolo had not been involved in the pornography, that he had been shocked and angry when she confronted him with the photograph. He wasn't there when Angelotti took that photo; at least I knew that for certain. And then, as to gambling, when

I saw him at the club, he looked just like any harried waiter serving dinner. I never saw him go into the gambling room. I planned to tell whoever would listen that he had been forced to participate in his parent's business and that we had decided to run away together to escape from his bondage to them. It might not be what I thought at the time of the storm and when he abandoned me, but I'd convinced myself that it had been his intention all along.

Annabel and I had walked from the trolley stop on Houston to Hester Street, through the narrowing streets, past the crowded tenement buildings. I could sense her hanging back. I took her hand and pulled her along. "We need to hurry! The arraignment is at nine this morning."

The farther we got into the Polish neighborhood, the less comfortable Annabel appeared. She looked around suspiciously and flared her nostrils in distaste. "It smells awful here. And these people...are they Jews?"

I knew little of Annabel's background except that she had been on the stage from quite a young age and had come from Vermont. "Are there no poor people in Vermont? Is everyone a Methodist?" I said.

She snapped her mouth shut as we climbed the stoop and entered the building. "You're not..." she said.

"No. But why would that matter?" I didn't see that being Jewish should have any bearing on friendship. It didn't for my mother, clearly, who, as an ardent Catholic, had a Jew as her only friend.

My mother answered the door to us and peered warily at Annabel. "It's all right. She knows everything, and you can trust her," I said before greeting her with a kiss. She stepped back to let us in, but I could see she was still on high alert to danger. I had told her a little about Annabel the other day but had given no indication that she was acquainted with our sordid secrets.

I then quickly explained to my mother what I wanted us to do that day. "So, you see, we need to go there together, with Annabel too, to mention how Paolo came to Vitagraph to get me so we could finish our plan of running away from New York."

"*Es tu fou!*" I recognized that anger in my mother's voice. If she stood her ground, it would be hopeless. "If he was there in that den of crime that family runs, he is as guilty as his parents. And don't forget what he did to you." I caught her quick glance in Annabel's direction. I guessed she wasn't certain I had told her about the money.

"Annabel really does know everything, now," I said.

It took some persuasion, but eventually she agreed to accompany us to the Tombs. The Bonnanos were to be arraigned there that morning. A magistrate would determine how they would be charged.

"What shall I tell Aaron?" she said. "Taking such a long time out of my day will make it impossible for me to finish the waists. And Mrs. Bonnano...I hoped I would never set eyes on her again in my life."

"But this is for Paolo. He tried to help. You said so yourself." I picked at the frayed cuffs of my coat without thinking. "Here," I said, "I brought back your coat."

"Yours is hardly fit to keep you warm," she said. "You look like a poor tenement dweller."

She was right. I'd gotten by so far that autumn by wearing the jacket with the hidden bills, which was quite warm enough, or borrowing something from Annabel or Alice.

"I made something for you yesterday. I'll be back in a moment." She went to the bedroom, and when she returned, she was carrying a beautiful, dove-gray coat in the latest fashion, with two tiers, a deep collar, and in the chic wraparound style that buttoned below my waist. I was almost too stunned to say anything, but when her face started to cloud, I reached out for the coat. "It's beautiful!"

"I copied a design by Coco Chanel that Aaron brought me. No one will listen to you in a tired old coat such as factory girls wear." The coat was lined with silk. I'd never worn anything so luxurious.

"The material must have been very expensive." I examined my mother's face to see if there were any signs of embarrassment, any indication that she'd had to pay for it herself in some manner, and I hated myself for thinking it.

Annabel stepped forward, mouth agape, to touch the luxurious, soft wool. "So that's where you learned it. But I thought this plan, going to The Tombs, just came about yesterday."

"This one did. I was originally coming here for something else, but that will have to wait."

Aaron's soft knock at the door silenced us. I had hoped we'd be gone by the time he arrived but persuading my mother had taken longer than I expected.

He entered, carrying two items. One was his usual sack of pieces to be transformed into the finest shirtwaists in Manhattan by my mother's skilled hands. The other appeared to be a very elegant hatbox. "Ah! I see you are—" He stopped talking abruptly when he saw Annabel, who stood like a gaudy pillar in the middle of the small parlor.

"Annabel, this is my mother's friend, Aaron Silverstein."

He nodded in her direction. She gave him a shaky smile and glanced nervously around the parlor. "Is there a clock? Goodness, time has flown. I mustn't be late for my appointment." Annabel bustled over to the door. Mr. Silverstein stepped aside so she could pass by him. Before I knew what she was doing, she went out. "See you back in Queens!" she said, trying to sound nonchalant, but I knew something was wrong.

"Annabel, wait!" I called after her, but I could hear her rapid, light steps fading as she hurried down the stairs.

"Why did you bring her?" My mother's words had a sharp edge to them.

"Because she knows about Paolo and the money, and I didn't want her gossiping if she stayed behind. Besides, she's the one who brought me the article so I would know about the arraignment."

"The arraignment?" Mr. Silverstein looked confused.

"There's no time to explain. We must be going!" I held my mother's coat for her, and she slipped her arms into it.

"You will also need this." Mr. Silverstein put the hatbox down on the table and opened it. He gently lifted out a magnificent hat that matched the coat my mother had made me and held it out to her. "You help Sylvie put it on."

"Why?" I said, looking back and forth between them. With that coat and hat, I was wearing something Anne Morgan, or any of the society ladies I had met at the Colony Club, would have been proud to wear.

My mother stepped close to me, put her two hands on either side of my face, and gazed into my eyes with such love. "Because you are now a woman, and to succeed in the pictures, you must look the part."

She had heard me. She wasn't angry or disappointed.

"We'll bring the other package," Mr. Silverstein said, "I see no reason to completely alter our original purpose."

My mother nodded her agreement and fetched a parcel wrapped in brown paper from a corner of the room.

I was too intent on what was to come to inquire further into the original purpose Mr. Silverstein mentioned, but I suspected my carefully sewn jacket and skirt were in that parcel, and that my mother and her friend had come to a decision about how to rid me of the stolen money.

Mr. Silverstein insisted we take a cab down to the tombs. He clutched the parcel tightly to him all the way, which only confirmed my suspicions about what it contained.

We arrived at the main entrance of a building that looked like a fort and a prison, impenetrable and inescapable. A smell emanated from the walls that hinted of rot and despair. Mr. Silverstein found out where the arraignments took place—because he was a man, guards and officers listened to him instead of just staring and ogling, as they did at us—and we found our way there somehow through a warren of ill-lit hallways and steep stairwells. By the time we at last arrived at the magistrate's court, I had already begun to doubt the wisdom of my impulsive plan. Who was I to change the course of justice?

The three of us filed into the back of the crowded courtroom. About a dozen men and women were already in the holding area, but I saw no sign of Paolo and his family.

The magistrate entered, and everyone rose. I cast my eyes around to examine the other spectators, a strange combination of grubby men scribbling on notepads with pencil stubs and genteel ladies, noses held high as if to get to a more salubrious level of the atmosphere. "Temperance, or vice," Mr. Silverstein whispered into my ear to explain who they were, just as the first person was called.

One by one, the prisoners stood up in front of the magistrate to answer to charges and were handed down either a sentence or a fine, or simply a harsh talking-to. One time, the crime was bad enough, and the accused insisted he wasn't guilty, so his case had to go to trial at a later date. Each time before his decision, the magistrate would ask the gaping crowd if there was anyone to post bail or to speak on behalf of the criminal in front of him. Only once was his question not greeted with silence. A large lady marched forward and took hold of a man who apparently had been drunk and disorderly, cuffed him on the ear and said, "I'll take him home. Here's your fine," and plopped down a bag heavy with coins on the magistrate's desk.

Her shouts of, "Serve you right to spend a night in jail!" and "You'll never amount to anything!" made several in the room laugh and talk, and it took some time for the magistrate to silence everyone again.

The last person who had been waiting in the holding pen went before the magistrate, and still, Paolo and his family had not entered. I began to worry that I had somehow gotten it wrong and dragged my mother and Mr. Silverstein all the way here for no reason. Many of the other spectators had left too, obviously certain no more entertainment or news was to be had that day.

"I'm so sorry," I whispered to my mother. "Let's go. We'll do whatever it is you had been planning for us to do."

At that moment, the door at the front by the bench opened, and a guard led three people in. They were chained together and handcuffed. I recognized Mr. and Mrs. Bonnano from the illustrations in the paper. Paolo, of course, I would have known anywhere, even if his face wasn't freshly imprinted on my mind. My heart turned over, and my mouth went dry. He stared at the floor in front of him as he walked, not looking up, even as his parents stared hard at the assembled audience. Everyone shrank back a little as if trying to get out of their reach.

And then, the woman—Paolo's mother—spotted us, and glared at us so fiercely it felt like a blow.

The atmosphere in the courtroom changed from restless interest to intense, focused silence. The magistrate read the charges.

Illegal gambling. Pornography. Vice. Extortion. All through it, I stared straight at Paolo, but he kept his eyes to the ground. *See me!* I thought, willing him to look up, wanting to somehow convey to him that I was there to help, and didn't believe he had done anything wrong that he hadn't been forced to do.

Angelotti should have been there too. I wondered why he wasn't if they'd found all the dirty postcards in his storage room. I was so absorbed in my thoughts that I jumped when I felt the touch of a hand on my shoulder. I looked around, and there was Annabel. "I'm sorry," she said. "I feel foolish. I didn't know what to do."

"Just stay with me now." I gave her hand a squeeze and refocused my attention on the proceedings.

"Enrico Bonnano, how do you plead?" The magistrate's voice rang out more strongly than it had for any of the other criminals brought before him.

"Not guilty."

"Magdalena Bonnano, née Angelotti, how do you plead?"

I gasped. Of course. The connection. She must be the photographer's sister.

"Not guilty."

"Paolo Bonnano, how do you plead?"

At that moment, Paolo finally looked up. He must somehow have known I was there because he looked straight at me, fixing me with the intensity of his deep brown gaze. "Guilty," he said.

The courtroom erupted in murmurs and gasps. Before I knew what I was doing, I leapt to my feet. "Not guilty!" I cried.

The magistrate peered over his spectacles from the paper before him, casting a glance around before finally settling on me. "Young lady, do you have something to say in this lad's defense, or are you simply trying to disrupt my proceedings?"

My mother pulled my hand to try to make me sit again, but I wasn't finished. "He wasn't involved. I know it. He tried to help me, but it all went wrong. I don't know about his parents. I think he was afraid of them, only now you have them, and he can be honest."

I don't know what possessed me, but everything suddenly became clear. Paolo didn't rob the jewelry store. He was simply in the wrong place, and the police assumed he was involved. The money he gave me to keep could have been from any of his family's unlawful businesses. It didn't matter anymore. He had been stuck in his path just as I was, perhaps always looking for a way out but never finding one. I truly was not the only one running away that day of the snowstorm.

Mr. and Mrs. Bonnano's faces held thunder that I sensed could explode any moment. If they were not chained and I was not in the middle of a crowded courtroom, I think one of them would have leapt forward and put hands around my neck to squeeze the life out of me.

"Please sit down, Miss. One of the officers of the court will take your statement later."

"No!" I said, shaking my hand free from my mother's grip. "I have more to say." I bent down and snatched the wrapped parcel from the floor at Mr. Silverstein's feet and held it aloft. "I believe I possess something that will exonerate Paolo Bonnano." My mother gasped. "It's all right," I whispered.

"Officer, please fetch that package and bring it to me."

I clambered over the people seated between me and the aisle in the middle of the courtroom and met the uniformed officer.

More murmurs and whispers arose from the crowd as they craned their necks to see what the parcel would contain. "What are you doing!" Annabel leaned forward and whispered fiercely into my ear.

I didn't answer her. I was too busy watching the magistrate take out a small pocketknife and slide it under the twine to cut it away from the package. He peeled the paper back as though he were unwrapping a gift and lifted out the jacket, now neatly pressed and folded. He scowled. "Young lady, have you lost your mind! I am not interested in your laundry."

"Open the seams, sir."

While he used his knife again to pick at one of the piped seams, I let my gaze wander to Paolo. He was still watching me, his expression puzzled but not angry, or even unhappy. I could have sworn that the light had rekindled in his eyes, even as those of his parents became darker and more menacing.

"Look, it's money!" Someone in the crowd cried out as the

magistrate succeeded in getting two or three of the tightly coiled bills out.

He smoothed them on the wooden surface in front of him. "What is this?" he asked me. "Where did this come from?"

"Ask Paolo Bonnano," I said. I had made a leap of understanding that I knew might be completely misguided. But I had to give Paolo the opportunity to let everything come out into the open. It had been his burden as well as mine.

"Young man," the magistrate said, addressing Paolo, "Do you know how much money is sewn into these garments?"

"I think maybe five-hundred dollars, more or less."

Another collective gasp had the magistrate banging his gavel. "And do you know where this money came from?"

Paolo's father tried to take a step toward him, fists clenched, but the officer who had led them in restrained him. Paolo noticed, and I thought I saw him waver. I willed him to look in my direction, so I could send courage from my eyes to his.

But in the end, it wasn't necessary. He straightened up and looked directly at the magistrate. "It's money that was stolen from a jeweler's shop last March."

I held my breath. He hadn't said *that I stole*. I hoped it meant what I thought it did.

"The money you stole, you mean? And for which you were detained for some months?"

"No...I mean, yes...I mean..."

"Well, which is it?"

"I didn't steal it, but I took the rap. I had to."

Now the courtroom burst into a din of talking that drowned out what the magistrate was saying to the officer. When he finished, he hammered the gavel until the room quieted again. "The Bonnano family case will go to trial."

My heart dropped into my feet—or felt like it anyway. We stood and started to file out, but the officer who had taken the parcel from me stopped me. "Magistrate wants to see you in chambers," he said, taking a firm hold on my arm.

"No!" my mother cried out.

"It's all right," I said. "All will be well." I caught Mr. Silverstein's eye, and he nodded. He understood what I was doing. He would take care of my mother. "Make sure Annabel gets home," I said. "I don't know how long I'll be."

CHAPTER
THIRTY-SIX

Ending

Sylvie

It's funny. When I think back to that day, I realize I was never frightened. I know I should have been, since without fully realizing it, I'd exposed a layer of criminal activity in the Bonnano family that, even if the police suspected it, they hadn't been able to prove.

And when I returned to my mother's apartment late that night after talking for hours to the magistrate and the detective, I learned of her part in leading the police to the warehouse and ultimately enabling them to close the trap they had been trying to lure the family into for over a year. No wonder she hadn't wanted to go to the Tombs with me.

Paolo walked me back to my mother's apartment when

everything was over. He was not charged with anything and never would have been, but I didn't know that at the time.

"I guess you probably hate me now," he said.

We were at the bottom of the stoop, he had his hands thrust into his pockets, and I could see they were clenched into fists. "You were very brave."

Paolo shrugged. "I did what I had to. It was that picture of you sent me over the edge."

"I need to know: the day of the storm when I found you, and the police were chasing you, had you—"

"Does it matter now? Everyone's got their money back, and those people...are locked up. Angelotti will be soon too, less he's hiked it out of town far enough."

"Will you have to testify?"

He looked down at the ground and nudged a dirty bit of paper into the gutter. "No. But I have to go away, as far as I can. There's guys out there who'll come for me. I got a reward. It's enough to get me started."

I wanted to ask him where he would go, and what exactly he would get started at, but a hollow space had opened where my heart used to be, and the words wouldn't come. He wasn't the thief I thought he was, even as I defended him in court. Not really. Everything he did, in the end, had been to protect me.

"Anyways, you'll be all right. You got your flickers, and your mama." He looked away when he said it. I can't imagine what it had cost him to betray his family that way, knowing he would end up being separated from them forever. "I guess I better go."

"You're not going to Delancey Street, I hope?"

"Hah," he said, without any humor at all. "No, they got me a room somewheres uptown. I'll be on a train west tomorrow."

I nodded. I wanted to say so much, I wanted once again to say, *Take me with you!* But I knew it was impossible for me, and too risky for him.

"So, bye then." He touched the brim of his cap and started walking away.

"Paolo, wait!"

He turned, and the sadness in his eyes crushed me. I ran to him. He put his arms around me and held me close. I tilted up my chin and put all my complicated feelings about him—distrust, admiration, and love—into my eyes, hoping they would say what I couldn't.

A moment later, the distance between us vanished as our lips touched, and then we kissed and kissed. The salt of my tears mingled with the taste of him.

When we separated at last, I spoke. "I don't hate you, in case you couldn't tell." That made him smile. "None of the good things of the past nine months would have happened without you, either. We'll meet again, I'm certain." My voice cracked a little at the end.

I stood there and watched him leave. He didn't look back. When he turned the corner, I climbed the stoop to go home to my mother's apartment for the night.

#

Justine

So much has changed in the last month. I know where Sylvie is, although she chose not to come and live at home. She persuaded me to go out to the studio in Brooklyn with her and see her new world, her new family of friends. I met the French woman called Alice, and I liked her. We understood one another, and I understood why Sylvie admired her so. I confess I was a little jealous to hear my daughter talk about her with such enthusiasm.

"Come and work at my studio. I have plans to open in Fort Lee," Alice said to me. "You could make costumes instead of piecing shirtwaists together for pennies."

It was a tempting thought. But I could never do that. The cinema was Sylvie's world, not mine. Or rather, Sarah Potter's. That was the name the studio—Mr. Blackton, at least—said should be shown in the credits at the end of the pictures she was in from now on.

Alfonse sailed for Paris a few days after the arraignment. He agreed never to tell anyone of his relationship to Sylvie in exchange for a promise that she would come to Paris sometime in the next year. The two of them spoke privately for several hours. Sylvie told me she would never call him father, but that just as I could be forgiven for my past actions, so should he.

Aaron's knock roused me from my reverie.

"Are you ready?"

His smile, his kind face, was once again untroubled and serene. I couldn't help but smile in answer. "Of course!"

Aaron helped me into my coat and waited patiently while I settled my elegant new hat on my head and pinned it in place. We walked out together as we often did now, arm-in-arm. People in the neighborhood stared at us in disbelief. A Jew and a Catholic. Good friends. The very best of friends. Possibly a little more. And business partners too. The fashionable skirts, coats, and gowns I had made in the last month had been eagerly purchased by the best department stores, and I had commissions for many more.

It was Christmas Eve, but I was not going to Mass. That habit mattered only when my heart was heavy with secrets so shameful I could hardly breathe. No, this evening we were going to the new picture palace on Twenty-Third Street.

We arrived in plenty of time. Aaron paid for our tickets, and we took seats right in the middle, close enough to see everything. We didn't speak as the theater filled up with couples and families, all kinds of people out for the pleasure of escaping their dreary lives for an hour. There would be three short pictures that evening.

The gaslights in the house were turned down, and the bubbling conversations around us hushed as the pianist over to the side started playing. The projector at the back whirred, and the empty screen flickered to life with the title of the first picture. *A Midsummer Night's Dream*, from Vitagraph Studios.

I knew Sylvie's part in this was a small one, but it was her first, even though other pictures where she had bigger roles had been playing in the nickelodeons for weeks. I watched for her in the scenes with the fairies, hardly noticing the other actors or even the story.

The camera caught her eyes at one point, and I felt as if she were looking directly at me. How could I not have noticed that ambition? Why did I not understand that her vision was so much grander than the meager future I thought would be hers?

Sylvie had become a woman with purpose and drive, with the will to seize opportunity with both hands. She would achieve great things, more than I ever thought possible in my narrow view of the world.

In my heart, though, I knew one thing for certain. Whatever else she became, however else she defined herself and her life—actress, wife, mother, director—she would always and forever be the courtesan's daughter.

And that was all right with both of us.

ACKNOWLEDGMENTS

Many thanks to Colleen Alles, whose expert editing eye helped me take this book to the next level; to Claire Barnhart, who wrangled my commas into submission; and to the entire team at Atmosphere Press.

ABOUT ATMOSPHERE PRESS

Atmosphere Press is an independent, full-service publisher for excellent books in all genres and for all audiences. Learn more about what we do at atmospherepress.com.

We encourage you to check out some of Atmosphere's latest releases, which are available at Amazon.com and via order from your local bookstore:

Dancing with David, a novel by Siegfried Johnson

The Friendship Quilts, a novel by June Calender

My Significant Nobody, a novel by Stevie D. Parker

Nine Days, a novel by Judy Lannon

Shining New Testament: The Cloning of Jay Christ, a novel by Cliff Williamson

Shadows of Robyst, a novel by K. E. Maroudas

Home Within a Landscape, a novel by Alexey L. Kovalev

Motherhood, a novel by Siamak Vakili

Death, The Pharmacist, a novel by D. Ike Horst

Mystery of the Lost Years, a novel by Bobby J. Bixler

Bone Deep Bonds, a novel by B. G. Arnold

Terriers in the Jungle, a novel by Georja Umano

Into the Emerald Dream, a novel by Autumn Allen

His Name Was Ellis, a novel by Joseph Libonati

The Cup, a novel by D. P. Hardwick

The Empathy Academy, a novel by Dustin Grinnell

Tholocco's Wake, a novel by W. W. VanOverbeke

Dying to Live, a novel by Barbara Macpherson Reyelts

Looking for Lawson, a novel by Mark Kirby

Yosef's Path: Lessons from my Father, a novel by Jane Leclere Doyle

ABOUT THE AUTHOR

Susanne Dunlap is the author of more than a dozen works of historical fiction for adults and teens, as well as an Author Accelerator Certified Book Coach. Her love of historical fiction arose partly from her PhD studies in music history at Yale University and partly from her lifelong interest in women in the arts. Susanne earned her BA and an MA (musicology) from Smith College and lives in Biddeford, Maine, with her little dog, Betty.

CPSIA information can be obtained
at www.ICGtesting.com
Printed in the USA
JSHW031115020123
35602JS00002B/98